PENDRAGON

JOURNAL OF AN ADVENTURE THROUGH TIME AND SPACE

Book Ten:

The Soldiers of Halla

PENDRAGON

JOURNAL OF AN ADVENTURE
THROUGH TIME AND SPACE

PENDRAGON

JOURNAL OF AN ADVENTURE THROUGH TIME AND SPACE

Book Ten:

The Soldiers of Halla

D. J. MacHale

Aladdin

New York   London   Toronto   Sydney

ALADDIN
An imprint of Simon & Schuster Children's Publishing Division
1230 Avenue of the Americas, New York, NY 10020
Copyright © 2009 by D. J. MacHale
All rights reserved, including the right of reproduction
in whole or in part in any form.
ALADDIN and related logo are registered trademarks
of Simon & Schuster, Inc.
The text for this book is set in Apollo MT.
Manufactured in the United States of America
First Aladdin hardcover edition May 2009
2 4 6 8 10 9 7 5 3 1
Library of Congress Cataloging-in-Publication Data
MacHale, D. J.
The soldiers of Halla / D. J. MacHale. — 1st ed.
p. cm. — (Pendragon ; bk. 10)
"Journal of an adventure through time and space."
Summary: Each of the Travelers returns home to learn the truth about their
origins before being reunited for a final, ineveitable confrontation with Saint
Dane, whose efforts to control Halla are destroying its very foundations.
ISBN: 978-1-4169-1420-4 (hardcover : alk. paper)
[1. Adventure and adventurers—Fiction. 2. Space and time—Fiction.
3. Fate and fatalism—Fiction. 4. Diaries—Fiction. 5. Fantasy.] I. Title.
PZ7.M177535Sol 2009
[Fic]—dc22
2008053573

*For Rob, Julie, Peter, Michael, Richard, Lisa, Ellen, Rick,
and everyone else who first said "yes"*

This is it.

It's been about eight years since I first came up with the idea of Halla and the story of a guy who was destined to protect all that is, was, and ever will be. I know that to many of you that seems like a lifetime ago. To me it feels like last week. It wasn't. Eight years is a long time in anybody's life. In those years I experienced the birth of my daughter and the death of my father. Evangeline and I were married. I saw nieces and nephews grow into adults, produced a TV series, and saw the world change in dramatic ways. Some of those changes were great; others weren't. But no matter what happened over that time, whether it was good, bad, or in between, I always had one constant . . . Bobby Pendragon. As real-world events swirled, I always knew that I could close my eyes, step into the flume, and have a blast while imagining new challenges for Bobby and the Travelers.

Not anymore.

It's a fact of life. You always know when you're doing something for the first time, but you rarely know when you're doing something for the last time. (Unless you're jumping off a bridge, I guess.) That's a good thing. Life is full of possibilities, and it's exciting to know that all avenues are open; it's a bit sad when you realize that a door is about to close. It doesn't happen often, but when it does, it's tough. I know. It was difficult typing the two words that only a few short years ago seemed light-years away. "The End." But type them I did. Bobby Pendragon's story has come to an end.

As with Bobby, before looking forward I'd like to take

a short look back to once again thank some of the many people who help bring the Pendragon saga to life.

Liesa Abrams is the third and final editor of the Pendragon books. She came on board at the exact right time. Not only has she worked incredibly hard on the Pendragon novels, she has also been editing the Before the War prequel books and the Pendragon graphic novels, and she has been overseeing all things Pendragon at Simon & Schuster Children's Publishing. Thank you, Liesa, for taking care of Bobby and helping me make his story the best it can be.

All my friends at S&S deserve special thanks. Carolyn Reidy, Rick Richter, Rubin Pfeffer, Bethany Buck, Mara Anastas, Ellen Krieger, Justin Chanda, Lucille Rettino, Paul Crichton . . . the list goes on. And on. These are only a few of the people behind the publishing of Pendragon. Without their support and confidence in the series, you would not be holding this book. I owe a debt of gratitude to them all.

Heidi Hellmich, Ace Copyeditor is the only person in the world besides me who has pored over and analyzed every single word of every single Pendragon novel. Thank you, Heidi, for sticking with it and getting Bobby to the finish line.

I still remember the first conversation I had with Richard Curtis, the man who was to become my agent and good friend. I had written a proposal for a book series. I'd never written a book series before. It was new territory, so to speak. The proposal included an overview, sixty pages of the first book, and outlines for nine more. Richard read the proposal and, in his calm, measured way, said, "You should write the entire first book before we look for a publisher." Good advice. The right advice. I didn't take it. I had what I thought was a good story and wrote it down for fun. To be honest, I didn't think anybody would want to publish it. So I told him, "Nah. If I write the whole book, I'll be taking it way too seriously and be really disappointed if it doesn't get published." I thought he'd tell me to get lost and find another agent. Instead, in that same calm, reassuring voice, he said, "All right, let's see what I can do." Well, Richard, you did good. There's nothing more to say but thank you.

As always, Peter Nelson and Mark Wetzstein are due big thanks for keeping the business of Pendragon running smoothly. You guys are the best.

Danny Baror has continued to spread Bobby's story throughout the world. The list of languages the books have been translated into is always growing longer, thanks to Danny.

As always, I have to thank my wife, Evangeline, for being the first sounding board for Bobby's adventure. From the very beginning I've relied on her good taste and story sense to keep the story on track . . . and my head in the game. Thanks, Evander.

My daughter, Keaton, is still a bit too young for Pendragon. I showed her a fairly innocent *Are You Afraid of the Dark?* episode recently, and it freaked her out for days. Oops. It will be a few years before she can start fluming. The gratitude I owe her is for being the nutty girl she is and making sure I continue to think like a kid. It's a valuable skill . . . for both of us.

I've had the good fortune to travel quite a bit and meet many booksellers who have recommended Pendragon to their readers. I'm grateful and honored. I've also met many teachers and librarians who have encouraged their students not only to read Pendragon, but to read in general. They know, as we all do, that reading makes you smarter. Simple as that. We all owe them a debt of gratitude.

Between appearances and e-mails I've spoken to thousands of readers' parents. It's a great feeling to know there are so many engaged parents who are encouraging their kids to read. To all you parents, especially the ones who bring their kids to see me and then have to sit through a talk about quigs and territories and Travelers, you are all heroes.

A great big thanks goes to all you readers who have been faithfully visiting the website and posting on the forums. Some of you have been there since the beginning, while new acolytes are showing up every day. It's been a blast having you be part of the Pendragon adventure. I hope you continue stopping by for a long time to come.

The final piece in the puzzle is . . . you. I guess it's kind of obvious to say, but without you guys there wouldn't be a Pendragon adventure. For those of you who have been there from the start, as well as those who have recently discovered Halla, I thank you for joining me on this journey. It's been the ride of a lifetime. Thank you.

What lies beyond Pendragon? Lots. You're not getting rid of me that easily. Since this preface is about this book, I won't make a list. All I'll say is that when we meet again, it won't be in a flume, but on a mysterious highway known as the *Morpheus Road*.

Have I covered everything?

Oh yeah. Almost forgot. The book. Right. That.

Over the years I've been asked the same questions thousands of times. They took many forms, but all boiled down to this: "What's going to happen to Bobby and the Travelers?" I think the number one question was "Will we ever see Uncle Press again?" Of course I knew the truth from day one, but I had to keep answering the same way: "Sorry, no spoilers." "You'll see." "Keep reading." You know, duck, dodge, weave. After avoiding the question for so long, I really enjoyed writing the last chapter of *Raven Rise*, because I was finally able to stop dodging and give the real answer.

At the end of Book Nine, Bobby hit bottom. He failed. Halla was lost. Saint Dane had won. Game over. Right?

Well . . . no. For those of you who have been paying attention, you know that Saint Dane winning wasn't necessarily the worst thing that could happen. I always knew that when things got as bad as they could possibly get, Bobby would feel a tap on his shoulder and hear the words "Havin' a rough day?"

Yeah. Uncle Press finally came back. Along with the nine other Travelers. How was that possible? Where had they gone? Where were they now? How could so many have died, only to return? Where was the previous generation of Travelers? Were Mark and Courtney dead? What's going to happen to the territories? To Halla? To Bobby? Ahhhh!

Well, kids, the wait is over. No more questions. No more cliff-hangers. No more "To be continued . . ." It's all here. The conclusion of an adventure through time and space. It's no longer about individual books and separate stories. With this book, the Pendragon saga takes full shape. It's all one story now, and this is the finale.

For me, the Pendragon saga is complete. For the rest of you, there's one more chapter to go. One more trip through the flume. One more adventure.

Bobby Pendragon is not finished yet.

Neither are you.

Not by a long shot.

I ask your indulgence in allowing me to say for one last time:

Hobey ho, let's go!

—D. J. MacHale

PENDRAGON

JOURNAL OF AN ADVENTURE THROUGH
TIME AND SPACE

Book Ten:

The Soldiers of Halla

THE END

Yeah. The end. Or pretty close to it, anyway. The battle for Halla is over. For sure this time. No more surprises. No more twists. No more false hope. It's done. I promise. I guess it's not a big surprise to say that I'm still around. Not that my survival was a lock or anything, it's just that if my existence had ended, I wouldn't be writing this, would I?

Still, a very big question remains. What's next? What will become of me now that my job as a Traveler is complete? Things aren't the same. The battle with Saint Dane has altered Halla, and I'm no longer sure what my place is. The future I'm looking at now scares me more than anything I've encountered over the past few years. That's really saying something.

So I guess I lied. It's not really the end. The final chapter of the existence of Bobby Pendragon has yet to be written. I know that I will have to deal with that at some point, but not just yet. Before I can face the future, I must first deal with the past.

I'm writing this journal in a small, sparse room that has become my temporary home. I have no idea how long I'll be here. My guess is that I'll be allowed to stay for as long as it takes to finish this journal. I'm not sure if I should pick up the pace and get it done, or string this out for as long as possible to avoid dealing with the next phase of life. As always, there's a certain comfort that comes from writing these journals. I think that's because when I write, I already know what happened. Writing is safe. There are no surprises. Though reliving these events is reassuring, it can also be painful. I'd just as soon forget about much of what has happened to me and my friends. But that's not the point. Writing isn't just about Bobby therapy. It's about documenting what has happened on my adventure through time and space. This is what I do. It's what I've always done. Why stop now? The last chapter needs to be written.

Whoever you are, reader, if you're up to speed and have seen my previous journals, you'll know that I didn't have many opportunities to sit and write. Things were happening too fast. It wasn't until I found myself in this room that I could take a breath, collect my thoughts, and get it all down. I wrote several of my previous entries here as well. I deliberately concluded my Journal #36 where I did because it seemed like a natural place to finish one major chapter before beginning another. When I spin my memory back to that moment, it's with mixed emotions.

I was at the lowest point imaginable. Second Earth was lost. Scores of people had been sucked into a monstrous flume created by Alexander Naymeer. Mark and Courtney were gone. Patrick Mac was killed. Alder was killed. Saint Dane's Convergence was complete.

And I had become a murderer. I killed Alexander Naymeer. I acted out of anger. Out of weakness. It was exactly what Saint Dane wanted me to do. That one heinous act gave him his final victory. Halla was his. He no longer needed the flumes and they were destroyed. I was flung through space and found myself in a desolate wasteland. Beaten. Lost. Alone. I couldn't have been in a lower place. I had failed. Miserably.

So why exactly are those emotions "mixed" for me? Though I had reached bottom, I soon discovered that I wasn't alone. Uncle Press kept his promise. He came back. So did all the other Travelers. My friends. I had seen many of them die, including Uncle Press, but somehow we were all brought together again. How was that possible? Were we all dead? It didn't matter to me at that moment, because it seemed like a dream. But it wasn't. We were truly together.

It was then that Uncle Press gave us our final challenge. He once told me that Saint Dane could not be beaten until he felt as if he had won. There was no question in my mind. Saint Dane had won. Going by Uncle Press's reasoning, that was good news. How twisted is that? As we all stood in that mysterious, empty place, Uncle Press asked me a question that was simple, but carried a load of weight: "Will it end here?"

I looked to the other Travelers. Gunny Van Dyke. Vo Spader. Elli Winter. Siry Remudi. Patrick Mac. Aja Killian. Kasha. Alder and Loor. Their looks back to me were unmistakable. They weren't ready to give up. It was their conviction that gave me the strength to decide that, as grim as things had gotten, as many mistakes as I'd made, as badly as we'd been beaten, there was still some fight left in the Travelers.

It gave me the confidence to say to Uncle Press, "We are *so* not done yet."

That's where I ended my previous journal and where I will begin my next. Journal #37. The final journal of Bobby Pendragon's adventure through time and space.

Before I can look forward, I must look back.

One last time.

1

The missile hit without warning.

We didn't know we were under attack until, well, we were under attack. It was fast. It was violent. I had no idea what it was all about, other than the fact that I had only been on this strange territory for a few minutes, and I already wanted to leave.

Uncle Press was walking maybe forty yards ahead of the Travelers. The small missile screamed in and thumped down in the space between us. If it had landed twenty yards farther ahead, Uncle Press would have been liquefied. Twenty yards back and every last Traveler of Halla would have been obliterated. Our final stand against Saint Dane would have been over before it had the chance to get started. We were lucky.

Lucky? That's a relative term. After the first *boom*, good luck seemed to be in short supply.

"Down!" Uncle Press screamed as he ran back through the burning debris that hung in the air.

Too late. I was already down. The force of the blast had knocked me off my feet. My eyes stung from the cloud of dirt that hit me. My ears rang. Since I had been leading the group, I hoped that I had taken the worst of it. I rubbed my eyes with the sleeve of my Second Earth sweater, desperate to clear my vision and get back some control before another missile arrived.

Again, too late. Two more explosions erupted, though not as close as the first. I was halfway to my feet and got knocked down again. I heard a scream of fear. Not of pain, of fear. That was good. Fear was better than pain. It sounded to me like Elli. She was an older, frail woman. She hadn't experienced anything like this before. If any of us needed help, it would be her.

"You okay?" Uncle Press yelled at me.

"Yeah, where's Elli?"

"I got her," he said, then screamed out to the others, "Scatter! Find cover in the ruins!"

Ruins? What ruins? All I had seen of this wasteland was a bunch of dust in the air. At one point I caught a glimpse of a tall, tilted building through the haze, but it was too far away to reach while trying to dodge a storm of incoming missiles. I wiped my tearing eyes to scan for something closer.

I heard a loud *whoosh* and sensed, more than felt, a dark shape swooping by overhead. Looking up, I caught the fleeting image of a low-flying aircraft. It could have been a small helicopter, but it seemed more squat than that. I didn't hear the typical sound of a chopper engine, either. Whatever was powering this thing, it was pretty quiet. Was this the beastie shooting at us? It flew by at treetop level. That is, if there had been any trees in this barren place. As I watched in wonder, I was hit with the beam of a powerful light. Turning quickly I looked up to see two more of these flying craft headed toward us. Each had a single headlight that swept the ground. Searching.

"We must find shelter," came a calm voice at my shoulder. It was Loor. She was still in one piece, I'm happy to say. Looking around I saw that none of the Travelers seemed hurt. Uncle Press had an arm around Elli's shoulder and was hurrying her off to . . . somewhere. Everyone else was following Uncle Press's instructions and moving in different directions to find shelter.

Kasha, Gunny, and Spader scrambled together in one direction, Alder and Patrick in another. Siry led Aja off, holding her hand like a protective brother. To him she was a living legend from the distant past of his own territory. I knew he would protect her. They all disappeared into the swirling smoke and sand. Only Loor and I still stood in the path of the oncoming aircraft.

Boom! Boom!

Two more missiles tore at the ground. These flying craft weren't just searching. They were attacking. I grabbed Loor's arm and ran. I didn't know where we were going, but we ran. We sprinted blindly through the thick dust that hung suspended in the air. I heard the sounds of more explosions. Some distant. Some closer. The only thing I knew for sure was that nobody was shooting back at them. These craft were hunting, uncontested. I was totally disoriented. The only thing that felt real was the deafening roar and the shaking ground as the missiles exploded around us like a violent fireworks display.

"Structures," Loor announced, looking ahead.

Through the dust I saw the outline of several small stone buildings. None looked higher than maybe two stories. They were clustered together around a central, open area that could have been a courtyard at one time. I say "at one time" because these buildings were bombed out. Destroyed. Empty. Whatever they were, they were no longer. This war we found ourselves in the middle of wasn't new. We were surrounded by destruction. The derelict buildings looked to be made of gray stone, much of which was shattered and scarred. As we got closer, I saw that the courtyard area held a large, empty hole in the dead center. It wasn't a bomb crater; it looked like a man-made pool of some kind. Or a moat, since it was basically a trough surrounding a pile of large boulders. There was no water in it though, only dirt and debris.

"We can take shelter in there," Loor suggested.

The two of us ran to the edge of the trough and jumped in. The sides were just above head level. I had to stand on tiptoe to peer back out.

"Where are we?" Loor asked. She wasn't even out of breath. "What is this territory?"

"I was hoping you knew."

"I do not. Nor do any of the others."

"The flumes exploded," I told her. "I saw them. It was like I was floating in space and they just . . . self-destructed."

"I know," she said calmly. "I saw it as well. We all did. Wherever we are, Pendragon, we will not be leaving."

Two of the dark helicopters swooped overhead. We ducked. We didn't need to. We weren't the targets. The marauding shadows headed for what seemed to be a long, low building around forty yards from us. They hovered over the dilapidated structure. Their headlight beams cut through the dust, trained on a large, jagged wound in the wall that had probably been a doorway at one time.

An amplified voice blasted from one of the gunships.

"Walk out of the building," came a no-nonsense command.

The dust seemed to be clearing. It gave me a better view of the ships. They were indeed helicopters, but without the familiar tail and rear rotors. Instead, a single overhead rotor controlled the craft. Two pontoonlike skids hung beneath. Affixed to the sides of these pontoons was the bad news. The rocket launchers.

Who were they? Why were they coming after us? Where the heck were we in the first place? My momentary thrill of being reunited with Uncle Press and the rest of the Travelers had turned into a confused nightmare.

"I want to get a closer look," I said to Loor, and made my way around the boulders in the center of this dry pool. She tried to stop me, but I was already moving quickly toward the far side of the moat, closer to the building that was being targeted. Loor followed. The two of us stood peering up over the lip as the scene unfolded.

"Did any of the Travelers go in there?" Loor asked.

"No idea. Maybe. They ran off in all directions."

The amplified voice boomed again. "There is no option. You must surrender immediately."

"Or what?" I whispered to Loor.

I sensed movement to my left. Somebody was creeping up on us. I tensed. Loor did too. I gave her a quick glance, as if to say, "Ready?"

She nodded. She knew.

We quickly dodged in two different directions. If somebody was going to attack, they wouldn't get us together. I hit the inside wall of the trough, crouching, ready. Loor swept her wooden stave from behind her back and held it out, poised to fend off whoever was dumb enough to attack us. We froze. Neither of us understood what we were seeing.

Actually, I understood it better than Loor, but that didn't mean I wasn't confused.

What we were both squared off against, ready to battle, was a penguin. I'm serious. A two-foot-tall, black and white penguin. The goofy little bird stood in the center of the trough, staring at us as if to say, "Who are you two clowns?"

"Is it dangerous?" Loor asked, confused.

It was actually funny seeing Loor coiled up, ready to battle a little penguin. I guess it's more funny now as I think back on it. At the time I didn't feel like laughing.

The amplified voice boomed one more time. "You have been warned."

What followed can be best described as obliteration. Both flying vehicles unloaded their weapons on the building. One drifted slowly to the right, the other to the left, as they launched a series of missiles at the already damaged structure. Sharp pieces of stone flew everywhere. That broke the penguin's cool, and it waddled off quickly. Fire erupted inside the building, licking out of the glassless windows. Thick black smoke billowed from every crack, new and old, like blood pouring from open wounds. If any of the Travelers were in there, they were going to get hurt. Badly. I made a move to jump up onto the lip of the trough to see if anybody needed help, but Loor held me back.

"What would you do?" she said calmly.

She was right. There was nothing to do but watch and hope.

"Look!" she declared.

On the far left end of the building, people were crawling out of a window, escaping. People we didn't recognize. They wore raggy, nondescript clothes. I guess back home in

Connecticut I'd say they looked like homeless people. They didn't quite look Flighter nasty, but they were definitely people who were having a rough time. A few of the men actually wore what looked like ragged business suits. Some women wore blue jeans and sweaters. There were a couple of kids, too.

A powerful-looking guy with long black hair that touched his shoulders stood outside the window, helping the others out. He wore jeans and a faded, torn sweatshirt. It looked as if he were in charge. At the very least he was taking control of the situation. He seemed more worried about getting the others to safety than about his own getaway.

The gunships hadn't seen them. Yet. They continued their methodical move toward each end of the building, firing away.

The guy with the black hair was doing all he could to get those still inside to hurry. He was too far away for me to see exactly what he looked like. He wasn't big, but he was strong. His chin was covered with thick beard stubble. He pulled the others out of the building, mostly helping the smaller children to safety. He waved for them to pick up the pace. No sooner did he help one person down than he reached back to get the next.

"Brave man," Loor said under her breath.

From Loor that was high praise.

"He'd better get out of there," I said.

The missiles were drawing closer to the escapees. The brave guy kept glancing at the approaching helicopter, calculating how much time he had, trying to get as many people to safety as possible before jamming out of there himself.

The barrage stopped. For a second I thought it was over. It wasn't. I quickly realized what was happening. Whoever was piloting the craft had finally spotted the runners. The second gunship stopped firing and flew quickly to join the first. They must have been in communication. They hovered, side by side, their rocket launchers rotating slowly toward the window where the frightened people were making their escape.

The brave guy didn't stop pulling people out. As each new person dropped out of the window, they jumped up and ran off, leaving him to his work.

"There is no longer a need to fire," Loor announced. "They have found their quarry."

"I wonder if he's going to surrender," I said.

The attackers didn't make another announcement. They didn't ask the people to stop running and come forward. They didn't land and take prisoners.

They opened fire.

Both gunships unloaded on the building. The people in the window jumped back inside, but there was no way they could survive the barrage. The brave guy who helped so many escape dove around the corner of the building. I didn't know if he lived or died. One thing was for sure, whoever these people were, they did not want to be taken alive, though from the looks of things, the attackers weren't there for prisoners.

"It's a slaughter," I declared.

Another sound broke through the torrent of rocket fire and exploding stone. A sound that made no sense. It was hollow and haunted, like the bellow of a forlorn animal. It was loud, and it was coming from behind us. I turned quickly to see that we were no longer alone in that deep, concrete trough. Standing a few yards away was a very large, very angry polar bear.

Loor and I froze.

Its eyes were wild and scared. It seemed to be just as terrified of the bombing as the victims were. Maybe more so. There was nowhere for us to go. The trough was only five yards wide. Its walls were too high for us to scale quickly. At least, quickly enough to escape if the bear decided it didn't like us. We could always turn and run, but judging from the size of the bear, it would be on us with a single leap. We both realized that we had only one choice. If the bear were to attack, we would have to fight.

"Maybe it's tame," I whispered, without taking my eyes off the behemoth.

As if in answer, the bear reared up on its hind legs, towering over us. It held up two mighty paws with dangerously long claws, howled . . . and attacked.

It wasn't tame.

2

We had no time to react. Loor brought her stave forward. I turned sideways, poised to deflect a mighty swipe from the bear's huge paw. Or to duck under it. The monster's front paws hit the ground, and it bounded through the trough, charging us.

It never made it.

With a snarl and a flash, a large jungle cat leaped from the boulders encircled by the dry moat, landing on the bear's back. The surprised animal reared again, but the cat didn't back off. It dug its own claws into the bear's neck, locking its teeth onto the animal's shoulder. This was no ordinary cat.

It was Kasha, the Traveler from Eelong.

She clung to the polar bear tenaciously as the angry animal swung its head to try to fling her off. It was a disturbing sight in more ways than one. These were two wild animals, locked in battle. There were no rules. No restrictions. For all I knew it would be a battle to the death. It was gruesome. Making it all the more surreal was the fact that one of the animals was Kasha. I had seen her die a few years before, when she was crushed by falling rocks as the flume on Eelong crumbled. Yet there she was, about as alive as you can get, locked in a vicious blood battle with an enraged bear.

Loor tried to get in a shot with her stave to help Kasha, but the fight was too violent. The huge bear thrashed wildly. There was nothing she could do. One stray swipe of the bear's claws and she could have lost an arm. I pulled Loor back and shoved her toward the outer wall of the trough. We both jumped up, grabbed the edge, and hoisted ourselves up and out. The fight was left to Kasha. She would either triumph or die. Again.

She clung tenaciously to the back of the bear. The bear knew it was losing. It did all it could to shake her. Finally the behemoth hurled itself against the inner wall. Kasha wasn't ready for that. She was jolted and flung off the bear's back. She landed in the bottom of the dry moat, stunned but not out. She quickly sprang back to her feet, or paws, ready to attack again.

Blood streamed from the bear's wounds, glowing crimson against its dirty white fur. A tense moment followed. Would it attack or retreat? I think the bear was debating the same question, and finally came to the right conclusion. It had had enough. It didn't want any part of Kasha. With one last tortured bellow, it reared up, spun, and bounded away, headed for the far side of the trough. In a surprisingly graceful leap for an animal so immense, the white bear launched itself off its hind legs and clawed its way out of the cement moat. Once out, it lumbered off quickly to lick its wounds somewhere else.

"Hobey, Pendragon. What kind of natty place is this?" came a voice from the rocks that were surrounded by the dry moat.

Looking up, I saw Spader sitting there, wide eyed. Next to him stood the penguin, looking equally wide eyed. Or as wide eyed as a penguin can get. A penguin. A freakin' penguin. And a polar bear. Why were these cold-weather animals hanging around here? It wasn't cold at all. In fact, it was kind of hot. I spun the other way to look at the building that was being targeted by the gunships. The attack was over. Both helicopters had stopped firing. They rose straight up and soon disappeared into the clouds. A few seconds later I no longer heard their engines. Whatever their mission had been, it was complete. In their wake they left the remains of an obliterated building. I didn't want to know how many people lay dead or wounded inside.

"Are you okay?" I called to Kasha.

The klee rose up on her back paws, standing like a human. "Of course," she answered with confidence. "That beast was nowhere near as vicious as a tang." She wiped a smear of blood from her mouth.

Yeah. Disgusting.

I looked at Loor. Loor shrugged and raised an eyebrow. She was impressed. Kasha was Loor's kind of girl. Or klee. Or whatever. "We must find the others," she declared.

"I'll find them," Kasha answered. Before I had the chance to thank her for saving us, she dropped back down onto all fours, sprang out of the trough, and ran off in search of the other Travelers.

Spader, Loor, and I remained. I couldn't speak for them, but I was shaken. The events that had occurred over the last few hours were nothing short of impossible.

We had lost the battle for Second Earth. Naymeer and his Ravinian cult had lured seventy thousand people into Yankee Stadium, then created a monstrous flume to swallow them up. I had killed Naymeer by dropping him from a hovering helicopter into the mouth of the giant flume. It was the act that gave Saint Dane his final victory. The helicopter was then sucked into the massive flume, along with Saint Dane, Nevva Winter, and me. Instead of crashing, I found myself floating, alone, in space, where I witnessed the destruction of the flumes.

Soon after, I found myself on this barren territory, where Uncle Press and the other Travelers showed up. Dead friends were suddenly, well, not dead, and together we chose to make a final, desperate stand against Saint Dane.

That's when the gunships attacked, though we weren't the target. Those odd helicopters were after the people who were hiding in that building. We got caught in the cross fire.

Oh yeah, and Loor and I were nearly mauled by a polar bear.

And Spader was hanging out with a penguin.

So I guess it's understandable when I say that I was a little shaken.

"Pendragon, are we dead?" Loor asked, breaking the silence.

Good question. It was definitely on my top ten list of explanations for what was happening. In fact, it was in the top two. The other was that it was all a dream. But dreams never lasted this long. Or made me cough. I really wanted a third good explanation, but I couldn't come up with one.

Spader had left his penguin pal and crossed through the dry moat to join us.

"None of this makes sense," he declared. "One minute Gunny and me were patching up a wonky boat on the river in Black Water, the next thing I know we're wandering around here in . . . Where might we be, mates?"

I glanced around at the squat, derelict buildings. I had absolutely no idea.

"Better question," I said. "Where is Uncle Press taking us?"

"He's taking you home," came the answer from a soft voice behind us that I instantly recognized. I hadn't heard that voice in years, but I knew it for sure. I looked at Loor. She gasped. Her eyes went wide. Loor never registered surprise, but at that moment, she was definitely surprised. She stared at me. It was as if she didn't want to look and learn that it was a mistake.

It wasn't.

"Hello, Daughter."

We all looked to see Osa, Loor's mother, walking slowly toward us. The Batu warrior was as beautiful as the day I had last seen her—the day she died while protecting me from Bedoowan knights. She no longer seemed as tall, but that was because I had grown. Her dark skin was impossibly clean looking, in spite of the dirt and dust that swirled around us. She wore a long, red wrap that draped off one shoulder and stretched to the ground. She looked every bit as strong and graceful as I remembered her.

"Mother?" was the only word Loor could get out. I'd never heard her so tentative.

"I have missed you, my sweet girl."

Loor did something that was aggressively un-Loor like . . . and absolutely perfect. She dropped her wooden stave and ran to her mother. The two joined in an embrace that melted away years of sorrow. For that brief instant Loor became a little girl. Tears rolled down her cheeks.

"I am so proud of you," Osa whispered to her daughter.

She looked up to us and added, "I am proud of you all."

I didn't know what to say. I *really* didn't know what to say. I didn't feel like I deserved her praise, but more than that, my head was still trying to wrap itself around what was happening. Osa had died in a fury of arrows. I was there. There was no mistake. Yet there she was, as alive as we were. Assuming we were alive, that is.

Loor pulled away from her mother, but still clung to her. "Help me understand," she said through her tears.

Osa gave her daughter a warm smile, which she then shared with Spader and me.

"You are all going home," she said. "That is where you will learn."

"Home?" Spader said, surprised. "Hobey, I don't even know where home is anymore."

"Then it's time I showed ya, spinney fish," came a gravelly man's voice I didn't recognize.

Spader did. He spun on his heel to see a man wearing an aquaneer uniform striding toward us.

Spader stared at the guy and gasped, "It's me *dad*!"

"Who else would it be, now?" the man declared. He looked like Spader, only an older version with streaks of gray in his hair. He even had the same Aussie-sounding accent that Spader had. But Spader's dad had been killed by the poisoned food supply on Cloral. Of course we all knew who was ultimately responsible for his death. Saint Dane. His father's murder had sent Spader off the deep end. He became driven by the need for revenge. More than once he lost control of his own emotions and put us all in trouble as his anger outweighed his good sense. But that was in the past. Now his father was back. Somehow.

"Let me have a look at ya!" the gregarious man bellowed,

and wrapped his arm around Spader's neck in a friendly bear hug. "You got bigger, you did, but still not big enough to take me on."

Spader clutched at his dad. He was overcome with emotion.

"How?" was all he could get out.

"How indeed, spinney fish. Let's be off now," he said, while leading Spader away.

Spader pulled away from his father and looked back toward us.

"But, Dad . . ." He let the word trail as he gestured to us.

"No worries, mate," Spader's dad assured him. "You'll see 'em again, you will. Trust me on that."

Spader looked at me with confusion. As much as he wanted to be with his dad, he didn't want to leave us.

"It is all right," Osa assured him. "You will all be together again."

Spader nodded, dazed. Just as quickly, the smile returned to his face, and he threw his arm around his father. The two strode away, arms around each other like old chums, laughing. They walked into the swirling dust and seemed to disappear. I mean that literally. I wasn't sure if the dust swallowed them up, or they actually disappeared.

"The same is happening with all the Travelers, Pendragon," Osa said.

I caught a glimpse of two men walking together on the far side of the moat. It was Gunny, along with another black guy who looked even older than he was. The man had a hand on Gunny's shoulder in a fatherly way. I couldn't hear what he was saying, but Gunny was listening and nodding. A moment later they disappeared into the swirling dust.

"Where are they going?" I asked.

"I told you, they are going home," Osa answered. "They all are."

"To their home territories?" I asked.

"No," she answered. "They are going *home*. You will be too."

With that, she led Loor off.

"We cannot leave Pendragon," Loor protested. "Our destiny is to be together."

"Indeed it is, and you shall be," Osa assured her. "First you must learn."

Loor looked to me, waiting for my opinion.

"Go," I said. "I'll be okay. I think."

"He will be," Osa said. "You all will be."

Loor relaxed. She trusted her mother. After all, she was the Traveler from Zadaa before Loor. As Spader's dad was the Traveler from Cloral before Spader. As Uncle Press was the Traveler from Second Earth before I was. If we couldn't trust them, who *could* we trust? The weight of the world, no, the weight of Halla had been on our shoulders for a very long time. It was nice to know there was now someplace we could look for guidance. And help. And maybe even relief.

Loor nodded in understanding and followed her mom. The two warriors walked away from me, looking more like each other than ever before. A moment later they were gone. Had they simply walked farther away? Or had they disappeared too? I didn't know. I hoped that answer would come soon. I glanced around, wanting to see one of the other Travelers. There was no movement. No sound other than the hollow wind. I glanced over at the destroyed building. As much as I wanted to know what that was all about, I couldn't bring myself to investigate. I figured I'd find out soon enough. I didn't want to run into that angry polar bear again either.

"Uncle Press?" I called out.

No answer. Where was everyone? I feared that some of the others might have been hurt in the attack.

"Elli? Kasha?"

Still no answer.

The penguin hadn't moved from where he'd been standing next to Spader. What the heck was that about? Where was I?

As if in answer to my thoughts, the wind picked up slightly, rustling my hair. Slowly the floating dust in the air began to clear. I could make out more shapes around me. I stood near the moat in the center of the circle of low, battered stone buildings. What was this place? Some kind of lonely outpost in the middle of nowhere? As the dust cleared, I was able to see beyond the buildings. There didn't seem to be much out there other than open, arid land. It made me feel as if I were standing in an oasis. I remembered the tall building I'd caught brief glimpses of earlier, and hoped that the dust would clear enough for me to get a better view of it.

I turned slowly, doing a one-eighty, looking off in the distance to see if I could spot the tilted building. Now that the air was clearing, I began to see that I wasn't surrounded by open land after all. Far from it. I sensed massive shapes that stood between me and that mysterious, tilted building. There were other structures, larger than the ones near me, though they looked just as battered. It soon became clear that I was in a ruined city. It all felt vaguely familiar, yet not. Had I been here before? Was I on Earth? Rubic City? The city of Rune? None of the above?

The dust cleared further. I expected to see a Lifelight pyramid, or perhaps the castle where Veego and LaBerge ran their violent games. I squinted, racking my brain, trying to understand why it all seemed so familiar.

I'm not sure what made it all come together. Maybe it was something subliminal that I couldn't consciously place. Maybe it was a smell, or the shadows made by the sunlight that tried to peek through the gray clouds. It could have been any of those things, but I'm thinking it was the penguin and the polar bear. The two oddest clues helped me realize the truth.

I was indeed standing in an oasis. At least that's what many people considered it to be. It was a magical place that existed in an amazing city. I had been here before. Many times.

"We first brought you here the day before Shannon was born," the familiar voice of a woman said. "Remember?"

I froze. Was it possible? It was the last thing I expected. I'm not sure why. Maybe it was because it felt like too much to ask for. Maybe I had given up hope. Maybe I didn't want to open myself up to the possibility, only to be disappointed and crushed. I felt something nudge the backs of my legs. I didn't jump in surprise. I knew exactly what it was. I had felt it hundreds of times before, in another life. Memories like that become part of your being. Poking his head between my legs from behind, looking for attention, was my dog, Marley. His big, brown golden retriever nose pushed its way forward, followed by those big brown eyes. I could feel his whole body rock, as his tail wagged happily. I reached down and held his head with both my hands.

"Hi, Marley-Mar," I said through my tears. "Where've you been?"

That's when I knew where I was. The buildings. The polar bear. The penguin. I was standing next to the sea lion pool in the zoo that was on the edge of New York's Central Park. At least, what was left of it. The huge, tilted building in the distance was now all too familiar. It was the Empire State Building. I was on Earth. What I still didn't know was *when* I was. At that moment, I really didn't care.

"Did you have to grow up so fast?" the woman said.

I had to hold myself back from breaking out in tears. Or bursting with joy. It's a fine line. I turned around to see them. My family. Mom. Dad. My little sister, Shannon. Though she wasn't so little anymore. How old was she now? Thirteen? She was now a young lady in jeans and a pink sweater. She looked perfect. They all did.

We stood facing one another, nobody really sure of what to do. I was suddenly hit with a fearful thought. I had been down this road once before, and it didn't have a happy ending.

"Is this a Lifelight jump?" I asked.

"A *what*?" Shannon asked with a wiseass look that can only come from a thirteen-year-old girl who has been working long and hard to perfect it.

"No, Bobby," my dad answered. "It's us. For real."

I couldn't move. It was too much for me to comprehend. I hadn't seen my family since the day they'd left me at home to go to the basketball game at Stony Brook Junior High. They had disappeared. My life had disappeared. Finding them was one of the driving forces behind everything I had done as a Traveler. Maybe the only driving force. And now, they were standing in front of me.

"So who won the game?" was the first question that came to mind.

Shannon rolled her eyes. "You're such a dork." But she gave me a sly smile. I loved Shannon.

"Stony Brook lost," Dad said. "Bad. They needed you."

"And I needed you," I replied.

"I know," Mom said, barely holding back her own tears. "That's why we're here."

That did it. I ran to them and threw my arms around my family. The moment I had longed for all those years had finally arrived. We were back together. The Pendragons were a family again. I don't know how long we stayed hugging that way. It could have been a week for all I cared. I wasn't going anywhere. I didn't want to let go, for fear they'd disappear again.

Dad put his hand behind my head and held my neck. His eyes were as red as mine were. "I'm proud of you, Son."

I nodded in thanks and burst out in tears. I couldn't help myself. The floodgates of emotion and relief were open. Things were going to be okay. When I finally got my act together, I straightened up, wiped my eyes, and said, "So what the hell is up with Uncle Press? You gonna tell me what that guy's about or what?"

"We are," Mom said with a chuckle. "You're going to learn everything. But first we have to go home."

"To Stony Brook?" I asked hopefully.

"No," Mom answered. "We're going to the place where you were born."

I let that sink in, then added, "Something tells me we're not going to Second Earth."

"We're not" was Mom's simple, direct answer.

It was the right answer. The only answer. Though it scared me to death. I was finally going to learn the truth.

About me. About the Travelers. And maybe most important, about Saint Dane.

"Then let's go," I said.

Dad led the way. Mom kept her arm around my shoulders, Shannon's arm was around my waist. Marley ran in front of us, his big bushy tail wagging.

We took maybe two steps when I realized . . .

We weren't on Earth anymore.

3

We had stepped out of one strange situation, directly into another.

There were no flumes involved. No journey that I could tell of. I didn't get the sense that we had traveled any distance at all. Except that one moment we were walking through the windswept ruins of the zoo in Central Park, and a second later we were in an environment I can best describe as being alien. Though I guess "alien" can mean a lot of things. I stood in wonder, looking around at the most barren, forlorn chunk of real estate I had ever seen.

The air was clear. That's the best thing I could say about the place. It was night, though there was plenty of light to see by. The sky was full of stars. More than I could imagine. I didn't recognize a single constellation. The night sky was alive with thin, wispy clouds of all shapes and sizes that moved quickly overhead. At least, I thought they were clouds. They weren't like any clouds I'd ever seen. Some glowed with color. Reds, greens, oranges, and yellows. Others were dark shadows. None were so thick that they blocked out the stars, yet they definitely had substance. I could see right through these translucent bodies that shot across the heavens impossibly fast. Many blazed with light, as if they were somehow charged with energy. It was a tightly choreographed fireworks display in the vast night sky.

On ground level I felt as if I could see for miles, yet there was nothing to see. The landscape was made up of nothing but jagged gray rock. I saw peaks in the distance, chasms beneath them, miles of flat land in between. I thought of the lava field we once visited in Hawaii where the molten lava had spread and hardened, leaving a jagged world of gray. That's pretty much what this was, multiplied by about a million. There were no buildings. No trees. No sign of civilization. We stood at the bottom of a mountain of rock that jutted up higher than I could see. There seemed to be levels everywhere. Were there caves built into this dark matter? Could people live on this rock?

Dark matter. That's what the flumes were supposed to have been made of. The oldest known substance in the universe. The gray rock that made up this strange world looked exactly like the rock from the flumes. Was there a connection?

As much as this desolate world seemed dead, it wasn't empty. This is hard to describe, but I'll try. I sensed life. It's not like I saw people crawling around on the various levels of rock. I didn't. But I felt the presence of life. What I saw were shadows and light that moved quickly past on the edge of my vision. When I tried to look at them, they'd be gone. A few times I thought I actually saw the image of a person, but by the time I turned to focus . . . nothing. These maddening images danced beyond my ability to actually grasp them and understand what they were. Who they were. It seemed as if I were surrounded by ghosts.

Oddly, I wasn't scared. Confused maybe, but not scared.

The only thing normal about this place was my family. Though seeing them standing in that desolate place was about as abnormal as I could imagine. Dad had on his usual dark green khakis and his favorite faded Villanova sweatshirt. Mom wore a jean skirt and a black turtleneck under a white sweater. I already said that Shannon had on jeans and a pink sweater. Marley wore his blue collar that was embroidered with fish shapes. They looked about as normal as I remembered them. They were a typical-looking family from Connecticut . . . standing together on Mars.

They let me take in the surroundings without a word. I guess they were waiting for me to get used to the place. Yeah, right. Fat chance that would happen. After seeing all I thought there was to see, which wasn't much, one question jumped out ahead of all the others.

"So, uh, this is where I was born? Not exactly homey."

"It wasn't always like this," Dad replied. "This is what it has become."

"What territory is it?" I asked.

"It isn't a territory," Mom answered.

"Then what is it?" I asked, growing anxious.

"We call it Solara," Dad said. "Though others use different names. It's the essence of Halla."

I guess I should have followed that up with a surprised, "What the heck is that supposed to mean?" I didn't. Though I had no idea what he meant, I felt as if it were right. It made sense, like I already knew the truth. But I didn't. Or did I? At least, I was confident that it would eventually make sense. I didn't panic. I needed to learn. I kicked at a gray stone, sending it skittering across the rocky surface. I had a million questions. The trick was to figure out which I needed answered first.

"Do you know what happened to me?" I asked. "I mean, about what happened after I left home?"

I was surprised that Shannon was the one to answer. "We know it all, Bobby. Everything. More than you, in fact."

I didn't like the idea that my little sister was so well informed, but what the heck. If that was the worst of my problems, I figured I was doing okay.

"What happened to you guys?" I finally asked. "Where did you go?"

All three exchanged looks. It was time. I was going to find out why my family had disappeared.

"Let's sit down, Bobby," Mom said softly. "We have so much to tell you."

That made me nervous. It was as if she were getting ready to break some bad news and wanted me to be prepared.

"I'm good," I said. "I'll stand."

Shannon sat down on a hunk of rock, hugging Marley, keeping him happy, which wasn't too hard to do. Marley was a good dog.

Mom began, "Before we go any further, we want you to understand something. No matter what you hear, what you learn, you must remember that we love you. We have always loved you. Nothing will change that."

Yikes.

"You're starting to worry me, Mom," I said. "And after what I've been through, that's really saying something."

"But you must know that," she repeated. "It's important to us."

"I know, Mom," I assured her. "And I love you too. Tell me what happened."

Dad began. "Once you learned that you were a Traveler, we were no longer needed. In fact, it was important for us to leave. If we hadn't, you might never have accepted your destiny."

"So, you knew all about this from the get-go? Like, my whole life? You always knew I'd be chosen as a Traveler?"

"You weren't chosen to be a Traveler," Shannon said. "You were *created* to be a Traveler."

I changed my mind. I sat down.

"You weren't alone," Mom added. "It was the same for all the Travelers. They were each put on their territory to grow up there, learn about its culture, become part of the world. It was all in preparation to try and stop Saint Dane."

Dad said, "On each territory it was the job of the previous Travelers to mentor the new Travelers. To guide them and to give them a moral compass, based on their particular world, that would guide them during their difficult mission."

I saw something on the edge of my vision. This time when I looked, I thought I caught a fleeting image, far in the distance. It looked like Kasha walking upright with another klee. It was Seegen. Her father. The Traveler from Eelong before her. Was she getting the same talk I was? Were all the other Travelers here in this barren, forsaken place learning of their true history?

"So the Travelers before my generation didn't battle Saint Dane?" I asked.

"No," Dad said with certainty. "They were preparing you and the others for the battle."

I nodded, letting this sink in.

"But you guys aren't Travelers. Or are you?"

"Not exactly," Dad answered. "But we are the same as you. It was planned for you to have a Traveler mentor, but circumstances changed. Saint Dane saw to that. He was already at work before you became a physical part of Second Earth. Things had to change. We became your family, and Press was given the task of mentoring you."

"So who bailed? Who was supposed to be my mentor if it wasn't you guys or Uncle Press?"

"Alexander Naymeer," Dad said flatly.

It was a good thing I was sitting down.

Naymeer was definitely a Traveler. But like Nevva Winter, he was corrupted by Saint Dane.

"Do you know what happened to him?" I asked tentatively. I hoped they didn't, since what happened to him was that I had killed him. That was the kind of nasty tidbit you wanted to keep from your family.

"I told you," Shannon said with a hint of thirteen-year-old impatience. "We know it all."

So much for keeping things from my family. I jumped up and paced nervously. Though I had wanted to know the truth for so long, hearing it wasn't easy. It was a lot to get my head around, and we were just getting started.

"Saint Dane told me we were illusions," I said. "I don't know, maybe I'm in denial, but it's kind of hard to accept that none of us are actually real."

"Because we *are* real!" Mom said with passion. She quickly stepped forward and took both my hands. "I told you before, sweetheart, the love we have for you, and that I know you have for us, isn't a fantasy. Or a mirage. All that happened before you left Second Earth was reality. Everything we did. Everything we shared. It was real. We were given a gift. We spent more than fourteen years living on Earth, experiencing all that world had to offer. That can never be taken away from us. We were as human as anyone else."

"But not anymore?" I asked.

She didn't answer. At least not with words. Her sad eyes said enough.

It was an odd feeling to know that my family had known the truth all along and had been keeping it from me. I guess that was all part of the deal, but still. They were my family! Mom and Dad taught me not to lie. As it turned out, they were lying to me every day.

"You couldn't know," Mom said, as if reading my mind. "I'm sorry that we kept this all from you, but you needed to be a part of Second Earth. It was all about your being a normal person with the perspective and experiences of your territory. You were fighting for the people of Second Earth. In order to do that, you needed to believe you were one of them."

I looked up at the starry sky, watching the colorful, charged clouds flying by. It was beautiful. Though as spectacular as that sight was, the ground around us was a total contrast. It was dark. Bleak. Desolate.

"What is this place?" I continued. "I'm afraid you're going to tell me we're really little green aliens from the planet Nimrod or something."

When I looked down at my mom for her answer, I blinked. She stood in front of me, holding my hands, but I could see through her. Literally. I could see Shannon and Marley right through my mom.

"Mom?" I gasped.

"It's all right," she answered soothingly.

It wasn't all right. Mom was disappearing. Her hands no longer had substance. I quickly glanced to Dad and Shannon. They too were flickering, as if they were lights that were slowly running out of power. Dad walked toward us, wavering between solid and transparent.

"I told you that Solara wasn't always like this," he said soberly. Sadly. "This is what Saint Dane has wrought. His only hope of controlling Halla is by destroying all you see around you. Or at least destroying what it should be."

I heard a quick bark from Marley. When I looked to my dog, he was gone. Disappeared.

"What's happening?" I asked in a panic.

Dad said, "Our ability to exist as physical beings comes from all that surrounds us here. We are fed by the essence of Halla. It's that very essence that Saint Dane has been methodically destroying."

This was all getting a bit too cosmic for me. I needed answers, and it didn't look as if Mom and Dad were going to be around much longer to give them. Shannon jumped up, ran to me, and kissed me on the cheek. It felt like nothing more than a soft, sweet breeze. She was nearly gone.

"I miss you, Bibs," she said. "Don't worry about us. Kick some ass, all right? We'll be watching."

She had called me Bibs since she was a baby and couldn't pronounce Bobby. That had to have been real, right? I reached out for her, but too late. She'd disappeared. My sister was gone. Again. In the sky above me, I heard what sounded like rumbling thunder. I glanced up to see one of the dark clouds suddenly glow bright red.

"Mom?" I gasped in desperation.

My parents stood together. They were nearly gone.

"This is right, Bobby," Mom said reassuringly. "You don't need us. We only came to see you again, and let you know that we're fine. That *you're* fine. You don't have to worry about us any longer."

"But . . . where are you going?"

"Nowhere," Dad answered. "And everywhere. Shannon

is right. We'll be watching. Your job isn't done just yet."

"You can't go!" I cried. "I've got more questions now than before!"

"We love you, Bobby," Mom said. "We're proud of you, and maybe most important, we believe in you."

"I don't want to lose you again!" I screamed.

"Then make things right," Dad said.

A moment later they were gone. I had lost my family. Again. At least, I thought I had. In the dark sky above I saw two more dark clouds crackle with light. One flashed yellow, the other deep blue. What the heck was that about? I found myself standing alone on a shelf of gray rock on a desolate world that was supposedly my birthplace. Not at all how I thought the day would play out. But was I truly alone? As I said before, I felt the presence of life around me. It was more like a feeling of energy, or spirit, than anything physical. I know, that's weird. It felt weird to me, too. But I wasn't afraid. Not even when I caught glimpses of figures that could have been people who floated by. I kept turning, hoping to bring one into focus, but that didn't happen. Could one of them have been Shannon, or my mom or dad? Was that what they meant when they said they weren't going anywhere? Were they still right beside me, only in some kind of spectral form? Or had they flown up and become colorful clouds in the sky?

Solara. What was this place? *Where* the heck was this place? Okay, *when* was this place?

"Guys?" I called out. "You still here?"

I didn't expect an answer, but I got one.

"Who you talking to?" came a deep voice.

I spun to see Uncle Press standing a few yards from me, with his hands on his hips and a smile on his face.

"Uh, Mom and Dad. I think," I said, not really sure that that made sense.

"Try not to be upset with them," Uncle Press said. "For keeping the truth from you, I mean. For that matter, try not to hold it against me, either."

"I don't," I said sincerely. "I really don't. But I'm a little numb right now."

"It would be strange if you weren't," he said. "After all, your frame of reference is based on your life on Second Earth. That was the whole point. For all intents and purposes, you are from Second Earth. Right now all the Travelers are learning the truth about their real lives, just as you are."

"So, they all came from here—wherever *here* is?"

Uncle Press nodded and gazed off into the distance. I saw sadness in his eyes. "I never thought it would come to this," he said softly.

"Is it my fault?" I asked in a small voice.

Uncle Press shot me a look. "No. We may not have been as successful as I'd hoped, but it was not your fault. Nor was it the fault of any of the Travelers. This was brought on by Saint Dane."

"Are you going to tell me who he is?" I asked.

"I am."

"Are you going to tell me what this world of rock is?"

"I am."

"One more question—"

"Only one?" he asked playfully.

"Okay, lots more questions. But one that matters more than any other."

"Go for it."

"Do we really have a shot at stopping him?"

Uncle Press glanced around at this strange world once

again. An odd feeling came over me. I sensed that I wasn't the only one who wanted that answer. Whatever forces were at play here, whatever beings inhabited this lonely rock, they all wanted to know what the future held.

"I'm afraid there's only one person who can answer that, and it isn't me," he finally said.

"Then who?"

"That would be *you*, Bobby."

4

My heart raced.

This was it. I was going to learn the truth. The whole truth. About my existence. About Halla. About Saint Dane. As I stood with Uncle Press in that stark, dark place called Solara, I realized that I was finally going to learn it all.

"Just tell me right off," I said. "You're not going to give some mysterious half answer that's going to drive me nuts, and say something like: 'Don't worry. You'll learn it all in time,' and then disappear again, are you? Because that would really piss me off."

Uncle Press laughed. It seemed odd under the circumstances. Then again it was so perfectly Uncle Press. At least that part felt right. I needed to hang on to anything familiar when it happened by. Those little things were my lifeline to sanity.

"No, it's time you knew it all," he answered.

Phew. Great. Except that's when my heart *really* started racing. I guess I wasn't so sure I was ready to know it all. I liked being Bobby Pendragon from Stony Brook, Connecticut. I liked my old life. The hope of getting it back kept me going for years. Now it seemed the biggest illusion of all was that I actually had a shot at returning to normal. Or at least what I thought was normal. I had to hope that the new "normal" was going to be something I could learn to accept. Not that I had a choice.

"Let's walk," Uncle Press said, and led me across the surface of the mysterious, dark world. We walked casually, as we had done so many times together at home. Or rather, on Second Earth. Every so often I glanced up at the dazzling, colorful clouds that careened across the sky. It was a constant reminder that this was *nothing* like home.

"Solara is the essence of Halla," Uncle Press began, gesturing.

"Yeah, that's what Dad said," I replied quickly. "Gotta tell you, not impressed so far. Though the whole cloud-light-show thing is kind of cool."

Uncle Press smiled and continued, "I guess you could say we are on the outer edges of existence. But not in the physical sense. The fact is, Solara is everywhere. Or at least, everywhere that intelligent life exists. We are as old as humanity, and we will exist for as long as humanity exists."

I didn't comment. I figured it would be better to just let him roll it all out.

"Solara was created from the energy that is mankind. All mankind on all the worlds of Halla. Solara is their spirit. It is the sum total of all intelligent life that ever was."

He fell silent, letting that sink in.

"Oh?" I responded nonchalantly. "Is that it? Wow, I thought it was something more complicated than that. I thought maybe we were aliens or superheroes or something else that was, oh, I don't know, tricky to understand. Phew."

Uncle Press gave me a sour look.

"What the hell are you talking about?" I snapped. "Created from energy? What is that supposed to mean? If that's your whole explanation, I'd just as soon you didn't bother."

He smiled. My tirade didn't throw him. I guess it's hard to throw anybody who represents the sum total of all intelligent life that ever was. Whatever that means. Sheesh.

"Give me a chance," he said, cajoling. "I know this is hard to understand."

"You have no idea."

He continued, "Each life that exists in Halla is unique. Everyone is different, no matter what world they are from. Everyone chooses their own course. One person could be a criminal, while someone else becomes a judge. One person cares for others, while others only care for themselves. One individual might have the talent to create a painting that stirs emotions, while someone else can't draw a straight line. But the person who can't draw a straight line might have an aptitude for mathematics that would make the artist's head spin. Some of that is inherited. Some of that is learned. There are so many paths to travel. So many choices to make. What drives it all is the spirit inside each individual that makes him or her unique. To understand Solara, Bobby, you have to know that that spirit, the force that makes an individual who they are, is so powerful it cannot die. Even after a person's physical body gives out, the spirit that made them who they are lives on . . . and becomes part of Solara."

"You're telling me this is . . . heaven?"

"No," Uncle Press said quickly. "This is not a reward. This just . . . is."

"Good," I replied with a chuckle. "Because it looks more

like hell." I was trying to be glib. I think it was a defense mechanism, because what I was hearing was kind of freaky. Uncle Press didn't laugh with me. He was suddenly all business. I gave up on glib.

"We exist because mankind exists," Uncle Press explained. "The sum of energy that animates and informs mankind is such a powerful force that, once released from its physical shell, it creates its own reality."

"Solara."

"Yes. Solara isn't governed by time or by space. It is pure intellect. It is not just a reflection of life, it *is* life. All life. The world you see here exists on the outer edges of physical reality. This rock is the foundation of all that is. It is the most elemental form of life. It is the beginning, but not the end, because there is no end. Halla is always expanding, therefore, so is Solara. From here we can observe every time. Every place. Every thing that has ever existed. Like I said, it is the spirit of all there is. Solara is the essence of Halla."

I stopped walking and stared at my uncle. How else was I supposed to react?

He gave me a sympathetic shrug and said, "I know it's hard to fathom because you're looking at things from the perspective of someone from one of those worlds. From Earth. This isn't exactly something that's taught in school."

"Yeah, I must have missed that class," I replied. "But I'm from *Second* Earth, right?"

"There is only one Earth, Bobby. The territories existed in different times because of the turning points Saint Dane targeted. But let's not get ahead of ourselves."

"No, wouldn't want to do that," I shot back. "So you're telling me that every person's life force leaves his or her body when they die and becomes part of this greater entity? Solara?"

"That's exactly it."

"And when you say 'mankind,' you mean everyone in Halla? The klee and the gar from Eelong, too?"

"Absolutely. From all worlds. When I say 'mankind,' I'm referring to all intelligent life."

"So, what are you? A ghost?"

"You feel the energy that surrounds us, don't you?"

I nodded. "I see things, but not really. But I know something is there."

"More than something. You're sensing the life forces that make up Solara. They're all around us. They don't have physical form, at least not the way beings exist throughout Halla. But they are just as real."

"And you?"

"I'm one of them, Bobby. I'm part of Solara."

Somehow, in spite of all that I had seen, hearing that Uncle Press was a spirit was difficult to accept. That's not the kind of thing you hear every day. Then again, he was dead. I saw him killed in the flume on Cloral. But here he was, alive and kicking. As was Kasha. And Alder. And Patrick. And Osa. And . . . and . . . and . . . They had all died, but none were gone. It explained a lot. Sort of.

"So you're not my uncle. You're a spirit who floats around with all these other spirits at the edge of the universe? Is that what you're saying? This is all one big haunted hunk of rock?"

Uncle Press chuckled. "That's one way of putting it. But this isn't a ghost story. It is very much about life. I've been around almost as long as there has been intelligent life in Halla."

I whistled. "Wow, you look good for somebody who's, what, a couple million years old? Nice."

"Thank you, but of course this physical body isn't that old."

"No, of course not. How could it be? That wouldn't make sense. Any idea when I'm going to wake up from this dream?"

Uncle Press gave me a friendly shove.

"You're doing fine," he said warmly, sounding every bit like my uncle Press and not some ancient spirit.

"So, if you're a ghost, why do I see you?" I asked. "Why do you have a physical form and nobody else does?"

"You're getting ahead of me. Let's get back to understanding Solara."

"Okay," I said. "What's the point? What are all these spirits doing floating around here, bumping into one another? Does Solara have a purpose?"

"Absolutely. There are seven populated worlds in Halla. Forget the territories. Think worlds. Or planets. Intelligent life has developed on seven of them. Each has its own unique history. But as different as they are, the one thing they have in common is intelligent life. Intelligence does not die. Spirit does not die. Solara holds the collective knowledge and wisdom of the ages. It's what we are. And as such, we act as the conscience of mankind."

"Explain that."

"Solara only exists because mankind exists. We aren't separate or distinct. Solara evolves right along with mankind because we *are* mankind. At the same time, we are able to observe the physical life on all seven worlds."

"Who is 'we'?" I asked. "Do you mean that every life that was ever created still exists?"

"Yes."

"Isn't it getting a little crowded?"

"Physical space is not a factor."

"And who's in charge?"

"It's not that rigid. It just is."

I frowned. I was trying to understand. I really was.

Uncle Press continued, "Though we exist on an entirely different plane, our existence and that of the physical worlds are not separate. Solara is a direct reflection of the physical life that exists on the seven worlds of Halla."

I looked around at the bleak surroundings. Believe it or not, I was starting to get it. Sort of. At least I was beginning to understand how Saint Dane's quest might have affected this place.

"We do not interfere with the physical world. However, since we possess the wisdom and intellect of the ages, we act as guides. That's our responsibility. I guess some people on Earth would call us guardian angels. We offer balance. Harmony. We don't interfere or make judgments on what is right or wrong; we simply offer insight."

"Uhhh, how?"

"Our physical abilities are extremely limited. We're spirits. When individuals are facing critical junctures and aren't sure of what choices to make, we visit their dreams to show them all sides of their dilemma. You've heard of people who dreamed of being visited by people in their past? They really *were*. Sometimes just the calming presence of a lost loved one will help someone see clearly and be confident with his or her choices. Most times people don't consciously remember these dreams. But our guidance was there. We don't tell them what to do, or even *suggest* what they should do. We offer clarity. And confidence. We assure them that whatever decision they make will be the right one, and to not be afraid to trust their instincts. Our goal is not to change the course of human existence, but to help ease the way. It has been this way since the dawn of mankind."

The odd thing was that the more he told me, the more I felt as if I already knew it all. When I looked at what he was saying from the perspective of Bobby Pendragon from Stony Brook, Connecticut, it all seemed like a fantasy. But when I let it just wash over me and not fight it with my usual skepticism, I felt as if I had known it all along.

"I'm afraid I might know where this is going," I offered.

"Tell me," Uncle Press said with enthusiasm.

"You're talking about people facing critical junctures. Making choices that affect their future. Helping them find their own way without actually influencing their decisions. That means the people of Halla are still deciding their own fate—you're just helping them see the whole picture. It sounds like you really are guardian angels."

"That's exactly right."

"But having that ability can be tempting. If you actually *did* want to influence the decisions that people made, you could."

"Yes, we could. But we haven't."

"Until now," I said soberly.

Uncle Press took a deep, tired breath. "Yes, until now."

"Saint Dane is from Solara, isn't he?" I asked.

"Yes, he is, Bobby."

"Which means he's got more power than I ever realized."

"Yes, but there's something else you should know."

"What's that?"

"He isn't the only one with that power."

Uncle Press stared at me with a knowing smirk. He was waiting for it to sink in. It didn't take long.

"Are you telling me—"

"Yes," he said quickly. "The fate of Solara and the future of Halla has been trusted to you, Bobby Pendragon. You have more power than you can imagine."

I nodded thoughtfully and said, "Tell me about Saint Dane."

5

Uncle Press leaned over and picked up a baseball-size chunk of gray rock. He held it in the palm of his hand, weighing it. For a second I thought he was going to throw it. Instead, he placed it back down reverently. I guess you don't go around chucking the stuff that is the foundation of all there is.

"Saint Dane is part of Solara," Uncle Press began. "One of its oldest souls. He helped guide mankind throughout the ages."

"Guide?" I shot back. "You call what he did guide? I thought you said you weren't supposed to interfere or decide on what was right or wrong?"

"We aren't," Uncle Press said quickly. "And he didn't. But over time he grew restless. His name isn't really Saint Dane, by the way. Once things started to change, he took that on. He called it 'ironic.'"

"So what's his real name?"

"We have no real names. Like I said, we aren't physical beings."

"But you're Press Tilton."

"Because I needed to be."

"Okay, never mind the names. What happened with Saint Dane?"

"Like I said, we aren't about influencing or changing the natural course of events. Since we are reflections of man, our only purpose is to help bring balance to their lives and allow people to reach their full potential, whatever it happens to be. That wasn't enough for Saint Dane. I don't know why. Perhaps he had seen too much. Or had too many difficult experiences. But he actually grew angry at mankind. Which is an odd concept because we *are* mankind. He became obsessed with what he considered the mistakes made by people on all worlds. Instead of rejoicing in man's various achievements, he dwelled on their errors."

"Sounds like a 'glass is half empty' kind of guy," I offered.

"The trouble began when he decided that we should start playing a greater role in shaping Halla's destiny. Instead of allowing people to find their own way, he started to influence their choices."

"Because he thought he knew better," I added.

"That is exactly right. He felt Solara had the only true perspective on how mankind should evolve, and that it was our duty to steer the worlds of Halla in the right direction. Or at least, what he thought was the right direction. He thought we were more important and more knowing than mankind. That alone was wrong. We aren't gods. We don't know all."

"Yeah, try telling him that," I said, scoffing.

"I did. Many did. But he would not be convinced. He was appalled by the state of mankind, or so he said. He thought we were all weak for not taking the responsibility of guiding the very life that created us."

"Kind of like the Frankenstein monster turning on the guy who made him."

"Except that Saint Dane considered himself to be superior. What he didn't accept was that there is no right or wrong. There is just life. With all its flaws and triumphs. To alter that is to change the natural course of evolution, which could lead to the end of it all."

I had heard a lot in the past few minutes. The past few years. Nothing hit me harder than what Uncle Press had just said.

"Wait, you're saying that altering the natural course of life could lead to the end of all life?"

Uncle Press stepped away from me and gestured out to the wasteland that was Solara.

"Your dad told you that Solara wasn't always like this. It wasn't. Solara was a wondrous place of light and harmony. Since it isn't a physical existence, its nature is different for each of us. Solara is whatever you want it to be."

"Like Lifelight?" I asked.

"In a way. In fact, that is one of the influences Saint Dane made. He planted the concept of Lifelight in the head of Dr. Zetlin on Veelox. He wanted to gift mankind with the kind of existence we share here. And you know how that turned out."

"Yeah. Yikes."

"Exactly. Saint Dane wasn't all about power and conquest. At least not at first. He actually thought he was doing the right thing by bestowing his wisdom on the people of the territories. He wouldn't accept the fact that he might not have all the right answers, and even if he did, he shouldn't be imposing them on the worlds of Halla."

"Sounds like his typical arrogant self. So what happened to Solara?"

"Like I've been saying, we were created by the spirit

of mankind. It not only created us, but it powers us. What they are, we are. We are the spiritual reflection of the state of Halla. We have very little physical power."

Uncle Press pointed to the roiling, colorful clouds above us. "You're looking at the base elements of matter. Halla is constantly expanding. This is where it begins. What you see up there is matter that will soon become part of the physical Halla."

I had new respect for the light show in the sky. They weren't clouds at all. Those electric images in the sky were the seeds of all that is. Or about to be.

"Uh, wow" was all I could squeak out. Kind of an understatement, I guess.

"Saint Dane injected himself into the natural cycle," Uncle Press said with a touch of anger. "Like I said, we aren't gods. We don't create. But Saint Dane crossed a line that is taboo. He manipulated that material to create matter. Physical matter."

"He had that kind of power?" I asked, aghast.

"Not at first, and not alone. He brought other spirits together, creating forces greater than any individual life. He didn't want them for their ideas or wisdom; he needed their energy. He became stronger, far stronger than any single entity in Solara. That power allowed him to manipulate matter on the physical worlds. The first thing he did was create an actual, living being for himself. He became the man you know so well."

"Too well."

"But he wasn't truly human. He could manipulate that physical being, becoming any form he chose. Any person, any creature. He continued gathering power from Solara and created the flumes."

"Saint Dane made the flumes?" I asked, stunned.

"To connect the worlds. That was a critical part of his plan. To gather together the strength of Halla, he needed to make it one. But to do that, he needed a way for the worlds to physically join. That's why he needed the flumes. And the quigs to guard them."

"All that was done using the spiritual power of Solara to manipulate physical matter?"

"Yes. It was not only wrong, there was a stiff price to be paid. With each physical creation, with every manipulation he made to the worlds of Halla, he killed a little bit of Solara."

"Killed?"

"Solara is dying, Bobby. Saint Dane's actions have drained its spirit. Each time he manipulates matter, a bit more of Solara dies. From creating that massive flume in Yankee Stadium on Second Earth, to turning himself into a raven. It all drains a bit of life from Solara. You know that he saved Courtney Chetwynde from dying, right?"

"Yeah, I do."

"That act alone nearly brought Solara down for good."

I didn't know how to react to that. Talk about conflicting emotions.

He continued, "I told you that the spirit of mankind is so powerful it cannot die. That isn't entirely true. Using Solara to physically manipulate Halla is slowly destroying that life force. The reflection works both ways. If Solara dies, Halla dies."

"Yikes, talk about interfering in the way things are supposed to be."

"It gets worse."

"Worse than the total destruction of Halla?"

"Saint Dane doesn't want to destroy Halla. He wants to

control it, and thereby control Solara. His quest has been to change the mindset of mankind. I think you understand, Bobby, that mankind is basically good, with positive goals and the desire for peace and order. Yes, there are wars and strife and every kind of conflict that you can imagine, but taken as a whole, mankind strives for good. Saint Dane has slowly changed that. By finding the turning points on each of the territories and altering their destiny, he has turned Halla into a dark, dangerous place. People live in fear. So many have died, and those who remain fight for survival. Then of course, there are the chosen. Saint Dane has created a superior legion on each territory that live in peace and safety, but even they are consumed with keeping their own power."

"The Ravinians?" I asked.

"Yes."

"But doesn't Saint Dane realize what he's created? I mean, did he really want to create such chaos?"

"I don't believe that he cares one way or the other about Halla."

"Uh, what?" was all I could get out.

"Maybe at one time he did. Maybe he actually did feel that he knew what was best for mankind. But his goals have evolved. I believe he has set his sights on an even greater prize."

"I thought Halla was everything? What could be greater than that?"

"By crushing the spirit of mankind, he will ultimately control Solara. If that happens, the existing worlds of Halla will mean nothing, because he will have the ability to use the power still held by the spirits of the ages to create his *own* Halla."

"What!" I shouted.

"That is Saint Dane's ultimate goal, Bobby. He won't have to bother with what has gone before and the molding of existing worlds to his liking, because he will be able to create his own worlds. Multiple worlds. Why stop at seven evolved worlds when he can create ten? Twenty? A hundred? All would be created according to his vision. Simply put, he *will* be a god, because he will have the power to create. That is what Saint Dane has been after, Bobby. He has turned Halla toward chaos in order to give himself the power to form an entirely new universe. One that he alone controls."

I looked around at the bleak world with renewed wonder. I had been right from the start. This was a dead place. Or at least a place that was dying. Saint Dane was killing it. All that had happened was done to break down the positive spirit of mankind, which would in turn cripple Solara and allow him to control its power.

I had thought the guy was an arrogant, egotistical tyrant. I had no idea how right I was. The scope of his vision was so far beyond anything that I had expected, it was almost laughable. Almost. Each territory, each battle, each turning point was just another building block in the foundation of the most incredible crime of all time. Saint Dane didn't want wealth. Or to rule a group of people. Or to control a country, a world, or even multiple worlds. He wanted to create his own personal universe. From all that Uncle Press told me, it looked like he was going to succeed.

"I've got a dumb question," I said.

"Go for it," Uncle Press shot back.

"It sounds like you've known what he's been up to for a long time."

"From the beginning. He and I were together for eons. I

believe I knew him better than any other in Solara. I suppose in some strange way you could say that we were friends."

"Okay, odd, but if you knew what was happening, why didn't you try to stop him?"

Uncle Press smiled. That was an odd reaction, considering that we were on the verge of Armageddon.

"You're right, that was a dumb question," he said.

"Why?"

"Because we *did* do something to stop him. In an act of total desperation that in many ways went against the nature of Solara, we created the one thing we hoped would stop his mad plan."

"What was it?"

"We created *you*, Bobby."

6

From the first moment I left home to go with Uncle Press so long ago, there were very few times when I actually felt I was up to the challenges put in front of me.

Sure, there were times when I had plenty of confidence. I had become a decent fighter. I think I did pretty well figuring out Saint Dane's schemes. At least some of them, anyway. I had faith in my fellow Travelers. We made a good team. But whenever I turned my thoughts to the larger, more cosmic issues, I always felt I was behind. I didn't know why I had been chosen to be the lead Traveler. I was just a kid. I always felt as if they should have picked somebody better equipped to match up with Saint Dane. Hearing all the incredible things that Uncle Press had to say about Solara did nothing to change my mind. The battle against Saint Dane was no longer about a tribe or a city or a country or a world. It wasn't even about Halla. It was about trying to stop a guy who had taken on the power of a god and was about to create his own universe. How the heck was I supposed to compete with that?

As we stood together on that mysterious world at the

edge of reality, I really hoped that Uncle Press had a good answer.

"I don't mean to criticize," I said to my uncle. "After all, you have the combined knowledge and wisdom from all time, and I'm just a basketball jock. But, how do I say this? What the *hell* were you thinking? You're trying to stop a demon who has the power to control the power of all that ever was, and you chose *me* to stop him? Doesn't seem like the brightest move, if you ask me."

"It was the only move," Uncle Press answered.

"Then Saint Dane won before the game even began" was my conclusion.

"Not true. I've watched you, Bobby. I've seen your every move. We made the exact right move."

"You saw it all? Everything? You know exactly what happened?"

"Everything. Solara is everywhere, remember?"

"Everywhere. Right. You even saw me when I was, like, going to the bathroom?"

He gave me another sour look.

"Sorry, habit. If I don't make fun of what's going on sometimes, I'll explode."

"I know that, too."

"So if you saw everything, you know I was outmatched every step of the way. Even when I thought we'd won, he turned it back on us. It's been totally futile."

"But it hasn't been. Saint Dane knew that you and the Travelers were the only threat to his plan. Stopping you was as important to him as swaying the destiny of the territories. He could have ignored you, but he didn't."

"He kept asking me to join him."

"Of course he did. I think you can see why now."

"Not exactly."

"I know you've wondered how the battle was supposed to play out. What Saint Dane told you is true. He was trying to prove the rightness of his way of thinking. That was the battle. His philosophy of control and elitism, versus your thinking that people should be free to choose their own destiny."

"Yeah? Then who the heck were we trying to convince? Is there some kind of grand judge on Solara? A panel? An executive council? The bosses of the ages, who are going to pass judgment on who won and who lost?"

"In a way you were trying to prove yourselves to the most important judges of all. The only judges that counted."

"Who?"

"The people of Halla."

"Uh . . . huh?"

"Saint Dane's plan was to turn the territories upside down. Mankind is inherently good. Saint Dane wanted to change that. He wanted to create an atmosphere of mistrust. Of constant competition and pervasive desperation and fear. On each territory he appealed to the lowest instincts of man. Greed, arrogance, self-absorption, paranoia. But for his ultimate goal to succeed, it had to happen on a universal scale. On *all* the worlds of Halla. That's why he found those turning points in the histories of those worlds. He needed to find the moment in time of each territory that would have the maximum negative impact on that world. By turning a territory away from its natural destiny, which was to follow the positive instincts of man, he forced the territories into chaos. That, of course, brought out their worst. Since Solara is a reflection of mankind, the spirit of Solara changed right along with those worlds. The high thinking and positive energy that created us changed. It's why you can barely feel the spirits of Solara. They are growing weaker and dying off. The desolate world you see now is a direct result of Saint Dane's meddling with the nature of man."

"So how was I supposed to stop that?"

"Not just you. You and the other Travelers. Saint Dane became a physical presence in Halla. For him it was no longer about visiting dreams and whispering guidance. Once he determined the turning points, he became part of their societies, seemingly helping them make decisions, but actually leading them toward disaster."

"Yeah, I know all that."

"The only way to stop him was to create our own actual presence in Halla. We took ten souls and gave them physical life. One on each territory."

Uncle Press stopped talking. He must have seen the look on my face.

"What do you mean 'took ten souls'?" I asked cautiously.

"You're from Solara, Bobby. All the Travelers are from Solara."

I knew he was going to say that. It's exactly what my parents had told me. But hearing it put so plainly was still a shocker. Maybe in the back of my mind I was hoping for another explanation, but that was just wishful thinking.

"So I'm really not Bobby Pendragon" was my sober response.

"Oh no, you are very much Bobby Pendragon. That was the whole point. We chose a strong, wise, caring spirit and gave it life on Second Earth. We created a family to raise and nurture that spirit, teaching him the ways of that world. The same happened with each of the territories. Each Traveler was given a mentor from Solara to prepare them for the conflict with Saint Dane. It's why I became a physical being. I bounced between territories, ensuring that the Travelers were being properly prepared and ultimately telling them of their true destiny."

"That's why Press Tilton was born," I said.

"Not exactly born. More like created. The only hope we had of countering Saint Dane's influence was to do so with actual, living beings. But instead of just one, we chose ten. Saint Dane had grown too powerful; there was no way we could match what he had become with only one Traveler. Our intent was for the Travelers to bond and work against him, which is exactly what happened."

My mind flashed to a million different questions.

"But wasn't that just as bad as what Saint Dane was doing? I mean, the spirits of Solara aren't supposed to monkey with reality, right?"

"You're right. By creating the Travelers, we were also sapping the strength of Solara. In some ways what Solara has become was also our doing. The tools we gave the Travelers came at a cost. We showed you all how to use Saint Dane's flumes. We marked them with stars and created rings to help locate them. We advised you to write journals and send them to your acolytes. Whenever you stepped into a flume, we ensured that you arrived where you needed to be, when you needed to be there, in order to continue the struggle with Saint Dane."

"And we could heal one another," I added.

"Yes, as much as you were human, you had that ability as well. But each time it was used, another piece of Solara slipped away. It was a price that had to be paid. The alternative was far worse, which was to hand Solara over to Saint Dane without a fight."

"Why didn't you just tell us all this from the get-go? Maybe we would have had a better chance."

"No, in spite of our manipulation of physical reality, your mission retained the spirit of Solara. You were behaving exactly as natural inhabitants of the territories would act because that's what you were. Everything you did, every decision you made, came from your experience as a living being, with all the flaws and fears and strengths that every being has. We counted on your strength and character to triumph. And it did. You had many victories, Bobby. Each time, Solara was given a new, positive shot of life. It was restored not only because you kept a territory on its natural course, but your own personal spirit returned strength to us. You personified the triumph of the spirit of mankind."

We walked a bit in silence. Uncle Press was letting me process the information. It was all beginning to make sense. It was incredible, but it was making sense. My questions were being answered. I can't say I liked any of the answers, but at least I was getting them.

"You gotta know how impossible this all seems to me," I finally said. "You tell me I'm an ancient spirit from an alternate universe on the edge of reality, but I still just feel like Bobby Pendragon. I mean, I have no memory of being anything other than Bobby Pendragon. I'm half expecting you to burst out laughing and tell me it was all a goof, and you can't believe I fell for it. Psyche!"

"You feel like Bobby Pendragon because you *are* Bobby Pendragon."

"Lead Traveler," I added.

"Yes, lead Traveler. You above all were created to be the heart of the Travelers. It was based on the strength of your spirit long before you set foot on Second Earth."

"And I blew it all by killing Alexander Naymeer," I said soberly.

Uncle Press frowned. "What you did is exactly what Saint Dane wanted you to do. You gave in to the darker nature of man. First by brazenly mixing the destinies of the territories—"

"What was I supposed to do?" I shot back. "Let the dados destroy Rayne?"

"Yes."

Oh.

"I couldn't let that happen."

"I understand, but it cost. That was the beginning of the final slide. With that battle, Solara grew dark. Not only because of the tak you brought to Ibara, but because you reintroduced that weapon to the Milago and Bedoowan tribes of Denduron, who then used it to invade and enslave the Lowsee tribe. The fall of Solara mirrored your own. As it grew weaker, we relied more on your own personal spirit to hold on. The final blow came when you killed Alexander Naymeer. You had hit bottom, and so has Solara. Out of desperation, we destroyed the flumes."

"*You* destroyed the flumes?" I asked, shocked.

"It was all we could do. With Halla crumbling, we felt that preventing the Ravinians from traveling between territories might slow the fall. I'm afraid it was too little too late. Saint Dane didn't need them anymore to achieve his goals. His Convergence was a success. Each territory was already on its own downward spiral."

Great. I was more or less responsible for letting Saint Dane destroy all that was good about Halla, and allowing the ultimate evil to take control.

"I'm sorry," I said softly. What else could I say? It felt pretty inadequate, but it was all I had. I sensed movement nearby. I expected to look up and again catch the fleeting image of a spirit. Instead I saw Spader. He stood on a rock outcropping, staring at me. He looked shaken, which wasn't like him.

"Quite the natty tale, isn't it, mate?" he said. "Not at all what I expected, no sir."

Loor walked up behind him. She had a totally blank look on her face. I'm guessing that she was just as stunned as I was. She was quickly joined by the other Travelers. Gunny, Patrick, Kasha, Elli, Siry, Aja, and Alder. None of them looked very good. When we were last together, they'd each had a spark of defiance in their eyes that said they were still ready to fight. Now they looked as if they had all seen a ghost. Which they had. Except that they had been looking at themselves. Once I saw that everyone had arrived, I turned to Uncle Press.

"So I guess that's it," I said. "I blew it."

"*We* blew it, shorty," Gunny called out.

"Whatever," I snapped back. "It doesn't matter. It's over. All that's left is for Saint Dane to return to Solara and take control of the wreckage."

"That's his plan," Uncle Press said. "Once Halla has totally turned, the negative forces that have overcome mankind will create a rebirth of Solara. A much different Solara. It will still be filled with the spirit of mankind, but it will be a dark, negative spirit. After that, Saint Dane can use it as he will to manipulate matter and create an entirely new Halla. That's the road we're on."

Siry called out, "And what happens to us?"

"That's your choice," Uncle Press answered. "You can accept what's happened as inevitable and become part of this new Solara, or you can make one last stand."

Aja huffed and said, "There isn't much left to stand on."

Uncle Press gave us one of those sly smiles that I knew so well. He knew something. He hadn't shared it all.

"Saint Dane isn't infallible," he said. "You've all seen that. In spite of the high opinion he has of himself, he *isn't* a god. He's made plenty of his own mistakes."

"And yet he's still won," Elli pointed out.

"Not yet," Uncle Press replied quickly. "There is one territory left. It may be hanging by a thread, but it hasn't been lost."

"Third Earth," Patrick said with reverence.

"Saint Dane made a mistake," Uncle Press said, enjoying himself. "A huge one. It's up to us to make sure that it was a fatal one."

"So we're not done yet?" I asked.

Uncle Press gave me a wink and said, "Do you really think I'd have brought you all together like this if I thought we were done?"

7

We were all back together.

We were a little wiser and maybe somewhat overwhelmed by all that had been revealed to us. But at least we were together. It was good to know I wasn't the only one who had to deal with getting knocked over the head with a big fat reality stick.

Uncle Press addressed us all. "In spite of all you've heard, Solara is not dead. At least, the Solara that has always been is not dead. You all sense the presence of the spirit here, don't you?"

I looked around to see my friends nodding.

"Solara is at its lowest point. The toll of this battle has been huge. The spirit is dying. You've met your loved ones here—the spirits who became Travelers to help guide your way on your home territories. Giving them a physical presence so they could speak with you was an added drain. The only reason we brought them forward now was to help ease your transition. They're still here, but we can't continue to maintain their physical selves."

I thought back to how my family flickered and disappeared.

It seemed like a lightbulb running out of power. Turned out it was exactly that. The same sort of thing must have happened after I left Second Earth the first time. Every piece of evidence that my family existed had vanished. It must have all been created by the spirit of Solara, and then removed when it was no longer necessary.

How weird is that?

Uncle Press continued, "The worlds of Halla have fallen. Each territory is in chaos. The darker nature of mankind has triumphed, just as Saint Dane wanted."

Gunny stepped forward and asked, "So then, why is Solara still hanging on?"

Patrick asked, "Because there's still hope for Third Earth?"

"There *is* still hope for Third Earth, but I don't believe that's the reason. Third Earth has become a war zone. That's where we all gathered before coming here."

That made sense. The zoo, the shattered buildings, the tilted Empire State Building. Third Earth was a mess, worse than when Patrick was last there.

Elli asked, "Do you believe that saving Third Earth will stop Saint Dane?"

"I don't know. I'd be lying if I told you otherwise. Truth is, it's all we've got left. But I'll tell you something I *do* believe. I don't think that saving Third Earth is as important as *how* we save it," Uncle Press answered.

We all exchanged confused glances. We had no idea what he was talking about, which was pretty much par for the course even at this late date.

"Make no mistake, we are on our last legs," Uncle Press continued. "The spirits of Solara no longer have the ability to move through the physical worlds. They are all here now. Or at least, what's left of them. There is no way of knowing what is happening throughout Halla, except through your eyes."

"Us?" Siry said in surprise. "How can we know what is happening out there? We're trapped here too. And the flumes are destroyed."

"You've all heard how the creation of the Travelers was our only hope to stop Saint Dane. That is still true now. More than ever. The spirits of Solara have gathered back here in order to channel their remaining energy to you. To us. I'll be with you until the end."

"Well, there's one spot of good news!" Spader declared, trying to be positive.

"That's how we will be able to maintain a physical presence and make our final stand. The remaining positive spiritual energy that exists in Solara is being channeled to us. The Travelers."

Aja looked glum. "Nothing like a little pressure."

Alder said, "But if there are no flumes, we will be unable to travel."

"You don't need the flumes anymore," Uncle Press declared.

That made everybody start talking at once. I was right there with them. What the heck did that mean?

"Whoa, whoa!" Uncle Press called out, trying to get everybody to settle.

I said, "I think you better explain that."

"Saint Dane created the flumes to connect the territories. He wanted technology and physical items, and ultimately people, to travel freely and blend all the worlds. To converge. He was able to travel between territories whenever he wanted and from wherever he happened to be. He stepped from one world into the sea of time and space, and right into the next world, instantly, effortlessly. You all experienced it yourselves when you arrived here from Third Earth."

That was exactly what happened. My family and I took two steps—the first on Third Earth, the second here in mysterious lavaland. But the idea that we could have been doing that all along made me a little, oh, what's the word? Angry. Yeah. Angry is a good word. None of the other Travelers looked too happy either.

Loor was the only one who had the discipline to ask the question calmly. "Was there a reason that we were not told of this ability?" she asked.

Uncle Press answered with equal calm. "Because you didn't have it before."

"Why not?" was my obvious follow-up. "It would have made things a little simpler, don't you think?"

"For one, we wanted to maintain the illusion that you were natural to your own territory. By hitchhiking through Saint Dane's flumes, you didn't need to know of your true origins."

"Not a good enough answer," I said, testy.

"But the main reason is that the flumes were there. They worked. Changing your physical selves to step in and out of the sea of time and space would have been too great of a drain on Solara. The same would have happened if you changed your physical beings the way Saint Dane did. Each time he became a different person, he took more of the spirit of Solara along with him. If you all did the same thing, we wouldn't be talking to each other right now. That's how draining it is for us to manipulate matter."

Spader jumped forward. "You mean we have the same spiff powers as Saint Dane?"

"No," I countered. "No way. I tried to change myself,

more than once. Unless there was some secret switch or something, it didn't work."

"Because we didn't allow it," Uncle Press replied. "We wanted you to behave as normal beings, not spirits."

"But Nevva Winter could change," I said.

"Because Saint Dane allowed it. As I said, he is slowly controlling the power of Solara. We didn't allow you to use that ability or to travel without the flumes because it would have caused untold damage to Solara."

"And now?" Gunny asked.

"Now there are no flumes," Uncle Press said. "And you all have the same abilities as Saint Dane. The spirits of Solara will see to that. But we must be cautious with how we use them. Our resources are very near the end. It's risky, but hey, things have gotten a little desperate."

I could guess what everyone was thinking. It was an amazing feeling to know we could travel between territories without having to worry about finding a gate to the flumes. But it was also pretty scary. How badly would we be hurting Solara each time we used that ability? However things played out, we wouldn't be able to rely on flashing between worlds at will. Or turning into ravens. Whatever the final battle would be, it would be like all the others. In real time. With our physical selves. Win or lose.

I was the first to speak again. "You said that Saint Dane made a mistake."

Uncle Press looked up at the sky. I followed his gaze. Was I imagining things, or were there already fewer color-charged clouds floating by?

"Halla has fallen," Uncle Press said bitterly. "The nature of mankind has turned. Even with Third Earth still in doubt, Solara should be dark. But it isn't."

Aja said, "Of course not. Ravinia may dominate the territories, but there are still people out there who haven't given up. Their spirit must be feeding Solara."

"That's not it," Uncle Press countered. "Halla is in chaos. For those few who lived through the Ravinian revolution, life outside of the conclaves is brutal. Like I said, survival is their only goal. They forage for food. Disease and despair are rampant. They live in constant fear of being attacked and killed for what little they have. There is no joy. No working toward a better future. That's the kind of spirit that now feeds Solara. Think of the Flighters on Veelox. Their existence has become the norm. There is little positive spirit coming from Halla anymore, which is exactly what Saint Dane wanted."

Siry asked, "So then, what is keeping Solara alive?"

Uncle Press answered, "There is a strong, focused source of light. Of hope. It's like the last trickle of water in a dried-up oasis. It isn't much, but it's out there somewhere. It's real and it's keeping Solara from crumbling."

"What is it?" Aja asked.

"It's Saint Dane's mistake," Uncle Press answered. "On Second Earth, as the Ravinians were about to take power, they made a single dramatic purge of thousands of their enemies. A massive group of those who opposed Ravinia were sent into a flume."

"The Bronx Massacre," Alder said.

"Seventy thousand people went into that flume," I said.

Patrick added, "History said it was a mass execution."

"That's what most people believed. Seventy-some-odd thousand people became victims of Ravinia in order to intimidate those who dared oppose them. It was diabolical, but it worked. Ravinia soon controlled Second Earth."

"So what was the mistake?" Patrick asked.

"Saint Dane used those people to help him gain power on Earth, but if he truly wanted to be rid of them, he should have killed them."

"So . . . he didn't?" Patrick asked hopefully.

"No. I believe they are still out there living in exile. These were the only people in Halla who, as a group, were brave enough to stand up to Naymeer and try to put an end to Ravinia. I believe they are still alive. Somewhere. They are the last significant source of positive, spiritual energy that is keeping Solara alive."

"Where are these people?" Siry asked.

"I don't know," Uncle Press answered. "We have no way of knowing. Are they on one territory? Or scattered over several? How many are left of the seventy thousand? What kind of shape are they in? Wherever they are, I believe they represent the last living beings of the old order who have not been corrupted by the Convergence. Their strength of spirit is proof of that. Without them, Solara would cease to exist, and the darkness would rise."

"And what about Third Earth?" Patrick asked.

"The Travelers are the last hope for Third Earth. The exiles are the last hope for the Travelers. If we want to stand up to Ravinia on Third Earth, we are going to have to rely on the positive spirit of the exiles to continue energizing Solara, which in turn gives us the ability to maintain our physical selves and to travel. If something happens to the exiles, game over."

"Then they must be protected," Alder said.

"Yes," Uncle Press said quickly. "But first we have to find them and ensure their safety before turning our sights to Third Earth."

I guess it came as no surprise to any of us that it was going to come down to Third Earth. The final territory. What was Saint Dane up to there? We had no idea. But unless we found the exiles and kept them safe, it wouldn't matter what he was doing, because the Travelers wouldn't have the ability to stop him. Finding the exiles and protecting them seemed like the right thing to do. The *only* thing. But there was one other reason that I believed in the plan. I didn't share it with the others because, in the long run, it didn't matter to anyone but me. I kept my feelings to myself. They energized me. They gave me confidence. Of course I wanted to find the exiles and have one last shot at Saint Dane. But there was another reason. A personal one.

Finding them might also mean finding Mark and Courtney.

8

Find them," Uncle Press announced, all business.

Siry looked shaken. "But, how?"

"I can't answer that. I don't know. You each have more knowledge about your home territory than anyone else. Use it. Return to your homes and track down the exiles. But I have to warn you, things have changed. Everywhere. Saint Dane's Convergence has seen to that. It will be dangerous."

Siry said, "But that shouldn't matter. Not if we have the power of Solara to protect us."

"You do," Uncle Press replied. "But if you do not use it wisely, you will do more harm to Solara than good. Resist the temptation to use your powers as a tool, except in the most dire of circumstances. Solara can't stand to be depleted much more."

Elli asked, "If we locate the exiles, what should we do?"

"Do all you can to ensure their safety, then come back here. All of you. We will reconvene as a group and determine our next step based on what you've found. Hopefully by then, we will have determined what Saint Dane is doing on Third Earth. Maybe our only course of action will be to keep the exiles safe. If that's the case, so be it. The one thing I do know is that their spirit can be the nucleus of a revived Halla. It has to be. They are all we have left. No, that's not right. We have them . . . and you. This is the final mission of the Travelers. One way or another it will soon be over."

Aja said, "And what happens to us when this ends?"

Uncle Press sighed. "The better question is, what will be left of Halla and Solara when this ends? That answer depends on all of you."

Alder spoke up. "Then we should get to work."

We shared looks. All of us knew what we had to do, sort of, but it didn't look as if anybody knew how to begin.

Spader was the first to admit it. "Uh, not to be a bother, but how is it exactly that we're supposed to travel? I'm a wee bit unclear on that."

Uncle Press smiled and answered, "It's easier than you can imagine. No, that's not right. It's exactly what you can imagine. Focus on where you want to be and take a step. The spirits of Solara will guide you to where you need to be."

Spader scoffed uneasily. He didn't believe it was possible, and I think if we took a poll, he wouldn't be alone. It couldn't be as easy as that.

Could it?

"Not that I don't trust you, mate," Spader said. "But that sounds a bit wonky."

"Try it," Uncle Press answered with confidence.

Spader looked around, chuckled nervously, closed his eyes, took a step forward . . .

And disappeared.

Elli gasped. I think we all took a step backward in surprise. Before anybody could comment, a rumbling was heard in the sky. Above us, another cloud went black. The rumbling continued, and Spader reappeared, taking a step out of nowhere.

"Hobey!" he shouted, his eyes wide. "I was on Grallion! I was truly there!"

The rumbling grew louder and another cloud went dark.

"You see?" Uncle Press pointed out. "But those two trips cost Solara. That's how important it is to use this power sparingly."

"There was something else," Spader said. He looked shaken. "Grallion was in flames. People were scattering every which way. I think there was a crash. It may be sinking."

"Like I said," Uncle Press intoned soberly. "Things have changed."

There was a silent moment. It was all sinking in. The truth. Our history. Our future. Our mission. It was a lot to understand, let alone accept. I'm sure there were doubts all around. I know I still had them. My mind searched for other possibilities. Other explanations. Other ways that we might be able to end this war and save Halla.

I came up empty.

The way to go was clear. It was time to get started.

I walked up to Spader and said, "This is finally it. You're back in the game."

Spader stood up straight. The fear was gone. In its place was that look of confidence I knew so well.

"Like I've been telling you, mate, I'm ready." He glanced around at the other Travelers and called out, "Doesn't hurt, by the by. It's quite spiff actually. No worries. Speed and luck to us all!"

He looked directly to me. "Been a long time since I've said this to you, mate."

"Said what?"

He smiled, winked, and exclaimed, "Hobey-ho, let's go."

I'd missed Spader. "Hobey-ho."

He looked to the others and added, "No time for second guesses. No room for hesitation. Nothing left to lose. If you're asking me, there's only one thing we can do."

"And what's that?" Gunny asked.

"Mates," Spader replied, "let's get dangerous."

He took a step backward, and was gone. Above us, thunder rumbled. I didn't look up. I didn't want to see another light go out.

"Guess I should be on my way too," Gunny said. "Haven't been home in a while. Anything I should watch out for?"

"I wish I had an answer for you, Gunny," Uncle Press said.

Gunny shrugged and looked at me. "Then I'll just have to take a look for myself. Take care of yourself, shorty."

"See you soon," I answered.

Gunny closed his eyes, took a step, and was gone.

Thunder rumbled.

One by one the Travelers took off. Elli, Aja, Siry, and then Kasha. They all gave a quick farewell and left Solara to begin their final mission. Each time they left, the rumbling returned. It became so intense that the ground shook. That wasn't good.

Alder called to me. "I do not want to leave you, Pendragon."

"Nor do I," Loor said. "Perhaps we should travel to our territories together."

"We make a superior team," Alder added.

"And you'll be a team again," Uncle Press said. "For now you'll have to be with each other in spirit. You know that to be true now. None of you are ever alone."

Alder nodded. He understood. "Then I will say good-bye and be careful." He took a step forward and disappeared.

Loor folded her arms and walked right up to Uncle Press. "Where will you be?" she demanded to know.

"Third Earth. Patrick and I will return there to try and learn what Saint Dane is planning for—"

"No," I interrupted.

Uncle Press gave me a surprised look. "Excuse me?"

"You should stay here for when the Travelers return with news of the exiles."

"Bobby," Uncle Press said patiently, "you heard what I said. Third Earth is still in play. This is it. It may all come down to this last territory. I have to go."

"No, you don't," I said forcefully. "*I* have to go. *You* have to stay here."

The two of us stared each other down. I don't think Uncle Press knew how to react to my demand. He had everything figured out, except for me.

Patrick stepped between us. "Uh, I kind of like the idea that Press comes to Third Earth," he offered meekly.

Uncle Press added, "Bobby, go to Second Earth. That's your territory."

"The exiles aren't there," I argued. "Why would they be? That's where Naymeer started sending them into the flume."

This gave Uncle Press pause.

"He's right," Patrick said thoughtfully. "The Ravinians shot those people through the flume in the early twenty-first century. Unless they somehow boomeranged back, they aren't on Second Earth. If our mission is to locate the exiles, going to Second Earth would be a waste of time."

"It's not just about the exiles," Uncle Press argued. "We have to track down Saint Dane on Third Earth."

"Exactly," I shot back. "And who better to do that? I've been chasing that creep around Halla for years. You may know his history, but I know how he thinks."

Uncle Press looked to Loor. Loor nodded. She was on my side.

"Uncle Press, do you remember how you got me to go with you that night back in Stony Brook?"

He gave me a small smile, remembering. "Sure. I told you that some people needed our help."

"And I went because I wanted to help them. I still do. Maybe now more than ever. As impossible as everything is that you told me, I believe it. All of it. It's hard to get my head around the fact that I'm anything other than Bobby Pendragon from Second Earth, but maybe that's okay, because Bobby Pendragon has unfinished business. I'm the lead Traveler, remember? Saint Dane told me more times than I can count that this battle is between him and me. Heck, you told me the same thing. I get it now. I understand. I went with you that night because I trusted you, Uncle Press. Now I'm asking you to do the same. Trust me. This battle is mine. Let me finish it. I think that's the way it was meant to be."

We all looked up to the sky, drawn by an encouraging sight. Several clouds that had been dark, sparked to life. Brilliant color blazed from the heavens.

"You did that, Pendragon," Loor said in awe.

Uncle Press laughed and shook his head. "I guess we've come full circle. I had to drag you into the fight, and now I can't drag you out."

"We haven't come full circle yet," I cautioned. "Not until I stop Saint Dane."

The sky crackled with energy.

Uncle Press smiled. "I was right about one thing. The spirit of Halla isn't dead. It lives in those exiles, and it flows from you Travelers. From you, Bobby. You represent all that Halla is about. You aren't perfect. Far from it. But you understand that to find the greater good, you have to look inside each individual. That's why you are the lead Traveler. This *is* the way it was meant to be. I should have known that."

"You did know. You just want to stop him as badly as I do. As we all do."

"It's true. You're right. Go to Third Earth."

I felt a strange shift. Not a physical one, but more to do with my own attitude. Uncle Press had been my mentor. He'd helped create the Travelers to battle Saint Dane. He'd chosen me to be the leader. But I never felt much like a leader, until that moment. I always felt Uncle Press was the light we should follow, even if he wasn't physically around. He set the standard. He knew what the game was all about. Now we all knew. The spirits of Solara had called upon me to lead the Travelers in the battle against Saint Dane, and for the first time there was no question in my mind: I wanted the job. Uncle Press had given us what I hoped would prove to be the most important power of all. He'd given us knowledge. It was up to us to use it wisely. It was up to *me* to use it wisely.

Gulp.

Loor said, "There is a battle coming, Pendragon. I feel it. If the exiles are on Zadaa, I will find them and return here. I want to be by your side in the end. Not like on Ibara."

"You weren't on Ibara because I wanted you safe, in case

you had to lead the Travelers into the future. The future is here. We'll face it together."

Loor and I hugged. It felt good, and a little strange, because for the first time I was her physical equal. I had grown. I was strong. I was a warrior. Together we were going to do some damage.

"Find him," Loor ordered, pulling away from me. "When you do, we will take him down together."

She nodded to Uncle Press and to Patrick. With one hand she reached back and grabbed her wooden stave. She held it out across her body, ready for whatever she would find on Zadaa.

"Be careful," I said.

"Always," she replied, took a step forward, and was gone.

I ignored the rumbling in the sky.

Uncle Press, Patrick, and I were the only three left.

"Are you sure Press shouldn't come with us?" Patrick asked nervously. "I mean, I agree that you should come, Pendragon, but the three of us could—"

"No, Bobby's right," Uncle Press said. "When the other Travelers return, I should be waiting for them."

"Do you know anything about what's happening on Third Earth?" I asked.

Uncle Press shook his head. "Only what we saw when those gunships attacked."

"Third Earth wasn't like that the last time I was there," Patrick offered. "When I was still . . ."

He didn't finish the sentence. The memory was tough for him. He had been killed on Third Earth. Saint Dane told me.

Saint Dane.

I was going to get one last shot at him. If he thought the war was over when I killed Alexander Naymeer, he was in for a very big surprise. The Travelers weren't finished. We were going to follow Spader's advice. We were going to get dangerous.

"This is it, Bobby," Uncle Press said. "Our last chance."

I stood next to Patrick. He looked squeamish. Patrick wasn't built for conflict. He was a teacher. A librarian. But he was brave. He had proved that many times over. With his brown hair falling in his eyes, he looked much younger than a guy in his twenties. Twenties? Did I actually write that? Who knew how old Patrick really was? Or any of us, for that matter. We were spirits. We were from a world other than the one we had grown up in. We were Travelers.

And we had one more shot at finishing the job we were born to do.

"You okay?" I asked him.

"I am," he said, taking a deep breath. "I really am."

"Then let's go get him," I said. I took Patrick's arm and looked at Uncle Press. "And so we go."

We both stepped forward on Solara. . . .

And were instantly barraged by the sound of rolling thunder as we stepped into the swirling sand of the zoo in Central Park on Third Earth. As much as I knew that it was exactly what was supposed to happen, it was still a strange experience. I was disoriented. It didn't help that the thunder didn't stop rolling. At first I was afraid that by all of us traveling back to our home territories, we had done serious damage to Solara. That wasn't it. Maybe that would have been better, because the truth wasn't so good. It wasn't thunder we were hearing.

The gunships were back.

Two of the dark, deadly helicopters were flying in low, headed right toward us.

"Go!" I shouted at Patrick and shoved him out of the path of the incoming birds of prey. We hid under a crumbling brick archway that was not more than twenty yards from the long building that the helicopters had pulverized earlier. The helicopters continued on, passing overhead, heading off to who knew where. I'm happy to say that they weren't firing any more rockets. Once they flew off, I moved to step out from our shelter, but Patrick pulled me back.

"Wait," he whispered. "Look."

There was movement on the ground. The air was so full of swirling dust and dirt that I couldn't make out what it was at first.

"Please tell me that's not a polar bear looking for lunch," I whispered.

Actually, it would have been better if it were the polar bear. A line of men appeared, headed our way. The first detail I noticed was the glint of gold off their helmets.

"Dados?" I asked Patrick.

Patrick shrugged.

There were ten of them. They carried silver rifle-looking weapons. Their uniforms were dark red.

"Ravinians," Patrick whispered.

"They're looking for something. Or somebody," I added.

"I hope it's not us."

"There's never a polar bear around when you need one."

The patrol was definitely searching for something. The long building that had been shot up by the helicopters was still burning. That meant the attack had just happened.

"I don't think they're looking for us," I whispered. "But I'd just as soon they didn't find us."

Suddenly the loud chime of church bells sounded directly above our heads. I jumped. Patrick jumped. I think the soldiers jumped too. They were just as startled as we were.

And they turned our way.

I grabbed Patrick and pulled him back into the ruins of the building. The bells continued, and I realized that they were playing a tune. "Twinkle, Twinkle, Little Star." Or the "Alphabet Song." Whatever. Same tune.

"It's the clock," I whispered.

It probably wasn't the exact same machine I had seen back on Second Earth. After all, this was three thousand years later. They must have restored it through the ages, because on top of the arches over our heads was a fanciful clock, with bronze animal sculptures that rotated around it to mark the hour, while the bells chimed out a nursery rhyme. It was kind of a sweet thing. That is, for a little kid on a sunny afternoon. For us it meant trouble, because it was drawing the soldiers' attention our way.

"They're coming," Patrick whispered.

There was no way to get into the building we were hiding next to. The doorway was blocked with debris. We were trapped.

"We'll have to fight," I whispered.

"I—I don't fight," Patrick stammered.

"I'll get the gun from the first one. Just stay out of the way."

I pushed Patrick farther back. It looked as if our mission on Third Earth would begin with violence. The lead soldier drew closer. I tensed up, ready to spring.

"Here!" one of the other soldiers called.

The soldier who was nearly on us stopped and ran back to the others. If he had taken one more step, I would have pounced. I had to force myself to back down. It's tough committing yourself to attack, and then have to pull back. Kind of like being all set to sneeze and then it doesn't come. Okay, maybe it's not exactly like that, but you get the idea.

"They found someone," Patrick announced.

The two of us peered out to see two soldiers dragging a man out of the ruins of the long building they had destroyed. The guy was a mess. I couldn't tell if he was sick or unconscious or dead. They had him by his shoulders and pulled him along with his feet dragging on the ground. When they got him to the center of the group, they dropped him down like a bag of laundry. The guy hit the ground and bounced. Ouch. When he went down, he let out a grunt.

"He's alive," one soldier growled.

Without hesitation another soldier hauled off and kicked the guy square in the gut. The poor man grunted and doubled over in pain. He was alive all right. Who knew how long he'd stay that way around these sadistic goons?

"How many are left?" the soldier who kicked him asked.

The guy's answer was a cough that sprayed blood. He was dressed in rags, much like the people I'd seen jumping out of the window to escape the attack. His hair was unkempt, and it looked like he had a short beard. Again, he wasn't Flighter-nasty, but he definitely hadn't seen a bar of soap in a while.

"Where are they?" another solder asked angrily.

The first soldier kicked him again. I guess he was the designated punter. Creep. The victim answered again with a pained grunt and a wet cough. The placekicker was about to launch another kick when he was stopped by one of the other soldiers.

"We do not want to lose him," he told his sadistic friend. "Bring him to the conclave."

He immediately pulled out what was probably a walkie-talkie and barked some orders into it.

"Did he say conclave?" Patrick whispered.

He was thinking the same thing I was.

A moment later the sound of the helicopter returned. The chopper flew in low over our heads and landed next to the dry sea lion pool. The soldiers dragged the beaten victim toward the gunship and threw him inside. Two soldiers jumped in with him, and the chopper lifted off. It wasn't on the ground for more than twenty seconds. The remaining soldiers trudged off in the same direction from where they had come. Their work was done. . . .

And "Twinkle, Twinkle, Little Star" hadn't even finished playing.

"He did say conclave, didn't he?" Patrick asked.

"That's what I heard."

"Is it possible? Could the Conclave of Ravinia still be at the flume in the Bronx? It wasn't there the last time I was on Third Earth."

"Things have changed, Patrick," I said, stepping out from our hiding place. "I think we're going to find a lot of things that weren't here the last time you were."

"But if the Conclave of Ravinia is there, it means Ravinia is still active."

I looked around at the ruins of what was once a beautiful series of buildings inside a lush, green park. This was once a place of joy for all ages. It was now rubble.

"And if Ravinia is still active," I offered. "Can Saint Dane be far away?"

"We're going to the Bronx, aren't we?"

"Yeah," I declared. "We're going to the Bronx."

As we began our journey north, a troubling question

kept nagging at me. I didn't mention it to Patrick because he was already on edge. I didn't want to push him over. It was about the concept of Solara, and how its positive spirit empowered us. I actually understood that, sort of. But if Solara's spirit was nearly depleted, and Saint Dane was a spirit from Solara, where was he drawing his power from? I couldn't help but wonder if the answer to that question would be the key to Saint Dane's defeat or the proof that he had become invincible.

To find that out, we first had to find Saint Dane.

9

It was a good thing we landed back in the zoo.

Not because I loved zoos and getting chased by polar bears, but because it was the only proof that we were actually in New York City. Once we left the ruins, there was nothing that even looked close to the New York that either Patrick or I knew. The city was destroyed. As we walked north toward the Bronx, we passed block after block of forlorn shells that used to be buildings. It reminded me of pictures I'd seen of Europe after the bombings during World War II. Compared to this new New York of Third Earth, Rubic City on Ibara was a vacation spot.

We walked like a couple of zombies, numbed by the sight of the carnage that surrounded us. There were no people. None. Not even creepy ratlike Flighters living in squalor. The city was dead. Of course that raised the question of what the polar bear had been eating to stay alive. I didn't want to think about that.

"It's like a bomb fell," I finally whispered. "Or a thousand."

"Maybe that's what happened," Patrick replied. "This is far worse than the New York I left."

"I wonder what year this is. I mean, did Third Earth change again, or did this happen after your time?"

Neither of us had the answer, and it wasn't like we could grab a newspaper to find the date. All we could do was keep moving north. As we trudged through the rubble, the air began to clear. I kind of wished it hadn't, because it gave us a better view of the destruction. At one point I glanced at Patrick and saw tears in his eyes. He noticed that I was looking at him and quickly wiped them away.

"Sorry," he said, embarrassed. "It's kind of a lot to handle, you know?"

I nodded, though I wasn't sure if he was talking about the destruction of his city, or about all the truths that had been revealed to us. Probably both.

"I guess it's finally my turn," he said with an ironic chuckle.

"For what?" I asked.

"Third Earth. My territory. Last but not least."

"Yeah, home sweet home," I said, trying to make light.

Patrick smiled, but his heart wasn't in it. Another tear fell. He wiped it away quickly. "I don't know if I can do this," he finally uttered.

"Yeah, you can," I said with confidence. "You've already proved that."

"I'm a teacher, Pendragon. I'm not a warrior like Loor or Alder . . . or you."

"You're a Traveler," I said quickly. "Don't think of yourself as 'Patrick Mac the teacher.' Think of yourself as someone who has the power of Solara at your command."

He looked at me sideways. "That's just odd."

I had to laugh. "Yeah, tell me about it. It sounded good though, didn't it?"

Patrick shrugged and laughed. Neither of us had gotten over the shock of all that we had learned in Solara. I was still Bobby Pendragon from Second Earth, and he was still Patrick Mac from Third Earth.

"You know something," I said. "I think this is the way we're supposed to feel. I mean, we're handling this like normal people from Halla, right? That was the whole point. The only thing that can stop Saint Dane is the spirit of mankind. Real, physical mankind. Flaws and all. If the spirits, or whatever they are, from Solara could have stopped him, they would have. But they didn't. That's why we're here. They made us into real people. I think we're supposed to be scared. And unsure. And angry. And indignant. And freaked out and all the things that real people feel. It's like we represent mankind. And if mankind can't save itself, then maybe it can't be saved."

Patrick nodded thoughtfully. "Nice speech," he finally said. "But it doesn't make me feel any better."

I laughed. "Really. This is freaking scary."

For the first time Patrick seemed to brighten. "But hearing you say that *does* make me feel better. If you're scared, at least it means I'm not the only one who feels out of his league."

I was scared all right. About a lot of things. But there was one fear I didn't want to share with Patrick. It went beyond the battle that lay ahead. I was afraid of what would happen to us once the war was finally over. No matter which way it came out. In some ways, losing to Saint Dane would be easier. Seriously. If that happened, I had no doubt that we would cease to exist. I don't know if that could be considered "dying" or not, but if the final positive spirit of mankind was snuffed out, I felt certain that the Travelers would be snuffed right along with it. As frightening as that was, I understood it. What I didn't understand was what would happen to us if we won. What would life become? Would we turn into spirits and float around someplace called Solara to guide mankind? What the heck would that be like? It didn't stop me from wanting to beat Saint Dane, but still. Yikes.

Patrick stopped. He stared ahead with wide eyes. I looked too, but didn't see anything unusual.

"What?" was my obvious question.

"What is that?" he asked.

I didn't see anything out of the ordinary. The swirling dust and fog in the air had gotten thick again. As it moved, I caught glimpses of something solid. At first it looked like a group of vertical pillars floating in the air. Barren trees? Light poles? I couldn't tell. It took a weak gust of wind to blow away some of the dust to give us a better view. In seconds the structure had substance. It was a bridge. Or at least what was left of a bridge. It was one other touchstone that I remembered about New York. We had reached the water that surrounded the island of Manhattan. I figured the structure ahead was the railroad bridge that spanned the distance between Manhattan and the Bronx. We were getting closer to the conclave.

"We'll have to walk over that wreck," I said.

Patrick shook his head nervously. He didn't want to go.

"I think it's the only way," I added.

"That's not what I'm worried about," he croaked without taking his eyes away.

I wasn't sure why the bridge didn't bother him. It worried me plenty. At one time the metal span had to withstand the pounding from hundreds of trains that rumbled over it every day. Now it didn't look strong enough to withstand the pounding of our feet. The steel structure swayed and squealed in the wind. It was more wreck than bridge. It looked as if one good sneeze would send it crashing into the river.

"No problem," I said, trying to sound sure of myself. "We'll make it across."

Patrick swallowed and said, "What are we going to do about *that* when we get there?"

He continued to stare ahead. I was definitely missing something. I looked again, trying to see anything that would scare him like that. All I saw was a white wall of fog on the other side of the bridge. . . .

That wasn't fog.

"Yeow" was all I could say.

On the far side of the river, set back a few hundred yards from the bank, was a wall. A huge wall. No, an immense wall. It was so gigantic that I thought it was a bank of fog. I had never seen anything so vast. It must have been twenty stories high. It spread out before us for what seemed like miles to either side, like a gargantuan dam. It was a monster.

"I'm guessing that wasn't on Third Earth when you were here," I muttered weakly.

Patrick shook his head without taking his eyes off the structure.

Whoosh. Whoosh.

Two helicopters flew by above us. They were coming from the south, headed for the wall. They were traveling fairly low, which meant they had to quickly gain altitude or they would smash into the flat, smooth surface. The dark vehicles lifted higher and cleared the top of the structure with expert ease. Once over, they dropped down out of sight. It looked as if they were headed in for a landing on the other side.

"Any guesses?" I asked, numb. I was officially as stunned as Patrick.

"It looks like a fortress," he said. "No telling how big it is, but I'm thinking it covers the spot where the Conclave of Ravinia is. Or was."

I took a deep breath and said, "We could stand here forever wondering. There's only one way to find out what that big boy's all about."

Patrick finally broke his gaze from the wall and looked at me. "How are we supposed to get over that bridge? It's a wreck."

Turned out he was nervous about the bridge after all.

I started walking toward the structure. "I don't know. But we won't figure it out standing here staring at it."

I led Patrick toward the decrepit bridge. We soon found that we were walking on the remains of railroad tracks that hadn't seen a train in a very long time. Most of the ties were missing, and every few yards there were rusted gaps in the rails. When we reached the twisted structure of bridge itself, my heart sank. Up close it looked even flimsier than from a distance. And believe me, it looked pretty bad from back there.

"If this crashes, it's over," Patrick pointed out.

"Yeah," I said. "Good thing we can't die."

"Our bodies can die, Pendragon. Trust me. I've been there. It isn't pleasant."

"Sorry," I said quickly. I'd forgotten that he had been killed on the old Third Earth. Could life get any stranger?

He added, "Maybe we should try to turn into birds and fly across."

"Last resort," I said quickly. "Uncle Press told us to use our abilities sparingly."

"But if we can't get across—"

"We'll get across," I said, and started walking.

The second I looked down through the rails to the river below, I changed my mind. I was no longer sure that we would make it. The ties were rotted, but didn't necessarily look it. Some seemed porous, but were actually strong. Others looked solid, but crumbled under my weight. The only way to tell was to step on a tie and hope that it didn't crack. Much of the bridge bed below the tracks had fallen away, leaving gaping holes. We had to move like a couple of tightrope walkers on the rails that spanned these gaps. It was terrifying.

Each step brought with it a new, ugly sound. Metal groaned. Pipes snapped. Chunks of cement fell away and crashed into the churning water far below. I wasn't just worried about where we stepped, but about the bridge as a whole. How stable was it? If things started to sway, it would go down for sure, and we'd be crushed in tons of twisted steel. That would hurt. It came down to a test of our own inner strength, and balance. It must have taken an hour to cross the hundred yards of bridge. It felt like a hundred miles. But we made it. The gaps below the rails became smaller with each step. My confidence grew. I hopped the last few yards until my feet were once again on solid ground. I turned quickly to see Patrick not far behind. He was looking down, concentrating, with his arms out wide for balance.

"You got it," I said.

He too hopped the last few yards, joining me on the far side of the river.

"Let's not go back that way," he declared, panting.

We turned together to look ahead.

"Whoa" was all Patrick could get out.

Yeah. Whoa.

The massive wall was a few hundred yards from where we stood. Still, it towered over us. It really did look like a dam. The surface was light gray and smooth, with an etched pattern of rectangles that revealed it was constructed with a series of blocks. It must have taken years to build. Like the great pyramids. Looking left and right, I couldn't see where it ended. Was it a straight wall? Or did it turn on an angle to enclose whatever was on the other side? That would have been even more incredible. If this wall continued around, it would have to be the largest structure ever built by man.

"Eighth Wonder of the World," I said. "I have no idea what the other seven are, so don't ask."

Rising up from the base of the structure every fifty yards or so were huge, red vertical rectangles that could have been massive doors. Or decorations. I couldn't tell. They each looked about twenty yards high and half as wide.

"We aren't alone," Patrick pointed out.

I'm not sure why I didn't see them at first. It must have been because I was too busy gaping up at the monstrous wall. But at the base of this structure, were people. Even from as far away as we were, I could see that they were Ravinian soldiers. They had on the same red jumpsuits and golden helmets that those guys wore who beat up the man in the zoo. They walked in a line, maybe thirty yards apart, along the base of the wall. Other than the helicopters, it was the first sign of life we'd seen since the zoo.

"They look like guards," Patrick pointed out.

"Yeah, but are they trying to keep people out or in?"

"It could be a Horizon Compound," Patrick offered. "Naymeer built walled cities to keep the lower classes separate. I heard they were horrible places."

"I guess," I said, thinking. "But would the Ravinians really need to build something that extreme just to separate people? I mean, that thing would hold back King Kong."

Patrick and I exchanged nervous looks, both thinking the same thing. Could that wall have been built to hold back something monstrous?

"No way," I finally said. "That's just . . . fantasy."

"You mean like everything else we've been hearing isn't?"

I was about to argue why I didn't think we had to worry about a giant ape when the ground began to rumble. I have to admit, for a brief second I thought that it might have been from the thundering footsteps of a monster monkey.

We were near the river. The area between us and the wall was a wide stretch of concrete. It reminded me of an empty parking lot at a stadium. That's how big it was. Weeds grew up through the spiderweb of cracks that spread out everywhere.

"Earthquake?" Patrick asked through chattering teeth.

As if in answer, we heard a grinding, machine sound. To our left the cement surface began to shift. One of the cracks wasn't a crack. It was a seam. It split apart, creating a gap that stretched from the bank of the river in front of the destroyed bridge, all the way to the wall. The two sides lowered and retracted beneath the ground to either side, creating a gap that was maybe five yards wide. At the bottom of this gap, running the length of the newly formed channel, was a single metal track.

"Get down!" I yelled, and pulled Patrick toward the river's edge. Not knowing what we were dealing with, I figured it would be better if we weren't seen. We jumped down beneath a cement ledge and peered back at the wall to see what the Ravinians might be up to. We were looking the wrong way. The sound of rushing water pulled our attention back to the river. It looked to me like a whirlpool was forming, creating the sucking sound. A moment later something rose up out of the water in front of the bridge.

"Did King Kong swim?" Patrick asked, transfixed.

A wide tube pushed up from out of the center of the whirlpool. Its steady movement showed that it wasn't alive. It was mechanical. I heard a faint whirring sound beneath the sounds of swirling water. The tube rose up from beneath the surface at a steep angle, until it reached the edge of the long trough that held the rail.

Another mechanical sound followed. Gears were turning. It was coming from the direction of the wall. One of the huge red rectangles began lifting up like a garage door. The rail led right up to it.

"This is our chance," I announced. "We gotta get in there."

"What?" Patrick shouted in horror. "What if it's a prison? What if it's one of the Horizon Compounds?"

"We have to know," I answered while looking between the tube that had come up from the water and the rising door.

"But we can't just run over there and walk through!" Patrick whined. "There's no protection. Nowhere to hide. How are we supposed to get there without being seen?"

"I'm thinking."

"Hey!" he announced. "We have the power. Why don't we turn into birds and fly in?"

I gave him a sharp look. "For one, I don't know how that

works, and I don't want to try. And two, we're not supposed to be using that power, remember?"

"Then come up with a better idea!"

A shrill whistle sounded. It was coming from the water tube. I felt another slight rumble. The whistle sounded again. It was coming closer.

"It's a train," I declared. "That track must run along the same route as the old ones. The bridge is history, so they went underwater."

A moment later a sleek, golden train glided up out of the tube. It looked to me like a cross between a fancy, old-fashioned steam engine and a monorail from Disneyland. It had to be electric, because it moved silently on the single track. The nose came to a point, with a cockpit just above. The body of the train was covered with fancy golden sculptures that looked like vines. They didn't seem to have any other purpose than to be decorative. The engine was short, and pulled two more longer cars, where I guessed the passengers rode. This was not a freight train. It was a mode of transportation for people who traveled in style. It moved slowly and smoothly. I glanced ahead. The massive red door was open. The train was almost all the way out of the tube. I felt sure that once it was out, it would pick up speed.

"Now or never," I declared.

"Now or never what?" Patrick replied with surprise.

I scrambled to my feet and climbed up over the lip of the cement embankment. Patrick didn't.

"Pendragon!" he wailed. "You'll get us killed."

I turned back to him but kept moving. "So what?" I said. "We'll just end up in Solara and come right back here. That's what you did, right?"

"Yes, but . . . it hurt!"

"So then, let's not get killed."

I ran for the train. A quick look back told me Patrick was doing the same. The train was picking up speed. If we were going to jump on, it would have to be right away. The only place that seemed logical to do it was the space between the two passenger cars. I sprinted to the spot where I guessed it would be when I reached the train, and miscalculated by a few feet. The train was accelerating faster than I thought. Instead of grabbing on to the platform between the two cars, I grabbed on to a chunk of the decorative sculpture that was affixed to the side of the train. I trusted it was strong enough to hold me. I jumped, using my arms to climb the sculpture like a jungle gym. I found myself dangling off the side of the train car as it gathered speed. My idea suddenly didn't seem so bright. I looked back to see Patrick sprinting to catch up. I didn't think there was any way he would climb up the way I did, so I made my way forward, scrambling carefully along the sculpture until I reached the front of the car. From there I swung my legs over the safety rail, onto the small platform in between. I was on!

"Let's go!" I yelled to Patrick.

The train was speeding up. Patrick wasn't.

"Can we please just turn into birds?" he gasped.

"No! Pick it up!" I yelled.

Patrick dug in and sprinted forward. He reached out to me. I grabbed his hand and strained to hoist him up and onto the platform. We were on. That was the easy part. We still had to get past the wall, and the guards. We both crouched down, so as not to be seen from inside either car.

"I hope this wasn't a mistake," he wheezed.

Mistake or not, we were on our way. The monorail train continued on toward the mysterious wall.

"What do we do if we get in?" Patrick whispered.

"Let's worry about that once we're in," I answered.

Truth was, I had no idea what we would do. Or what we would find. Though I felt certain we were in the right place. Whatever this monster wall was, whether it was keeping somebody in or out, it had to have something to do with Saint Dane. That much I was sure about.

A moment later we arrived at the massive wall. I held my breath, as if that would do any good. We both pushed ourselves flat against the platform to try and look as inconspicuous as possible. Neither of us moved. Patrick looked one way, I looked the other. When we reached the entrance, I saw two Ravinians standing next to the track, looking the other way. I winced, expecting an alarm to go off. Or a guard to shout that there were stowaways sneaking in.

There were no alarms. We weren't seen. Seconds later we glided through the door and into another world.

10

The first thing I noticed was the smell.

It was good. Sweet even. Until I caught a whiff of the air beyond that wall, I hadn't realized how truly dead the city we had just left had become. On this side of the wall, the world smelled alive. It gave me hope that we hadn't entered a prison. Or one of the Horizon Compounds. The smell alone told me that this was a better place than the one we had left. The golden train glided slowly over the single rail, bringing us deeper into this new and mysterious place.

"We gotta get off," I whispered to Patrick. "This thing is probably headed toward somewhere with people. Until we know whose side they're on, we better be invisible."

Patrick nodded and looked over the safety rail of the moving platform. He swallowed hard. He wasn't thrilled about having to jump off a moving train.

"Don't think about it," I warned. "Go."

I grabbed the rail with both hands, jumped up, and launched myself up and over with both my legs to one side, like vaulting over a pommel horse in gymnastics. I hit the ground and rolled backward to absorb the shock. It was disorienting, but I bounced back to my feet quickly and turned toward the train to spot Patrick. He wasn't as quick about it as I was. He stood grasping the handrail, looking nervous, moving away. I wanted to shout "Jump!" but I was afraid of who might hear. All I could do was will him to move.

He did. It wasn't exactly graceful. He landed on one leg, tumbled sideways, and fell on his shoulder. Ouch. I ran to him, hoping that he wasn't hurt. Of course, I knew if something had happened, I could fix it. A healing Traveler hand would do the trick. But that would have sapped more strength from Solara.

"You okay?" I asked.

Patrick sat up, rubbing his sore shoulder. "It would have been easier to turn into birds," he complained.

I didn't argue the point. He knew what was at stake. I think he was just complaining for the sake of it. That was okay. He deserved to. The train kept moving. No alarm was sounded. No shouts of "Hey! Who are you guys?" Wherever we were, we had arrived unnoticed. I realized that we were sitting on grass. Soft, green grass. It was a welcome, physical sign of life. There would be more. Many more.

"Wow," Patrick said. "I didn't expect this."

That was an understatement. Once the train cleared our field of view, we got a good look at our surroundings. I don't know what better word to use to describe what we saw other than "beautiful." Okay, maybe I can think of a few others. Lush. Green. Idyllic. Maybe even perfect. We were sitting next to the single rail that cut through an absolutely spectacular park. At least, I thought it was a park. There were leafy trees, a meadow covered in wildflowers, a narrow stream that meandered quietly along the length of the track, songbirds darting about, and sculptures. Many sculptures. A few yards from the side of the track there was a massive white statue of a naked guy. It was like three times life-size. It was awesome, in more ways than one.

"*David*," Patrick said with a gasp.

"Who?"

"It's the statue of David by Michelangelo. It's a pretty good replica."

"Maybe it's the real one," I suggested.

"That's impossible. The *David* is in Florence, Italy. It's eight thousand years old; it would never be here and definitely not kept outside like this." He gave me a dark look and added, "At least, I hope not. The *David* is one of the great art treasures of all time."

We crossed over the rail and found a path that wandered through the grounds. We passed many other elaborate sculptures and fountains and footbridges that spanned lazy brooks. Oddly, the air was clear and the sky was blue. I wondered how they were able to keep the dirt and grime that swirled through the air outside from descending here.

"It's like paradise," Patrick said.

"It definitely isn't one of those Horizon Compounds," I added. "That answers one question. The wall is to keep people out, because I can't imagine anybody wanting to leave this place. Especially knowing what's outside."

We passed a few buildings, though calling them "buildings" doesn't come close to describing them. They were more like palaces. Or mansions. Whoever lived there was definitely living large.

Eventually we saw people. At first we hid behind trees, so as not to be seen, but we soon realized it wasn't necessary. There were kids playing touch football on grassy flats.

Couples strolled around, holding hands. Mothers pushed baby carriages. It all looked so normal, like a park. A really incredible park. I was still wearing the brown sweater and khakis I had glommed from the Chetwyndes' boat on Second Earth. Patrick wore jeans and a blue short-sleeved shirt, which is exactly what he was wearing the day I met him. Oddly, our clothes were totally clean. Except for whatever dirt we'd picked up on our trip from the zoo, it was like our visit to Solara had refurbished everything. The people we saw wore a variety of normal-looking Earth clothing. This could have been a park on Second Earth, which meant we didn't stand out.

Besides seeing the people who were enjoying the day, we also saw workers. They wore dark green khaki uniforms with short pants and pith helmets. I didn't think they were dados because they didn't all look the same. There were all types, all races, and both men and women. They were trimming trees, cutting the grass, and sweeping the pathways. Yes, sweeping the pathways. Not a leaf was out of place or blade of grass too long. The place was immaculate.

I asked, "You think if I pulled a flower petal and dropped it, somebody would come running to sweep it up?"

"Look," Patrick said, pointing to a man who was polishing a bronze statue of a giant guy holding what looked like the world on his back. It looked familiar but I couldn't place it. "Look at the guy's arm."

My mouth went dry. The man had a cloth patch on his sleeve. It was a red star. The symbol of Ravinia.

"I guess Ravinia is alive and well," Patrick said soberly.

"I want to know how big this place is," I said.

"For that we have to get up high," Patrick offered.

We kept walking, looking for some sort of structure that

would give us a bird's-eye view. I was thankful that Patrick didn't suggest that we turn into birds and get an *actual* bird's-eye view. We needed to get up high the old-fashioned way. It didn't take long for us to find what we needed. I'm not sure why we didn't see it until we were almost on it. Maybe it was because the trees were too dense. Maybe we had been too close to get perspective. Maybe there was so much to see on ground level that we hadn't been looking up. Maybe we were just idiots. Whatever. When we stepped out of a thick stand of trees, it was my turn to gasp. We were staring at one leg of a giant, golden, four-legged structure. Though I had never seen it in person, I recognized it for what it was. It was impossible, yet it was there.

"Is this a replica too?" I said, my voice cracking.

Patrick was staring straight up at the giant golden tower. "It has to be," he declared. "What other explanation is there?"

People strolled casually through gardens that were situated under the massive structure. A small orchestra played classical music. Vending stands with festive red and white awnings were set up, offering drinks and ice cream, though it didn't look like anybody was paying for the treats. They just walked up and got what they wanted. It was like some big, private party . . . happening beneath the Eiffel Tower.

"We're not in Paris, are we?" I asked, stunned.

"Let's find out," Patrick answered, and walked toward the closest leg of the tower, and an elevator that would take us up and give us the view we needed. Neither of us said a word as we entered the red elevator, where a woman wearing a dark green khaki worker uniform greeted us.

"Which level?" she asked with a smile.

"Uh, first stop is fine," I answered awkwardly. I had never been to the Eiffel Tower and figured going up to the first observation level would be plenty high enough. The elevator clattered as it ascended through the golden trusses.

"It can't be the real deal," I whispered to Patrick. "The Eiffel Tower isn't golden, is it?"

Patrick shrugged. It only took a minute for us to rise to the first level. The worker opened the door with a smile to allow Patrick and me to exit.

"Thanks," I said to the woman.

She gave me an odd look, as if I had said something strange. How could that have been strange? All I said was "thanks." Odd.

"It must be a replica," Patrick said as we walked across the wide expanse of the first observation deck to get a view out and over the edge. "Who would go through the trouble and expense to transport such a huge tower across the ocean and—"

The words caught in his throat as we got our first glimpse of the world we had been exploring on the ground. We were looking out over an enormous sea of trees, all enclosed by that mighty wall. What we had seen from the ground was only one small section. The wall did wrap around. There was no telling how many acres were enveloped by the massive structure. Hundreds? Many hundreds? It was a vast oasis within a dead world. To our right and left I could see beyond the walls, where there was next to nothing. I made out faint outlines of some of the destroyed buildings, but other than that there was desolation. The swirling dust that blanketed the ruins of New York City were somehow kept away from this lush environment. The contrast of this green world against that bleak gray was like night and day. Life and death. Real and surreal. Though I'm not exactly sure which was more surreal—the gray, destroyed city on the outside, or this impossible paradise.

The Eiffel Tower wasn't the only recognizable structure. There were others spread randomly throughout this park. I saw the Clock Tower from London's Parliament, where Big Ben chimes. The Greek Parthenon sat on top of a massive rocky hill, though this wasn't an ancient ruin. It looked fully restored, with gleaming marble and colorful friezes. Directly across from where we were, maybe a mile away, was a structure that looked as if it were the center of this strange universe. It sat high above the trees, gleaming in the sun, looking down on all those below. It was the Taj Mahal. Or at least a building that looked like the Taj Mahal.

"One thing's for sure," I said. "We aren't in France."

"Is it possible?" Patrick mumbled. "Could these be the actual buildings that were somehow brought here?"

"What else is down there?" I added. "Maybe that statue was the *real David*. Could there be other works of art? Sculptures? Paintings? Have the Ravinians brought all the great treasures of the world to this one spot?"

"If that's the case," Patrick thought out loud, "they've taken the best of what the people of Earth have created, and brought it here to decorate their own paradise."

The moment was broken by the sound of a shrill whistle. We both looked to the ground to see a man running through the garden below. The guy looked scared. He bumped into a few people, nearly knocking them over as he desperately tried to escape from . . . Who? What? A second later we saw two red-suited, golden-helmeted Ravinian guards sprinting out from under the tower, chasing the guy.

"I wonder what he did," Patrick said.

I thought for sure the guy would get away, because he looked to be running for his life, while the Ravinians were jogging with no urgency. Turned out the two guards weren't the only ones in pursuit. Four more Ravinians closed in on the guy from up ahead. He was surrounded. He changed direction. The Ravinians countered and cut off his escape. Moments later they had him.

"They must be dados," I said. "They all look pretty much alike."

"We should get down there and see where they take him," Patrick said.

He started to run off, but I saw something that made me stop him.

"Wait," I said.

We both looked down to see that instead of hauling the guy off, the Ravinians forced the guy to his knees. The garden was full of people, but in spite of the drama going on right under their noses, very few seemed to care. They all went about their business of enjoying the day, without so much as glancing at the action.

Only one other person seemed to care. It was a young girl, no more than six. She ran toward one of the soldiers and pulled on his belt as if to get him to leave the runner alone. The soldier turned quickly and loomed over the girl threateningly. The girl froze in fear. Instantly a woman who must have been her mother ran up and grabbed the girl to protect her. The little girl started crying. Her mother bundled her up and sped her away as the soldier turned his attention back to the prisoner. It was then that I noticed that the other people hanging around weren't necessarily oblivious to what was going on. I caught several people throwing nervous glances over their shoulders, as if they didn't want the soldiers to know that they were being watched.

"What are they afraid of?" I asked Patrick. "That they'll be next?"

"Next for what?" Patrick said. "What are they doing to the guy?"

The answer came quickly. One of the Ravinians strode up to the man. He was holding a three-foot-long silver wand with a black handle that I thought might be a silver weapon like the dados used on Second Earth. I didn't think he needed it. That guy wasn't going anywhere. I didn't realize how right I was. The guy was kneeling with his head down, being held by two Ravinians. The guy with the silver weapon stood behind the man and pointed the silver end of the wand at the back of his head. He held it there as the two guys who were holding the prisoner stepped away.

"Wha—" was all Patrick got out.

We heard a sharp, shrill sound that cut through the air like a laser. *Paf!* There was a brilliant flash of light. An instant later the guy on his knees had turned to black dust.

"My god!" Patrick cried.

It was a horrific sight. A small, thin tower of ash hovered in the air where his body had been. It hung there for a second, then crumpled into a small pile that the Ravinian with the weapon stepped on and crushed into the ground.

"They killed him," Patrick cried. "They just . . . killed him."

My stomach twisted, not just because of the gruesome execution, but at the thought that no matter what the guy had been accused of, the Ravinian guards had the ability to act as judge, jury, and executioner. The six Ravinians strode away as if nothing had happened. None of the people who witnessed the execution reacted. If anything, they turned away from the soldiers, so as not to make eye contact.

"I guess paradise comes with a price," I said softly.

"What has Earth become?" Patrick whispered.

I didn't know, but I had an idea of where we would find out. I looked back out over the green oasis to the awesome building that looked down over it all. The Taj Mahal. This opulent building was in the center. It was a place of importance. I felt sure that whatever answers we needed, we would find there.

I also felt that along with those answers, we'd find Saint Dane.

11

We took the elevator back down from the first observation level of the Eiffel Tower and started walking in the direction of the Taj Mahal.

How bizarre a sentence is that?

We walked among the people who were enjoying the day, seemingly unfazed by the fact that they had just witnessed a swift, grisly execution. Or maybe they were in denial. A few guys threw a Frisbee. A family had a picnic on a flowered blanket. A couple sipped wine while laughing at some secret joke. It was all so creepy. Seeing such normal activity after what had happened was almost as chilling as the execution itself. Did they truly not care? Or was it an act they put on for the Ravinians, to avoid stepping into their sights as well?

"The Taj Mahal is set up to be the center of this strange Eden," I said to Patrick. "I'm thinking we'll find answers there."

After walking quickly (but not so quickly as to attract attention) through the winding paths, we found the train that had been our vehicle into this world. It was stopped at a small building that looked like a replica of an old-fashioned brick train station, complete with a green-shingle roof and a wrought-iron fence around it. Like the rest of the place, it was immaculate. The paint sparkled like new, as if the station had just gotten a fresh coat that very morning. An overhead sign ran the length of the shelter roof. In elegant golden letters were the words "Taj Mahal."

"I guess we're here," Patrick declared.

"Where?" I asked. "Disneyland?"

A flagpole rose up next to the building, holding a flag that fluttered in the breeze. Looking up I hoped to see an American flag. Or a New York State flag. Or any flag other than the one that was there.

It was a red flag with the Ravinian star.

The train was parked on the far side of the station. Beyond that was a row of tall, thick trees that blocked our view of what lay beyond. Patrick and I walked past the train and onto a platform on the far side. We followed a brick path that left the station and snaked through the tall trees to reveal . . .

The Taj Mahal. As with the Eiffel Tower, I'd never seen the real thing, but I'd seen enough pictures to know that this was either a pretty good replica, or the real deal. You couldn't miss that single, huge onion-shaped dome that crowned the gleaming white building. Smaller domes surrounded the center one, while four circular towers stood tall like sentries, one on each corner of the foundation. A long reflecting pool stretched out before us, leading to the grand structure. To either side of the pool was grass and trees and more sculpture gardens. Lined up in rows to one side, it looked like hundreds of statues of life-size Chinese soldiers.

"I've seen those before," I said. "Like in *National Geographic* or something."

"It looks like some of the Terra-cotta Army of Emperor Qin," Patrick answered. "They were created to guard him in the afterlife. I think it was in something like two hundred BCE."

I gave him a sideways look. The guy knew his stuff.

People strolled around the statues and enjoyed the gardens here as well. But I noticed something a little different. There were more Ravinian guards hanging around. Each had a silver weapon strapped to his back. They walked in pairs, which said to me they weren't out to enjoy the day. They were working. They were there to provide security.

That meant we were in the right place.

Patrick and I walked casually, trying to look like we had no purpose other than to check out the statues and enjoy the day.

Patrick spoke softly. "Is it possible that the Ravinians transported all this from around the world?"

"I don't know" was my answer. "I guess they could have built their own. Either way, this place is all about living large. I haven't seen a single house that isn't like, awesome."

With each step we took toward the massive domed structure, my feeling grew stronger that we were getting closer to Saint Dane. Maybe it was instinct. Maybe it was wishful thinking. Or maybe I was beginning to consciously tap into the whole spirit of Solara. I can't say, but I felt sure it wouldn't be long before we once again faced the demon. Our goal was to find out what he was up to on Third Earth.

When we reached the high platform that the building stood on, we saw that the Ravinian guards had increased. Instead of patrolling randomly, they were stationed at entryways built into the box.

"Do we turn into birds now?" Patrick asked.

The solitude was broken by the sound of a helicopter. We turned to see two tailless choppers heading our way. They descended quickly and landed near one of the archways that led into the base of the building. No sooner did they touch down than several Ravinian guards sprinted for them. Two left their post at the entrance to the building, directly in front of us.

I looked to Patrick. "Could it really be this easy?"

We walked quickly for the building. Before ducking under the arch, I took a look back to see that the Ravinian guards had opened the side doors of the choppers and pulled out four people who seemed to be prisoners. The guards grabbed them by their arms and dragged them toward the building. In that brief instant I recognized one of them. It was the powerful guy with the long black hair, who had helped all those people out of the building at the zoo. My stomach sank. He was a hero. Now he was done. At least he was still alive. For the time being, anyway.

"C'mon," I ordered, and we ducked inside.

All I knew about the Taj Mahal was that it was built by some emperor in India to be a mausoleum for his wife back in the day. Not that I know much about mausoleums in India. Or mausoleums for emperors. Or their wives. Or anything about any mausoleums, for that matter. But what we saw inside looked nothing like a place for the dead.

It was a palace. Seriously. The walls were lined with ornate tiles that depicted all sorts of detailed scenes of idealized countrysides. Hanging in what would be the sky of these scenes were paintings. Paintings that I recognized. Again, I don't know much about art, but in the fourteen years I lived on Second Earth, you kind of couldn't miss seeing the big, famous paintings of the world. I didn't know any of their names or who painted them, but they sure looked familiar.

"Van Gogh," Patrick uttered. "There's a Degas. And a Picasso. Those two are by Cézanne. Dali, Matisse, Lautrec, and Jackson Pollock. My god, Pendragon, these are some of the greatest paintings of all time."

I guess Patrick knew art, too. Heck, he was a teacher.

"I know that one," I said. "*Mona Lisa*, right?"

Patrick nodded, dumbfounded. "They can't all be replicas. They're too . . . too . . . good."

"So maybe that big statue we saw outside really was the original *David*. And those soldiers really were pulled out of a tomb in China."

"And maybe these buildings aren't replicas, either."

The idea was staggering. Did the Ravinians steal great artworks from around the world for their own personal collection?

"There is something odd, though," Patrick commented, frowning.

"Gee, you think?"

"All the artwork we've seen dates from the early twenty-first century and before. I haven't seen a single piece of notable art that was made in the three thousand years since then."

"And you'd know it if you saw it?" I asked.

He gave me an impatient look. Of course he would.

I shrugged. "Okay, genius, what do you think that means?"

"It could mean that from the time the Ravinians took power on Second Earth, no notable art was created."

"That's kind of, I don't know, scary," I said.

Patrick nodded. It was a sobering thought.

We heard the sound of a heavy door being thrown open, followed by the scuffling of feet. The sounds were coming from deeper in the building. There was a small forest of tall pillars ahead of us. Patrick and I used them to hide behind as we made our way toward the sounds. We only had to move a few yards before we came upon the dead center of the Taj Mahal, directly under the massive dome. The central area was open, with ornate mosaic tile work on the floor. The whole area was ringed by marble columns. I nudged Patrick and pointed to the floor inside the ring. He looked, and winced. The tile pattern formed a giant, red Ravinian star. To our left was a wide set of stairs covered with rich red carpet. On top of these stairs was a platform, upon which was a heavy golden throne. The detail on it was incredible. There were intertwining vines and flowers that looked to have been molded from solid gold. On the seat and the back were rich red cushions.

"So who's the king?" Patrick asked.

I didn't know. But I had a pretty good idea.

Opposite the throne, across the center area, light blazed in from the doors that had been thrown open. A group of people hurried in—the Ravinian guards with their prisoners from the helicopters. The poor guys weren't putting up a fight. They looked too beat up for that. The guards dragged them inside the ring of marble columns, but stopped before entering the circle that contained the Ravinian star.

I heard a woman's voice call to them. "Stop there!"

It made the hair go up on the back of my neck. I knew that voice. My first reaction was to scream. I didn't, because it was also good news. Sort of. It meant that we were in the right place.

"Bring their leader forward," the woman commanded.

Patrick and I carefully maneuvered around the pillar where we were hiding to see her. She stood next to the throne on top of the platform, looking down on the guards and their victims. She wore a long, deep red robe with golden trim. Her dark brown hair was piled up on top of her head like some kind of fashion model, as opposed to the way she normally wore it, which was straight down. Under other circumstances, I'd say she was beautiful. These weren't other circumstances.

I wanted to leap onto that platform and strangle Nevva Winter.

Two Ravinian guards stepped forward, holding one of the victims. It was an older guy with shaggy gray hair and a salt-and-pepper beard. His face looked swollen. A trickle of blood oozed from the side of his mouth. He'd been beaten. The red-shirt guards dragged him to the center of the Ravinian star and pushed him down onto his knees. He didn't resist. Of the four prisoners he looked to be the weakest. The other three each had two guards holding them. One of them was the powerful-looking hero guy with long black hair. His head was down, his chin against his chest. He may have been beaten up, but he was alert. I saw him stealing quick glances, sizing up the situation. I guess he didn't want the Ravinians to know that he wasn't done yet. It made me like this guy even more.

Nevva drifted down the stairs and approached the man on his knees. Her eyes were locked on him. He didn't lift his own eyes to meet her gaze. When Nevva spoke, she actually sounded as if she had sympathy for the guy. I knew better. Nevva was heartless.

"It would be better for all of you if you told us what you

know," she said softly, as if trying to put him at ease.

The guy took a deep, pained breath and twisted his head to look up at her.

"Better?" he rasped. "Are you saying that Ravinia will show compassion?"

"I'm saying that if you refuse to speak, things will go badly for you. For you all."

The guy chuckled. It made him cough. It was a sickening, gurgling hack. There was blood down there. I could feel his body tense in pain. I thought back to the guy at the zoo that the Ravinian guards were kicking. These guys must have gotten the same treatment.

"I don't see how things could get much worse than they already are," he wheezed.

A voice boomed from on top of the platform. "Believe me, things can always be worse."

I felt Patrick tense up. I must have done the same. That voice always had that kind of effect. My instincts were right. We were definitely in the right place. We both looked up to the platform to see the proof.

Saint Dane stepped in front of the throne.

It was definitely the demon, but I had to do a double take. He didn't look the same. He was still thin and stood very tall. He still had those cold blue-white eyes. His voice was the same. But the guy standing there looked more like Saint Dane's younger brother than Saint Dane.

His hair was back. It was as long as I remembered from when I first met him, before it burned off, leaving a bald, scarred dome. It was parted in the middle and fell straight past his shoulders. But it wasn't gray. It was black. Jet-black. He wasn't wearing that familiar black suit, either. The cut of the suit he now wore was the same as the old one. It still buttoned tight under his chin, but it was deep red with golden braids around the cuffs and collar. The strangest thing of all was that he looked younger than I remembered. If I were to guess, I would have said that Saint Dane always looked like he was in his fifties. He now looked to be in his thirties. He didn't seem to be playing a role, either. It was definitely Saint Dane as himself. But it wasn't. I hate to write this, but I have to be true to what I saw. This new and improved Saint Dane actually looked . . . yikes . . . handsome.

Patrick was every bit as stunned as I was. He looked at me as if to ask, "Is that really him?"

I nodded. It didn't matter what color his hair was or what kind of silly suit he wore; it was him.

The demon walked casually down the stairs, headed for the kneeling man.

"You are quite brave," Saint Dane said to the man. It was a compliment, but it was cold. "You are all brave. I commend you. However, you must know that your cause is lost. How many of your rebel band are left? A few dozen? How many have you seen die? Too many. Such a waste. Don't you want that to end?"

The guy on his knees was breathing heavily. He kept his eyes on the ground.

"Look at me," Saint Dane said softly.

The guy didn't.

"I said *look at me*!" he bellowed while grabbing the guy's chin and forcing his head up.

Nevva took a step back. I wasn't sure if she was bothered by this or she didn't want to get in the way if Saint Dane started swinging.

"You have a choice," Saint Dane said, once again calm.

"You always have a choice. You can tell us what you know. A simple answer. One word. That's all I need, and your suffering will end."

"I don't know what you're asking me," the guy seethed. He was holding back anger. I knew the feeling.

"Of course you do," Saint Dane said jovially. "When you entered the flume, you did not come here. That much I know for certain."

I grabbed Patrick's arm. What was Saint Dane talking about? Who were these guys?

"I'm not sure how you ended up here," Saint Dane continued. "Obviously it was before the flumes were destroyed. That is of no interest to me. What I want to know is where you were sent when you first entered the flume. Is that so much to ask?"

My heart raced. These guys weren't Travelers. But who were they? My heart leaped. Was it possible? Could these guys be the very people we were looking for? Were they some of the enemies of Ravinia who were sent into exile? I was excited and terrified at the same time. Excited that we may have found them. Terrified because Saint Dane had found them too.

"So tell me, my friend," Saint Dane said to the man on his knees. "All I need is a word. The name of a territory. Where is it that you ended up when you entered the flume? Tell me and your suffering will end."

"All right," the guy wheezed. "I'll tell you."

I saw the other victims tense up. The Ravinian guards held them tight.

"Wonderful," Saint Dane exclaimed.

"Come closer," the guy said with a raspy voice.

Saint Dane walked up to the guy and towered over him.

The guy whispered something so softly that I couldn't hear. Neither did Saint Dane, for he bent over to get closer. When Saint Dane was down on the same level as his prisoner, the guy spit in his face. Even from where we were, I could see that there was more blood than saliva. Saint Dane didn't flinch. The Ravinians started to pull the guy back, but Saint Dane held up his hand.

"Leave him be," he said calmly.

The demon got right back in the guy's face. He didn't even wipe off the blood and spit that dribbled off his chin. He locked eyes with the poor guy. I knew what that felt like. The guy was in serious trouble.

"I will kill your three friends first," Saint Dane said icily. "It will be slow. It will be painful. I will break their bones with my own hands, starting with their feet and working my way up their spines. They will bleed. The best they can hope for is that the pain will cause them to pass out, for drowning in your own blood is a horrible way to die. Is that the fate you wish to condemn them to? The choice is yours, my bold friend."

The guy didn't look away from Saint Dane, though I felt his fear. He wasn't being bold; he was desperately trying to hold on to his sanity. He started to whimper. His body shook as he was overcome by emotion. Still, he didn't break eye contact with Saint Dane.

"Tell me," Saint Dane said with mock kindness. "Tell me. The truth will be your salvation."

Finally, in a haunted voice that seemed to come from a tortured place, the guy muttered the single word that Saint Dane was looking for.

"Cloral."

"Cloral?" Saint Dane repeated.

The guy nodded and dropped his head in defeat.

The other three prisoners seemed to deflate.

Saint Dane allowed himself a small smile. He backed away. Then, with one quick movement he grabbed the long silver weapon from one of the Ravinian guards and pointed it at his victim.

"No!" Nevva shouted.

The prisoner let out an anguished cry.

Saint Dane didn't react to either of them.

Paf!

The sound of an electric charge cut through the room as the weapon fired a deadly charge. The two Ravinian guards backed off quickly, so as not to be burned. The prisoner tried to dive away, but it was too late. A moment later he was a cinder. As with the guy we saw under the Eiffel Tower, the victim's body became a thin tower of ash that dangled in the air for an impossible second, then fell to the ground in a heap of black soot.

Patrick let out a small, pained gasp.

My head spun. Saint Dane had killed the man with no more thought or remorse than if he had swatted a fly.

"Kill them all," he commanded while casually tossing the weapon aside. It clattered onto the tiled floor, its deadly work complete. Saint Dane strode for the stairs that led up to the throne, his mission accomplished.

"You can't," Nevva called after him.

Saint Dane slowly turned back to her.

"Why is that? I am keeping my promise. I told him that their suffering would be over. His most certainly is, and theirs will be as well."

"I'm just saying that there may be another way," she said, regaining her icy composure. For a second I thought I actually sensed compassion from Nevva. It didn't last long.

"There is no other way, Nevva dear," Saint Dane said patiently. "They must die. They must all die. As distasteful as that may be to you, it is the only way that we will—"

He stopped himself in midsentence. His eyes flashed. He was suddenly on alert. He looked up, his eyes scanning everywhere and nowhere, as if trying to make sense of what he was feeling.

"What is the matter?" Nevva asked.

Saint Dane held his hand up to quiet her. He looked around, as if confused.

"Impossible," he said aloud, but it seemed more like he was talking to himself.

Something was wrong. Something he hadn't expected. There were very few times that I had seen Saint Dane thrown. He always had every angle figured. Every move was calculated, planned for, and anticipated. Not this time. Whatever was bothering him, it had come as a complete surprise. This might be going too far, but in that moment Saint Dane seemed nervous.

I was pretty sure I knew why.

"Get back to Solara," I whispered to Patrick. "Tell Uncle Press everything you saw."

Patrick's eyes were wild. "What are you going to do?" he whispered back.

"I'm going to shake things up a little."

I knew what Saint Dane was sensing. I knew why he was confused. He thought I was done. He thought *we* were done. He was wrong, and that's what he was sensing. He felt our presence. I figured I might as well confirm things for him.

"Pendragon, don't—," Patrick warned.

I stepped out from behind the pillar into the light.

"Man, that suit is just *wicked* cool!" I called out.

Saint Dane spun toward me. I was right. I was the last person he expected to see wandering into his palace.

"Hi, Nevva," I said casually. "You guys get your hair done at the same place? Cute. Love the outfit, too. You've got a kinda retro, sixties *Star Trek* thing going on."

Nevva opened her mouth but couldn't speak. They both looked as if they'd seen a ghost. Maybe they had. Since the moment I'd let Alexander Naymeer fall from the helicopter, I had seen the impossible. I had learned more truths about Halla, Saint Dane, and myself than I could have imagined. I can't say that I was at peace with any of it. At least, not yet. Most of the news that Uncle Press had given us about the struggle against Saint Dane was bad. Our backs were to the wall. We were running out of time and opportunity. We all knew that this was our last stand. Up until that moment I had been moving forward semi-numb, going through the paces. It all seemed so futile.

Until that moment.

I saw fear in Saint Dane's eyes.

That told me we may have been down to our last chance, but it was a good chance. He feared us. He feared me. My confidence soared.

This really wasn't over.

12

Every eye in the place was on me. I'm sure that the Ravinian guards and their prisoners had no idea who this wiseass intruder was. You'd think they would have jumped me, but they were waiting for orders from their boss.

The order didn't come. Saint Dane stood there with his mouth hanging open. It was awesome. This might be a weird thing to say, but I was enjoying myself. I felt for the first time in, well, the first time *ever*, that I was one step ahead of him. I had to make sure that I stayed there. I strolled around the circle, acting all nonchalant, looking at the opulent surroundings.

"I like what you did with the place," I said, all friendly. "Nothing like a little artwork to freshen up a tomb."

Saint Dane and Nevva kept their cycs on me. Nevva looked dumbfounded. Saint Dane just looked confused. I liked that.

"And look at you!" I said to Saint Dane. "All young and regal looking. What are you now? King? Emperor? Grand Pooh-bah? I had you all wrong. Here I thought all this time you had some master plan for the good of Halla because only you knew what was right for mankind, and all you really wanted was to live in a palace and wear fancy king clothes. Gotta tell you, I'm disappointed."

"Be careful, Pendragon," Patrick warned as he stepped out from behind the pillar.

Nevva and Saint Dane both shot him a surprised look. I was almost as surprised to see him. I thought he had left for Solara. I didn't want him there. I had a plan and knew that Patrick would only get in the way. Oh well. I had to stay in control, so I needed to act like this was part of the plan.

"Yeah," I announced casually. "Patrick's back. We're all back, in case you were wondering. Did you miss us?"

Saint Dane still hadn't recovered. I knew that wouldn't last long.

"Patrick," I said calmly. "You should go now."

"I—I can't leave you here. Not like this!"

"Why not? What could happen?" I asked innocently. "These goons could zap me, there'd be a big ouch, and I'd just end up back in Solara."

Nevva and Saint Dane both snapped a look to me. Yes, another shocker. We knew all about Solara. This was fun.

"It's true," I said to Saint Dane. "We're all back and pretty much up to speed, thanks to Uncle Press. Hard to believe that you and Uncle Press were friends once. I don't get that one."

Saint Dane winced with each new revelation, like I was shooting tiny little arrows at him.

Patrick took a step toward me. "Pendragon, I—"

"Patrick," I said firmly. "Go. I'm serious. Now."

I may have sounded casual, but my look told him that I was dead serious. He took a quick, apprehensive look around and nodded. He stepped backward . . . and disappeared.

.I heard Saint Dane gasp. He actually gasped. It was awesome.

"Oh, right," I teased, pretending to have just remembered something important. "We've all got the same tools now, demon boy."

Saint Dane gathered himself up, stood tall, and fixed his cold blue eyes on me. "Then by all means," he said, "use them."

So much for keeping him off balance. His act was back together, and he was calculating his next move. He knew we couldn't use the spirit of Solara more than necessary because we would only weaken it.

"So what's the deal?" I asked. "Did you get the Ravinians to steal this cool stuff from all over Earth? I mean, Big Ben? The Eiffel Tower? Is that what this has all come down to? Gathering a bunch of famous stuff and creating a little Ravinian theme park? It's good to be king, isn't it?"

"It's much more than that, Pendragon," Nevva said, her voice cracking. Unlike her boss, she was still off balance.

"Don't bother, Nevva," I snapped at her. "I know all about it."

"And you are correct," Saint Dane said, almost jovially. "I have enjoyed taking human form. And why not? If I am going to be the salvation of mankind, why shouldn't I enjoy a little reward? Is that asking too much?"

"Nah!" I replied sarcastically. "You're worth it! And man, you look good for somebody who's got to be, what, a couple hundred thousand years old? Talk about a makeover. Yikes. The long hair is especially slick. A little glam-rock, but still. Nice."

As I spoke, I kept scanning the group, looking for my chance.

"I *am* surprised to see you," Saint Dane growled. "With the collapse of the flumes I felt certain that the last light of Solara would have been dimmed, along with you and your kind. Apparently I was mistaken."

I held my arms out and shrugged. "Sorry."

"If you know as much as you say," he continued slyly, "you also know that your existence is hanging by the thinnest of threads."

I wanted to ask him where he was getting his own spiritual power from, if it wasn't Solara, but I didn't want to admit how much I still didn't know. I walked toward the three prisoners who were being held by the Ravinian guards. They were the reason I was still there. I had to try and rescue them. If they were exiles, they might know more about the others. It's why Saint Dane had them there. It's why he tortured them for information. One thing that Saint Dane said was absolutely correct. If his final conquest of Halla was going to succeed, he had to kill the exiles. Or as many of the seventy thousand as he could find. As long as they lived, Solara lived. Saint Dane was hunting for them just as the Travelers were.

"That thread isn't so thin," I lied. "Solara isn't in as bad a shape as you think." Another lie, but what the heck. "I'm actually feeling pretty good about things. You know why?"

"Please," Saint Dane said sarcastically. "Share with me."

I stopped at the first prisoner and looked into his eyes. I needed to know what kind of shape they were in. If they couldn't move, or were badly injured, there was no way I'd get them out of there. The guy raised his chin and looked at me. There was fire in his eyes. I gave him a small nod. I hoped he knew what that meant. I moved on to the next guy and saw the same thing. They were just waiting for their chance. I intended to give it to them.

I looked at the guard that was holding the second prisoner. My suspicions were correct. It was a dado. The eyes were a dead giveaway. Or should I say the dead eyes were a giveaway. Saint Dane was being protected by an army of dados.

"We're in a different place now," I said cockily. "What is it you like to say? Oh yeah. The rules have changed. Since the day I found out about the whole Traveler thing, I was scared for my life. I was afraid I'd never see my family again. I was afraid of what might happen to each territory and eventually what would happen to Halla. But now? Well, now the stakes are very different."

"And why is that?" Saint Dane asked. He actually sounded curious.

I looked to him, gave him a cocky smile, and answered, "Because now I have nothing to lose."

A second later I ate those words. I stopped at the third prisoner. It was the brave guy who helped rescue those people from the building at the zoo. His long dark hair fell in his eyes. I felt pretty sure he'd be as ready to go as the others. What I saw was something else entirely. He was ready all right. But after looking into his eyes, I wasn't so sure that I was anymore. He lifted his chin and locked eyes with me. My throat clutched. I froze. Yet again, I was hit with the impossible.

The guy gave me a small smile and whispered, "About time you showed up."

My head spun. I had to fight to keep my balance. I blinked, but what I saw didn't change. I was staring into the eyes of my best friend. It was Mark Dimond. But it wasn't the same guy I had grown up with. He had changed since the last time I saw him. On Second Earth he and Courtney and a group of protestors were thrown into the flume in the Conclave of Ravinia. Whatever happened to them after that, I'd yet to find out. But the change it had made in Mark was dramatic. Gone was the book-loving, carrot-eating genius who shied away from anything physical. He was still shorter than me, but his shoulders were broad and strong. He looked older, too. Was it possible that he was now older than I was? I think the biggest change was in his face. This was a guy who had been through a lot, and gained strength from it. I knew that from what I'd seen at the zoo, when he stayed until the very last second to help rescue those people from the helicopter gunship. This was a different Mark.

Trouble was, I now had something to lose. I still wanted to rescue the three prisoners, but the stakes had suddenly become much higher.

"You up for this?" I whispered.

Mark winked. "Say when."

My confidence rose.

"When."

I instantly fell on my back, rolled into a backward somersault, grabbed the silver weapon that Saint Dane had tossed onto the floor, and continued rolling until I was almost on my feet. While still moving, I flung the weapon at the nearest Ravinian guard. I had no idea how to fire one of those things, but I knew that the weapon itself was charged. If the silver end hit the dado, I hoped it would have the same effect as it had on those poor victims. The silver wand sailed toward the guard, who didn't react in time. The business end nailed him in the gut, and with a short, sharp electric sound, the guy was fried. He fell to the ground along with his own weapon. Unlike the other victims I had seen killed, the dado didn't vaporize. I guess robots didn't burn.

I dove for both weapons, hoping to get one before the others had the chance to react.

Mark and the other prisoners came to life. I was right. They weren't nearly as hurting as I'd first thought. They each turned on the guards who were holding them, fighting to get their electric weapons before they were vaporized.

I slid across the tile floor and scooped up one and then the other wand that had fallen to the ground. By this time the second guard, who had been holding the guy who was killed, came after me. I jumped up, holding the two wands out for protection. He came at me with his own weapon, swinging it wildly. I knew that one touch from that thing, and I'd be back on Solara with Patrick and Uncle Press. I held each of the weapons with one hand, knocking away his blows. I tried to counter with an attack of my own, but the dado was quick. I was trained, but he knew how to use these weapons. He flashed the electric wand, easily repelling each of my attacks.

I heard an electric charge sound coming from behind me and stole a quick glance to see that Mark had nailed one of the dados with his own weapon.

Mark. Unbelievable. In some ways hearing the truth about my own history and the revelation of Solara was easier to accept than Mark being a badass. Yet he was. He punched out the second dado that had been holding him, sending the guard careening backward. The dado slammed into one of the marble pillars. Hard. If it hadn't been a dado, I'd guess that it would have hurt. But dados didn't hurt. It stood up and went right for Mark.

I had my own problems. The dado I had been fighting

was coming after me, aggressively. What drove me was knowing how important it was to get those guys out of there. To get Mark out of there. No matter what, I had to stick around, which meant not being killed. The dado lunged at me. I knocked his attack away, forcing him off balance as he followed through. It gave me a short window. It was all I needed. I hit the guy on the back of his head with the other wand. A short zap later, he was done.

"Bobby!" I heard Mark shout.

I turned in time to see that I was being attacked. Not by a dado. By Saint Dane. Nevva had run to the top of the platform next to the throne, safely out of harm's way. Saint Dane, on the other hand, was coming after me with his own electric prod. I turned and threw my two weapons up to repel his attack. I didn't have to bother. Oddly, he stopped. The others continued to battle the dados, but Saint Dane stopped. He stood there with a confused expression, as if trying to process new information—which is exactly what was happening.

"'Bobby'?" he repeated, as if the word were alien to him. Then a look of recognition.

Uh-oh.

"Mark Dimond!" he said aloud as the truth hit home. "Well, Pendragon, it looks as if you have something to lose after all."

Rest time was over. He came at me, swinging his weapon furiously. He was even faster than the dado. I had no chance to think about how to attack. It was all I could do to keep the wand away from my body.

With each swing Saint Dane growled out a word. "You . . . will . . . go . . . back . . . to . . . Solara . . . and . . . watch . . . it . . . die."

I was getting tired. Saint Dane wasn't. He knocked one of the wands out of my hand, and followed up with a backhand. His prod was about to hit me in the stomach. I reacted quickly. It had to have been out of some ingrained instinct, because I certainly wasn't taught to do what I did. Saint Dane's swipe came parallel to the ground. In a second it would slice right through me, sending me back to the edges of Halla. I couldn't let that happen. I had to get Mark and the others out of there. What I did was out of desperation— not to save myself, but to save my friend.

Saint Dane's electric weapon swept right through me. I had willed myself to become smoke, and I did. I didn't feel any different. In fact, the moment his attack swept through me, I was back and ready to fight. Maybe I had only changed my midsection. Whatever. It had worked. I had used the power of Solara, the same way that Saint Dane had used it for so long. I'd like to say that I was invincible, but that was wrong. I couldn't keep on using that power. Solara couldn't handle that.

The effect it had on Saint Dane was instant. He was stupefied. He stood frozen, his weapon still at the end of its arc.

"So you *do* know the truth," he said in awe.

I answered by nailing him with both of my wands. I brought them together like cymbals, hitting both his shoulders at the same time. The reaction was instant. Saint Dane turned to ashes. Not smoke. Ashes. His remains fell to the ground just as the others had done. He had been so surprised by the demonstration of my newfound ability that he didn't use his own power to save himself.

The dados reacted instantly. They left their individual battles and ran to the pile of soot that was the remains of their leader. I wasn't sure why. What did they think they were going to do? Put Humpty Dumpty back together again? I didn't feel bad for Saint Dane. He was a spirit from Solara. I may have killed his body, but I knew it wouldn't be for long. As soon as he hit the cosmic reset button, he'd be back. I didn't want to be around when that happened.

"Outta here!" I shouted to Mark and the others.

They immediately ran for the door. Before following them, I looked up to Nevva who hadn't moved from her spot near the throne. She didn't do anything to try and stop me. On the other hand, she didn't try to help Saint Dane, either. It seemed as if she was in shock.

"Is this the way you wanted things to be?" I asked.

"I'm afraid this is the way it must be" was her melancholy answer.

"Don't bet on it," I said, then turned and ran.

As I sprinted after the fleeing prisoners, my head was already spinning forward to our next move. We were going to get out of the Taj Mahal, but we would still be in the middle of Saint Dane's luxury theme park. How would we get out of there? Run all the way back to the wall? That was a long way, with lots of dados between here and there. Once we got there, would there be any hope of opening those big doors? There would certainly be more Ravinian dado guards there. What chance did the four of us have against them? We needed an advantage, and not the kind that came from being a spirit from Solara. That wouldn't help Mark and the others. Right now, it was all about those guys. I had to keep them safe, but the truth was, I didn't know how.

Fortunately, Mark did. He and the others hit the door before me and blasted outside. We found ourselves in the wide-open garden that Patrick and I had crossed to get to the building. Mark knew exactly where to go. He sprinted straight for the helicopters that had brought them there. It seemed like the perfect means of escape, except for one thing. Mark wouldn't know how to fly a helicopter. He'd never even gotten his driver's license.

That was the old Mark. The new Mark had learned a few new tricks.

"Keep 'em back!" he shouted to me and the others.

"Keep who back?" I called after him.

He didn't have to answer. From around both corners of the Taj Mahal, Ravinian guards were headed our way. The two helicopters were parked square in the middle of one side of the building, which meant the guards from both sides had about a seventy-yard sprint to get to us. Mark jumped into the pilot's seat of one chopper and started confidently flipping switches. With a tortured whine the overhead rotor began to turn, though painfully slowly. The other two guys stood on either side of the chopper, holding up their stolen electric prods, ready to repel an attack. I didn't think they'd do so well against a swarm of dados, but I wasn't going to point that out.

I jumped into the seat across from Mark. "You can fly this thing?" I shouted above the growing whine.

"We captured one a year go," he answered. "We taught ourselves."

"A year go?" I shouted. "How long have you been here?"

"Been here? Or since we got dumped into the flume?"

"Since the flume."

"Five years. Give or take."

That news hit me like a punch to the head. It had been five years since Mark and Courtney were herded into the flume on Second Earth. Five years. That meant Mark was twenty-three years old. The buddy I had grown up with was five years older than I was.

"We've got a lot to catch up on," Mark said with a smile, which was pretty amazing under the circumstances.

"We'd better get the chance," I shot back.

The rotor was picking up speed. So were the dados.

"Come on . . . come on . . . ," Mark coaxed the machine.

We didn't have much more time.

"Get in!" I shouted to the others.

They didn't listen. They were focused on the incoming dados.

"Uh, Mark," I said with fake calm. "It would be good to get airborne."

"Couple of seconds . . . ," he said, concentrating on the RPM reading on the controls.

I heard a scream. We had less time than I thought. The dados from inside the Taj Mahal had regrouped and descended on the two guys outside the helicopter. Mark's friends both jumped away from the chopper, flailing their weapons at the dados.

"Get in!" I shouted to them.

"They won't," Mark said, with a calm that I'd never heard from him. Especially given the circumstances.

The helicopter shuddered, the rotor whined. I felt a lurch. We were starting to lift off. I turned to call the others again. It was too late. They fought valiantly, but were quickly overwhelmed. I saw one hit by a silver wand and turned to ash. The other went down seconds later. They had sacrificed themselves so Mark could get away. That is, *if* Mark could get away.

The swarm of dados arrived from both sides. They

jumped at the landing skids of the helicopter. A few caught on and were lifted into the sky along with us.

"We've got hitchhikers," I announced.

"Not for long."

Mark lifted the chopper straight up, then quickly shifted the joystick. The helicopter made a sudden counterclockwise turn, flinging off the dangling guards. They fell to the ground, landing on their pals.

"Outta here," Mark said, and accelerated our ascent.

My stomach hit the seat, not only because of the sudden acceleration, but because of something I saw. Standing on the first level of the Taj Mahal, watching us, was Nevva Winter. Standing next to her was Saint Dane. He was already back, no worse for wear. It didn't surprise me, though it made me wonder again where he was drawing his own power from.

What really made me sick was something else I saw on the ground.

The rotor of the second helicopter was starting to turn. We weren't going to be the only chopper in the sky.

13

We accelerated quickly and flew high over Saint Dane's mini-kingdom. Seeing it from the sky gave me an even better idea of how huge the place was. It was a sprawling green oasis surrounded by that gigantic wall . . . in the middle of a dead, gray city.

"They're coming after us," I said to Mark.

"I hope they do. Maybe we'll snag another one of these babies," he answered while staying focused on flying.

Unbelievable. It was Mark, but it wasn't. I was thrilled to see him, though totally thrown by how much he had changed. Up until that moment, Mark and I had been aging at the same rate. It didn't matter that we were on different territories. For whatever reason, our time lines had been the same. Not anymore. Did that mean I had spent five years on Solara? Or floating in space? Or was that the wrong way to look at it? Maybe when I left for Third Earth, the spirits of Solara put me here, five years past the time when Patrick was killed. If that was the case, did that mean that the turning point of Third Earth had shifted? I was always sent where I needed to be, when I needed to be there. Thinking this way actually gave me hope. Third Earth was definitely still in play.

All my confused questioning ended abruptly when our helicopter was rocked by an explosion.

"Whoa," I exclaimed. "What was that?"

"They're shooting from the ground," Mark said calmly. "It won't last. As soon as we get past the wall, we'll be out of range."

I looked down out of the window to see that we were about to cross out of the green and into the gray. Two more explosions rocked us. The helicopter shuddered but we weren't hit. A moment later I looked down to see the wall passing underneath us. We were back over the dead city of New York.

Whoosh! Something flew by to my right, barely missing us. It left a smoke trail in its wake.

"I thought you said we'd be out of range?"

"Yeah, of their ground guns," Mark replied. "That came from the chopper that's chasing us."

Oh. Swell.

"I saw what those rockets can do," I said nervously. "I was at the zoo when you helped those people out."

Mark gave me a quick glance.

"Where have you been for five years?" he asked.

"That is a very long story."

Whoosh. Whoosh. Two more rockets passed by, one on each side.

"I gotta concentrate," Mark said, and pushed the joystick forward. We immediately went nose down, headed for the ground. I put my foot out to brace myself. It wasn't that I didn't trust Mark's flying, it was just that, well, okay, I didn't trust Mark's flying. But then again, I trusted the guys behind us even less, so whatever Mark did was okay with me.

"We'll lose them in the haze," Mark announced.

The air was once again filled with the same brown, dusty clouds that swirled through the zoo, which meant that the visibility quickly dropped back to near zero. Mark pushed the helicopter down toward the river. After a nauseating plunge, he leveled us out and sped southward. We couldn't have been more than ten feet above the water, skimming the surface.

"This is, uh, dangerous," I said, trying not to show how terrified I was. At the speed we were going, we wouldn't see anything solid in front of us until a second before the crunch.

"Yeah, it is," he said with no trace of fear. Or stutter. That was good. If Mark didn't stutter, it meant he wasn't nervous. That made one of us.

"You, uh, you've done this before?" I asked, hoping that my skepticism didn't bleed through.

"Couple times," he answered. "The bad visibility will make us tough to hit."

He seemed confident at the controls. I mean, he wasn't like a fighter-jock or anything, but on the other hand, he wasn't looking around with a "What's this button do?" attitude. I figured that as long as we didn't hit anything, we'd have a chance at getting away. The helicopter behind us stopped shooting. I guessed it couldn't see us anymore. Mark knew what he was doing. I watched him for a few seconds, amazed at the transformation that had happened over the past five years. It kind of made me sad, because the time had been rough on him. You don't become toughened like that by hanging around reading books and eating carrots. Mark had definitely been through some stuff.

A huge shadow passed overhead. Or should I say, we passed under something huge. I ducked. I know, dumb. It was an involuntary reaction. I saw through the bubble roof that it was one of the wrecked bridges that had connected Manhattan to the rest of the world.

"Where are we going?" I asked.

"Home" was his answer. "But not until we shake this guy. We don't need to show him the way."

Another shadow flew overhead. I ducked again. This time it wasn't a bridge. It was the other helicopter.

"Did he see us?" I asked.

"Let's find out."

Mark pulled back the joystick. We immediately shot skyward. I was pressed back into my seat, fighting nausea all the way. It was like being on a ride at Playland. A really sickening ride that could end in certain death at any second. Knowing that didn't help the nausea. It was a reminder that as much as I was a spirit from Solara, I was still very much a human being. At the moment I was kind of wishing that I was a little less human. The wrecked tower of another bridge appeared out of the haze. Mark veered us to the left. We would pass by safely, but too close for my taste.

"So? Did we lose—"

Two rockets hit the top of the bridge's tower. It exploded, sending off a cloud of smoke and a shower of metal shrapnel. Mark banked hard to the left and flew down. Chunks of metal hit the chopper, pinging the surface, rocking us.

"No," Mark said.

"'No' what?"

"No, we didn't lose him."

Mark dropped us down to the river again. We leveled off and flew over the choppy, dark water.

"Why don't we go over land?" I asked.

"Because I don't want anything falling on anybody."

Good answer. I hoped we wouldn't be the ones doing the falling.

"So we just try to lose him in the haze?" I asked.

"That. Or I'll drop him in the harbor."

Mark said that so matter-of-factly I actually believed he could do it.

"You have a plan for this or are you just winging it?"

He didn't answer. Not good. We were approaching another bridge. The roadway loomed overhead. No sooner did we pass under it, than the roadbed exploded. The chasing helicopter was above us. Still shooting.

"You ever play chicken as a kid?" he asked.

"No, and neither did you."

Mark laughed, as if remembering the geeky kid he used to be. That kid was long gone. "He's not giving up. We're going to have to play."

There was a reason I never played chicken. It was dumb. It was a test of wills. There was no point to it other than to prove who was the bigger idiot. But this was Mark's show. I wasn't going to argue. We flew under another bridge. It could have been the Brooklyn Bridge. It was hard to tell. We were going too fast and I didn't care anyway. Mark accelerated and drove us skyward again.

"We've got to get far enough ahead of him to make this work," he explained.

The haze cleared a bit once we were over New York Harbor. It was still pretty thick, but visibility had increased slightly.

"He can see us now," I cautioned.

"Good. I want him to."

Up ahead I saw the last bridge before open ocean. It was the long Verrazano Narrows Bridge that connected Brooklyn and Staten Island. Its two towers still stood tall.

Mark explained, "For whatever reason, this bridge is still pretty much intact."

I twisted and looked back to see that the chasing helicopter had fallen far behind us. I caught glimpses of it through the haze to see it was just clearing the Brooklyn Bridge.

"Maybe we can lose it now," I offered hopefully.

"No way. We're in the open now. It's going to have to end here. One way or the other."

We flashed over the bridge, directly between the two towers. Mark pressed the chopper on, headed for open ocean.

"Now what?" I asked.

"Now we play."

Mark banked the chopper hard, doing a one-eighty. In seconds we were on our way back toward the bridge, and directly for the other helicopter. We drifted to the left, headed toward the south tower.

"If we're lucky, he won't know this bridge is still in such good shape," Mark growled. His calm was gone. He was now focused and intent.

"What if we're not lucky?" I asked.

"Then we'll see who's chicken."

I couldn't see the other helicopter through the haze. But at the speed we were traveling, it couldn't be more than thirty seconds before we'd cross paths. Or collide head-on. Mark gripped the joystick and fired a rocket. It sailed straight ahead, hitting nothing.

"What was that for?" I asked.

"I want him to know where we are."

Our helicopter continued to drift to the left until we were lined up directly on the south tower of the bridge. It looked as if we were flying at an altitude just above the roadbed.

"Look out!" I shouted.

A rocket was incoming, shooting out of the mist. Mark easily dodged it.

"I guess he knows where we are," he said.

"This is crazy!" I shouted. "Let's just try to lose him."

"We won't, Bobby. He'll keep coming. Then other choppers will join him. We've got to end it here."

That's when I saw it. Maybe a half mile ahead, directly in front of us. We were on a collision course with the other helicopter. Chicken time. I figured the odds were fifty-fifty.

"Shoot it!" I screamed.

Mark fired off a shot, then another. The oncoming chopper dodged them easily and fired back. Mark dipped our chopper and veered left, ducking both missiles. He then brought us back up to the same level as the enemy helicopter. On this course we would fly just over the roadbed of the bridge, inside the south tower . . . and crash head-on with the other chopper.

"Keep shooting!" I shouted.

"Don't need to," Mark said calmly.

The chopper fired another rocket. It missed us, and didn't let off another shot. It was starting to look as if our hunter didn't care about shooting us down anymore.

"He wants to kamikaze into us," Mark said, reading my mind.

"That's not how you play chicken!" I screamed.

"He doesn't know the rules."

The oncoming chopper was about to reach the bridge.

"Mark, I can't let you die."

Mark smiled. "I won't. We've got him."

Huh?

I looked ahead. We were a couple of seconds away from flying head-on into this guy. In seconds we'd be wreckage. I squinted. It was going to hurt.

Suddenly the oncoming helicopter exploded in midair. One second it was bearing down on us, the next there were chunks of wreckage scattering every which way.

"Gotcha!" Mark shouted.

The doomed chopper's rotor spun wildly off on its own. The skids flew in opposite directions. The remainder of the rockets exploded, followed by a violent eruption that had to have been the fuel tank.

Mark pulled back on the joystick, and we sailed up and over the carnage.

"Whooooo!" he yelled, totally psyched.

"What the heck happened?" I shouted.

"I told you, that bridge is pretty much intact. It's a suspension bridge. All of the cables are still there that connect the two towers. Trouble is, you can't see them through the haze."

I looked back over my shoulder in time to see the shattered helicopter hit the bridge roadbed, bounce off, and plummet toward the ocean below.

"So you lured him into a spiderweb," I said. "That's why you were flying so close to the tower." I punched him in the shoulder. "You could have told me, you know."

"I could have, but I didn't want to look bad if it didn't work."

"If it didn't work, looking bad would have been the least of your worries. That was awesome, Mark."

"Thank you. Now we gotta get down before they send more choppers after us."

I sat back in my seat and tried to catch my breath. I don't know what was more shocking: The fact that we had nearly been killed by that chopper, or that Mark Dimond was the cool pilot who set the trap and calmly sprang it, saving our lives. We flew back toward Manhattan, staying low to the water in case any other dado pilots came looking for us. I remembered the tip of Manhattan as being a place that was loaded with tall buildings. It was like a whole separate city. Not anymore. It looked as if the buildings had all been sheared off around the tenth story. It wasn't like Rubic City on Veelox, where the city was simply crumbling from age and neglect. No, something had happened here. Something bad.

"What's the story here?" I asked Mark, gesturing to the sad remains of a once-great city.

Mark nodded. "They didn't officially give it a name, but they should have called it World War Three," he said. "Except that it wasn't about countries. It was Ravinia against the rest of the world."

"Who won?"

"Nobody. Though I guess you could say it was Ravinia. Once it came to power, Ravinia thought it had crushed all of its opposition. But a revolt was brewing. It took centuries to grow strong enough to challenge the Ravinian authority. Up until then, if you weren't a Ravinian, you lived in squalor. The people finally grew strong enough to fight back in numbers large enough that it scared the Ravinians. So this is how they dealt with the revolt."

"By destroying the city?" I asked.

"Many cities. But not before moving the most valued possessions of the world to their various conclaves."

"So that really was Big Ben back there? And the Taj Mahal and the *Mona Lisa*?"

"Yup. They have hundreds of those garden spots all over. Once they looted the world of its treasures, they unleashed Armageddon. Basically, the entire arsenal of mankind was ignited. I think in some places they even used nukes. Like in Washington DC. From what I heard, it only took a few days, and the entire non-Ravinian world was laid to waste . . . along with most everyone in it."

Looking down at the devastation, Mark's story seemed possible. It truly was Armageddon.

Mark continued, "They didn't kill everyone, of course. There were survivors. But not in any numbers, and certainly not enough to stand up to the Ravinians."

"When did it happen?" I asked.

"I'm not exactly sure. I think it was about four years ago."

That rocked me. "Four years ago? That's all?"

Mark turned away from his flying long enough to give me a dark look. "I think it was the turning point of Third Earth, Bobby."

I couldn't breathe. Was it possible? Had we been sent back too late? Was the battle for Third Earth, and Halla, truly over before we'd had a chance to stop it?

Mark looked back ahead. He had tears in his eyes. "I just don't get it," he said. "Obviously this is all about Saint Dane, but what does he gain by destroying most of the population of Earth?"

I didn't answer. I knew of course, but it wasn't the time to give Mark a crash course in Solara. Still, he deserved an answer. Every last survivor deserved an answer.

"Because it's about more than just Earth," I said. "And

it's about more than Halla, believe it or not. What Saint Dane is doing is crushing the positive spirit of man. Once that happens, he can rebuild a universe any way he chooses."

Mark frowned and nodded. There was no way he could understand exactly what my words meant, and maybe it didn't matter.

"But there is hope," I added.

"Is there?" he asked, sounding tired and a little more than skeptical.

"The hope is you, Mark. And everyone like you. It's about all those who were exiled through the flumes."

Mark gave me a surprised look.

I added, "Why do you think Saint Dane wants you dead?"

"Because we're all that remains of the opposition."

"That's more true than you know. What happened to you when you went into the flume in the Bronx on Second Earth? Where did you go?"

Mark's expression turned dark. "Cloral," he said softly. That was all he said at first. I think it was tough for him to wind his mind back to that time. He was struggling to keep a lid on his emotions. I didn't want to press him, but I had to know.

"I messed things up pretty bad, Bobby."

"You?" I said, trying not to laugh. "Mark, with all that's been going on, I don't think there's anything you could have done that would make it any worse."

He didn't believe me. Something was eating him up.

"Tell me," I said.

After another minute Mark got himself together and told me his story.

"A couple dozen of us ended up on Cloral in that underwater cave. I was the only one who knew enough to swim out. But once we got to the surface, it was nuts. It wasn't like the Cloral you described in your journals. There were battles between barges. The raiders were everywhere. Each barge was like its own fortress trying to defend itself. We were picked up by some raiders and forced to work on their ships. It was nasty." He looked me dead in the eye and said, "It's where I learned to fight. You don't want to know why."

There was one question I had to ask. I had been holding off because I was afraid of the answer, but I couldn't wait any longer.

"What about Courtney? Was she with you?"

Mark shook his head gravely. "No. I don't know what happened to her. We went into the flume together, but she didn't land on Cloral. Once other exiles started arriving, I started piecing together what must have happened. We figured that the Ravinians were tossing their enemies into the flume and sending them to other territories randomly. A few more showed up on Cloral. There may have been others, but I had no way of knowing."

Mark hadn't yet heard about the Bronx Massacre and the multiple thousands of people that Ravinia tossed into the flume that black day in Yankee Stadium.

He added, "I haven't seen Courtney since we went into that flume together."

"We were afraid you were all executed," I said.

"Sometimes I wish we had been."

My heart ached for my friend.

"How did you end up on Third Earth?"

"I didn't know what had happened on Second Earth, but from the way things were going with Ravinia, I was pretty sure it was lost. That meant Third Earth was the only territory that Saint Dane hadn't brought to a turning point. As dumb as this sounds, I still felt as if we were on the mission, Bobby. I wanted to get here to try and stop Saint Dane. I gathered together a bunch of the other exiles, and we mutinied against the raiders. We stole a couple of skimmers and took off to the flume. I hoped that a Traveler would come by, maybe even you, and get us out of there, but nobody showed. I knew that traveling without a Traveler would damage the flume, so we sat and waited. I don't know for how long. Too long. I was beginning to think we'd have to live in that underwater cavern, eating the fruit from the walls forever. I finally couldn't take it anymore and called *"Third Earth"* into the flume. I knew it was wrong, but I guess I was going a little out of my mind. I expected things to start rumbling, but nothing bad happened. The flume activated normally and we were on our way here. Twenty of us. At first I thought it was okay. I hoped things had somehow changed. It wasn't until we got here that I realized I was wrong. As soon as we set foot on Third Earth, the flume started rocking. It was like Eelong all over again, Bobby. The flume collapsed. It was my fault. Bringing those guys here was wrong. I'm the one who destroyed the flumes."

I smiled. Mark gave me an odd look. I guess that's what happens when you bare your soul to your best friend, and all he does is smile.

"You didn't destroy them, Mark. It would have happened anyway."

"But . . . what?"

I wanted to put his mind at ease, but I didn't want to start the whole lesson on Solara just then.

"The flumes were destroyed, Mark," I said. "All of them.

It had nothing to do with you. Trust me. There are bigger forces at work."

Mark stared at me a long time, trying to understand. He wanted to believe, but he was having trouble. "Are you serious or just trying to make me feel better?"

"Both."

"You're not kidding?"

"No. It wasn't you, Mark. I swear."

He relaxed. It was like the weight of guilt was physically lifted off his shoulders. Mark may not have understood it all, but he believed me. Probably because he needed to.

Although, his story raised questions. I knew exactly how the flumes were destroyed, but now I wasn't so sure *when* they were destroyed. I had thought it happened right after I was sucked into the flume on Second Earth. But if Mark had lived on Cloral for so long, the time lines didn't match up. As confusing as that was, it actually fit with what I was seeing. Sort of. Mark aged when I didn't. Though it felt like minutes, I may have been floating in time and space limbo for years. Or maybe time didn't matter once you left a physical world. Or maybe now that I knew I was a spirit, any pretense of living a normal physical life didn't matter anymore. Or maybe I should stop freakin' worrying about things I couldn't control. Yeah, that was the way to go.

"Tell me what happened after you got here," I asked Mark.

"We barely got out of the flume before it was crushed under some big, marble building I'd never seen before. I figured it was a new flume on Third Earth until we started exploring. It was the flume in Stony Brook, Bobby. But it wasn't the Stony Brook we grew up in."

I didn't want to hear those details. I knew they couldn't be good.

"The place was deserted, so we made our way toward the city. We found some survivors, and that's how we found out about the war. That was around three years ago. We've been fighting to survive ever since, waiting for something to happen. Or maybe I should say, we were waiting for you to come. Are you serious about the flumes?"

"Yes. So there are only twenty exiles here on Third Earth?"

"No. After today we're down to twelve. I don't understand it. There are plenty of war survivors, but the Ravinians only target us."

"That's because the exiles are the last thing standing in Saint Dane's way."

Mark gave me a confused look. That made no sense to him, and I wasn't so sure my explanation would help much.

We stopped talking for a while as he brought the helicopter in for a landing. We touched down in an empty lot on the Upper West Side of Manhattan. No sooner did we hit the ground than a group of men and woman ran toward us. I tensed up. Were we under attack again?

"It's okay," Mark assured me. "They're my guys."

Mark and I climbed out of the chopper. Not a word was spoken because everyone knew exactly what to do. Four small flatbed dollies were dropped on the ground. Half the group went to one side of the chopper, half on the other. They didn't even wait until the rotor stopped turning. Everyone lifted the small helicopter up and placed it onto the dollies. Soon we were under way, pushing the helicopter toward the open doors of a derelict garage.

Once the chopper was wheeled inside, four more people ran back out to scuff up the tracks from our journey, while the others pushed the huge door shut. The whole operation didn't take more than a couple of minutes. The helicopter was hidden away, safe from the prying eyes of Ravinians.

Once the job was done, I turned to look into the garage and saw a half dozen other choppers, along with a number of yellow taxicabs.

"What do you think of our collection?" Mark asked with a smile. "The choppers are courtesy of the Ravinians."

"You stole them?" I asked in surprise.

"There's more, too. Hidden all over the city. We've been acting like guerrillas since the minute we arrived here, Bobby. We hope to put this stuff to good use someday." Mark looked me right in the eye and asked, "Is today that day?"

I debated about how much to tell him. The truth about Halla and Solara was a huge, impossible story. I decided that the details would wait for another time. There were more important things to do. So I told him what I thought he needed to know. We sat on the far side of the garage, away from the others. I knew they'd have a million questions, and they deserved answers, but they would have to wait.

"This is the deal, Mark," I began. "Saint Dane and the Ravinians exiled thousands of people. From what I've heard and what you tell me, they were sent all over Halla. Those people are now the last hope. The Travelers have been sent back to their home territories to find them. But Saint Dane wants to find them too. Desperately. That's why he tortured that poor guy today. He's afraid of you, Mark.

I don't think the turning point on Third Earth was that war. I think it's you."

"Me?" he echoed, shocked.

"You and all the other exiles. You represent the future of Third Earth and of Halla. That's why Saint Dane wants you dead."

"Why us? What can we do to him? There's only a handful of us left."

"There's more than that. Way more. Seventy thousand people were dumped into a flume on Second Earth. I was there. I saw it. The exiles are the ones who stood up to Ravinia so long ago, and it's your collective spirit that's keeping the battle going. It's that spirit that Saint Dane wants to kill. You represent independence. Free will. Unique thinking. Everything that goes against his ideal. You and the others are the last positive force in Halla."

Mark nodded thoughtfully.

"You're getting a little cosmic on me," he said with a small smile.

"I know."

"Seventy thousand?" he asked.

I nodded.

"Man, I'd love to have half those people here with us. We've been coming up with ideas on how to bring down that Ravinian conclave. None of 'em work with a few dozen of us. But seventy thousand . . . that's a whole different ball game."

"Maybe you'll get the chance."

Mark had a gleam in his eye. He was imagining the possibilities. "There were more exiles on Cloral," he said. "Do you think the rest could be there?"

"I don't know, but I'm going to find out. I'm going to Cloral."

"What should we do in the meantime?"

"Stay alive. That's the most important thing. Once I know the other exiles are safe, I'm coming back, and we'll take our last shot at Saint Dane. Together."

"There's something else you have to do," Mark said.

"What's that?"

"Find Courtney."

Courtney. Where could she be? After seeing Mark, I had no doubt that she would still be alive. I had to believe that. If anyone represented the positive spirit of Halla, it was Courtney. Heck, she could probably keep Solara going all on her own.

"I missed you, man. There were so many times I wished you were with me."

Mark and I finally broke down and hugged. He was my best friend. The guy I grew up with. The guy who was loyal to me throughout everything. He was my acolyte. Now he was one of the forces that would try to save Halla. I was certain of that. It was the way it was meant to be.

"Why did you take so long to come back?" he asked.

"I didn't, Mark," I explained. "I feel as if I've only been gone for a short time. Maybe hours."

He gave me a confused look.

"Strange, huh?"

"Uh, yeah."

"You know something," I added. "I think that's good news."

"How's that?"

"Because I've been sent here to Third Earth five years after Patrick's time. That tells me that the turning point may have shifted. I'm here because I need to be here. Now. I think we've still got a chance."

Mark nodded thoughtfully. "You gonna explain all this to me a little better some time?" he asked.

"Yeah," I said, smiling. "It'll make your head explode."

"Seriously?"

"It's incredible. I know it all, Mark. Everything. And I found my family."

"Really!" he exclaimed. "Where are they?"

"They're safe, but I don't want to explain it now. You've got enough to worry about."

"I'm happy for you, Bobby," he said with total sincerity. "I know what it's like to lose your family."

"I know you do," I said. There was nothing more to add, so I stood and took a deep breath. "I'll be back as soon as I can."

"Better not be another five years," Mark cautioned.

"I don't think that'll happen. This is where I need to be. This time. I may not be gone very long at all."

"However long it takes, we'll be ready. We've been ready for a while."

"For what?"

"To bring down that conclave. That's what we're going to do, isn't it?"

I laughed. "Listen to you, getting all macho on me."

Mark shrugged. "What can I say? I'm ready for this to end."

Mark and I hugged one last time.

"Find them," he said softly. "And find her."

"I will."

We pulled apart and he said, "Hey, how are you going to get to Cloral if the flumes are destroyed?"

"I'll find a way."

Mark shrugged and turned toward his friends. If he

had looked back at me a second later, he would have been surprised to see that I was no longer there. I had stepped off Third Earth. . . .

And onto the deck of a burning barge on the territory of Cloral. It took me all of five seconds to realize that it was under attack.

14

I was totally disoriented.

Fire and screaming and explosions that rock the deck hard enough to knock you off your feet will tend to do that. I thought it was broad daylight, but the sky was dark. That didn't add up, until I realized I was surrounded by fire. It lit up the world so completely that it seemed like day. Whatever was happening on this barge, it wasn't good. People ran for cover, desperate to get below, away from the firestorm.

It had been years since I'd been to Cloral. At the time, it wasn't on fire, so it didn't exactly seem familiar. What barge city was I on? Who was attacking? Who were the good guys and who were the bad guys?

I heard the whistling sound of an incoming missile. But from where? What was the target? Who was firing? I decided not to move, figuring I'd just as likely be running into the missile's path as getting out of the way. I stood there, closed my eyes, and braced myself. A second later the one small building that wasn't on fire exploded. The missile hit it dead-on, blowing out windows, shattering glass, and spewing flames from within. It was a good thing I hadn't run for cover, because if I had, I probably would have gone into that building. Phew.

It was then that I got my head together enough to remember what Spader had said. He was the first of us to leave Solara and said he had gone to Grallion, and that it was on fire. Was this Grallion? Had I arrived at the same time as Spader? I ran along the deck, between two rows of burning buildings. I needed to get to someplace that would give me a view of the whole barge habitat.

I dodged several people who scrambled for protection. It was chaos. Nobody seemed to know where to go. When I got to the end of a long line of burning buildings, I found an observation tower that hadn't been hit. I had to climb. Of course, if it was a target, I'd end up back in Solara. Do not pass Go. Do not collect two hundred dollars. But I had to take the chance. I sprinted up the stairs, taking two at a time until I got to a level high enough to allow me an overview of the habitat.

I was definitely on Grallion. Or a habitat much like it. Grallion was a floating farm. Spread out in front of me were acres and acres of farmland. Half of it was on fire. It was a nightmare. I saw several brave aquaneers and farmers using hoses to try and douse the flames. Buildings could always be rebuilt, but the farms on Grallion provided food for many thousands of people.

What was happening? Who could be doing this? When I left Cloral, the mythical lost city of Faar had recently risen from the depths of the ocean to become a center for academics and art. On Second Earth, Alexander Naymeer said that Faar was going to become the center for Ravinia on Cloral. Had that already happened? Did this attack have something to do with the Ravinians taking over Cloral?

Another whistling missile came rocketing in, landing square in the middle of the farm, spewing fire. Burning crops. This kind of weapon was something new to Cloral. When I had been here, they had destructive weapons, but the ammunition was compressed water. Those weapons were destructive, but they didn't create fire. Whatever these weapons were, they were new. But how new?

When was I?

I turned to look in the direction the missile had come from to witness a frightening sight. The tower I was standing on wasn't too far from one end of the giant barge. From here I could look out over the vast ocean that covered Cloral. The night was clear. The sky was loaded with stars. . . .

And the sea was loaded with ships. War ships. Grallion was surrounded by a string of midsize ships armed with fixed, lethal guns. Of course I could only see a fraction of these ships from my vantage point, but it was clear that this was where the attack was coming from. The line of marauders was probably half a mile off the habitat, which was plenty close enough for their guns to do some damage. They looked like modern, fast vessels. As I watched, two of the big guns unloaded. The night air was pierced by the shrill whistle. Moments later two more explosions erupted on the farm below me.

What was the point? Were they trying to sink the habitat? I didn't think so. The guns were doing some serious damage, but it didn't seem as if they packed enough power to actually sink an entire floating habitat. I wondered if they were softening up the people to board and take over the barge. During the brief time that I'd been there, I hadn't seen any fighting actually happening on board. If they were going to board the habitat, it hadn't happened yet. Which meant one thing: Yet again, I was sent to the right place at the right time. Whatever this battle was about, it would probably play into the overall struggle for Halla.

I had to find Spader. I was about to start down from the tower when the sky lit up with a massive barrage from the guns. It had to have been coordinated, because it seemed as if every ship had unloaded at once. Over and over again, missiles screamed through the air and impacted on Grallion. It was so loud I thought my eardrums would burst. It suddenly felt like a really dumb thing to be on that tower. I scrambled to get down. All around me, bombs hit. The tower shook. I lost my balance and stumbled down the stairs. Another explosion erupted, and the tower started to go over. I was still ten feet from the deck and had to dive off the tower or I would have been crushed beneath it. I hit dirt, luckily, and rolled. The tower crashed down not far from my head. I was spinning through a world of light, dirt, and ear-shattering noise. All I could do was put my arms over my head, assume the fetal position, and hope that I'd survive the onslaught.

Suddenly it all stopped. Just like that. Done. The sound of the multiple explosions echoed over the ocean. It was replaced by the sounds of crying and of things burning. I heard the distant sound of people screaming out instructions to one another. I couldn't make sense of anything, but it was pretty clear that they were scrambling to pick up the pieces and care for the wounded.

That sound was quickly replaced by another. An amplified voice boomed over the water. It was so loud I had no doubt that every last person on Grallion could hear it.

"People of Grallion," the man's voice boomed. "You are protecting individuals who are guilty of crimes against

Ravinia. Harboring fugitives is a capital offense for which the entire population of Grallion will be held responsible. If you do not release the fugitives to us, we will have no choice but to continue our attack with much more drastic consequences. We have the authority, and we will sink this habitat with all on board. There will be no survivors. The choice is yours."

Ravinia. It was alive and active on Cloral. That pretty much told me who the good guys and the bad guys were. Question was, who were the fugitives they wanted so badly? Could it be the exiles? Even if it wasn't, if somebody was an enemy of Ravinia, they were a friend of mine. I had to find them. I pulled myself to my feet. I was wobbly but not hurt. Knowing that the aquaneers ran the habitats, I knew I had to start by finding them. I hoped that Spader would be with them.

I ran toward the stern of the giant barge. As I got my wits back, I began to recognize some details about Grallion. The burning buildings where I had first arrived were the stores near the aquaneer living quarters. I was sorry to see that square in the middle, nearly gutted by flames, was Grolo's. It was the tavern where Spader had first introduced me to the strange bitter-sweet drink called "sniggers." People wearing the familiar, light-colored clothing of Cloral were doing all they could to put out the flames. It was no use. There would be no more sniggers flowing at Grolo's. My heart went out to these people. I wanted to stop and help, but there was more than a lost tavern at stake.

My goal was to get to the aquaneer station at the stern of the barge, belowdecks. That was where the defense of Grallion would be plotted. I would have bet anything that Spader was there. My route was guided by memory. I soon found a hatch that led below, climbed down the stairs, ran along narrow catwalks, and finally found myself in the large, four-story bay in the stern where the aquaneers docked their skimmers and speeders. The stern of the giant habitat opened out to the sea. Several levels below me I saw dozens of skimmers tied up, bobbing on the water. Looking out onto the ocean, I saw the shadows of the gunboats. They floated like ominous predators, silently waiting to spring on their prey. Two levels up from the water, and one level below me, a ring of aquaneers had gathered. They all wore the black, formfitting swimskins that were the uniforms of the sailors who piloted and protected the habitats. Spader was nowhere in sight, but I was relieved to see someone else I recognized.

Wu Yenza, the chief aquaneer, was in the center of the action. Yenza looked pretty much the same as I remembered her. Her dark hair was cut very short and practical. Her eyes were focused and intense. She wasn't that tall, but she was still a physical force. She was the boss. Maybe best of all, she was Spader's acolyte. She knew about Halla and Saint Dane. She understood the larger context of this battle.

Unfortunately for her, she was in the middle of an attack, and it wasn't coming from the Ravinian gunboats out on the sea.

"Give them up!" a tall, angry aquaneer shouted at Yenza. "You can't sacrifice the safety of Grallion to protect strangers."

"It doesn't matter if they're strangers, they aren't traitors. They're victims," Yenza countered.

"So what?" a woman aquaneer shouted. "Our job is to protect Grallion. How can you justify risking the lives of so many to protect so few?"

"It's not just about those few," Yenza lectured. "It's about what Ravinia has done to Cloral. Do you think we're better off now that they dictate our every move? Who's to say if these people are guilty of anything other than being an enemy of Ravinia?"

"What if they're killers?" the woman aquaneer asked.

Yenza countered, "And what if their only crime is to have opinions that differ from the Conclave of Ravinia? Do you want to be the judge? If we give them up to the raiders, you'll also be their executioner. Is that what we've come to?"

Raiders. I remembered those guys. They were pirates that attacked random ships. They definitely didn't have the kind of firepower or organization that those gunships displayed. Was it possible that the raiders had become the muscle of Ravinia on Cloral?

Yenza continued, "We are at a turning point here. I know you people. I know what values you have. You don't agree with what Ravinia is turning us into any more than I do. If we give up those poor people now, who knows where it will end?"

"Who are they anyway?" another aquaneer asked. "Where did they come from? I spoke with them, and they couldn't answer the simplest questions about their own habitats. They're hiding something."

The hair went up on the back of my neck. Things were coming clear. I had a feeling I knew who they were, and why they didn't know much about Cloral. And why the Ravinians wanted them so badly.

"Does it matter where they come from?" Yenza asked. "I believe they are victims, and if we give them up, we're giving in to Ravinia. Who knows where that will lead us?"

I knew. I'd seen it on other territories.

The aquaneers were uncertain. Sure, Yenza was convincing. Her words rang true. I wanted to back her up and tell them all about how Ravinia destroyed Earth. But I didn't think that would have been cool.

"So then what do we do?" the tall aquaneer asked, softening. "We're a farming habitat. We don't have the muscle to repel an armada of raiders."

The woman added, "They've already knocked out many of our defenses, and people are scrambling to put out fires all over the habitat."

The man added, "Do you feel so strongly that you're willing to let Grallion die to make a statement against Ravinia?"

Tough question. I really wanted to hear Yenza's answer. Her response was odd. She looked at her watch. The other aquaneers were just as confused as I was.

"Soon it won't matter," she replied.

The aquaneers looked at one another, not sure of what she meant.

Yenza continued, "Before the raiders began their attack, I loaded the fugitives into a hauler submarine and sent them off the habitat. By now they should have cleared the blockade. They're gone."

The aquaneers erupted in anger. "How could you do that?" "It wasn't your decision alone." "You have sentenced us all to death."

The woman aquaneer didn't argue. She ran to the edge of the platform and looked down to the level below. "Go!" she commanded.

Instantly a skimmer came to life. An aquaneer was aboard, powering up.

Yenza ran to the woman aquaneer. "Who is that? What's happening?"

"You have just saved Grallion," the woman replied, smug.

"What do you mean?" Yenza demanded to know.

"All they want is the fugitives," the woman explained. "They have no issue with Grallion, unless of course, the Conclave of Ravinia decides to punish us for harboring them. Once the raiders find out about the hauler, they'll leave Grallion alone and hunt the fugitives down."

Yenza stared the woman down. "You're a Ravinian."

The woman lifted up her right sleeve. Tattooed on her arm was a green star. The mark of Ravinia. "There are more of us here than you know."

Yenza wound up and slugged the woman square in the jaw. It was awesome. The woman fell backward, both feet up in the air. It was almost comical. Almost. The aquaneer on the skimmer pulled away from the dock, headed out to sea. Headed for the raiders to tell them where to find the fugitives.

The exiles.

I had no doubt that they were some of the exiles we were charged to find and protect. The aquaneer had to be stopped, which meant I had to come out from hiding. I slid down the ladder, too fast for safety. My goal was to get a skimmer and chase the guy down before he got to the raiders. Yenza had the same idea. She left the other aquaneers, some of whom were probably Ravinians, and climbed down toward the dock level. We hit the bottom level at the same time. She heard my feet hit the deck and turned in surprise. When she saw me, her eyes went wide.

"Pendragon?" she gasped, stunned.

"We gotta stop him!" I yelled to her. No time for reunion talk.

Yenza took off toward the edge of the dock and the line of skimmers. I was right after her. As she ran she yelled, "By the time we power up a skimmer and take off it may be too late!"

The loud hum of a fully powered skimmer suddenly echoed through the dock area. Yenza and I both looked to see a skimmer flying in at full throttle. I thought for sure that it was going to crash into the dock.

I shouldn't have been worried. The driver spun the water-craft, making an impossibly tight turn that threw up a wave of water. The craft side-slipped forward until it kissed the edge of the dock with a safe, gentle thump. At the controls was a smiling Vo Spader.

"Good to be back on the water, mates," he called to us.

I had to smile. "You've got your wish, Spader."

"What wish is that?"

"You're back in the game."

He gave me a huge smile and said, "You have no idea how badly I've wanted to hear those words, Pendragon."

Yenza and I leaped onto the skimmer and barely had time to grab on to something before Spader gunned the engine and launched from the dock. If anybody could catch this guy, it was Spader.

The Traveler from Cloral was going to have another wish come true.

We were about to get dangerous.

15

The Ravinian aquaneer was nearly halfway to the nearest gunboat.

We had some catching up to do. Spader stood at the motorcycle-like controls of the skimmer and opened up the double-pontoon engines. The small craft lurched forward and seemed to fly over the water. Yenza and I knelt on either side of Spader, holding on to the rails. We knew that if we so much as hit a small swell, we'd be launched.

"When's the last time you drove one of these?" I called to my friend above the whine of the engines.

"No worries, mate," he said while staying focused ahead. "What is it you say on First Earth? It's like riding a bike." He gave me a quick look back and a sly smile. "I like riding bikes."

I knew that. If the aquaneer was catchable, Spader would catch him. His long dark hair flew back in the wind. His almond-shaped eyes were focused dead ahead. It was good to be back together.

Yenza called to me, "Spader says the exiles are fugitives from another territory."

Her words surprised me at first. The last time I was with Wu Yenza, she didn't know anything about anything. But since then she had become Spader's acolyte. She had read his journals. She was up to speed. It still felt weird, but it also felt good. We needed as many people on our side as possible.

"Are they worth risking Grallion for?" she asked.

I looked her straight in the eye. How could I answer that? I didn't want to see Grallion sunk. That would be a catastrophe beyond imagining. But I had also seen the horror of what Earth had become. I had no doubt that the same kind of fate would hit Cloral.

"Yes" was my simple answer.

Yenza nodded. She accepted my word.

"I told them to navigate the hauler out beyond the raiders' ships and to wait for us to join them," she explained. "I thought we'd hide them in Panger City. If the raiders learn they're in a hauler, they'll hunt them down for sure."

"Let's make sure that doesn't happen," I said.

"We will," Spader called back. "We're almost on this woggly."

I looked ahead to see that we were catching up to the Ravinian spy. He kept glancing back like a runner who was nearly out of gas and desperate to get to the finish line before his nearest challenger caught up. Our skimmer had much more power. We were going to get him.

"Who is he?" Spader called back to Yenza.

"Never seen him before," she replied. "He isn't one of my aquaneers."

I added, "Then you won't mind if he gets hurt."

Both Spader and Yenza gave me a quick, surprised look.

"Bold words, mate," Spader said. "You've changed a might."

"You have no idea."

At the rate we were closing, I figured we'd reach him with a hundred yards to spare. Spader was that good. I stood up next to Spader and yelled, "Pull up next to him, so I can jump aboard!"

Spader gave me another smile. "You really have changed."

I shrugged. If he was surprised at my words, he was going to be totally shocked when he saw me lay into that renegade aquaneer. Unfortunately, our plans quickly changed. We were suddenly bathed in bright, blinding light from the closest gunship. They had trained high-intensity spotlights on us. It got worse. I shielded my eyes in time to see that the aquaneer had stopped his skimmer and had grabbed a long, silver water rifle. He had decided to make a stand on the water.

We weren't ready for that.

"He's gonna shoot!" I shouted just as the first blast erupted.

The shot hit our skimmer square in front, nailing the steering column. The force pulled the handles out of Spader's grasp, and we spun sharply to our right. Yenza didn't hesitate. With an impossible sense of balance that could only have come from spending years on the water, she pulled up the floor panel to grab for her own weapon. It was going to be a shoot-out.

Spader grabbed the handles back and started maneuvering evasively. I crouched down, trying to make a smaller target. While Spader spun us every which way, I caught glimpses of the aquaneer who was our quarry. His skimmer was dead in the water, his back was braced against the steering column, his rifle was up and aimed at us.

He was no longer our quarry. We were *his* quarry.

Boom. Boom.

I remembered the sound of those sleek, silver water guns from the last time I was on Cloral. They were no water pistols. They fired highly compressed rockets of water that could tear somebody in two. Spader kept us moving and spinning. I heard and felt the water projectiles fly by. Yenza had her rifle up and ready. She took to one knee and fired back. Her aim wasn't great, which didn't surprise me, considering we were randomly spinning one way and then the other. It also didn't help that the guy was in silhouette because of the bright spotlights from the gunboat behind him.

Which also meant we were lit up like ducks in a shooting gallery.

"You still want on that skimmer?" Spader asked.

"Can you get me there?" I called back.

"I'll take that as a challenge." He laughed.

Unbelievable. We were in the midst of a deadly water fight and Spader was as calm as if we were playing Marco Polo.

"Need a couple of shots to his left," Spader called calmly to Yenza.

"Done," she called back calmly and started squeezing off a series of shots that forced the aquaneer to dive down and take cover on the right side of his skimmer. But he wasn't done shooting. He lay flat on his stomach like a sharpshooter and took aim back at us.

"Stand by, mate," Spader called to me. "I'll swing around his bow."

Spader gunned the skimmer and launched forward. The aquaneer saw what was happening and tried to swing his rifle toward us, but Yenza let loose with a volley of shots that made him duck down below the rails of his small craft. Spader was now flying on a straight line, which made it easier for Yenza to take aim.

"If he pokes his head up," she growled without taking her eye away from the barrel of the gun, "he's done."

"Right," Spader announced. "Off you go, mate."

He swung our skimmer around the bow of the enemy. The aquaneer tried to sit up and raise his rifle, but Yenza nailed his gun with a shot of her own. His silver rifle clattered to the deck of his skimmer. I had my window. Spader barely slowed as we crossed the bow. I sprang forward, launching toward where I hoped the skimmer would be when I landed. I left our moving boat and landed with both feet on the deck of the aquaneer's skimmer.

The guy scrambled for his rifle. There was no way he'd be able to get it up to aim and fire, but that wasn't his plan. He used the long rifle like a bat and swung it at me, nailing my right knee. Ow. It didn't cripple me, but it sure hurt. I lashed out with a backhand to his head. I really nailed him but the guy didn't react.

Bad news.

It was a dado.

There were dados on Cloral.

Swell.

He swung his rifle back, trying to hit my other leg. This time I was ready. I grabbed the rifle with both hands before it made contact and yanked him to his feet. I didn't know how strong this dado was, so I wasn't sure if I had a chance against him. I couldn't knock him out, that much was for sure. My best hope was to throw him over the side, where Yenza could finish him off with a couple of shots.

The two of us struggled, both with two hands on the

rifle. The dado was strong, but not superhuman. On the other hand, he fought dirty. He lifted his knee to nail me where it hurts. I saw it coming and pivoted to my left, catching his knee with the back of my leg. It hurt, but at least he didn't jangle anything. What it mostly did was make me mad. I drove my right elbow back into his chest. Again the guy didn't flinch. He drove the palm of his left hand forward, hitting me square in the chest. It threw me off my feet. Yeow. It was like he bruised my heart. I lay on my back on the deck, looking up at him as he lifted his leg to kick me in the head. I had to fight through the pain to protect myself. I caught his foot, twisted, and brought the guy down to the deck with me. I leaped onto his back like a wrestler. I wanted to roll him off the skimmer and into the water. The guy was flat on his stomach, making it impossible for me to get leverage. I snaked my arm under his, trying to get my hand up and onto the back of his neck for a half-nelson wrestling hold. As I struggled to get control, I looked up to see Yenza on the skimmer, with her rifle up and aimed . . . at us. I didn't care how good of a shot she was, she could easily have hit me instead of the dado. I opened my mouth to yell at her to stop. Too late. She fired. I flung myself off the dado to protect myself.

It was the wrong move. Yenza wasn't shooting at the dado. Behind me I heard an explosion, and one of the big spotlights from the gunship went dark. Yenza was shooting out their eyes. Of course, I didn't know that and had let go of the dado. Oops. He was now coming at me. He launched, I spun away, but kept my arms out in front of me. I grabbed the guy by his bogus aquaneer uniform and kept him moving forward and right over the edge.

"Shoot him!" I shouted before he even hit the water.

The result was way more dramatic than I had expected.
BOOM!

A shot was fired that was bigger than anything that had come from either rifle. A second later the water erupted not five feet from me. A wave hit the skimmer and nearly knocked me off my feet. What the heck was that?

"Hobey, Pendragon! Jump!" Spader shouted.

He had finally lost his cool. That meant trouble. A quick glance toward the gunboat told me why. The shot hadn't come from a water rifle. We were in the sights of the ship's big guns. I dove off the skimmer as one of them fired again. I was still in the air when the little skimmer exploded. I ducked under the water to protect myself as sharp pieces of destroyed skimmer flew all around me. I felt the sting as they hit me, even underwater. Then I felt somebody grab my ankle from below.

The dado was back.

He held me underwater, pulling me farther down. Did dados need to breathe air? Could this guy stay under, holding me down until I drowned? I didn't take any chances. I coiled my other leg and kicked down on his arm. Hard. The force made him lose his grip, and I swam for my life.

"He's pulling me down!" I yelled as soon as my head broke the surface.

I looked about frantically, trying to sight Spader and Yenza. The sea had turned violent. Explosions kicked up everywhere. There was so much smoke I couldn't see my friends.

"Hey!" I shouted.

No response. Had they taken off? Worse, had they been hit?

I heard one smaller pop, after which another light went

out. My heart raced. Though I couldn't see them, Yenza was still shooting. A few seconds later another pop came and another light was out. The last one. We were in the dark, but that didn't stop the raiders from trying to blow us out of the water. They knew where we were, more or less. I didn't know which way to swim, because I didn't know where my friends were. I decided to tread water and let them find me. . . .

And got pulled under again. This time the dado yanked on my Second Earth khaki's, pulling himself up. Or me down. Whatever. He had me in a bear hug several feet below the surface. There was nothing skillful or clever about his attack. He was going to hold me down until I ran out of air. I struggled to get free, but it was no use. He held me tight from behind, with his hands locked in front of me. There was nothing I could do but drown.

I felt a short, violent lurch, as if the dado's body had been hit by something. He instantly released his grip. I pushed myself away from him, kicked for the surface and spun around, ready for the robot to come after me again. He didn't. He couldn't. He no longer had a head. The thing floated there with its arms out. Dead. Or turned off. Or incapacitated. Or whatever it is that happens to a dado when the lights go out. It may have been a mechanical device, but it was still a gruesome sight.

I felt a strong arm grab the back of my sweatshirt. A second later I was lifted out of the water onto the deck of Spader's skimmer. Spader stood over me. Yenza was next to him, holding her rifle, smiling.

I guess she was a better shot than I thought.

"He won't be talking to the raiders anytime soon," she confirmed.

Explosions continued to churn the water around us. Spader dropped to his knees and opened up the hatch of the skimmer. He pulled out three round air globes.

"We'll have a better chance in the water than on the skimmer," he said.

I hadn't put on an air globe in a very long time, but I knew how they worked. The clear shell made a form-fit over your head. The small silver device at the top took oxygen in from the sea and allowed you to breathe. And speak. It was an amazing device. It looked as if we were going to have to rely on them to save us.

"We'll swim back to Grallion," he said. "Let them keep pumping shots at the skimmer. We'll be long gone."

We barely had time to put the globes on when the water next to the skimmer began to boil. All three of us looked in wonder at what could be causing it.

"That's not from the guns," I declared.

Yenza realized the truth first. "No," she bellowed. "No! No!"

I didn't know what she was getting all bent about, until I saw a large, clear dome break the surface of the water. If we were anywhere else in Halla, I would have been panic stricken, thinking it was some kind of sea beast. But we were on Cloral. I knew what it was.

"They shouldn't be here!" Yenza shouted.

It was a hauler submarine. Inside the dome I saw the faces of three scared individuals. It looked to be a family. A man, a woman, and a little girl that couldn't have been more than four years old. The man was at the controls. He waved frantically, motioning for us to get inside the sub.

The barrage of water-cannon fire stopped. There was a strange calm.

"Did they give up?" I asked.

A moment later we were again bathed in light as multiple spotlights from other gunships hit us. During the confusion two more gunships had drifted closer. We were now surrounded on three sides by raider ships, all with their lights trained on us and all with their guns locked in. They had hit the jackpot. They no longer needed information from the dado aquaneer. They had us. They had the hauler. They had the exiles. We were seconds away from being turned into liquid.

Spader leaped from the skimmer onto the body of the hauler, behind the cockpit bubble. He motioned to the people inside to dive.

"Down!" he screamed. "Down! Down!"

The pilot wasn't sure what to do. He wasn't an aquaneer. He probably had only learned to drive a hauler that day. He looked to Yenza. Yenza made the same move.

"Dive!" she shouted, and jumped on the back of the hauler.

I did the same. There wasn't time to board the craft. We were about to go for a ride. Bubbles boiled up from around the vehicle as the hauler began to sink. The back of a hauler had plenty of places to grab on to, so I grabbed. Tight. No sooner did my head go below the water than I heard the sounds of cannon fire. I was nearly ripped off the hauler by the force of the multiple impacts. The vehicle twisted and spun, but continued to dive. Yenza pulled her way forward along the back of the hauler to the cockpit bubble. She banged on the glass to get the pilot's attention and motioned for him to continue down. The water was deep around Grallion. If we got enough depth, there was no way that the water-cannon fire could reach us. I looked above to see the surface explode in a brilliant kaleidoscope of light from the ships. As we dropped farther away, the muffled explosions grew more distant. My confidence grew. We had escaped.

Yenza looked back to Spader and me. We could hear her clearly through the device on top of her air globe. "They could drop depth charges."

Oh. We hadn't escaped.

Yenza knocked on the hauler bubble again. The pilot turned to look, and Yenza made a motion in the direction she wanted the guy to drive.

"Uh, that's back toward Grallion," I announced.

"I'm hoping they'll think we broke for open water," she said with confidence. "If we hide below Grallion, it will be harder for them to find us with their deep scan."

I looked to Spader and shrugged. "Sounds good to me."

The hauler was nearly on the ocean floor. We moved swiftly and silently across the sandy bottom until everything grew dark. I figured that must have been because all light from above had been blocked by the massive barge city of Grallion. We traveled a few more minutes, with Yenza scanning the surface ahead while riding on top of the bubble like a circus performer on an elephant. Finally she seemed satisfied, and motioned for the pilot to stop and rest on the bottom. With a gentle thump, the hauler nestled safely on the ocean floor.

"We can get in through the air lock," Yenza explained.

The haulers I knew from Cloral didn't have air locks. This hauler was larger than any I'd seen, so I figured it was a more advanced model. Yenza led us along the hull toward the stern until she came to a hatch. She turned a red wheel that was recessed below the outer skin of the submarine, pulled open the door, and floated inside. A few minutes later we saw her appear in the cockpit bubble along with the exiles. Spader instructed me on how to get in.

"The compartment inside is flooded," he said. "Once I close the hatch on you, there's a green wheel that will clear the chamber of water. When it's dry, spin the release on the door inside and board. Then close the hatch, and I'll be right after you."

I did as I was told. Within minutes I joined Yenza in the large cargo area of the hauler. She closed the inside hatch after me, flooded the small compartment again, and Spader repeated the action.

Within ten minutes we were all safely inside the cargo bay. Yenza opened the hatch that led into the cockpit, and I got to meet the exiles.

"We had to come back," the man said. "The idea of Grallion being attacked because of us was too much to bear."

"You shouldn't have," Yenza declared.

Spader added, "But if you hadn't, we'd all be dead, so thank you."

The woman was nervous. She held the little girl on her lap protectively.

"Is that your daughter?" I asked.

The woman nodded. "Her name is Maggie."

"Where was she born?" I asked.

The man and woman looked to Yenza, as if not sure of what they should reveal about themselves. I put them at ease.

"I'm from Earth," I said. "My name is Bobby Pendragon."

They both looked relieved to hear that. "My name is Peter," the man said. "This is Carolyn. When were you exiled? Was it in Yankee Stadium?"

As much as I knew the origin of the exiles, it was still a shock to hear it from a different point of view.

"No, but I was there," I answered. "I saw what happened."

Carolyn said, "Maggie was born here, on Cloral. She never knew Earth."

"How many more exiles are there on Cloral?" I asked. It was the most important question of all.

"Just us," Peter answered.

"Are you sure?" I asked, trying not to sound too disappointed.

Peter and Carolyn nodded.

My heart sank. As happy as I was that these people were safe, I was hoping that there would be more. Lots more. On Third Earth there were originally twenty that arrived, including Mark. But eight had been killed. Here there were three, including the young girl, Maggie, who technically wasn't an exile. Was it possible that the spirit of so few exiles could keep Solara alive? I doubted it. Seventy thousand people were pulled into the flume that night in Yankee Stadium. Where did they go?

"There were more of us," Peter said. "Thirty in all. We were taken in by raiders and treated like slaves."

"I heard the story," I said with sympathy. "From my friend Mark Dimond."

Both Peter and Carolyn lit up. "Mark?" the woman said with a smile. "Have you seen him?"

"I have. He's okay."

They looked relieved to hear that. "Did he make it back to Earth?" Carolyn asked.

I gave a simple answer. "Yes." I didn't want to explain the trouble he was in. Or that he was actually three thousand years ahead of their own time.

Carolyn said, "So then there's still hope for us. We might be able to return someday."

I didn't say anything. Why should I ruin their dream?

Peter added, "If not for Mark, we'd all be dead. He was our leader. He took a lot of punishment that was often meant for others."

I nodded. Mark hadn't gone into the details of his ordeal, and I wasn't so sure I wanted to hear them.

Peter continued, "He led the mutiny. All thirty of us got off the raider ship. We stole skimmers. Some went searching for the flume, but we stayed behind."

"Why?" Spader asked.

Carolyn held Maggie close and gave a simple answer. "I was pregnant."

"We've been hiding from the Ravinians for years," Peter added.

Yenza jumped in, saying, "We're going to get you to Panger City. It's a busy place. You'll blend in there."

Something didn't add up. "You said thirty of you got off the raider ship. Did others die?"

"Not that we know of," Peter answered.

"So if thirty escaped, and you two stayed here, that means twenty-eight people went for the flume. But only twenty made it to Earth."

The man and woman exchanged looks, as if they had something to say but weren't sure if they should.

"You really should tell me everything," I said.

"There was another exile," Peter finally admitted. "He didn't originally land here with us on Cloral. He was first sent to another territory, but he came here in search of exiles. He said there were many more where he first landed, and he wanted to bring us all together. There was a debate over whether we should go with him or try to get back to Earth. That was before we were captured by the raiders. He ended up dying in the hold of that horrible ship."

I tried not to get too excited. If there were more exiles on another territory, maybe they had all begun to gather there before the flumes were destroyed.

"What was the name of the territory he came from?" I asked.

Carolyn answered. "If I remember right, it was called . . . Zadaa."

I had the information I needed. I was on the wrong territory. I instantly shot a look to Spader. "I'm going to Zadaa."

Spader replied, "I'm going with you."

"No!" I said quickly. "You have to keep these people safe."

"I can do that," Yenza offered with confidence.

"If there's a big group of exiles on Zadaa, that's where we should be, mate," Spader said.

I was about to argue, but the sound of thunder stopped me. We all heard it. Maggie held her mother close, terrified.

"Thunder?" I asked.

"Cannons," Yenza said soberly. "It sounds like they're unloading on Grallion."

"Hobey, would they really punish an entire habitat just because we were protecting this family?" Spader asked.

"I think they would" was my awful answer. "That'll give you an idea of how great the importance of every last exile is."

"Us?" Peter asked. "Why?"

"Do you want to see the Ravinians defeated?" I asked.

"It's all I think about," the guy answered.

"Then stay safe," I said. "If we hope to fight back, we need each and every exile to have faith that it's possible."

The thundering guns grew louder.

Yenza swallowed hard. "I fear what's happening up there."

"Protect them," I said to Yenza. "I can't begin to tell you how important it is."

"I believe you, Pendragon. They'll be safe with me."

"Uh-oh." Spader gasped.

He was looking toward the surface through the bubble of the hauler submarine.

Yenza gasped, "She's breaking up."

We all looked up to see cracks appear in the black mass that was the hull of the habitat Grallion.

"This is impossible," Yenza cried. "Why do they have such powerful weapons?"

"It's all about Ravinia," I answered.

The cracks grew larger. The barge was being wrenched apart. I think the realization hit us all at the same time that the giant city was going to sink . . . and we were directly beneath it.

"Get us outta here!" I screamed.

Yenza jumped into the bubble, pulled Peter out of the pilot seat and took over the controls. She toggled the water-fed engines to life, grabbed the control stick, and pushed us forward without bothering to ascend from the sea floor. We dragged up a bunch of sand, but we were moving.

Carolyn gasped, "It's coming down!"

All around us giant shadowy chunks of habitat were slowly floating toward the bottom. The pieces were of all sizes. Some were as big as houses, others looked to be a half mile across. The raiders had done it. They had destroyed a habitat. I didn't want to know what the rest of Cloral looked like.

"I hope they evacuated in time," Yenza said. Her voice cracked. I had never seen her show emotion of any kind. "I should have been there."

I didn't know how to tell her that as horrible as the loss of Grallion was, her mission to protect the exiles was about her entire world, not just one habitat. There was no way she'd understand that, so I kept my mouth closed.

"They were prepared," Spader said with sympathy. "You saw to that. The aquaneers were ready to get everyone off."

"This is all because of us," Carolyn said, sobbing.

I had no idea how to comfort her. I wanted to say how her survival was critical to the future of Halla. I wanted to tell her that she had the power to topple Ravinia. But that was all so impossible to grasp, especially as the remains of a destroyed city were raining down around us.

"Watch it," Spader calmly cautioned Yenza.

A massive piece of barge glided down in front of us. Yenza expertly guided the hauler around it. We all looked in horror to see a piece of decking with buildings still attached sink to the ocean floor. Like with New York, a city had been destroyed.

Ravinia was alive and well on Cloral.

Soon the water grew lighter as Yenza piloted the hauler safely out from beneath the sinking wreckage.

"Get them to Panger City," I said to Yenza. "Keep them safe and wait for word."

Yenza nodded. She didn't try to speak. I think if she had, she would have burst out crying.

"And me?" Spader asked.

I knew the answer he wanted, so I gave it to him. "You're coming with me."

Spader beamed. "That's what I like to hear, mate!" he exclaimed, clapping me on the back. "Just like old times."

Wu Yenza wasn't as happy about it. "But you've only just returned," she said softly.

For the tough chief aquaneer, that was a huge show of emotion. I didn't blame her. She had just witnessed the total destruction of her home. Besides that, I think she had a little "thing" for Spader. Spader leaned in and gave her a hug.

"I'm proud to call you my chief . . . and my acolyte. Thank you." He didn't say anything about coming back to Cloral again. He knew that wasn't a guarantee. "Take care of them."

Yenza nodded and gave him a weak smile. Spader let her go and backed into the cargo bay of the hauler.

"Be safe," I said to the others. "Please."

I touched the cheek of the beautiful little girl named Maggie. I hoped that the spirit held by the children of the exiles would be just as strong as their parents. I then touched Yenza's shoulder. I didn't know what to say, so I gave her a simple, "Good luck."

Yenza looked at me. Her eyes were red. "We do have a chance, don't we?"

"As long as we're alive, we have a chance."

She nodded. "Don't let him get into too much trouble."

"Spader?" I said, with mock surprise. "Does he get into trouble?"

She chuckled.

Carolyn asked, "Are you going to swim back to the flume?"

"Yeah, something like that," I answered, and closed the hatch leading to the hauler's cargo bay behind me.

Spader and I stood together in the empty tanker.

"Want to see a new territory?" I asked.

"Been a long time since we rode together, mate," Spader said. "Gotta say, I'm a touch excited."

"Then let's go," I said, and took one step forward on Cloral.

The second step was on the territory of Zadaa.

It was time to find Loor.

16

Spader and I found ourselves standing on the shore of a young ocean.

It was a familiar sight. I had witnessed this body of water being born when the pent-up rivers that ran beneath the desert on Zadaa erupted with spectacular fury. Fault lines had cut quickly and violently across the sand, sinking miles of desert that were soon replaced with water, gushing in from hundreds of underwater rivers. In minutes a desert had been transformed into an ocean.

Life now grew where none had existed for centuries. I didn't know how long it had been since I was on Zadaa, but time had definitely passed. The shore was now lined with palm trees and swaying grass. I saw what looked like small deer drinking from the freshwater sea. The day was clear. The sun was warm. For a brief moment I let myself believe that all was well with Zadaa.

A very brief moment.

A lone person sat by the shore, staring out at the dark green waters. One look at this woman told me that the spirits of Solara had put us where we needed to be. They had brought us back together with Loor. As relieved as I was to have found her so easily, it was strange to see her sitting alone, quietly, as if lost in her own thoughts. That wasn't like her.

"Loor?" I called.

She gave us a quick look, but showed no emotion or surprise. She nodded to acknowledge us, then went back to staring out at the sea.

I looked at Spader. He shrugged. I wasn't sure of what to say. Loor was obviously preoccupied. I didn't think it was right to jump at her, all excited, to say, "Hey! We heard some exiles were here. Did you find them? Did ya? Did ya? Huh?" There would be time for that.

Spader and I sat next to her. The three of us sat for a while, enjoying the warm breeze. At least I did. My clothes were still wet from Cloral, so I didn't mind letting the hot sun of Zadaa dry them. Finally Loor looked at me. I was surprised to see that her eyes were red. She had been crying. There was nothing right about that.

"What manner of evil has the power to change the course of so many worlds so dramatically?" she said.

We'd been dealing with that question since day one of this adventure. I wondered why Loor was just getting around to it.

"You've always known what Saint Dane is capable of" was my answer.

"It is not his intent that disturbs me so," she replied thoughtfully, as if trying to measure her own words. "I understand his quest. What I do not understand is why so many have chosen to follow him. Saint Dane would not hold the power he does now, he would not be on the verge of destroying Halla and creating his own universe, if not for those who have allowed him to do so."

"She's right," Spader added. "He may be a nasty woggly, but he's had a lot of help from the very people we're supposed to be protecting."

"It is a disheartening reality." Loor sighed. "It leads me to even darker thoughts."

Spader and I exchanged looks. What could be darker than what we had seen Halla go through? I wasn't so sure I wanted to know.

Loor continued, "Press said we are given power by what is left of the spirit of Solara. The positive spirit. If that is so, from where is Saint Dane drawing his own power?"

Turned out I wasn't the only one who was bugged by that question.

"I've been wondering that myself," Spader said.

Make that three of us.

"I don't know," I said. "But I've been giving it some thought. If there's one thing I've learned, it's that there's no such thing as absolute good or pure evil."

"Not so sure about that, mate," Spader interrupted. "I haven't seen a whole lot of good coming from Saint Dane."

"Not now, but according to Uncle Press, he started out with good intentions. He may have been arrogant and egotistical and ruthless, but his original goal was to help the people of Halla."

"But he was wrong," Loor complained. "His vision was wrong."

"I agree, but we're talking about his original intent, not his methods. His thinking was to save the people of Halla from themselves. His ideas may have been misguided, but in his mind he was doing something positive."

"I can't believe you're defending the bugger," Spader said.

"I'm not! What he's done is monstrous. I'm just saying

that in the beginning, in his mind, he was doing something positive."

Spader shrugged. "Then it didn't last long. Look at all the damage he's done."

"I think the real damage he did was to draw a hard line between good and evil. He's not allowing for the good in people to exist by only rewarding the darker side of human behavior. Look at Ravinia. What do they encourage? Pride. Aggression. Strength. Power. Those aren't necessarily bad things, unless you eliminate the other side. You can't have pride without humility. Aggression without tolerance. Strength without compassion. Power without restraint. That's what Solara has been about, balancing it all. Saint Dane has thrown that balance off."

"You may be correct, but that does not explain where he is getting his power from," Loor argued.

I stopped a moment before speaking. A theory had been tickling the back of my brain for a while. Listening to Loor's concerns brought it forward.

"I think he's created his own version of Solara," I said. "Uncle Press already told us that Solara wasn't about everyone being all peaceful and loving. That's not reality. There were always darker forces in Solara. It's the reflection of mankind, and mankind has two sides. There is no good without evil. Positive without negative. I think that by destroying the more peaceful, less aggressive spirit throughout Halla, it allowed another Solara to rise."

"You mean, like splitting it in two?" Spader suggested.

"Something like that. I guess. I don't know. I'm winging this. But I'm thinking that by doing what he's done, he's forced the spirits of Solara to take sides. Those who favor free will and tolerance are about to die off, and those who favor strength and aggression are building momentum. The exiles are feeding the positive side, and Saint Dane's Ravinian followers are feeding the aggressive side. Even the survivors of Ravinia must be feeding the negative side. Their lives are about fear and survival. Sounds like that could just as easily feed a dark Solara as a positive one. The balance that allowed Halla to thrive has been totally thrown off."

"And you think this other, dark Solara is where Saint Dane is drawing his power from?" Loor asked.

"What other explanation is there? If he were drawing his power from the Solara we visited, it would have died long ago, Saint Dane would be out of business. I think he won't be in total control until he's completely destroyed that place. The positive side of Solara. And that's where we come in."

Spader gave me a sideways look. "If you say so, mate. It all has me head spinning."

"The territories have turned," I added. "Everything we've seen tells us that Saint Dane's evil has taken over Halla. The balance has been tipped one way. The question is, how can we tip it back?"

"According to Press, it's all about the exiles," Spader said hopefully.

"And we have no idea where they are," I replied. "At least seventy thousand people were pulled into the flume on Second Earth. And we've only found . . . what? Twenty? I don't believe that number of people can be keeping Solara alive. There have to be more. Maybe they're here."

Loor dropped her head. She looked pained.

"What are you doing out here?" I asked her. "Why are you so upset?"

"Everything that you have said makes sense, Pendragon," she answered softly. "I have seen it here, on my own territory."

Spader and I exchanged looks. We both knew that bad news was on the way.

"How did Zadaa change?" I asked.

"My people are gone," Loor said, trying to keep her voice from cracking.

"Gone?" Spader asked. "You mean like . . . gone?"

"The Rokador have risen to power. They now control this area of the territory. I believe they have murdered the Batu tribe."

"Murdered?" I repeated. "You're saying the Rokador wiped out an entire tribe of Batu?"

"Not entirely," Loor answered. "Those who survived are now slaves. But they are a small portion of what once was. I understand your words, Pendragon, but it is hard for me to believe that pure evil does not exist. Perhaps it did not begin that way, but that is the way it has become." She pointed over our shoulders and added, "Look."

Spader and I turned to view a breathtaking sight. Spader had never seen the city of Xhaxhu, so I didn't think it would affect him one way or the other. But I was stunned. The whole time we had been there, I didn't think to turn around and look at the city that was Loor's home. It had changed. There was still a giant sandstone wall that surrounded the city, but that's where the familiarity ended. The tall, ornate pyramids that gave Xhaxhu its character were still there, but they were now covered with a silver metal skin. What had once been an ancient city of stone pyramids now had a strangely modern feel.

"The Rokador were always more advanced than the

Batu." Loor sighed. "The Batu were warriors who protected them in their underground homes. The Rokador provided technology in return. There were problems, but it was a good balance."

"There's that balance thing again," Spader said, trying to be helpful.

"So what is Xhaxhu like now?" I asked.

Loor stood. At her feet was a white Rokador robe. "I will show you, but I must wear this. Batu are no longer free to walk the streets."

That was an ominous statement. Loor took the wooden stave that was strapped to her back and tossed it to me. She then dropped the long robe over her head, and pulled up the hood so that she wouldn't be recognized.

"What about us?" Spader asked.

"You look like Rokador," Loor explained. "You will have no problem."

The Rokador were light skinned, mostly from living for generations beneath the surface of Zadaa. I definitely fit the profile. Spader was on the fence. It would have been iffy if he had spent the last several years under the hot, tropical sun of Cloral, but since he had been living in the jungles of Eelong, his skin had sufficiently paled up. We could easily pass for Rokador.

Loor led us across the grassy field that led to the city of Xhaxhu. The last time I'd been there, there was nothing but sand. Lots of it. It had now become a much more hospitable place. Unless, of course, you were a Batu. It took us a few minutes to walk the roughly half mile to the city gates. Standing guard were two Rokador soldiers. They stood like sentries at either side of the entrance. It had always been the job of the Batu to provide security.

Not anymore. For a second I thought they might stop us, but they didn't give us a second look as we strode into the city. . . .

And into a world I barely recognized. My memory of Xhaxhu was a city with wide, unpaved streets; soaring, ornate pyramids; elaborate statues of Batu warriors; and troughs of fresh, clean water that were fed by the underground rivers and ran along every street. It was a place full of bright flowers and towering palm trees. Xhaxhu was an oasis in the center of a vast desert.

The city was still an oasis, but the look had changed.

There were still palm trees and flowers everywhere, but I didn't see any open troughs. I figured maybe they had been buried under the paved streets. Yes, the streets were now paved, but they didn't look like any street surface I'd seen. They sparkled with color. To me it looked as if the roadbeds were made from billions of tiny bits of crushed quartz. The sun hit the millions of facets in different ways, making the streets appear to be paved with multicolored jewels. The pyramids were gone. At least, the pyramids I remembered. These new silver structures had a sharp, modern feel, as opposed to the crudely carved stone of the old Xhaxhu. The lines of these new buildings were clean and straight, with no intricate carvings at all. The Batu statues were gone. In their place were modernistic sculptures that looked like, well, I don't really know what they looked like because they were just kind of chunky pieces of metal.

This was not a modern city, but it was definitely moving in that direction. The place felt kind of, I don't know, cold. Which is odd to say because it had to be a hundred degrees in the shade.

I've described the physical city and how strange it was to see the changes, but there was something else about this new Xhaxhu that was much more disturbing than any new architecture. The old Xhaxhu was populated by the dark-skinned Batu tribe. Now everywhere I looked, I saw only light-skinned Rokador. It was like one whole population had moved out, and another had moved in. That's not to say that there weren't any Batu. There were. But I saw what Loor meant when she said they had become slaves. Where the Rokador were out enjoying the day or traveling along the roads or doing whatever, the Batu were working. I saw a few guys polishing the silver buildings. Others trimmed the flowers. There were no cars, so the Rokador moved along the streets in two-person rickshaws that were being pulled by sweating Batu tribesmen. As one passed I actually saw the Rokador lean forward and whack the Batu who was pulling him with a long stick to make him go faster. The Batu weren't just slaves, they were being treated like animals. I take that back—most right-thinking people wouldn't whack an animal with a stick, or make it labor in the heat of the day. I didn't see a single Batu who wasn't working. Hard.

There was one more change in Xhaxhu that told me how wrong things had become. It was probably the most dramatic of all. On top of each building, a flag waved. A red flag. With a Ravinian star.

I glanced to Loor. She was taking in the scene with dead eyes. She had gone beyond anger.

"Do you know what happened?" I asked.

"When the Rokador left the underground tunnels, they used their knowledge like a weapon. The Batu relied heavily on the Rokador to provide expertise in growing food and purifying water and giving medical care. Once they began living on the surface, that knowledge became power, and they used it to control the Batu."

I asked, "Didn't the Rokador still need the Batu for protection against enemy tribes?"

"No" was her quick reply. "They found another means of protection. The Rokador brought in an army from another part of the territory. They proved to be superior warriors to the Batu and wasted no time in gaining control over them. I did not know that such an army existed on Zadaa, but it did, and the Rokador brought them here to vanquish the Batu and take their place."

I saw a small group of these warriors marching together down the far side of the wide street. There were six of them, all marching in step. One look told me the truth.

"Dados," I said. "They didn't come from Zadaa. The Ravinians brought them here, just like they did on other territories."

"Whatever they are, they are demons," Loor said through clenched teeth. "They have destroyed my people."

"How did you find out about all this?" Spader asked.

"Come with me," Loor answered.

She walked quickly, keeping her head down so nobody would recognize her as a Batu. She led us on a winding path through the transformed city. We reached the far wall and continued outside again to the vast farmland that fed the people of Xhaxhu. I wasn't surprised to find that all the people laboring under the hot sun were Batu. There were men and women and even kids. Dozens of them. They all worked under the watchful eyes of several dado guards. It made me feel horrible to see how this once-proud tribe found themselves working on their knees to feed the very people they once protected. I could only imagine how it made Loor feel.

"I may be a spirit of Solara," she said, her voice trembling. "But I am still a Batu. This is not right."

The life she had known had been turned upside down. You could say that about all of the Travelers, but it must have been especially hard for her, knowing what a strong, proud person she was. I wished I could say or do something to make her feel better, but I had nothing to offer.

"What d'ya want us to see out here?" Spader asked.

Loor led us to several large carts that were piled high with what looked like potatoes. That's what the Batu were digging out of the dirt. Potatoes.

"Stay here, I will return," she said, and walked away from us.

"You're right, mate," Spader said to me wistfully. "Every territory has changed. We've lost every one of 'em."

"It's not about the territories anymore," I corrected. "It's about Halla."

Spader nodded thoughtfully, then added, "Do we have any chance of turning the tide?"

"I don't know" was my honest answer. "But it's not like we can stop trying."

"No," he agreed. "We're in this till the end. Funny thing though."

"What's that?"

"How are we going to know when the end comes?"

I was about to give him a quick answer, but stopped myself. The truth was, I didn't know. One way or the other. If Saint Dane found the exiles and wiped them out, would we all just stop existing? Would we even know that we had lost? And what if we won? What did that actually mean? Would things suddenly change? Would a gun go off and confetti fly, and we'd all pat one another on the back in congratulations? Probably not. Spader's simple question raised so many others. I decided not to deal with predictions. There was enough to worry about. One thing at a time. But Spader's words haunted me.

How would we know?

"Hello, Pendragon," came a familiar voice.

I turned to see that Loor had returned with one of the Batu workers from the farm. It was a woman, though that wasn't obvious, because she was dressed in rags and was covered in dust from head to toe. She was also drenched in sweat from her labors.

"It has been a very long time," the woman said. She sounded tired and beaten.

"Do I know you?" I asked, digging through my memory to try and remember who she might be.

"I have grown since you saw me last. I used to be a warrior. Now I dig in the dirt. But I am still an acolyte to Loor."

"Saangi!" I shouted, and threw my arms around her. I did it without thinking. If I had thought for two seconds, I probably wouldn't have hugged her. Saangi wasn't the huggy type. She was a tough little girl who wanted nothing more than to follow in Loor's footsteps. She didn't like me much either. She thought I was a wimp. I'd gained some respect after I went through warrior training with Loor and Alder, but I still had the feeling that she thought I was a step above useless.

I was surprised to find that Saangi hugged back. Yet another example of how much things had changed.

"What has happened?" she whispered in my ear, her voice quivering.

I felt a drop of her sweat on my cheek. Or maybe it was a tear. My heart ached. Saangi was beaten. She was a slave. Knowing the kind of strong girl she had once been made it all the more gut wrenching. She didn't let go of me. Instead, she cried. I felt her body shudder with emotion. All I could do was hug her closer.

"Saangi told me of the rise of Ravinia here, and the destruction of the Batu," Loor explained. "But there is more. Something you should hear."

Saangi pulled away from me and sniffed back a tear.

"There is talk of a group being held captive," she explained. "They are prisoners of the Rokador. Of Ravinia. We do not know all there is to know—that news only comes from overhearing the Rokador speaking when they do not think we are listening."

I gave Spader a quick, hopeful look.

"How many are there?" he asked.

"I do not know," she answered. "Many. Perhaps enough to fill a city."

I had to stop from shouting with excitement.

"Is it possible?" Loor asked. "Could these be the exiles we seek?"

"'Exiles,'" Saangi repeated. "I have heard that word."

"Hobey, this could be it," Spader cried with obvious excitement.

"Only one way to find out," I said, then looked to Saangi. "Do you know where they are being held prisoner?"

"Yes, I do, as do you."

"Uh, what?" I asked dumbly.

Saangi smiled. She actually smiled. That didn't happen much.

"It is a place you may not have fond memories of," she

said slyly. "For you it was a training ground. It has become a prison."

"Mooraj," I declared. I knew that place all too well. It was the abandoned Ghee warrior training camp in the desert, where Loor and Alder battered me into becoming a warrior. When the Rokador tunnels collapsed and the tribes joined together, Mooraj had become a playground for both Batu and Rokador children. From the sound of it, there was no more playing going on.

"It is heavily guarded by the new warriors," Saangi added. "If you seek those being held inside, it will be dangerous."

"Thank you, Saangi," I said. "I can't promise anything, but if these people turn out to be who I think they are, things might begin to change around here. For the better."

"There is something you can do for me," Saangi said.

"What's that?"

"Take me with you."

I wasn't sure about that. Saangi was a warrior in training at one time, but things had changed. She was older, and the time spent laboring in the sun had taken its toll. Saangi looked frail.

I frowned and shook my head. "I wish we could, but if things get tough, I don't think you'll be able to—" I didn't get the chance to finish my sentence. Saangi spun, kicked my right leg out and grabbed Loor's stave that I had been holding. With one swift move she knocked me on the side of my head. I fell to my knees, looking up at the girl who suddenly looked every bit as formidable as Loor ever had.

Spader laughed. "Can Saangi be on my team?" he asked.

I rubbed my sore cheek and looked to Loor.

She shrugged and smiled proudly. "A Batu warrior does not forget."

I looked back to Saangi. Her tears were gone. I slowly got to my feet and took the stave from her.

"Let's stop picking potatoes and see what's happening at Mooraj," I said to her.

Saangi smiled in relief. Like Spader, I wanted her on our team.

17

We needed a way to get to Mooraj.

It was too far to walk and there were no such thing as cars or trains on Zadaa. The solution came from Saangi.

With a satisfied grin she said, "I have been looking for an opportunity to use my skills once again."

I didn't ask what she meant by that. Spader and I were instructed to wait on the outskirts of the farm, while Loor and Saangi returned to Xhaxhu to carry out her plan. Whatever it was. All Spader and I could do was wait.

"Suppose we get there and find the place is loaded with exiles?" Spader asked. "Then what?"

"We go to Solara and bring Uncle Press back in," I answered.

"And what will *he* do?"

I shrugged. "Let's just find them first."

The truth was, I was forming a plan of my own. But I didn't want to talk about it, or even seriously consider it, until we found the exiles. Too much was up in the air for me to start getting everybody all worked up about something that might never happen. We had to stay with the mission, find the exiles, and make sure they were safe. Once that happened, *if* that happened, I'd reveal my thoughts.

We only had to wait a few minutes before two robed Rokador trotted up to us on horseback, each leading another horse. All four horses had wooden staves strapped to their saddles. The riders heads were covered by white hoods, but I knew who they were.

"How did you pull this off?" I called out.

Loor and Saangi took down their hoods. They both beamed. They were back in the saddle, so to speak.

"It seems," Loor explained coyly, "the new warriors are not as invincible as we thought." She threw down two white Rokador outfits. Spader and I now had white pants and white tunics with hoods. We would be as good as invisible. Spader and I quickly put on the new, lightweight clothing over our own.

Saangi said, "I do not believe those warriors are flesh and blood."

"They aren't," I replied as Spader and I mounted up. "And they aren't from Zadaa. But they're still going to come looking for their horses."

"By then we will be at Mooraj," Loor announced, and kicked her horse into gear. "I look forward to meeting more of those warriors."

"As do I," Saangi said, and followed after her.

Spader looked to me with wide eyes. "Those two scare me."

"Good thing they're on our side," I said with a chuckle.

The four of us rode across the wide-open countryside of Zadaa. The rivers that once flowed beneath the ground now provided enough irrigation to turn arid desert into rolling, grassy hills that stretched all around us for as far as I could see. There were no roads. We followed narrow trails that had been tramped by other horses. I'd like to say it was a huge improvement over what used to be, but it was hard to say that, knowing how Ravinia controlled it all. It was a steep price to pay for grass and wildflowers. I kept scanning the horizon, expecting to run into some Rokador. Or worse, a patrol of Ravinian guards. Being confronted wouldn't have been the end of the world. They had no long-distance communication on Zadaa. No radios. No cell phones or walkie-talkies. If we came upon a patrol, we would have to take them out. Simple as that. We couldn't risk them going to Mooraj, or back to Xhaxhu for reinforcements. No, if we happened upon random travelers, they would regret it.

It was hard to judge distance on rolling hills. It's not like there were signposts saying: MOORAJ—THIS WAY or ONLY FIVE MILES TO MOORAJ. I had to trust that Loor and Saangi knew the way.

Finally, after getting a little saddle sore, I saw the beginnings of the wall that surrounded the training camp.

"We must use caution to hide our approach," Loor advised. "We will keep to the troughs."

Loor led us on a winding route around the higher hills, using them to block any view of us. It was a good move, except that my butt was in agony. Riding was something you had to get in shape for, and I wasn't. At least, my butt wasn't. I looked to Spader, wondering if he was having the same trouble. As usual, Spader looked as fresh as if he had only been riding for a few minutes. He must have recognized the pain on my face, because he said, "I've been riding zenzens on Eelong, remember?"

I shrugged and grimaced. I didn't want to let on how sore I was.

Finally, mercifully, Loor motioned for us to stop. She got

off her horse and handed the reins to Saangi, then lay down on her belly and crawled to the top of a rise. She peered cautiously over the crest and motioned for Spader and me to follow. I got off the horse and had to stop myself from letting out a huge, relieved "Ahhhh." No way I was getting back up on that beast.

Saangi took control of our horses while Spader and I crawled up to join Loor. The three of us peered over the top to see we weren't more than a half mile from the walls of Mooraj. The place looked pretty much as I remembered it. There was a formidable sandstone wall that surrounded the camp. I could see only the hint of the tops of structures inside, but they didn't look any different from when I had been there to train. There were no silver buildings or weird sculptures. All looked normal, except for one thing.

"Hobey," Spader exclaimed. "Quite the tricky-do."

The place was surrounded by Ravinian guards. Dozens of them. For whatever reason, they didn't think they needed much security at Xhaxhu, but Mooraj was being guarded like a fortress.

"There's definitely something in there they don't want to let out," I observed.

"And that will make it difficult to get in," Loor commented.

"No offense, mates," Spader added, "but I don't think we stand much chance with swinging sticks against that army."

We were stuck. There was no way we could fight our way in. I thought that maybe it was time to do a little shape-shifting, but that had to be a last resort. Besides, the idea of turning into a bird or smoke or anything other than Bobby Pendragon kind of creeped me out.

"What's that?" Spader asked.

I looked to the right of the sprawling fortress to see a small, stone building about thirty yards from the wall.

"It is the entrance to the underground tunnels," Loor answered.

I looked at Loor. She looked at me. We were on the same page.

"Does the tunnel end there?" I asked.

"No," she said thoughtfully. I could tell that her mind was racing to possibilities. "The transfer trains are housed beneath Mooraj."

"It will be guarded," I cautioned.

"But with fewer warriors than outside the walls."

"We won't know how many until we get there."

"But it is our best opportunity."

Spader had been looking back and forth between the two of us, trying to catch up. He finally couldn't take it anymore and blurted out, "Stop! What are we talking about here?"

"I think we have a way in," I answered.

We let the horses go. We didn't need them anymore, and even if we did, it would have been impossible to hide them. My aching butt would have rebelled, anyway. So the horses were history. We crept through the valleys, doing our best to shield ourselves from curious eyes. In no time we found ourselves a few yards from the stone hut.

"I see no guards," Loor commented.

"Wait," I said, and quickly ran for the hut. Once there, I pressed myself against the far side, away from Mooraj. No alarms sounded. No Ravinian jumped out and tried to beat my brains in. I glanced inside the darkened hut. It was empty. Why weren't there any guards here? I waved the others to come forward.

"I will go first," Loor whispered. "Wait for my call."

I didn't argue. If she wanted to take on the first guard, that was okay by me. Heck, she probably needed to get out a little aggression anyway. After learning what happened to her people, I had the feeling she would welcome a fight. Loor held her wooden stave out in front, ready to do some damage. A moment later she entered the dark stairway. The three of us waited and listened. Loor descended silently. If a Ravinian guard was down there, he wouldn't know what hit him. I kept expecting to hear the sounds of a fight. Instead, we heard a single word.

"Come," she called to us.

I went first, followed by Saangi and then Spader. I remembered the stairs. We had taken the small train from one of the tunnels deep within Rokador territory to this very spot. These were the stairs I climbed to get my first sight of Mooraj, the camp where Loor and Alder taught me to be a warrior. Their vicious lessons served me well more times than I could remember. With each step down the stairwell, my hopes grew that this might actually be our way into the Mooraj camp, and our meeting with the exiles. We climbed down to a landing, turned, and continued into the dark. There was barely enough light for me to make out Loor's form standing on the next landing . . . in a foot of water.

"I should have known," she announced, defeated. "The tunnel is flooded, just like all the rest of the tunnels."

Of course. When the pent-up rivers of Zadaa had let loose, the water raged through every tunnel the Rokador had created over generations. The pressure became too much, and their tunnel system collapsed like a house of cards, creating the ocean near Xhaxhu. Many tunnels remained, but most were flooded, like this one.

"I guess that's why they don't bother guarding this entrance," I declared.

"We have to find another way," Saangi announced.

"Hold on, now," Spader said. He stepped down into the water and scanned the area. "How far below us is the cross tunnel?"

"It is just below us," Loor answered. "Perhaps a few feet."

"And this leads to an open area under the camp?" he asked.

"It is where they kept the transfer trains," Saangi said.

"Hobey," Spader exclaimed. "I can swim that."

"Impossible!" Loor blurted out. "No one can swim such a distance under the water."

Spader gave me a knowing look. I shrugged.

"I'm an aquaneer," he said with pride. "You may be a spiff warrior, but when it comes to playing in water, you're in my world."

"What if you make it?" I asked. "Then what?"

"Depends on what I find. If it turns out not too natty, I can lead you back myself, one at a time. Or maybe find a rope to pull you through quickly. Or it may be too far for any of that, but we won't know unless I get wet and give it a lookey loo."

Loor and Saangi frowned. They hated the idea.

I didn't.

"Do it," I said.

"There you go!" Spader declared and quickly pulled off his white Rokador clothing to reveal his dark swimskin. He gave a quick look to Loor and Saangi and saw how unsure they were. "No worries, mates. This is what I do."

They weren't convinced.

"If you get into trouble, you can always travel to another

territory," I offered, then smiled. "Or I guess you could turn into a fish."

Spader laughed. "You forget, mate, I'm already a fish."

He took a few more steps down until the water was up to his waist. He hyperventilated a few times to fill his lungs with oxygen, then started to dive into the water, but in the wrong direction.

"Wait!" Saangi called out.

Spader looked up at her and gave her a big smile. "Just wanted to see if you were payin' attention."

He turned in the other direction, jumped up, jackknifed, and dove into the dark. After one kick he was gone.

"He is an odd creature," Saangi growled. "But I like him."

I had to laugh. "Yeah, that's pretty much how I feel about him too. He's incredibly brave . . . and seriously crazy."

Loor had been oddly silent. She stared at the dark water, as if hypnotized.

"He'll be okay," I assured her.

"I believe he will," she said. "But you are forgetting something, Pendragon. I cannot swim."

Oops.

"I swim but not very well," Saangi added.

"That's okay," I assured them. "I'm a good swimmer, and I don't think I could make it that whole way underwater."

"Then why are we attempting this?" Loor questioned.

"Because if anybody can find a way to get us through, it's Spader. If he thinks we can make it, we'll make it. If not, he won't risk it. Whatever he says, I'll trust him."

My assurances didn't make them feel any better, but I was absolutely confident that Spader would give us an honest opinion. First he had to make it through himself. I was a little less confident about that, because he was swimming into the unknown. We waited for several minutes. I wondered how long Spader could hold his breath. Two minutes? Three? More? I could probably squeak out about a minute and a half, but no more. A lot less if I was swimming for my life. But Spader was a pro. I wouldn't have been surprised if he could lung-bust at least three minutes, even while swimming hard. But the tunnel was dark. He could be a few feet away from air and not know it. Or what if he hit his head? After ten minutes I was beginning to think it wasn't such a hot idea to have sent him into the unknown. After another five minutes I started looking over my shoulder, expecting him to walk down the stairs after having left this territory out of desperation, and returned where it was dry.

"What if he does not return?" Saangi asked.

I hadn't considered that possibility, but it was starting to look as if we should. Before I could turn my thoughts to Plan B, the dark water started to churn. Something was moving below. It didn't seem to be a swimmer, either. I felt the stairs shudder slightly. The others did too. We exchanged curious looks.

"I have no idea" was all I could say.

The water continued to churn. The rumbling grew slightly more intense, then stopped. Abruptly. We all looked down into the depths, not sure of what to expect, when Spader appeared. He swam up to us, broke the surface, and let out a loud "Whoooo!" of joy.

"It worked!" he shouted in victory. "Have to admit I wasn't so sure myself, but it did! It really worked!"

"What did?" I asked.

"It was just as you said, Loor. The tunnel led to a wide-open area, and I was able to surface. No troubles. It isn't even that far."

"It does not matter how far it is; we cannot swim," Loor cautioned.

"That's the beauty part!" Spader announced. "You don't have to. You're going to ride in style."

"Not following," I said, getting impatient.

"The trains, mates! They still run. I found the one that was on the track leading back here and figured out how the tricky thing works. That's what took me so long. Once I got the knack, I chugged the little trolley along the tracks back here. It's right down there, waiting for passengers."

Loor, Saangi, and I looked at one another. I don't think any of us knew how to react. It seemed impossible, yet Spader was there to prove it.

"Nobody has to swim, mates," he added. "All you have to do is hold your breath and hang on. You can do that, can't you?"

Loor and Saangi looked to me. I think they wanted me to confirm that Spader wasn't a nutjob.

"If Spader says it'll work, it'll work," I said with confidence.

"There we go!" he shouted. "All aboard!"

We all dropped our Rokador robes. They would be way too heavy underwater, not to mention the possibility of getting snagged on something. It was better to arrive alive and take our chances on the far side.

We then began the scary process of boarding the underwater train. I figured I could take care of myself, but it would be up to Spader to get Loor and Saangi on board. Loor bravely said that she would go first. I wasn't surprised. Going first meant she would have to hold her breath longer than her acolyte. As much as I trusted Spader, I was pretty nervous about this stunt. I couldn't imagine how scared

Loor was. She had to battle a deep-seated fear of water. I'm guessing that it helped her to know that if things got scary, she could travel to another territory. But that wouldn't make the trip any less terrifying. And Saangi couldn't travel. There would be no turning back for her.

Spader took charge. "Relax. Don't fight. I'll get you there. I'll take Loor first, get her set, then make it back right quick for Saangi. Pendragon, you follow Saangi and me. The train cars are open. I'll put Loor behind the engine, then Saangi next. Pendragon you grab onto a car behind Saangi. Can you take my weapon?"

I nodded.

"Good. Then all you have to do is hold on. I'll make this a snappy-do. No worries."

Loor continued to stare at the water, psyching herself up. She clutched her wooden stave so hard I saw her knuckles go white. For a second I thought she wouldn't be able to overcome her fear and bring herself to dive into the dark.

Silly me.

Loor took two deep breaths and said, "Now!"

Spader didn't waste a second. He took Loor's hand and the two dropped down underwater. She did as she was told. She relaxed. At least, she relaxed her body. Her mind had to have been in hyperdrive. Spader kicked off from the stairs, pulling the warrior girl down. She trailed behind him, clutching her stave. A moment later they were gone.

I put my hand on Saangi's arm. "It's gonna be okay."

Saangi nodded quickly. I sensed she was just as scared as Loor. She stared down at the water. No more than twenty seconds had gone by when Spader popped his head back up.

"Snappy-do," he announced. "Next!"

Saangi held out her hand, took his, and dropped below

the surface. It was my turn. I had been so worried about Loor and Saangi that I didn't think too much about how scary it was going to be for me, too. But there was no time to waste working up my nerve. I had to go right away. I held the two wooden staves in my left hand, against my body. I figured I'd need my stronger, right arm for pulling. After two deep breaths, I held the third and dove below. It was cold. That's what hit me first. It was dark, too. It wasn't easy to see underwater anyway, but the dark made it nearly impossible. I was really wishing for an air globe from Cloral. Or at least goggles from home. Anything. All I could do was follow the vague shadow of Spader and Saangi as they swam in front of me.

The descent was quick. I had only been swimming for a few seconds when I saw the dark outline of the small train. I remembered it very well. It reminded me of the kind of small train you'd ride in an amusement park. There were three cars behind an engine. It had been used to transport the Rokador through the tunnels and to move equipment. Through the murky water I could see Loor clutching to a handrail in the first car. Spader was moving Saangi into position in the second car. I took my place in the third. Once Saangi was set, Spader took a quick look back to make sure I was with them. I gave him an "okay" sign. That's what scuba divers did on Second Earth. I assumed it was universal. It must have been, because Spader was satisfied and quickly shot forward for the engine. A second later the train lurched, and we were on our way.

The little train moved quickly, even though it was working against the water that surrounded us. It couldn't have been better. We were moving. My lungs felt good. I figured we'd be underwater for another thirty seconds or so.

That wasn't too bad. After about ten seconds I felt certain that we would make it with no trouble.

I was wrong.

Without warning the train stopped dead. I looked ahead, wondering what had gone wrong. Had Spader hit the wrong switch and stopped us by accident? Was something in our way? I willed the train to move. Five seconds went by. Ten seconds. The realization hit that if we were able to move, we would have. Something had gone wrong. We were halfway between stops and going nowhere.

This had suddenly turned out to be a very bad idea.

18

My first instinct was to panic.

I kept hoping the little train would start moving again. For some reason that old kid's book came to mind. "I think I can, I think I can, I think I can." Well, in this case, the little engine couldn't. This was no fairy tale.

I felt a hand grab my shoulder. It was Spader. He motioned furiously for me to start swimming, then yanked me forward until I was next to Saangi. His intent was clear. I not only had to swim myself out of this, I was going to have to bring Saangi along with me. He left us and shot forward to go for Loor.

I dropped the two weapons. There was no way I could tow Saangi while holding them. I had to focus and stay calm. Saangi wasn't a Traveler. She didn't have the option of leaving the territory. Or being reborn. I had to get her to safety. My old junior lifeguard training kicked in, and I quickly flipped Saangi over and crossed my right arm over her chest and under her armpit. Focusing on saving her was a good thing. It kept my mind off the fact that I had to save myself, too. To her credit, she didn't panic or fight against me. Within seconds we were moving. But how much farther did we have to go? I figured that Spader knew, which is why he made the choice to go forward instead of back. That meant we were more than halfway there. I didn't know how long we had been holding our breaths. One minute maybe? That's a long time, especially when your heart is racing and you're burning oxygen. It didn't help that I had to pull Saangi along. It meant I couldn't go all that fast and had to burn even more oxygen. It wasn't like we had a choice.

It was hard to tell how far we had traveled. It was too dark and there was nothing to see but nothing. The cave walls had no detail, and it was all blurry anyway. I kept glancing forward to see Spader, but he was a better swimmer than I was, and he was soon out of sight. That's when I started to panic. My lungs were screaming. I kept pulling forward, but I couldn't tell how fast I was going. I glanced up, hoping to see light, but there was nothing but black. I wondered what it was going to feel like to die.

I felt a strong hand on my shoulder. Spader was back.

He grabbed the arm that I had been stroking with and started pulling. It felt as if we were tied to an engine, that's how strong a swimmer Spader was. I relaxed, letting him do the work. With my other arm I held tight to Saangi. We were going to make it. I could only hope that Saangi was still alive.

Seconds later I heard splashing. Spader had broken the surface. He let me go and grabbed Saangi, pulling her forward. I rolled over onto my back to see that we had barely emerged from the tunnel. The sandstone ceiling soared overhead. I rolled back onto my belly and saw that the water spread out to either side of us. Up ahead, rising from the water, was the train track, which meant the water grew shallow. Beyond that was a large, underground cavern that was filled with several other small trains like the one we'd just ridden in on.

Or maybe I should say, like the one that had died underwater.

My feet hit bottom. I walked the rest of the way, gasping for air. Spader pulled Saangi up onto the sandy floor, where Loor was on her knees, waiting, breathing hard. She was okay. Was Saangi? Spader sat her up, holding her chin with his hand. Saangi sat slumped.

"Breathe," he ordered. It didn't sound at all like something that would come from Vo Spader. There was no fun in it. No joke. No sly wink. He was dead serious.

Saangi didn't breathe.

Spader quickly laid her down on her back, pulled her chin up to clear her airway, and clamped his mouth over hers to try and resuscitate her. He gave two deep breaths, forcing her lungs to open up. After the second breath he turned Saangi's face to the side. She still didn't breathe. Spader repeated the process.

I had the fleeting thought that as a Traveler I might be able to save her. Didn't Saint Dane save Courtney from death? It was an agonizing decision. Should I try to save her? But what would that do to the little remaining spirit of Solara? I truly didn't know what to do.

Spader stopped breathing into Saangi's mouth and turned her head again. I knew that if she didn't respond soon, I would have to make a life or death decision. After an agonizing two seconds . . . Saangi coughed. Water spurted from her mouth, but she coughed. She was alive. I slumped down onto the sandy floor, spent, and about as relieved as I think I'd ever been in my life. Saangi rolled onto her side, taking deep breaths. As I write this now, knowing what happened, I still can't say what I would have done if she hadn't come around. I'm just happy that I didn't have to find out.

Spader looked to Loor and softly said, "I'm sorry."

Loor shrugged. "Why?"

"I thought the train would make it back. The water must have killed the engine."

Loor gave him a puzzled look. "You did exactly what you said you would do. You got us here. Perhaps you made it seem as if it would be simpler than it turned out to be, but if you did not do that, I am not so sure that Saangi or I would have gone under the water."

"I definitely would not have gone!" Saangi said, and coughed again.

"Do not be sorry, Spader. Pendragon told us to trust you, we did, and now we are here. You are to be congratulated."

Spader looked at me, not sure how to react.

I shrugged. "Don't look at *me*."

Spader turned back to the Batu warriors and said, "I am really, really happy that we're on the same side."

"I can say the same for you," Loor replied. That was as close to a compliment as Loor was capable of giving.

I took a few more breaths to get my head straight, then said, "Okay, that was fun. Now how do we get out?"

Loor stood and scanned the large train room that was half underwater. "There," she pointed. "Those stairs lead to a hut just inside the outer wall of Mooraj."

"How are you, Saangi?" I asked.

Loor's acolyte coughed one more time to clear her airway and stood up.

"Ready," she declared.

Amazing girls. Both of them.

Loor led us around the rows of parked trains, headed for the archway. I didn't think there would be any guards around. If they weren't guarding the hut outside, there would be no reason to guard this side of the tunnel. Still, we moved with caution. We followed Loor up the sandy stairs, moving quietly. With each step the stairwell grew lighter. The tunnel we had come through must have been angled upward, because we weren't as deep underground as when we had descended the stairs outside of Mooraj.

I had already forgotten about our harrowing swim. All that mattered was what lay ahead. The exiles. How many would there be? Was Mooraj full of them? Was this some kind of holding camp for the strangers from another territory?

When we reached the surface, we found ourselves in another small hut made of sandstone. At one time this was probably the work hut for the Rokador who ran the underground railroad. Not anymore. It was abandoned and empty. The four of us crept cautiously up from below and made our way to a window to get our first view of Mooraj. Or maybe I should say, what Mooraj had become.

There were a lot of ways to describe what we saw. Not all of them were good. Not all of them were bad. There was a feeling of total jubilation . . . and crushing disappointment. Relief mixed with sadness. There was reason for hope, but that was tempered by anger. I guess you could say that what we saw was a mixed bag of truths. I got all of that with one single look.

First off, we weren't looking at a camp filled with exiles. Our search would continue. Still, there was consolation. This camp was filled with other people, which was reason to rejoice. Mooraj had become the home of the Batu tribe. The Ravinians had not committed genocide. They had simply relocated thousands of Batu tribespeople to Mooraj.

Saangi was in tears. Tears of joy. Loor leaned on her arm against the window. I could feel her relief. Their people were alive. That's not to say they were in great shape. I believe this was the Zadaa equivalent of the Horizon Compounds on Earth. Mooraj had become an overcrowded, filthy slum. These once-proud people were sentenced to live in squalor. Even from where we were, it was obvious that this place was a nightmare. Kids ran around wearing nothing but rags. Most of the adults sat staring vacantly at nothing. We saw a fight break out between two men. Over what, I didn't know. It was vicious. The two beat each other bloody, and nobody made a move to stop them. They all sat quietly watching the mayhem with bored detachment. They were like zombies. No Ravinian guards came to stop the fight. That told me there was no order inside Mooraj. The guards kept them inside, but they were on their own when it came to keeping the peace. With that many people living on top of one another, I had to believe that it wasn't easy. The bigger of the two fighters finally delivered a knockout blow. The little guy fell to the sand, unconscious. The big guy hauled off and kicked him once, then strolled away, leaving the guy to bleed. Nobody helped the poor guy. Nobody cared.

When they lived in Xhaxhu, the Batu tribe may have been primitive, but they were industrious. They were proud. They had order. Not anymore. Ravinia had stolen their souls. I guess that's better than being wiped out, but not by much. This was living proof of what Saint Dane had accomplished. On the one hand he had created his superprivileged class of Ravinians. Their arrogance and selfishness fed the dark side of Solara. The same could be said for what was happening in Mooraj. The vicious, dangerous environment also fed the dark side of Solara. His control of Halla was complete. It was painful to see what had become of the Batu, but at least they were alive. Where there's life, there's hope.

But what of the exiles?

"Stay here," Loor commanded, back to business. "Saangi and I will learn what we can. There must be a reason why there was talk of exiles. We will find out why."

"Can't we come?" Spader asked innocently.

Loor gave him a quick look up and down. "These people are victims of the Rokador. You look like a Rokador. If you come, I cannot guarantee that we can protect you."

"Enough said," Spader said quickly, stepping back. "I like it here just fine."

Loor and Saangi left the hut to explore this new world, leaving Spader and me to wonder what our next move should be. We sat in the shadows of the hut, hoping none of the Batu prisoners would peek in and see a couple of Rokador-looking guys kicking back. That would bring more trouble than we could handle.

"This doesn't mean there aren't any exiles on Zadaa," Spader pointed out hopefully. "It just means they're not here."

I was discouraged. "Maybe. But how do we find them?"

"We will. We have to."

The two of us sat quietly, both lost in our own thoughts. After a few minutes I realized that something was off. I sensed a change. What was it? I looked at Spader. He felt it too. He was already sitting up, on alert.

"What is it?" I asked.

"It's gotten quiet" was his answer.

I don't know why I didn't realize it sooner. Mooraj was loaded with people and that created a natural din. That noise was suddenly gone. Alarms went off in my head.

"This isn't good," I said, and stood up.

No sooner did I get to my feet than we were attacked. A dozen Batu had surrounded the small hut and quietly closed the ring around us. When we jumped up, they jumped in. They flooded in through the door and dove in through the windows, screaming. We didn't stand a chance. I feared they would tear us apart, so I yelled, "We are not Rokador! We are not Ravinians! We are friends!"

I don't know if they believed me or not, but it bought us some time. We were both held by strong-armed Batu who at one time were probably Ghee warriors, because they knew exactly how to handle us.

"We are here with two Batu warriors," I called out. "Loor and Saangi. We are friends!"

That seemed to stop them. Or at least confuse them. I took another chance and said, "We are looking for exiles. Do you know them? Are they here?"

That got a reaction too. They were definitely confused.

"We're friends of the exiles," Spader added.

The men exchanged quick looks. Was it possible? Were the exiles living here in this Batu concentration camp after all? I couldn't breathe. I knew the next few seconds would be critical.

"Please," I said. "Loor is our friend. She is looking for the exiles too."

One of the Batu guys stepped forward. By the way he walked I could tell that he was in charge. Or at least as "in charge" as you could be with a bunch of angry, stir-crazy outcasts. He gave us both a long look up and down, sizing us up. He reached out to Spader's ear, and gave it a twist.

"Ow!" Spader screamed in pain. "What was that for?"

"I think he's checking to see if you're a dado," I said.

"All he had to do was ask," Spader shot back, indignant. Then to the Batu he said, "I'm real. See?" He opened his mouth and wiggled his tongue, saying, "Ahhhhh."

The ear-twister turned and strode from the hut. "Bring them," he ordered.

The other Batu instantly obeyed and dragged us out of the hut.

"This is good, right?" Spader called to me.

"I don't know," I answered. They didn't kill us. That was victory enough. At least for the time being.

We were dragged through the dusty, filth-strewn byways of Mooraj. I can't say that I recognized much from my training there. There were so many Batu lying around that there wasn't much chance to see any of the structures. Man, there were a lot of people crammed together in this compound. It was a dirty, overcrowded ghetto. It was hell. I didn't know how long they had been held prisoner there, but any time was too long. Everyone stared at us as we were dragged by. I'm sure they thought we were Rokador captives who were about to pay the price for having sentenced them to such a horrible life. I really hoped that wasn't the case.

We were brought to a long, low building that I thought I recognized, but couldn't be sure. We were quickly dragged inside, and I saw that both walls of this structure were lined with cots. It was the Mooraj hospital. It was a nightmare. The smell alone was enough to make you refuse treatment. There had to have been a hundred cots, all filled with people. Many more were on the floor. The only constant sound was that of people moaning in pain and misery. I guess I should have been repulsed, and I was, but the overriding feeling it gave me was anger. This was what Ravinia brought to those who didn't live up to their standards. This is what Saint Dane had directed his followers to create. This was what fueled Saint Dane's version of Solara. Pain, misery, anger. As I looked over the poor victims of Saint Dane's misguided quest, I wondered if my theory was wrong. Maybe there was such a thing as pure evil.

"Look," Spader called out.

Someone had entered the far side of the ward. It was a woman. She stood out mostly because she wasn't dark skinned like a Batu. She wore a light green smock and pants that made her look like a doctor from Second Earth. She knelt next to a bed that held an elderly man, using a damp cloth to gently wipe his forehead. Though she was caring for the sick and wearing clothes that made her look like a doctor, I knew she wasn't. The smock wasn't a doctor's smock. It was the uniform worn by those who were charged with caring for Mr. Pop, the repository that once contained the history of Quillan. The woman had long gray hair, tied back to keep it out of her eyes as she worked.

"Is it her?" Spader asked.

I called out, "Elli?"

Elli Winter looked up with surprise. At first she smiled, but her smile turned dark. She left the old man and came to us.

"I'm afraid it is too late. The exiles that came to Zadaa are dead."

19

Help me," an emaciated man gasped from the cot nearest us, holding up his hand weakly to Elli.

"Water," another begged in a raspy whisper. They were looking at Elli as if she were an angel sent to protect and care for them. Did they sense that she was a Traveler? I thought back to the way the gars looked at me as we were riding in that horse-drawn wagon on Eelong. They sensed there was something unusual about me. That's what it felt like here. Of course, it didn't hurt that Elli was a gentle, older woman with caring eyes, who showed them the kind of compassion that was in short supply around this hellhole.

"I'll be back," she said to both of them soothingly. "I promise."

She took both their hands and gently placed them back onto their chests. I don't think I'll ever forget the looks in their eyes. They were like wounded puppy dogs, desperate for any show of kindness. It broke my heart. It was hard enough to see anybody in such bad shape, but knowing the Batu were once proud, powerful people made it that much worse.

"Come," Elli said to us as she made her way through the tangle of sick Batu. As she passed the cots, hand after hand went up to her, begging for something. Anything. Elli touched each of them to give whatever solace that might provide. It seemed to help. A little. They appeared more at peace. Elli really was an angel.

She led us out of the horrific infirmary to a small room that was cluttered with trash. There were a few broken chairs, and a table that had empty bottles and cups strewn haphazardly.

"This is where I go to collect my thoughts. Do you like it?" Elli asked with more than a touch of sarcasm. "Make yourselves comfortable."

She gestured to the chairs. I didn't think it was possible to get comfortable in this nightmare ward, but I sat. Spader sat next to me. Elli leaned back on the dirty table. She looked tired and sad. No big surprise. I'm guessing she was near sixty years old, but at that moment she looked closer to a hundred. Her eyes were red. She was on the verge of tears. Having so many sick and dying people begging you for help will do that, I guess.

"I don't understand, Elli," I said. "How long have you been here?"

"That's hard to say," she answered thoughtfully, wiping her tired eyes. "There are no calendars or clocks. Time just goes by. But several nights have passed. I don't recall how many. Ten? Twenty? I've lost count."

That was odd. It's hard to measure time when you're bouncing between territories, but my own internal clock felt as if the Travelers had only left Solara a day or so before.

"The nights are the worst," Elli continued. "Outside

these walls it grows quiet, but in here the sounds of agony never end."

I couldn't imagine dealing with such sadness and despair.

"Why didn't you go to your own territory?" Spader asked.

"I did," Elli answered. "I spent nearly a month on Quillan."

Spader and I exchanged looks. We were both thinking the same thing. Time proved to be irrelevant. Again. It seemed as if Elli had been sent back to a time on Quillan that was further in the past than we had been living.

Elli continued, "There are no exiles on Quillan. At least not anymore. As soon as I arrived, I made my way through the underground, searching for information, just as Press asked. It wasn't easy. Blok controls every aspect of life on Quillan now. Throughout the territory. Most of the remaining revivors have been hunted down and . . ." She didn't finish the sentence. She didn't have to.

"What about Ravinia?" I asked.

"It is the new government," she said sadly. "Of course, they allow Blok whatever freedoms they wish for. The games are a thing of the past, by the way."

"Well, that's good, right?" I said hopefully.

"No" was her quick response. "It's because there are no people left to wager on them."

Oh. Not good.

She continued, "I did uncover one bit of information. I encountered a revivor who had escaped from a Ravinian prison. He was one of the few who survived. They'd beaten him unmercifully. Apparently the Ravinians are also looking for the exiles."

"Did he know about any exiles?" I asked anxiously.

"He did, and he was nearly killed keeping the secret. He stayed alive long enough to escape and share it with me."

Elli took a deep breath. Emotionally she was in rough shape. It seemed like she'd been through a lot since leaving Solara.

"Were there exiles on Quillan?" Spader asked gently, prodding her to continue.

"A few. They arrived in the city of Rune, looking for asylum. They found their way to the underground and actually connected with a few of the remaining revivors. But the entire time they spent on Quillan, they were on the run from Ravinian soldiers. They finally managed to escape back into the flume, and came here to Zadaa before they collapsed. That's what the revivor told me . . . just before he died."

Elli looked away from us. She was holding back tears. At least I understood why she landed back on Quillan when she did. She needed to get that information. If she had returned at a later time, that revivor would have died before meeting her. The power of Solara was an amazing thing. Time and again it put the Travelers where they needed to be, when they needed to be there. That was the positive power of Solara.

The dying power of Solara.

"So you came here looking for them?" I asked.

Elli nodded. "Six exiles left Quillan. They made the mistake of entering Xhaxhu looking for sanctuary and stepped into the lion's den. The Rokador took them in, offering them refuge. But they immediately turned them over to the Ravinians. When the exiles realized their mistake, they tried to escape, and were killed before they reached the outer wall of the city."

Elli couldn't hold back her emotions any longer. She

closed her eyes and sobbed. I walked over to her and put an arm around her. It was all I could offer and it wasn't much.

"It is all true," came a voice from the door.

Spader and I looked to see Loor and Saangi standing in the doorway.

Loor said, "We have just heard the same story from a Batu who labored in Xhaxhu. There are no exiles on Zadaa, Pendragon."

Elli buried her head in my shoulder. I looked at Spader, Loor, and Saangi. They seemed shell-shocked. We had reached another dead end, and Elli was falling apart.

"Let me talk to her alone," I said to them.

Spader nodded and walked to the door. "We'll be outside, mate," he said.

The three left, closing the rotted wooden door behind them.

"I am sorry, Pendragon," Elli said through clutched breaths.

"For what?"

"This is all more than I can bear. I can no longer continue as a Traveler."

I didn't respond. It was clear that she had a lot of pent-up emotion that had to get out.

"It pained me to see what Quillan had become," she continued. "It was far worse than when you were there. I couldn't stay. It was a selfish thing to do. I know. I shouldn't have come here. I should have gone back to Solara to let Press know what I discovered."

"Why didn't you?" I asked.

Elli wiped her eyes and leaned away from me, trying to get herself back in control. "To try and do something positive. For once."

"Everything you've done has been positive," I argued.

"It hasn't. You know that as well as I do, Pendragon. My life has been defined by a series of failures. My husband and I couldn't provide a better life for our daughter, so it drove him to gamble on the Quillan games, and he lost. Everything. He was sent to the tarz, where he died. But instead of being strong for Nevva, I abandoned her. I abandoned my only daughter! I should have stayed with her. Perhaps she wouldn't have turned to Saint Dane if I had been looking out for her."

"You don't know that," I said. "Nevva is a strong person."

"She is a traitor!" Elli snapped. "And I am responsible."

"Don't say that."

"And what did I do with my life instead? I dedicated myself to protecting the archives that were the history of Quillan. Mr. Pop. Another failure. It was destroyed, along with the future of our home. It was all for nothing. My life has been filled with one futile act after another."

"But then you volunteered to be the Traveler from Quillan to take Nevva's place," I offered.

"Yes, and a lot of good I did. Quillan is in ruins, save for the Conclave of Ravinia and Blok. I did nothing to effect any positive change there. When Press gave us the task of finding and protecting the exiles, I thought it was my last hope of actually doing something worthwhile. That's why I followed them here to Zadaa, only to discover that they had been murdered by the Ravinians."

"How did you end up out here at Mooraj?" I asked.

"When I first arrived, I wandered through Xhaxhu and saw how the Batu were being treated. It was appalling. They were slaves and I knew why. The Ravinian flags told me all I needed to know. I came upon a young woman lying in the street. She had been whipped by her Rokador master for not delivering fresh fruit to his door in a timely manner. He beat her for that, and left her to die. I helped her. I found other Batu, and together we smuggled her out of the city. The only place to go for sanctuary was here. This isn't much better than Xhaxhu, but at least here she wouldn't be beaten. The Batu realized that I wasn't a Rokador and let me stay. It was on the journey that they told me of the fate of the exiles. I'd only been here a short while before learning my quest was futile."

She took a deep breath and continued, "When I saw the state of this camp, I chose to stay and help. They are desperate, Pendragon. Their future is beyond grim. They have no hope. There is nothing more I can do for Solara except to offer kindness to the Batu here at Mooraj. It may not be much, but it is more than they have received in a good long while, and more than I have done as a Traveler, or a mother. I am done, Pendragon. However this final battle plays out with Saint Dane, I will learn of it here on Zadaa."

Everything she said was true. More or less. Still, she was being pretty tough on herself and taking a lot of blame she didn't deserve. I wasn't sure I could make her realize that. She was too upset. Still, I had to try. Whether she wanted to be one or not, she was a Traveler. We needed her.

"Caring for the sick Batu is noble," I said to her tentatively. "But you're wrong about there being no hope. Anything you do here to make them comfortable is only a bandage. If you really want to help the Batu, then you have to stay with the Travelers and help us defeat Saint Dane."

"I can't," she said sharply. "You don't need me anyway. I'm an old woman. I can't fight. I can't inspire anyone. I can barely take care of myself. I don't say that to make you feel sorry for me, Pendragon. It's the truth."

"What about Nevva?" I asked.

"What about her?" she said quickly, as if I had slapped her.

I didn't know where I was going with this, but I had to trust my gut. "If you believe she turned to Saint Dane because you abandoned her, maybe you should *un*abandon her."

Elli looked at me as if I were nuts. Maybe I was. I was grasping. Up until then Elli hadn't played much of a role in the war against Saint Dane. Her daughter, Nevva, was to be the Traveler from Quillan, but when she joined Saint Dane, Quillan no longer had a Traveler. So Elli stepped in and took her daughter's place. But since the turning point for Quillan had already passed, there was nothing for her to do. As I thought back on those events, something hit me. I hadn't thought much about it until then, because it really didn't matter. But now that we were revisiting Elli's past, things didn't quite add up.

"There's something I don't understand," I said. "Every Traveler from my generation was mentored by other Travelers who prepared them for the battle with Saint Dane. But your story is different. You had a whole life with your husband before you found out about being a Traveler."

"Why is that hard to understand?" Elli asked. "We all had lives before discovering we were Travelers."

"Not the Travelers from the previous generation," I shot back. "You told me on Quillan that Uncle Press told you you were a Traveler, but that was after Nevva was already around. How could that be? If your mission was to prepare Nevva, why didn't you know you were a Traveler before she showed up?"

Elli looked to the floor. I wasn't sure if she didn't know the answer, or was holding something back.

"I was adopted when I was a baby and never knew my natural parents," she explained. "I knew nothing of my future as a Traveler until after my husband died, and I'd already had my daughter."

"That's exactly what I don't get," I said quickly. "Wait. You *had* a child? On Quillan you told me you adopted Nevva. You did adopt her, didn't you?"

Elli looked pained. "No," she admitted. "I don't know why I told you that. Maybe it was to distance myself from the person she had become. I was so ashamed. But Nevva was not adopted. I gave birth to her."

Whoa. What the heck did that mean? Nevva was a Traveler, but she was also the biological daughter of another Traveler. As far as I knew, none of the other Travelers had biological parents. Including me.

"Was your husband a Traveler?" I asked.

"No," Elli said. "He was such a good man. I hope his spirit never discovers the truth about what Nevva has done."

I paced. Thinking. I didn't know what this meant. Maybe nothing. Uncle Press didn't think so, or he would have told us about it. Maybe it didn't matter. Still, there was a real, physical bond between Elli and her daughter that none of the other Travelers shared. Nevva was the physical offspring of a Traveler. She was the only Traveler who was actually born on her territory. The old-fashioned way. From what Uncle Press told us, the rest of us just sort of . . . showed up. All of us. From both generations.

Except for Nevva.

"You know what I think?" I finally said, still forming the thoughts. "I think you were always meant to be the Traveler from Quillan. But you fell in love and had a child before you found out your true destiny."

"Maybe," Elli said. "I suppose. Does it matter?"

"Well, for one it means that you didn't just fill in for Nevva. It was supposed to be your job. Things just got sidetracked because of the death of your husband. What's happening now might be the way things were meant to be for you."

"Knowing that doesn't change anything," she argued. "I still am not up to the task."

My thoughts were firing fast. Maybe I was spinning my wheels, but it was the first idea I'd had in a long time that felt as if it might have promise.

"You never got the chance to help Quillan," I said. "What if that wasn't what you were destined to do?"

"But you just said you thought I was always supposed to be the Traveler from Quillan."

"Yeah, but what if your true mission hasn't happened yet? What if you are exactly in the place you're supposed to be, when you're supposed to be here?"

Elli didn't like the sound of that. She turned away and busied herself with tidying up the messy room. "I can't imagine what that mission might be."

"I can."

She looked at me with a mixture of fear and curiosity. I paced again. Remembering. Putting myself back into the past. Re-creating moments from memory.

"It's about Nevva," I said, thinking out loud. "No question, she's a traitor. She bought into Saint Dane's vision of Halla and helped him at every turn."

"If you are trying to make me feel better, young man, you are doing a horrible job."

"There's something more," I said. "It happened more than once. In spite of all that Nevva has done, I've always had the feeling that somewhere deep inside, she has regrets."

I had Elli's attention.

"She believes in Saint Dane's philosophy, no question. But there have been moments, fleeting moments, where I felt a trace of humanity trying to peek through. It was like she believed in the vision, but not the methods."

I scoured my memory for those little moments that made me think there might be some truth to what I was saying.

"When she forced my friend Mark Dimond to give up his Traveler ring, Mark told me that she seemed upset. She got what she wanted, yet she was disappointed, as if she wanted Mark to hang on to the ring. And on Ibara, she truly seemed upset that I wanted to quit. It was like, like, she wanted me to be stronger and stand up to Saint Dane. Is that possible? Was she looking for another way?"

Elli shook her head. I was confusing her. Heck, I was confusing myself.

"In that final moment, when I was so driven by anger that I was willing to drop Alexander Naymeer from that helicopter, she tried to stop me. Saint Dane wanted me to kill him. It was the final event that completed the Convergence, but Nevva tried to get me to stop."

I didn't know where I was going with this, but I was getting excited.

Elli wasn't.

"Perhaps you're right, but it doesn't mean anything. Nevva may have doubts, but that hasn't stopped her from helping Saint Dane crush Halla."

"Maybe," I said. "Or maybe if she has some shred of

humanity buried somewhere, we can find it. Maybe *you* can find it."

Elli looked horrified. "Are you suggesting I speak with her?"

I shrugged. "Yeah, maybe I am."

"No," she shot back. "I cannot."

She went for the door, but I cut her off.

"Elli, I might be totally wrong, but maybe there's a chance to appeal to Nevva. She's your daughter. Your *true* daughter. You gave birth to her. That's a bond none of the other Travelers have. You said you wanted to do something positive? This might be it. You told me you feel as if all you've done has been for nothing. No, worse. You think your actions have created problems. Well, this might be the single most important thing you can do. This might be your chance."

Elli's eyes filled with tears, but she didn't cry. In that moment I felt the depth of her strength. Her love for Nevva. She always appeared to be a fragile woman. She wasn't.

"To what end?" she said softly. "Even if you're right, what do you expect me to say? What would you want Nevva to do?"

"I don't know," I admitted. "But we're running out of time. The last hope for Solara is those exiles, and we can't find them. What if they're all dead? That's seeming more likely by the minute. What then? Do we just sit around and wait for Halla to crumble? We could stay here and help care for the Batu and wait for the end, but that's all we'd be doing. Waiting for the end. I can't do that, and I don't believe you can either. We've come too far. If there's any small hope to turn things around, I think we have to go for it. If that means talking to the enemy . . . talking to your daughter . . . how can we not? This may be the way it was meant to be, Elli. This may be your moment."

Elli was trembling. Physically trembling. It was as if her body wanted to move—to run—but her willpower fought to keep her in place. Her eyes stayed locked on mine. I couldn't imagine what she was thinking. She blamed herself for the choices Nevva made. Now I was asking her to face the daughter she had abandoned. Face the enemy. For what? I didn't know. Saint Dane was in total control. We had to do something to change that, no matter how desperate it might be.

The door opened, bumping into me from behind. Spader poked his head in. "How we doing?"

I looked to Elli. She stared back blankly.

"Come on in," I said to Spader.

He stepped in, followed by Loor and Saangi. I didn't want Elli to feel as if we were ganging up on her, so I stood next to her.

As always, Loor didn't waste time. "What is our plan, Pendragon?" she asked. "There are no exiles on Zadaa."

I looked to Elli. She dropped her gaze to the floor, avoiding mine. I deflated. She wasn't as strong as I'd thought she was.

"We move on," I said, disappointed. "We have to keep looking. I'm thinking that we should go back to Solara and regroup. Elli will stay here to care for the Batu. Saangi, maybe you can help her."

"No," Elli snapped.

We all looked at her.

"Where is she?" Elli asked, looking right at me. Her gaze was strong. Her tears were gone.

"Who?" Spader asked.

"Third Earth," I replied to Elli. "Are you sure?"

"Like you said," she answered, "this may be my moment."

"What are we talking about here?" Spader asked with confusion.

"Change of plans," I announced. "Loor, Spader, I still think you should return to Solara and wait for word."

"And where will you go?" Loor asked.

"Elli and I are going to Third Earth."

20

Moving between territories is incredibly easy now.

It's like stepping through a sheer curtain and passing from one room to another. No more flumes. No more crawling through secret places to find hidden tunnels that carry us along on a carpet of light and music. Best of all, no more quigs. All we have to do is think about where we want to go, take a step and . . . hello. We're there.

Still, it's disorienting. It may be like stepping from one room to the next, but they are two very different rooms. And it's not like I can think, "I want to go to Third Earth at two thirty on Thursday afternoon and land on the bench that's behind the library." We still have to rely on the forces of Solara to put us exactly where we need to be and when we need to be there. I'm not really sure how the spirits know, but they've done a pretty good job so far.

This time was no different, though what happened when Elli and I first set foot back on Third Earth made me long for the familiar old gates at the end of a flume trip.

We held hands and stepped into the same hazy swirl of dust that we'd found on our last visit. There wasn't much else to see, but there was plenty to hear. A loud, angry grinding sound assaulted us. It was mechanical and it was getting louder. Elli and I froze. We didn't know where we were. We didn't know *when* we were. We didn't know what the sound was, or if we should be worried about it. In other words, we didn't know a thing.

"Look out!" came a desperate cry. Desperate cries were not good, especially if they came as a warning. "Heads up!"

We looked up quickly to see a shadow overhead that was coming our way. I didn't have time to register or to react. Luckily, Mark Dimond did. Elli and I were half tackled, half shoved out of the way. Mark wasn't being gentle, either. He manhandled us toward the wreck of a car and pretty much threw us behind it.

"What is it?" I gasped.

"Trouble."

Oh. I figured that.

I barely had time to peek up from behind the barrier to see what he meant. The shadow was a helicopter. I expected it to start firing at us, but its path was too steep. It was flying straight for the ground. Actually, it wasn't flying at all. It was falling.

Elli gasped. A second later the large black chopper smashed into the ground. The cabin crumbled and bucked forward. The rotor dug into the dirt. I was transfixed by the destructive violence. It was a good thing Mark was still thinking. He grabbed us both and pulled us down behind the car wreck. The next sound we heard was the squealing of tortured metal, followed by the sharp thumps of shrapnel that hit the far side of the wreck. The rotors had broken up on contact, spewing sharp pieces everywhere. The car windows exploded, raining glass down on us. Chunks of metal flew overhead and dug into the ground behind us. If we had been standing up, we would have been shredded. Elli clung to me in fear.

It was a rude welcome to Third Earth.

I looked to Mark. He was staring backward, his gaze fixed. This wasn't the Mark I knew. Besides being older, he had an intensity that I'd rarely seen. In anyone.

The grinding sound of the crash continued for a few more seconds, then ended. No more falling parts. No more screaming engine. All we heard was the soft hiss and tick of hot metal.

"Are the Ravinians attacking?" I asked.

Mark's answer was to jump up and sprint for the destroyed chopper.

"Wait here," I said to Elli, and followed him.

Mark ran straight for the wreck. A few others came running from other directions. A quick look around told me that we were back in the empty lot in Manhattan where Mark and I had landed the chopper we hijacked from the Conclave of Ravinia. The garage that held the stolen helicopters was off to our right. It looked as if this doomed helicopter barely cleared the top of that garage before crashing. The downed helicopter no longer looked anything like a flying vehicle. The engine was winding down. The cabin had become a twisted ball of black metal. The rotor was gone, having been flung in pieces every which way. I still didn't know who was inside. Was Mark running to make sure that a Ravinian dado wasn't going to jump out and attack? I didn't think so. It seemed like he was more worried about helping the guy who was inside.

He got to the wreck and yanked on the door. Or what was left of it. Mark had to pull with all he had. With an agonizing screech of metal, he managed to muscle it open.

"It's okay," he said to the guy inside. "We got you."

"No," came a cry from inside the chopper. "I can't move."

I made it to the wreck and looked over Mark's shoulder to the horror within. The pilot wasn't a dado. The blood and his pained expression told me that much. He didn't look like a Ravinian, either. His clothes were too shabby. This was definitely a friend. It was a gruesome sight, because his body was impossibly contorted inside the twisted wreck.

Mark reached for his arm and pulled. The guy screamed in pain.

"Don't!" he cried. "My back." The guy was in a seriously bad way. He took short, quick breaths as his eyes darted back and forth, focusing on nothing. I figured if his back was broken, there was no way he would survive. The blood wasn't a good sign either. There was lots of it. Medical care on the new Third Earth was nonexistent. At least, outside of the Ravinian conclave.

"Okay, okay," Mark said, trying to calm the poor guy. "We'll cut the wreck away from y-you."

Mark stuttered. He may have been all strong and in charge, but he was still Mark and he was under stress. He gave me a look that said it all. His friend wasn't going to make it. The others crowded around, trying to get a glimpse, but Mark put his arm out to hold them back. He took a breath to calm himself. There was nothing he could do to save the guy. It was now about making his last few moments less terrifying.

"You made it," Mark said, soothing. "You got back. I'm proud of you, Antonio."

The guy, Antonio, focused on Mark and smiled. "Don't

think we'll be able to use this chopper though." He spoke in pained gasps.

"Sure we will," Mark said, faking confidence. "There's only a couple of dings. We'll get it back in the air."

"Good," Antonio gasped. "We're going to need it. We're going to need everything we have."

"What happened?" Mark said, leaning in close to the doomed man.

"They're coming," Antonio said between labored breaths. I wasn't sure if his eyes were wild from pain, or from fear. "Worse than we thought." Antonio started to sob. He was out of his mind. "Get out, Mark. Get everyone out. Out of the city. Away from here. What we saw . . . it's impossible. But it's real. I saw it."

"What was it, Antonio?" Mark asked with a touch of desperation. "What did you see?"

"The factory," Antonio said. His eyes closed; he was losing consciousness.

"Antonio!" Mark barked. "What about the factory?"

"Where they build the choppers. We stole one . . . nearly got away . . . but they attacked. My guys . . . all killed."

"How many?" I asked Mark quietly.

"Four, including Antonio" was his answer.

"Were they exiles?" I asked.

Mark nodded.

Three more exiles had been killed. Of the original twenty exiles who came here with Mark from Cloral, nine were left. I was afraid it would soon be eight.

Antonio leaned forward. The small move was painful. I saw it in his eyes and the way he winced, but it didn't stop him. He needed Mark to understand.

"I think they've found them," he whispered.

"Who? Found who?" Mark asked.

"We heard them talking. After they finish us, they're going after them. That's what they've been doing. All this time, they've been getting ready to go after them."

"Who, Antonio?" Mark begged. "Who are they going after?"

Antonio could barely get the words out. His voice was growing weaker, but I heard. "They found the rest of the exiles."

"What!" I shouted.

Antonio didn't expect to hear another voice. His eyes looked around in confusion, searching for who had shouted. I pushed next to Mark, so he could see me. "Where are they, Antonio? Where are the other exiles? Are they here on Third Earth?"

Antonio shook his head. I don't know how he found the strength. Maybe it was easier than speaking.

"I don't know," he said, defeated. "After they come for us, they're going after the rest. Get out, Mark. Run. Hide. We can't stand up to what they've got. It's over."

Antonio closed his eyes for the last time. His face grew relaxed. He was at peace. I wondered if his spirit had joined the others in Solara.

Mark didn't move. He stared at his fallen friend. I didn't say anything. There was too much to absorb and process. I didn't know Antonio, but in those short few moments— his last—I found out that he was a very brave guy. A hero even.

Mark looked away from his fallen friend, to me. It was the old Mark. The young Mark. His expression was a cross between grief, confusion . . . and fear. I sensed he was looking to me for answers. I had one, but it wasn't the time to tell him. He glanced over his shoulder to see a few of his other friends watching. They were close enough to have heard all that Antonio said. They looked worse than Mark.

Elli was there too. She heard it all. She stood alone, looking lost and afraid.

"Let's get him out of here," Mark announced with authority. "Then we have to hide this wreck. We don't want anything to be seen from the air." He looked at me and added, "Are you here for a while?"

"For as long as it takes," I answered.

"Good," he replied. "You can help."

They put me in charge of digging the grave. It was an experience I'd managed to avoid up till that point, but I guess with all that had happened over the past few years, it was inevitable. I made sure that Elli was safe inside the warehouse, then found a shovel and walked across the street to a spot that Mark had directed me to. It was an empty schoolyard. I saw the vague outline of a baseball diamond. Toys were scattered around. A deflated kickball. A ballerina slipper. The arm of a doll. I wondered when the last time was that these toys had been played with. I had to force myself to stop thinking that way. As important as this job was, I didn't want to spend time looking back. There was trouble ahead. That's where we needed to focus. Burying the dead was looking back. Still, it had to be done.

I got to work digging a long, narrow hole among the sad reminders of a past civilization. The ground was soft, I was glad to discover. It allowed me to work fast. The mindless act of digging gave me the chance to dissect Antonio's last words. The Ravinians were planning an attack. That much was clear. It sounded like Antonio and his team had found the factory where they built their gunships and didn't like what they saw. It could mean that the Ravinians were building a lot more choppers, in order to launch some kind of massive aerial assault. Was this the final plan for Third Earth? Were the Ravinians going to wipe out every last non-Ravinian they could find?

Or was it going to be practice for their ultimate goal, which was to wipe out the exiles, and the remaining spirit of Solara along with them? If they were building helicopters, did that mean that all the exiles were somewhere here, on Third Earth? It seemed likely. That would be the ultimate turning point for Third Earth. If the last hope for Solara was here, destroying the exiles would give Saint Dane his final victory. Halla would be his.

The more I thought of this possibility, the more it made sense. The exiles had to be here. The Ravinians were preparing to attack them. And what was I doing? Digging a grave, not knowing what to do about any of it.

The sun was going down. Though I wasn't in an official graveyard, it still gave me the creeps to be standing in an open grave while shadows grew long. I finished the hole quickly and got the heck out of there. I brought the shovel back to the garage and saw that the wreck of the helicopter was gone. They probably salvaged any parts they could use on their own choppers, then ditched the carcass in one of the surrounding buildings. As I walked to the garage, a door opened. Six guys came out, carrying a body wrapped tightly in a white cloth. This was going to be Antonio's final journey. The procession went past me. I stood there and bowed my head out of respect. One of the guys came to me and took the shovel. I may have dug the grave, but the job of burying Antonio would be theirs. With a nod of thanks, he rejoined the funeral procession. I watched them for a few moments, then went inside.

Mark and Elli were sitting at a table among several of the stolen helicopters. He had put out food for her, but Elli wasn't eating. I wasn't much interested in food either, but I knew we had to eat when we had the chance. I sat down and looked over the feast. It was basically a bunch of canned fruit and vegetables that had been opened and spread out across the scarred, wooden table. A single fork was in each can.

Mark must have seen the look on my face. He said, "Not exactly the Manhattan Tower Hotel, but it's good. And it's safe. There's a ton of canned food all over the city."

"Looks good to me!" I said, lying. I picked up the least vile-looking can and scooped out a big chunk of something that looked like half of a peach. At least, I hoped it was half a peach. If it wasn't, I didn't want to know. I popped it into my mouth and tried to swallow it without chewing or tasting it. Not an easy thing to do. It was sweet, that much I could tell. It slid down and I didn't gag. I hated canned peaches.

"Try to eat, Elli," I said. "You never know when we'll get another chance."

She took a couple sips of water. Mark sat staring at the table. His mind was somewhere else.

"Who was he?" I asked.

"My best friend" was his answer. He quickly looked up at me and added, "After you, that is. We got shoved into the flume in the Bronx at the same time."

"I'm sorry" was all I could say. I didn't think it could even begin to help him feel better.

Elli looked sick, and I didn't think it was because of the

canned peaches. She had retreated into herself, hugging her waist in a way that looked as if she were trying to protect herself. As we sat there, I realized there was something we had to talk about. Neither of them were going to like it, but I didn't see any way around it.

"Mark, this is Elli. She's the Traveler from Quillan."

Mark looked up and nodded politely. I wondered how long it was going to take for him to connect the dots. He smiled at her, then his face went blank. The smile was gone. The dots had been connected in about three-point-two seconds.

"Elli Winter?" he asked, to confirm.

Elli nodded.

"Nevva's mother," Mark stated flatly.

I had to cut in. "This is Mark Dimond, Elli. He's been my friend since we were kids. We grew up together on Second Earth."

"I know," Elli said, her voice cracking. "You're the one my daughter's been manipulating."

"She's been manipulating a lot of people," Mark shot back.

I wasn't sure if he was angry or hurt. I also didn't know how he would relate to Elli, knowing that her daughter had threatened to kill his parents and generally made his life miserable. It was a tense moment. I didn't know what to say to diffuse it.

Elli took care of it for me.

"I'm sorry, Mark," she said kindly. "I've heard a lot about you and how you were tricked into helping Nevva. If I could undo the things my daughter has done, I would. It's why we're here."

Mark shot me a questioning look.

"It's true," I said. "We're scrambling, Mark. I thought Elli might be able to get through to her daughter."

"And do what?" Mark asked sharply.

"I don't know," I answered lamely. "Make her see reason. Show her another side to this whole thing. Maybe even shame her into acting like a human."

"There's nothing human about that witch," Mark spat. "She's heartless."

Elli winced.

Mark stood up, throwing back his chair. It clattered to the floor as he walked away from us. I went after him.

"Whoa," I said, heading him off. I got close to him, speaking softly but with intensity. Elli didn't need to hear what I was saying.

"I hear you," I said. "I know she's a witch. There are worse words to use. Nobody knows that better than I do, except for you. But Elli isn't Nevva. She's a Traveler."

"So what? Nevva's a Traveler too."

I thought about getting into the whole thing about Elli being Nevva's natural mother, but that would have meant explaining to Mark about Solara and the fact that none of the Travelers were actually from their home territories. I figured he had enough to deal with.

"I know. Nevva's a traitor. You get no arguments from me. But there were times, you said so yourself, that Nevva showed there might be more going on with her. Remember when she forced you into giving up your ring?"

"She threatened to kill my parents."

"Right, and when you gave it to her, you said she was disappointed, like she'd wanted you to fight for it. Saint Dane wanted that ring. Her mission was to get it. But she was disappointed when you gave it up."

"Yeah." Mark sniffed. "Because she probably wanted to kill my parents."

"Or maybe she was having second thoughts. I've seen it too, Mark. There might be some humanity in there somewhere. I figured if anybody could find it, it would be her mother."

Mark glanced over at Elli, who sat staring at the table.

"We have to do something, Mark," I continued. "Your friend died trying to get back here to tell you an attack was coming. If those Ravinians are coming after you and the rest of your friends, that's bad enough. But if Saint Dane knows where the rest of the exiles are, the ball game's over. It's all about the exiles, Mark. They are the last, best hope to save Halla."

"Why? How?" he asked.

"I can explain it all to you, but I think it would only make things more confusing. It'd be a lot easier if you just believe me. We have to find those people. We have to make sure they're safe. That includes you and your friends. I think Elli gives us a shot at doing that. I don't know how else to say it to you. It may be desperate, but it's the only thing I can think of doing."

"So you're just going to walk up to the gates of that fortress and ask if Nevva can come out and play?"

"I don't know. I haven't figured that part out."

Mark looked at me and nodded thoughtfully. "Did you find Courtney?" he asked.

"No" was my quick answer.

"She might be with the rest," he said hopefully.

"Maybe. I hope so. There are a lot of them out there, Mark. We have to find them and protect them."

I couldn't tell if I was getting through to him or not. I

was asking him to take a lot on faith. He had trusted me since we were kids. I hoped he wouldn't stop.

Mark took a tired breath and walked away from me, headed toward Elli. I watched nervously, not sure of where his head was or what he was planning to do. He knelt down next to her and put his elbow on the table.

"I'm sorry for saying those things about your daughter," he said with sincerity.

Elli couldn't bring herself to look at him. "Don't be," she replied. "They're true."

"When I thought I lost my mother and father, it made me do things I might not ordinarily have done."

"Nevva *did* lose hers," Elli replied sadly.

Mark nodded. "I know how important it was for me to get them back. Maybe it's time to let Nevva have her mother back."

That struck Elli. Her gaze lifted from the table. She looked Mark in the eye. He smiled warmly. Elli gave me a hopeful look, then touched Mark's cheek. "I'm sure your mother is very proud of you."

It looked to me as if Mark's eyes were filling with tears.

"She was," he said. "I miss them."

"I can't guarantee that Nevva misses me."

Mark held her hand and said, "Let's find out."

He stood up and faced me. "I can get you inside the conclave," he announced. "There's only one catch."

"What's that?"

"I'm going with you."

21

The plan was to get some sleep and leave before dawn.

I had been going nonstop for who knows how long, and my tank was empty. Two rooms were set up for sleeping on the second floor of the grimy garage. One for men, the other for women. They each had single-mattress beds lined up along the walls. It wasn't exactly cush, but it was far better than what the Batu had at Mooraj. At first I was reluctant to take one of the cots, thinking I'd be displacing somebody. That is, until I remembered that there were a bunch of people who wouldn't be coming back to sleep there that night. Unfortunately, there was plenty of room.

I made sure that Elli was set up and comfortable in the room they had for women. She was there along with three others. They saw to it that she had everything she needed, which wasn't much. Soon Elli was off to sleep. At least, I thought she was. She may have just been closing her eyes, so as not to have to deal with reality. Elli hadn't said much since we'd arrived on Third Earth. I hoped she was up to the task in front of us. In front of *her*. If she wasn't, our trip was for nothing.

When I finally settled into my own bed, Mark was waiting for me. He wanted answers. The thought of explaining the realities of Halla and Solara to him made me shudder. How would he react to it all? Getting Mark to understand and accept it was a job I didn't look forward to. All I wanted to do was sleep.

But he needed to understand why our mission to protect the exiles was so important. Heck, he was an exile himself, and he'd been part of this war as long as I had. He deserved something.

"I know it all now, Mark," I said as we sat facing each other on our beds. "Everything. Though I'm not sure how to explain it to you."

"Give it a shot," he said without hesitation. He didn't care that I was exhausted. I didn't blame him.

I racked my brain, trying to come up with the simplest explanation possible.

"There's life beyond our own," I began. "Spiritual life. The spirit that lives in every person doesn't die when their body does. It moves on and becomes part of a bigger reality that reflects our own."

Mark looked at me like I had just said cows could fly.

"Okay . . . ," he said with a huge dose of skepticism.

"I saw Uncle Press again. And Kasha. And Osa."

"They're dead," he said flatly.

"The physical beings they were when they were living in Halla are dead. Their spirit continues on in a place called Solara."

"An eleventh territory?"

"No, it's way more cosmic than that. It's been about Solara from the beginning. Saint Dane is trying to control it. To destroy its spirit. Once he does that, Halla doesn't matter anymore, because he can create his own physical universe. His own Halla."

Mark frowned. "Uh . . . what?"

"Yeah, this is where it starts getting complicated."

"Starts? I'd say we're already pretty far down that path."

I shrugged. What could I say?

"You're serious about this?" Mark asked tentatively.

I nodded. "That was a way simple explanation, but yeah."

"So why are the exiles so important that Saint Dane wants them dead?"

"Because after all that happened to Halla, after the dismantling of so many societies and civilizations, they're the last remaining group of people who stood up to Ravinia. To Saint Dane. When they were shot off of Second Earth, it was like they were taken out of the loop. They didn't experience the downfall of their own world. It was like Saint Dane inadvertently protected them, and now it's their collective spirit that is keeping him from his final victory. The collective spirit of the exiles is keeping Solara alive. Remember how Saint Dane kept talking about Denduron being the first domino to fall? The exiles are the *last* domino. If they are destroyed, Solara will be his."

"So, if the Ravinians hadn't sent us all into exile, Saint Dane would have won by now?"

"Pretty much. It was the biggest mistake he made. Now he's trying to correct it."

"And we're counting on it to come back and bite him in the butt."

"Exactly. The Travelers were sent out to find the remaining exiles and protect them. You're one of them, Mark. Courtney too."

"Okay, say you find the other exiles. Then what?"

"Then we move on Saint Dane here. On Third Earth."

Mark's eyes lit up. "*That* I understand."

"I thought you would."

"You think Elli can convince Nevva to help somehow?"

I rubbed my eyes. It was a point-blank question. I had to give him an answer that was just as direct.

"No. I don't. Nevva's hard-core. But who knows what'll happen when she sees her mother? It might get through to her somehow."

"Don't count on it," he grumbled.

"I hear you, but I'll try anything. I don't want to say that I'm desperate but . . . I'm desperate."

"Is it worth the risk? Going in there, I mean. You saw what happened to Antonio."

"I did, and it's another reason I want to get to Nevva. Antonio said there was an attack coming. If Saint Dane knows where the exiles are, they're dead and Halla is lost. We need to find out what's going on and try to scuttle it."

Mark nodded. I knew he was running Antonio's final words over in his head. I'd done it a hundred times myself.

"If he's building more gunships to go after the exiles," Mark said, thinking aloud, "it means they're probably here on Third Earth."

"That's what I was thinking."

"Are there really seventy thousand of us?" he asked.

"Saint Dane created a massive flume in the middle of a packed Yankee Stadium that sucked them all inside. Seventy thousand might be light."

Mark's eyes went wide. I figured he was trying to imagine the event. I, on the other hand, preferred to forget it.

Mark said, "It's easier to imagine that whole Solara-spirit

thing than to picture Yankee Stadium being sucked down a drain. Yikes."

We looked at each other, and laughed. It was totally inappropriate, but it broke the tension. For a second it felt like old times, when Mark and I would hang out for hours and talk about anything that came into our heads. It didn't last long.

Mark clapped his hands on his knees and stood up. "I'll send my guys out in a chopper at first light. If there are seventy thousand people hiding out somewhere, we'll find them."

"I don't know," I said skeptically. "It took Saint Dane a while."

"Yeah," he said slyly. "But we know where to look."

He strode for the door, then stopped and turned back, as if he had a new thought. He squinted, which was something Mark always did when he was having trouble understanding something. I liked those small, familiar moments. It meant that beneath that hardened exterior, my friend was still lurking around somewhere.

"The flumes were destroyed, right?" he asked.

"Every last one of 'em."

"So how did you and Elli get here? And how are the other Travelers getting around?"

"We don't need the flumes anymore. The Travelers can go wherever we want, anytime. But we have to be careful, because each time we do, it depletes more of the power of Solara."

Mark stared at me, still squinting. We stayed like that for a few seconds. I think he went into brain lock. What I had just said went beyond his comprehension. He finally shook his head and said, "Forget I asked."

"Forgotten."

He didn't move. Something else was on his mind. I hoped he wasn't going to ask me any more questions about Solara.

"What's the matter?" I asked. "Besides everything?"

Mark hesitated, choosing his words carefully. "I feel like, one way or another, this is it. I mean, it's finally going to be over, isn't it?"

"It is. One way or another."

He nodded. "I'm glad we're back together, Bobby."

"Me too."

"Courtney should be here."

"We'll find her," I said with confidence, but absolutely no authority.

He pulled himself out of there. I lay down on the bed and closed my eyes, hoping for sleep to come quickly. As usual, it didn't. My mind was too full of clashing thoughts, most of which were about what would happen the next day. I'd been on plenty of adventures since becoming a Traveler. My journals are loaded with the tales. It had become a way of life. A crazy way of life, but what can you do? That was the way it was meant to be. This time was different. Of all the things I've been through, either alone or with another Traveler, we were always able to take care of ourselves. More or less.

Not this time. Mark and I were setting out on what could be a suicide mission . . . with an older woman on our team. The closest I'd come to that was with Gunny, but he could take care of himself. Heck, he could handle himself better than I could. Elli was a different story. She was smart and resilient, no question there. But she was fragile. Physically and emotionally. I wasn't so much worried about something bad happening to her. After all, she was a Traveler. But we were going to have to move fast and react to constantly changing threats. Doing that with an older, fragile woman was going to be tricky.

Making it worse was the fact that Mark would be with us. He wasn't a Traveler. He could die. Like *really* die. And he was an exile. I had to make sure that Mark survived the ordeal . . . while watching out for Elli, and oh by the way, staying alive myself. Suddenly my plan didn't seem like such a hot one.

Needless to say, I didn't sleep much that night.

But I did get to sleep. Finally. My body and my brain needed it. I probably could have slept for days, but all we could afford was a couple of hours. Mark got me up before daybreak.

"Come on" was all he had to say.

I was up and ready to go in seconds. I followed him quickly and quietly, trying not to wake the other guys who slept in the beds around us. Elli waited for us in the garage near the helicopters. She had changed into nondescript gray pants and a black shirt. Standard wear for Third Earth. She stood stiffly, with her arms still wrapped around her waist. Her long gray hair was pulled back tight, out of the way. I'm not sure if it was the way her hair was, or the light, but for the first time I saw the resemblance between her and Nevva. She stood up straight. Her eyes were alert. Just like her daughter. They were definitely blood relatives.

I still had on my Second Earth clothes, and Mark had on the same raggedy pants and shirt I'd seen him wear the day he rescued those people from the building in the zoo. That seemed like years ago. For all I knew, it *was* years ago. I'd lost all sense of time.

Mark had three short, jet-black guns that looked like

miniature shotguns. The single barrels were wide. Beneath each was a thick, round disk where, I assumed, the ammunition was stored. Not that I was an expert, but it was like no gun I'd ever seen.

"These were stolen from the fortress," Mark explained. "It fires some sort of burst of charged particles. It's enough to knock a big guy off his feet, but it won't kill him. What it kills are dados. One shot and they go cold."

He kept one and gave one each to Elli and me. I held the weapon up, admiring it.

"I love this," I said in awe.

"I've never fired a weapon in my life," Elli said, holding the gun as if it were diseased.

"Be sure to hold the stock tight against your body, or the recoil might hurt you," Mark explained. "Each has ten shots. After that, it's done. We don't have reloads."

Elli looked sick. I wasn't even sure she knew which end to point at a dado. I took the gun from her.

"It's okay. You won't have to do any shooting," I assured her.

She looked relieved. Not relaxed, but relieved. I hadn't fired many guns either, but to be honest, the idea of nailing a couple of dados appealed to me. I didn't want to go looking for one, but if I had one in my sights, I didn't think I'd have any trouble pulling the trigger. The guns had shoulder straps, so I slung both weapons over my back.

"What's the plan?" I asked Mark.

He led us out of the garage to where one of the other exiles, a girl with red hair and freckles, named Maddie, was waiting behind the wheel of an ancient yellow taxi. She didn't look any older than sixteen. I wondered if she had her driver's license, though I doubted if anybody checked anymore. Just so long as she knew how to drive, I didn't care. We hurried into the backseat, slammed the door, and Maddie hit the gas. With a lurch we were off and flying. Fast. She knew how to drive.

Mark explained, "We have to get to the insert point before the sun comes up. Moving cars in daylight draw attention."

"Insert point?" I asked.

"The city is honeycombed with ancient tunnels," Mark said. "At all levels. They carried subways, sewage, electricity, pretty much everything that made a city work and that nobody wanted to see. There's a whole city below this city that most people never saw."

"It's still intact?" I asked.

"Most of it collapsed when the fireworks started. That's what they tell me, anyway. But the deeper tunnels survived, and we have maps. They're like gold. It's how everybody moves around without being seen by Ravinians."

"People live underground?" Elli asked.

"Some do, but mostly the tunnels are used as highways. There's a service tunnel that runs directly beneath the Ravinian fortress. They have no idea it exists. We don't use it that often, because we don't want to risk it being discovered and ruining the one advantage we have over them. But every once in a while we stage a quiet raid, like the one that got these guns. We're able to get right under their noses without them knowing."

Elli asked, "Is that how Antonio got to the fortress?"

Mark nodded.

I didn't want to dwell on that last mission. "Do you know the factory he was talking about?" I asked.

"Yeah. It's outside the fortress. It's a huge place where

they assemble the choppers. I think it's where they store weapons, too. I don't know for sure though. I've never been inside. Nobody has."

"Except for Antonio," Elli corrected.

"We should go there first," I said. "I want to see what Antonio was talking about. We have to know what we're up against."

"Done. I can get us in."

"Great."

"Tricky part is getting out again."

Oh.

On that depressing thought we all fell quiet. Maddie drove us quickly through the dead streets of Manhattan. It was a hairy ride. Our car didn't have headlights, and there were no streetlights burning, so it was hard to make out where the streets ended and the sidewalks or buildings began. That didn't stop Maddie. She charged down the streets and took corners as if she were wearing night-vision goggles. For the record, she wasn't. It was scaring the hell out of me. But I wasn't about to be a backseat driver. All I could do was dig my fingernails into the armrest and prepare for the jolt when we hit something.

We didn't, though I'm not sure why. Maddie pulled up to a two-story brick building that had no signage or markings. She hit the brakes, skidded to a stop, and looked back at us with a quick, "Go. Good luck."

"You too," Mark told her.

"That was great driving," I said to Maddie, trying to make friends.

"You should see what I can do in a helicopter," she replied with a sly smile.

I didn't necessarily want to experience that particular

pleasure. If she flew like she drove, I'd probably pass out from fear.

Mark said, "Maddie's flying the first leg to search for the exiles."

"Oh," I said quickly. "Then good luck to you, too."

She winked.

We all got out of the car. Maddie barely waited until I closed the door before taking off. She shot down the dark street, took a sharp corner, and was gone. She had to get back before sunrise. These people lived like vampires.

Mark wasn't wasting time either. He walked straight into the building. We followed. Of course the place was empty. I had no idea what it might have been used for, but if it was sitting over the entrance to an underground utility tunnel, it was probably a city building of some sort. Mark led us quickly across the empty floor that was covered with broken bits of furniture, glass, and I don't know what else. He knew exactly where he was going. I had Elli walk in front of me so I could keep an eye on her. Mark led us through a few doors, to a stairwell that disappeared down into the dark.

Elli hesitated.

"If Mark says it's okay, it's okay," I said, trying to reassure her.

Mark looked back and said, "This is the easy part."

That didn't make me feel any better, which meant it probably did even less for Elli. But like I said, she was brave. We followed Mark down several flights of winding, concrete stairs. After passing through another doorway, we came upon another stairwell. The deeper we went, the darker it became.

"Are we going to be walking the whole way in the dark?" I asked.

"Wait," Mark answered.

We had finally reached bottom. At least, I thought it was the bottom. I didn't see any other stairways around. I didn't see much of anything. It was nearly pitch-black. Elli had a death grip on my arm. Mark shuffled over to a far wall, moving slowly, so as not to walk face-first into something. He ran his hands along the wall until he came upon what looked like a box mounted there. He opened it, reached inside, threw a switch . . . and we had light. A line of overhead bulbs lit up an impossibly long tunnel that stretched out to either side of us. Dark pipes ran the length of the tunnel for as far as I could see. It was dizzying. We were standing at the foot of metal stairs, surrounded by electric juncture boxes.

"The survivors tapped the electricity that powers the Ravinian's underground train," Mark explained. "It's one of the advantages of living like a shadow."

"Yeah, no electric bills," I said, making a lame joke. Nobody laughed.

"This is the insert point that's closest to the fortress," Mark said. "I've made this trip only once, but it's not like we can get lost. We've got about a mile to go."

He turned right and started walking. Elli followed him and I followed Elli. It was tough getting my bearings after that breakneck cab ride courtesy of our night guide named Maddie. I figured that if we were headed toward the Ravinian fortress, then we were walking under the river. That was kind of creepy. But if this ancient tunnel had lasted through multiple centuries and a devastating war, the odds of it collapsing and trapping us were pretty slim. We didn't say much on our journey. I think we had all retreated into our own heads to prepare for whatever we might find on the other side. Every so often we'd come upon an area where the tunnel widened. These areas seemed to be where connections were made and service people worked. Kind of like crossroads. I could see that these areas had been used as homes. There were crusty, crumpled-up blankets, empty cans of food, and some long-forgotten books.

"Did the homeless live down here?" I asked.

Mark didn't even look back when he answered. "We're all homeless, Bobby."

Oh. Right. I started getting a clearer picture of what life was like for the non-Ravinians on Third Earth. They were in constant fear of being discovered by the Ravinians and lived like rats. They kept to the dark tunnels and could only move around without fear at night. They really were like vampires.

"So sad" was the only comment Elli made.

It wasn't much, but I was glad to hear that she hadn't checked out completely. Her head was with us, in the moment.

Our journey took about half an hour. It felt endless, since there wasn't much to look at. We reached another juncture point, where the only difference between it and all the others was a painted symbol on the cement wall. It was a crudely drawn red star. The star that marked the gates. The Ravinian star. Mark saw that I was staring at it.

"We painted that to mark the spot," Mark explained. "Kind of fits, don't you think?"

I nodded. I knew what he meant. Every trip I had taken through Halla had begun at a spot that was marked by a star. This time would be no different.

Mark continued, "Going up here would get us into the

conclave. You want to start here or check out the chopper factory?"

"I want to see what Antonio saw" was my answer.

"Then we keep moving."

Mark led us another few hundred yards until we came to another juncture. Our last. A narrow, metal ladder led up into the unknown.

"This is where it gets risky," Mark explained. "This is the route we sent Antonio's team on. The maps show that this comes up outside the fortress wall, next to the factory. We're going to climb up to a manhole that's buried under dirt and rubble. The thing is, there's no way to know if a Ravinian guard is standing nearby until we lift it up."

"So we might climb up into the middle of a bunch of dados?" I asked.

"Yeah, pretty much. This is outside the fortress, but it's inside their security perimeter. They don't expect anybody to be popping up out of the dirt. So if we run into somebody, it'll be bad luck."

"And what if our luck is bad?" I asked.

"Then we come out shooting."

I had to smile at my friend's bold statement. He hadn't only grown up, he'd become a guerrilla. "Are you sure you're Mark Dimond?" I asked.

He laughed. "I haven't been sure of anything for years. You guys ready?"

I looked to Elli. She nodded.

Mark went to another electric panel. "Gotta kill the lights. Too risky to leave them burning. Put your hands on the ladder."

Elli and I grabbed the ladder and Mark threw the switch. It was a good thing we were holding the ladder, because the juncture went pitch-black. I couldn't see an inch ahead of me. We would have bumped into one another looking for the ladder in the dark.

"Me first, then Bobby," Mark commanded.

I sensed him move past us and up the ladder.

"You going to be okay?" I asked Elli.

"I'm fine down here" was her answer. "It's what's outside that has me worried."

That made three of us.

We all climbed up. And up. And up. We kept reaching higher levels, where we transferred to other ladders. Luckily, the ambient light grew as we got nearer the surface, so it wasn't like climbing through ink. I kept glancing back, afraid that Elli might freeze. But she was right there with us. No problem. So far, she was rising to the occasion. We hit yet another level, and Mark waited for us to join him.

"This is it," he whispered. "The manhole is at the top of this next ladder. I'll go up and push the cover. Bobby, you stay behind me, but keep your eyes down. Dirt's gonna fall. Once I'm up, I'll check to see if it's clear, then call for you guys to follow."

"I should go first," I suggested. "This was my idea."

I was actually thinking that if we were to climb up under the feet of some dados, I didn't want them to get Mark.

"Sorry. I'm calling the shots here." He cuffed me on the arm. "Besides, I can't let anything happen to the lead Traveler."

I wanted to tell him that he didn't have to worry, but it was clear that his mind was made up.

"Fine. What do we do once we're on top?"

Mark shrugged. "Beats me. The map only gets us to here. After that we wing it."

I turned to Elli and said, "Stay down here on the platform. We'll call for you to come up."

Elli nodded and backed away from the ladder.

"Ready?" Mark asked.

I hitched the two guns up onto my shoulder and nodded. Mark scrambled right up the ladder. I followed close behind. In no time he was at the top. I leaned back and looked up to see the circular outline of the manhole cover. Mark waved for me to look away. I waved back for him to keep going and not worry about me. He shrugged and raised a hand up to the circle. Manhole covers are heavy to begin with, and if this thing was covered with dirt, it must have weighed a ton. I saw Mark strain to push with one hand. It barely budged. He had to use both hands, which wasn't easy while balancing on a ladder. He climbed up one rung higher so he could use his legs as well. Yet again, I was amazed at how much my friend had changed. He was now a powerful, confident guy. I hoped he was powerful enough to get us the heck out of there. I was about to climb up, to see if I could help, when I felt the first trickle of dirt fall in my eyes. I looked away, and not a second too soon because Mark had the cover in motion and a load of dirt hit me on my head. I saw Elli on the platform, looking up. She had to step back to avoid getting hit with the dirt shower. The sound of metal raking across metal meant that Mark was pushing the cover aside. More dirt fell on my head, but I didn't care. I wanted out of there. Fast. If there were any dados hanging around, we were in the worst possible position.

The scraping stopped and so did the cascade of dirt. I took a chance and looked up, to see a crescent of gray sky. Mark didn't waste time admiring the sight. He popped his head up and did a quick three-sixty around.

"Bring her up," he whispered down to me.

I looked down to Elli and motioned for her to climb. By the time I looked back up, Mark was already gone. I climbed quickly and squeezed myself through the sliver of an opening. Mark was right next to me, on his belly, his head near the open manhole.

"Stay down," he whispered. "It's clear, but who knows for how long?"

I scrambled out and got down on the ground next to Mark. The whole world looked gray, mostly because of the early-morning light that comes before the warm rays of the sun sneak over the horizon. We were in a wide alley between two high walls that ran parallel to each other. One, I realized, was the outer wall of the Ravinian fortress. It towered high over us like a skyscraper. I guessed that we were a couple hundred yards back from the front wall where the huge doors were. This wall had no doors. Or windows. Or anything. It was a sheer, stone facade that looked more like a giant dam than a wall. About thirty yards across from the fortress was the wall of another building. This wasn't anywhere near as tall. I'd say it was about four stories high. But it was still pretty huge. We were maybe fifty yards from the front of this building, but it stretched back the other way for several hundred more. I looked at the massive building, then to Mark.

He nodded. He knew what I was thinking.

"Yeah," he whispered. "The factory."

The best news was that there wasn't a dado in sight. We had made it through what Mark thought was the riskiest part of the trip. I had no doubt there would be plenty of risks ahead to make up for it.

Elli poked her head up out of the hole. Mark and I quickly

helped her out. After she was safely up, we struggled to push the manhole back into place and brushed dirt over it to hide our tracks. The ground between the walls was nothing but dirt, which made it easy to rebury the cover. We made sure to spread the dirt around enough to disguise the manhole. If somebody was looking for it, they'd probably find it. But if a random dado walked by, I was confident they wouldn't uncover anything. The whole time we were disguising the manhole I was thinking how there was no way we'd be able to use it to get out of there. Especially if we had to find it in a hurry. When it was time to get back to the city, we were going to have to find another route.

Mark was already scanning the building, looking for a way in. There were no windows in this wall either. No way to get a quick peek inside. It looked to me like the little brother of the much larger Ravinian conclave across from it. There was a set of double doors near the front of the building. Next to the doors was a metal ladder that ran up to the roof. We didn't need to discuss it. This was where we had to go. I looked to Elli. She nodded that she was okay, but her eyes were wild. She was scared. I was afraid that she was barely holding it together.

I motioned for Mark to go first. He jumped up and scampered to the wall of the factory and the double doors. I held Elli's arm and helped her run after him. My other hand was on the straps of the two rifles. I'd have preferred to have one of them pointed and ready, but I couldn't do that, hold the other strap, and guide Elli all at the same time. I had to trust that if a shot needed to be taken quickly, Mark would take it.

We got to the door in seconds. Mark tried it. It was locked.

"I guess that would have been too easy," he said with a shrug.

He tried to force it open. No go.

I looked at the ladder.

"We could climb, or we could head around the corner of this building to look for another door. I'm thinking that the longer we spend sneaking around, the better chance we'll be seen."

Mark didn't wait for any other opinions. He slung his rifle over his shoulder and climbed the ladder.

"One more climb," I said to Elli with a weak smile.

She went right after Mark. I was last in line. Climbing this ladder was hairier than any of the others. For one, we were totally exposed. Anybody coming by would spot us in a nanosecond. It was scary, too. Underground it was safe and closed. Out here we clung to the side of a building with nothing around us but air. We probably would have been hurt just as badly if we had fallen when we were down below, but being out in the open made this seem much more dangerous. I guess it's like the difference between walking a tightrope that's two inches off the ground . . . or thirty feet up. I made a point of not looking down.

We made it to the top with no problem. When I reached the lip and stepped onto the flat roof, I gasped. I actually gasped. The building was huge. Seeing one side wall didn't give the full perspective. Up on top we could see the whole thing, and there was a lot to see. The roof was completely flat, broken up by various air ducts and skylights that dotted the surface. From the front corner we could pretty much see to the far side. It was a long way away. The building was probably twice as long as it was wide. It was an enormous, sprawling structure.

"You could make a whole lot of helicopters here," I pointed out.

"I guess you need a lot to hunt down seventy thousand people," Mark added.

"Let's go see," I said, and jogged off.

We were totally exposed up there, but what else could we do? I ran toward the closest skylight, hoping it would give us access. The glass window looked like a small greenhouse structure on top of the flat roof. I got there first and peered down for my first look inside.

Sure enough, there were several rows of gleaming black, brand-spanking-new helicopters lined up, ready to fly. Each had rocket launchers in front. These choppers were assault weapons, no doubt about it.

Elli and Mark joined me and looked down.

"Wow," Mark exclaimed. "Armed for bear, too."

"It's monstrous," Elli gasped, numb.

A few feet beyond the skylight, I spotted a hatch with a handle. I grabbed the metal loop and pulled. The hatch opened.

"I guess they don't expect anybody dropping in from up here," I remarked.

Inside the building another small ladder led down to a metal catwalk. I climbed down first, then helped Elli. The catwalk ran along the wall, high above the factory floor. From inside we could look down to see the entire fleet of choppers. Or whatever it is you call a bunch of helicopters. They were all new. They were all armed. They were all ready for their deadly mission.

"Look," Mark said. "They're making even more."

He pointed to the far side of the space, where we saw several more helicopters in various stages of construction.

"Yikes. How many do they think they need?" Mark asked.

"Seventy thousand people is a lot of people" was my sober answer.

I scanned the vast factory floor, trying to take it all in. It was then that something struck me.

"This might get worse," I announced.

Mark said, "Worse than a few dozen attack helicopters armed with rockets?"

"I mean, this isn't the whole factory." I pointed to the right, which was the direction the building had stretched out before us when we were on the roof. "What we're seeing here isn't even half the factory. Look at the far wall. No way that's the end of the building. There's more beyond that. A lot more."

"Could there be even more helicopters?" Elli asked.

I saw that the catwalk continued on along the wall, high above the factory floor.

"Let's find out," I said, and moved quickly along the metal walkway.

I took one of the guns off my shoulder and held it against my hip, ready to shoot. I kept glancing to the factory floor to see if any workers or dados might be down there to sound an alarm. The place seemed deserted. I figured it might have been a day off. Did dados take a day off? Or maybe it was too early for the first shift to begin. After all, the sun had barely come up. We passed row after row of the attack helicopters. I was already planning some way to sabotage them. Maybe the rockets on board could be fired and that would create a chain reaction. Or something. We had to figure out some way of grounding this fleet of killing machines.

We made the long walk to the far wall, and to a door

that would lead us to whatever was beyond. I grabbed the door handle and turned. It was unlocked. I turned back to the others.

"You think we can do some damage down there?" I asked Mark.

Mark shrugged. "I don't see why not. There's plenty of live ammo around. Of course, if we start making noise, they'll know we're here."

"You think?" I chuckled.

I opened the door, stepped into the next factory space . . .

And all thoughts of helicopters left my head.

I dropped the rifle. That's how stunned I was. My arms went limp. The weapon clattered onto the metal walkway. I left it there, taking a few dazed steps forward, as if getting closer might make the image before me clearer, and prove it wasn't what it seemed to be. I hoped it was an optical illusion. Or a trick. Or anything other than what it looked to be.

There was a question I'd often wondered about but never bothered to try and answer. Since leaving home, I had to learn about and understand so many impossible things that some of them I just had to let go. It's how I felt about unique technology on all the territories. I never really wondered or cared about how they created power on Ibara. Or how the air globes of Cloral were created. Or what advanced technology would allow something like Lifelight to exist, or the amber crystals on Eelong that carried radio signals. These were all aspects of the territories that were interesting, but didn't need to be analyzed unless it could help us on our mission.

The same held true for what we saw on that factory floor. This is what Antonio and his team had discovered. This is what he meant when he said the Ravinians had been preparing to attack.

It had nothing to do with helicopters.

The factory did indeed go on. This second section had to be three times the size of the area that held the choppers. The lame choppers. The choppers that now seemed like toys compared to what faced us on that factory floor. I now had the answer to a question I'd never asked.

I now knew where the dados were made.

We stood above a sea of thousands of dado warriors. Shoulder to shoulder. Heel to toe. Row upon row upon perfect row. They were dressed in various uniforms. Some wore the green military-like uniforms with gold helmets from Quillan. Another whole section had on the deep red suits that showed them to be Ravinian guards. One huge section held dados that didn't have uniforms, but instead were dressed in normal clothing that would easily allow them to blend in with the people of Second Earth.

There was more. I saw dados dressed as Batu warriors and Bedoowan knights. Some wore the rags that made them look like Flighters from Ibara. Maybe the most jarring of all was the section of klees. They actually made dado cats.

As with the helicopters, one whole section of floor was an assembly line that held hundreds of dados that were yet to be completed. There were more to come. Many more. I saw multiple rows of legs and arms and hands—all waiting to be used to create more robotic warriors.

The dados all had the same, blank expression. Many were still made in Mark's image, but others branched out with different looks. The dados were looking more human than ever. But they weren't. They were machines. They were Saint Dane's army.

"This is what Antonio found," I said with a dry mouth. "This is how they're going to attack."

Mark looked just as stunned as I felt. "There could be seventy thousand exiles, or *seven hundred* thousand. It won't matter. They can't stand up to this army."

I went into brain lock. I didn't know what to do. About the dados. About Halla. About the exiles. I didn't even know what to do in the next second. I was frozen.

Wump!

A dull but powerful sound tore through the dead quiet. An instant later, a dado that had been creeping toward us along the catwalk fell off and plummeted to the factory floor. It looked like a mannequin because it was already dead. It hit, bounced, and crumbled like a doll. Mark and I both looked back in surprise to see Elli standing behind us with the gun I had dropped. She had it braced against her hip, her finger on the trigger.

She had dropped the dado with a single shot.

"Pick up your guns," she commanded with confidence. "They know we're here."

22

I don't know what was more stunning: finding the vast army of dados, knowing that we had been discovered and were in for a fight, or seeing Elli with a rifle on her hip after having blown away a dado.

I think it was Elli.

"Move!" she barked.

Mark and I both jumped to the side of the narrow walkway as Elli unloaded again. She shot from the hip, literally. She held the weapon at waist level, the butt against her hip. The rifle let out another dull *wump* as it discharged. For a fleeting instant I thought I sensed the charged particle as it shot past us. Maybe I'm crazy, but I could swear the hair went up on the back of my neck, as if I had been brushed by static electricity. A second later another dado was blown off its feet. It landed square on its back on the metal walkway. Dead. Done. Lights out. Whatever.

Farther ahead on the catwalk, more dados in red Ravinian outfits appeared and sprinted toward us.

"Back to the roof," I commanded.

We turned to run back the way we had come. Elli led the

way, her rifle out and ready to fire again. Who knew? We got as far as the doorway that led back into the helicopter section of the factory when Elli pulled up.

"They must have seen us on the roof," she gasped.

Sure enough, on the far side of the chopper factory, a dozen dados came flooding down the same ladder we had used to get down from the roof. We were trapped between two groups who were closing fast.

"Twenty-eight shots left," Mark said coolly.

"What if there's twenty-nine of them?" I asked.

"There's twenty-nine *thousand* of them!" Mark exclaimed.

"Climb down," Elli announced.

Without waiting for our opinions, Elli scrambled for a ladder no more than ten feet ahead of us that led down to the factory floor. She swung the rifle over her shoulder as if she had done it a thousand times before and quickly made her way down the ladder.

Mark looked at me with surprise, as if to ask, "Who woke *her* up?"

I shot past Mark and went for the ladder. The catwalk was high over the factory floor. The narrow ladder ran straight down with nothing around it but air. If we hadn't been on the run, I'm not so sure I'd have been able to climb down as quickly as I was. One slip and it would be over. As much as I didn't want to look down, this time I had to. We had to know if any bad boys were arriving below. I looked out over the sea of dados and my stomach flipped. It was like descending into a tank of piranhas. There were thousands of them. It was insanity. We were running away from a handful of dados toward an entire army. At least the army hadn't been activated. I hoped that they were no more dangerous than statues.

My foot slipped off a rung. I had to clutch the sides of

the thin, metal ladder or I would have fallen through. It was a dumb mistake. I was more worried about what we would find on the floor than about getting there safely. I had to force myself to look ahead and concentrate on my footing. One step at a time. Don't worry about the dados. There would be time for that soon enough.

I met Elli on the ground, followed shortly after by Mark. We all had our guns out and ready. But ready for what?

"They're coming down," Mark announced.

A quick look up showed that the dados from the roof had reached the ladder and were coming after us. The dados already on the catwalk were getting closer. I was happy to see that they didn't have weapons. At least they couldn't take shots at us from the high ground.

"Are you okay?" Elli asked me. She was focused and in control.

"I'm fine," I said, a little embarrassed. It made me realize that Elli wasn't the frail old lady I thought she was. What's that saying? "When the going gets tough, the tough get going"? Well, Elli was on her way.

"We've gotta find another way out of here," Mark announced.

The two groups of dados were about to join up and descend on us. I looked around but there wasn't an obvious way out. It became very clear, very fast, that there was only one thing to do.

"Needle in a haystack," I declared.

Mark looked at the sea of dados and smiled. He got it. "Right."

"What does that mean?" Elli asked.

"We'll get lost in the dados," I said. "C'mon."

The three of us ran for the army. They may have been

dados, but they looked like people. And there were thousands of them. Some even looked like Mark. My hope was to get far enough into the ranks so that the dados who were after us wouldn't know which way we had gone. It seemed like the best way to buy a little time until we could find a way out of that factory. The three of us plunged into the line of robots, barely grazing them as we moved as quickly and quietly as we could without knocking any of them over. We all knew enough not to speak. That would have defeated the purpose and given us away. Without planning it, we relied on hand signals.

Mark was on my right. Elli on my left. I took the lead and motioned for Mark to start moving diagonally toward the right. We made our way along, one dado width apart from one another. We didn't even have to duck down, because the dados were all at least a few inches taller than I was, and I was the tallest of the three of us. Still, I crouched a little, just in case. In seconds we were deep among the dados. I looked back to see if we were being followed. I was sure that we were, but they would have no way of tracking us. I didn't relax, but we had bought a little breathing room.

Moving through the field of dados was one of the eeriest things I'd ever done. Dados weren't human, but they sure looked like it. They were inactive, but looked as if they could spring to life at any second. I tried not to look at them too closely. I pretended they were statues and we were running through a museum. A really twisted museum where the exhibits might suddenly jump us.

Sheesh. Thinking like that wasn't helpful.

We kept moving quickly, putting as much space between us and our pursuers as possible. Every so often I motioned for everyone to change direction slightly, so we weren't moving in a straight line. The idea was to make it as tough as possible to track us. When I felt as if we were roughly in the middle of the dado sea, I motioned for the others to stop. I put my fingers to my lips to be sure they stayed quiet. We stood stock-still and listened. I wanted to know where the pursuing dados were. Strangely, we didn't hear anything. Had they stopped chasing us? From where we were, we could see up to the catwalk. It was empty. They were definitely on the factory floor. But where?

I got paranoid. Our plan was to hide ourselves among the dados, but it worked both ways. If the robots chasing us got close, we wouldn't see them until they were almost on us. They could be anywhere. They could be hiding from us as much as we were hiding from them, and we might not know they were on top of us until it was too late. We may have been like needles in a haystack, but they were like needles . . . in a stack of needles.

I scanned around, looking for any sign of movement. There was nothing. I motioned for the others to keep moving, but slowly. After a few more zigzagging steps, we came upon an open space where no dados were lined up. It looked to me like the spot where the dados first came off the assembly line. There was a conveyor belt that led down and under the floor to somewhere else. The space was ringed by silent dados who wore the dark green uniforms of the dados from Quillan, complete with golden helmets. They circled the open area, all facing the center. Pointed at us. It made my skin crawl.

When Mark saw the conveyor belt, he smiled. He was thinking the same thing I was. We might be able to follow the belt out of there. Wherever it would take us, it would be better than where we were, since we couldn't hide from the dados forever.

I got Elli's attention and pointed to the belt. She nodded. That was our way out. We made our move for the opening that led down below, when I quickly held my hand up, stopping everyone again. I had sensed something. Some movement. I did a three-sixty and saw nothing but the ring of inactive, mute dados. But I knew I had sensed something. It was fleeting, and I had only caught it out of the corner of my eye, but it was real. My Mooraj training was telling me so. Something was there. But where? Were there dados just outside this clearing, stalking us, getting ready to pounce? I stood stock-still. I wasn't looking for anything, so much as trying to sense something.

It happened again. This time I was ready for it. The movement wasn't on the floor. It was above us. I looked up quickly to see what looked to be a control room that hung down from the ceiling. It was an octagon, with glass windows surrounding it. It would be easy to see the entire dado-factory floor from up there, and that's exactly what the person inside was doing.

There was a dark figure inside, looking down on us. I couldn't tell who or what it was, but it was definitely active, and I had no doubt that it was looking right at us. Mark and Elli saw where I was looking and looked up as well. We all froze. What was this guy going to do? Sound an alarm? Direct the pursuing dados to our position? I didn't want to stick around to find out.

"Let's go," I commanded.

The need for secrecy was over. We ran for the conveyor belt and the hole that would take us below.

We didn't make it.

No sooner did we start to run than the lights in the

control room came on. I guess he didn't feel the need for secrecy anymore either. He also didn't feel the need to tell the few dados who were chasing us where we were. That was because he had plenty more to take their place.

All around us, the green-suited dados came to life. One second they were standing like statues. The next their heads slowly turned . . . and looked at us.

"It's the dado control room," Mark gasped. "He's turning them on."

The horrible truth of those words took a second to sink in. Whoever was up in that control tower was doing just that. Controlling. It was Dado Central. He had the ability to activate the dados. There were thousands of them, and all we had left were twenty-eight shots.

The dados closed in.

And we opened fire.

"Go for the ones near the conveyor," I ordered.

Wump! Wump! Wump!

All three of us let loose. The kick was a lot stronger than I expected. Each time I pulled the trigger, the gun bucked and punched me in the hip. The air instantly felt charged with electricity. Dados crumpled, one after the other. Elli was just as aggressive as Mark and I. She kept her rifle close to her hip and her eyes on her quarry . . . which wasn't hard, because there were plenty of them.

"Keep moving!" Mark shouted.

The dados weren't armed. If they had been, it would have been over in seconds. Even without weapons, our only hope was to keep them off of us long enough to escape down into the hole. Mark and Elli concentrated on the dados near the conveyor. I spun around and fired at those who were creeping up from behind.

Wump! Wump!

They fell, one after another. No sooner did one fall than two more came to life, turned, and moved toward us. It was like something out of *Night of the Living Dead*, except the dados weren't going to eat us. At least I didn't think they were.

We were moving closer to the conveyor tunnel, but not by much.

"If you can travel, get out of here!" Mark shouted at us.

No way that would happen. I couldn't leave Mark to the wolves. But Elli didn't need to be there.

"Go," I said to Elli. "Back to Solara."

Elli ignored me and kept firing. It was like she was possessed. She had a steely look in her eye that reminded me of her daughter. She was scared, no doubt, but it also seemed like she was taking some pleasure in blowing the dados away. She had been through a lot. Maybe she was taking some small measure of revenge. Whatever it was, she wasn't leaving.

"Elli! Go!"

She gave me a quick look and shouted, "We're almost there."

She backed toward the opening in the floor, firing as she went. There wasn't time to argue. Dados were closing in on her from the other side of the conveyor belt. I spun and fired to keep them back. Aim wasn't all that important. The charged particles that these weapons fired seemed to fan out like buckshot. Close was close enough. I dropped a dado with one shot, and saw a second fall at the same time. I fired again and dropped two more. But we were running out of ammunition, and time.

Elli's gun emptied first. Without hesitation she dropped the weapon, turned to jump into the hole . . .

And was blown off her feet by a shot from another weapon that was fired from somewhere else. She let out a sharp gasp, as if she had been punched in the stomach. She hurtled backward and hit the floor, hard, square on her back. I think she was unconscious before she landed. I had the brief feeling of relief that she hadn't been turned to cinder. Whatever hit her, it wasn't the same kind of charge that we had seen from the silver weapons in the Taj Mahal. But where had it come from?

I glanced up to the control tower to see someone inside with a rifle up and on his shoulder, leaning out of an open window like a sniper. No doubt he was the guy who shot Elli, and he was swinging the rifle toward me. I lifted my own weapon quickly and fired off three quick shots. I didn't worry about aim. The sight of Elli being so violently thrown by a shot from that guy made me lose it. I wanted him to suffer.

One of the windows of the control tower exploded from my first shot. The second hit the guy and knocked him back into the control room. The third blasted out a second window.

As I ran to help Ellie, I yelled to Mark, "Jump in the hole!"

Mark was out of ammunition. He fired two more times with no result, then threw his rifle at the approaching dados. No sooner did it leave his hands than he was knocked off his feet by another shot. I looked back up to the control tower to see another sniper leaning out of one of the windows I had shattered. Unlike his pal, he didn't hesitate to admire his marksmanship. By the time I looked up, he was already aiming at me. I was staring square into the barrel of one of those black weapons.

I lifted my own.

Wump.

I never fired. I didn't get the chance. My entire body went rigid. It felt like being Tasered by the Ravinian guards when Alder and I arrived at the Sherwood mansion on Second Earth. I'm sure I hit the floor, but I don't remember it, because an instant after feeling the jolt, I was unconscious.

Waking up from being rudely separated from consciousness is never easy. I should know. It's happened to me often enough. There's that initial feeling of disconnection, followed by the pain of whatever event caused the lights to go out, followed by the desperate need to understand exactly where I had landed and what situation I'd have to deal with. This time was no different. Once I started becoming aware of my surroundings, the first thing I realized was that I was paralyzed. I couldn't move. Not a pinkie. I didn't panic. I hadn't pulled far enough away from the land of the unconscious to feel as if it were anything permanent. I had been through this enough times to know I had to bring my brain back online before I could expect it to control my body.

One thing was clear. I may have been the illusion that Saint Dane said I was, but at that moment my body felt all too real. I hurt every bit as much as if I had been born in Stony Brook, Connecticut, instead of in some alternate universe filled with spirits. At that moment I kind of wished I was a little more spiritlike and a little less humanlike.

I opened my eyes and tried to focus. There wasn't a dado in sight, which meant I was no longer in that factory. I was flat on my back and looking up at a ceiling covered with white tiles. Was this a hospital? It didn't seem like a prison. I moved my head, which meant I wasn't paralyzed.

At least not from the neck up, anyway. Mark was lying next to me, still unconscious. Someone had covered us with dark green blankets. I saw that we were lying on thin mats and not directly on the floor. That was good. At least we were being treated semi-okay.

I felt control slowly returning. I twisted my head around to see that we were in a large, empty room. Windows were set high near the ceiling. There would be no way to get out that way. The walls were covered with ornate tiles that created mosaic patterns. If this was a prison, it was a fancy one. I rolled my head the other way and saw that someone was standing by the only door.

Nevva Winter.

"You'll be fine," she said without compassion. "The effects are temporary, which is better than what those weapons do to the dados. Where did you get them, by the way?"

Nevva wore a dark outfit that kind of reminded me of Saint Dane's black suit. But not quite as severe looking. She had a cloth belt that tied at the waist and an open collar. It looked more like a dark warm-up suit. Her hair was tied back too, which was different from the way she'd worn it on Quillan. This was more casual and made her look almost human. Still, she had those piercing eyes that made me remember just how cold and calculating she could be.

"Water?" she asked.

Elli. Where was Elli? I forced myself up to my elbows and scanned the room. Another body was lying against a far wall. Her face was covered, but I saw the end of Elli's gray ponytail poking out from beneath the blanket that was over her. She was here, but still unconscious. I hoped that the effects of the blast hadn't hurt her.

"No," I answered.

Nevva walked toward me. "Why did you come back?"

I put on my best smile. "I missed you."

Nevva didn't appreciate the sarcasm. She glared at me. "It's over, Pendragon," she said with a touch of impatience. "Halla has fallen. Anything that you and the Travelers do now is futile."

"So then you won't mind that we hang around a little longer," I replied.

"You can do whatever you like, but why would you bring Mark here and put him in jeopardy? That's just irresponsible. He's your friend."

I gave her a surprised look and said, "Wow. Do you really care?"

Nevva grimaced and turned away. It struck me that she hadn't said anything about Elli. Did she even know that her mother was lying only a few feet away? It didn't seem like it.

"Leave, Pendragon," Nevva said. "Take your friends with you and find someplace safe for them to live."

She said "your friends." She didn't know that Elli was one of them. I had to figure out a way to use that to our advantage. I also had to figure out a way to learn what Nevva knew about the exiles.

"Sorry," I said. "Monkeying with Saint Dane is a hard habit to break. I think I'll keep at it."

"But it's over!" she repeated with a touch of frustration. "Surely you understand that. You're fighting a war that has ended. The territories are no longer. Every world in Halla has been cleansed. There's nothing left to do now but rebuild."

I sat up. "Cleansed? Is that what you call it? What you mean is that the people Saint Dane considers worthy are living the life, and everybody else has either been killed or will be soon."

"We have rewarded excellence," Nevva said patiently. "That has been the vision from the beginning. Nothing has happened to the rest of the people of Halla that they didn't bring about themselves."

"You're kidding, right? Saint Dane manipulated the people of seven worlds into making decisions that led to their own destruction, and you're saying it's *their* fault? That's like pushing a puppy out into traffic and saying it was his own fault that he got hit by a car. Give me a break!"

Nevva took a breath. She was trying to control her emotions. "I know you don't feel that a guided future is right. You believe that people should be free to choose their own destiny. But time and again the people of Halla have chosen poorly. And not just where Saint Dane was involved. The people of Halla were flawed, and I have no doubt that if Saint Dane never intervened, their destruction would have occurred anyway. This way, we have separated those who are worthy of rebuilding Halla and protected them from those who are not. I know, the worlds of Halla are in shambles, but it was necessary. This is only the beginning. We are going to make it right this time, Pendragon. We are going to create Utopia."

I stood up. My head hurt and my legs weren't working that well, but I didn't want to be sitting on the floor to have this discussion. I wanted to be on Nevva's level.

"What about the dado attack on Ibara?" I asked. "Did the people of Ibara bring that on themselves?"

Nevva blinked. She didn't answer right away. I had struck a chord.

"They created the situation that allowed for it to happen," she finally answered.

"No, they didn't!" I shot right back. "They saw that

their society was in trouble, looked ahead, and did exactly the kind of thing that you're talking about. They created Ibara as a way to save Veelox. And they were going to succeed, until Saint Dane convinced the Flighters to attack and destroy the pilgrim ships, and then invaded the island with dados. Where was his grand vision there? The dado attack was sent as a conquering army. Plain and simple. It wasn't the people of Veelox who let that happen. It was all Saint Dane. How do you explain that?"

For the first time since I'd known her, Nevva looked unsure of herself. "It . . . it was about you, Pendragon. It was intended to put you to the test, and you failed."

"So what if I did? I'm not even from Halla! What was I being tested for?"

"The ends justified the means," she complained.

"No!" I shouted back at her. "You can't tell me this is all about doing what is best for Halla. Maybe at one time that's what Saint Dane thought. Maybe on some philosophical level he was right. Who knows? But it's not about that anymore. It's about his own selfish goals. He wants to be king, Nevva. No, he wants to be a god. He wants to create his own Halla. It's the ultimate power play. He's living in a palace. He likes being human. Look how he's changed himself. He's developed vanity. He wants to look good. Don't you see that? That's why he sent conquering armies, and that's why he's built another army of dados to do it again. Whatever noble thoughts he may have had at one time have been corrupted. If you think he's got any other goal than to be a god, you're kidding yourself."

Nevva looked stunned. I couldn't believe that my words had hit her that strongly. No way. She was too firmly committed to her mission to let a little argument like this change her mind. But something I had said got through, and shook her.

"What do you mean, 'he's built another army'?" she asked tentatively.

"Oh, please," I shot back. "Don't pretend like you don't know."

"Don't know what?"

"We saw the factory, Nevva. Where do you think we got shot by the dados?"

"You were found in the helicopter plant."

"Yeah, the helicopter plant that also happens to be building about eighty thousand dados. What do you think they're for? Washing windows and doing all the little chores you Ravinians think are beneath you? I'm not an idiot."

Nevva was shaken. Really shaken. I didn't think she was a good enough actor to fake that. And why would she want to? As far as she was concerned, the battle was over.

"Are you serious?" I asked without sarcasm. "You didn't know about the new army of dados out there, all polished up and ready to go?"

Nevva's eyes told the story. She really didn't know. It was a total surprise to her. She was about to get another one.

"Nevva," came a thin voice.

Nevva didn't look at first. She kept looking at me, but I saw the change in her eyes. She had heard a voice from the past. One I'm sure she never expected to hear again, and certainly not in a dim room on Third Earth. She held my gaze, silently asking if what she had heard was real. I motioned for her to look. Nevva had trouble turning away from me. It was as if she were fighting the pull of a magnet that wouldn't let her turn. But she had to.

Slowly Nevva turned to face her mother.

Elli was on her feet. She stood across from Nevva, tall and straight. Mother and daughter. It was like looking at the same person, though one was several years older. They locked eyes. Nevva opened her mouth to speak, but no words came out. Elli looked strong. Stronger than I'd ever seen her. As tough as it must have been to be reunited with her daughter this way, Elli was up to it. I was proud of her. My fears about her not being able to handle the situation were gone. Elli didn't say another word. I think she wanted Nevva to speak first.

Nevva was finally able to croak out, "Why are you here, Mother?"

Elli's answer was to haul off and slap her daughter across the face.

It was totally unexpected.

And totally awesome.

I wanted to bottle the moment to remember it forever. Unfortunately, something happened that made the sweetness short-lived. We heard a voice come from the doorway. A tall man with long dark hair stood in the frame.

"My," Saint Dane said with mock dismay. "Not exactly a touching reunion."

23

The demon strolled into the room as if he owned it. Which he did, I guess. He wore the same deep red, princely costume I had seen him in earlier. It still threw me to see his new look, complete with long black hair and the elegant suit. His eyes hadn't changed though. They still cut right through me.

"I feel sorry for you, Pendragon," he said with an air of superiority that made my blood boil. I guess I should have been used to it. "You've made such a valiant effort for so long, it pains me to see you unable to let go."

"Let go of what?" I snarled.

"Your coming back here smacks of denial. It's a pathetic attempt to prolong a battle that has long been over. And who do you bring along to help you on this desperate mission? A feeble woman. Is this what the mighty Travelers have come to?"

Elli ignored him. Her eyes were still fixed on Nevva. Nevva held her hand to her stinging cheek and looked to the floor. It was the first time I had seen Nevva Winter cowed. Instead of lashing back, she'd taken the slap as if she knew she deserved it. Her reaction to seeing her mother was what I hoped it would be. So far.

When Saint Dane reached Elli, he leaned down to her and whispered, "Did that make you feel better? Did it take away the pain of knowing the daughter you abandoned grew up to be one of the bad guys?"

It was a vicious thing to say. I wanted to hit him myself. I expected Elli to whirl and land one on him. Instead, she did something I never would have expected. She stepped forward and took Nevva into her arms. She closed her eyes and hugged her daughter.

"I miss you," she whispered.

Nevva didn't hug back, but she didn't pull away, either. There were tears in her eyes, though I couldn't tell if they were tears of emotion, or from getting whacked in the face.

"That's more like it!" Saint Dane exclaimed with sarcastic joy. "Together again! The woman who turned her back on her own destiny and the girl who never should have been." He smiled, as if realizing something for the first time. "Never been. Is that the origin of the name Nevva? How appropriate."

Elli held on to Nevva, but answered Saint Dane. "I do not regret having given birth to my daughter."

"No?" Saint Dane taunted. "The union between a creature of Halla and a spirit from Solara is just . . . unnatural. Then again, it is typical of your way of thinking. No thought to what is right. Or to the future consequences of your actions." He looked right at me and declared, "And yet you still wonder why you've lost the battle."

Saint Dane walked toward Mark, who hadn't yet budged. I'd almost forgotten about him. "Go away, Pendragon. Go back to your dying world and stop fighting a battle you lost so long ago."

Nevva gently pulled away from Elli. She stood up straight, regaining her composure. "Is it true?" she called to Saint Dane.

Saint Dane glanced at her. "Are you speaking to me?" he asked with surprise.

"The dado army," Nevva continued. "Pendragon says that you have created another large force."

Saint Dane stared at Nevva as if he couldn't believe she was questioning him. He stepped away from Mark to face her. "*I* have not created a large force. *We* have. Ravinia has. You are part of Ravinia, or have you forgotten?"

"Of course I haven't forgotten. I just don't understand why I wasn't informed."

"I'm sorry, Nevva. I wasn't aware that I needed to consult you on every decision I make. Forgive me." His comment dripped with sarcasm.

"To what end?" Nevva persisted.

This was getting interesting. Nevva was questioning Saint Dane. I'd never heard anyone do that before. Other than me, of course.

Saint Dane stiffened. "I don't believe I appreciate your tone, sweet Nevva."

Nevva left her mother and walked toward Saint Dane. She stood directly in front of him, still waiting for a direct answer. I was mesmerized.

"Must we discuss this here?" he asked in a low voice. He stole a quick look to me, as if to check whether I was watching.

I didn't budge, but my pulse was racing. Nevva was actually challenging Saint Dane. I wondered if it was because of the way he had insulted Elli. Or because he had more or less called her an unnatural mutant. Didn't matter to me either way. I was loving it. Saint Dane was off balance. That didn't happen often. Nevva had drawn blood. I figured I should rub some salt into the wound.

"It's a good question," I said. "If this war is over, why are you building another army?"

Saint Dane walked to me and looked me in the eye. He was still taller than I was, but not by much. I wasn't threatened by his physical presence anymore. I didn't flinch.

"Because I can" was his simple, blunt answer.

I chuckled.

"You find that amusing?" he asked.

I turned my back to him and faced Nevva. "See? Whatever lofty ideals this guy had, they are long gone. Now it's all about power. *His* power." I imitated him, saying, "'*Because I can*'! Ooh! What a badass!" I looked back to Saint Dane and scoffed. "Look at him. New hair. New face. Living in a palace. An outfit that makes him look like some goofy Disney prince—not that you know what that is, but trust me, it's a joke." I stood next to Elli and continued, "And he isn't above insulting a harmless lady like your mom. I don't know what kind of new Halla you think he's going to create, Nevva, but if you believe he's worried about anything more than elevating himself to some exalted position of power, you're dreaming."

Nevva looked unsure. For her, that was huge.

Elli must have seen it too. "There's still time, Nevva," she said. "You can still do the right thing."

"No!" Nevva snapped at her mother. "You don't have the right to say that. You gave that up a long time ago."

"Not because I wanted to," Elli replied. The words pained her. "I wasn't capable of raising you."

"But you're capable of jumping around Halla with the Travelers."

Elli dropped her head, as if embarrassed. "It's what I was born to do."

"Really?" Nevva pressed, upset. "What about me? What was I born to do?"

Elli didn't have an answer. She looked defeated.

"I guess that's pretty much what we've been fighting over," I said. "Is our destiny chosen for us? Or do we have a choice in the matter? What do you think, Nevva? If you had to do it all over again, what choices would you make?"

Nevva was shaken up. Things weren't happening the way she expected. She whirled on Saint Dane. "What is the army for?" she demanded.

Saint Dane was back in control. His emotions were in check.

"You know as well as I. As do Pendragon and his kind. Let's drop the charade. The remaining exiles of Ravinia must be dealt with the way that was originally intended."

"No!" Nevva shouted. "We were to leave the territory untouched. Unspoiled. This is not the way!"

"No territory is unspoiled, Nevva," Saint Dane explained patiently. "I was willing to allow you your little experiment, but circumstances have changed. They should have died, Nevva. You know that as well as I. One day we will learn how that mistake occurred, but as of this moment all that matters is that we have located them, and now we must cleanse Halla of their influence."

Nevva was trembling. She looked to be on the verge of tears.

Saint Dane gave her a twisted smile. "Don't you agree?"

Nevva started to answer, but stopped herself. She dropped her eyes to the floor. In a small voice she said, "Of course."

That was it. Everything we feared was true. Saint Dane had found the exiles and was planning to wipe them out. There was only one piece of the puzzle still missing.

"Where are they?" I asked casually.

Saint Dane gave me a sly smile. "Oh? You don't know?"

Oops. I was kind of hoping that since we were going to "drop the charade," everything was out in the open. Guess not. Now Saint Dane knew that we still hadn't found the exiles. I had made a huge tactical blunder.

Saint Dane strolled toward Mark. "I do realize that in large part the situation we now face is of my own doing. I should have seen to it personally that the dissenters from Second Earth were properly handled. But mistakes happen, don't they, Pendragon?"

"You mean you should have personally killed them. Nice. Really glad to hear that you're planning on running your own universe. Should be a real fun place."

Saint Dane shrugged. My sarcasm was lost on him. "No matter. My lack of diligence has only prolonged the inevitable."

"You are just ghastly," Elli gasped.

Nevva kept her eyes on the floor.

Saint Dane continued, "And now I must decide what to do about our situation right here. I don't believe there is anything you can do to stop me, Pendragon. Yet there have been so many times in the past where you have surprised me." He raised a finger and wagged it at me playfully. "You are quite the resourceful young spirit."

I wanted to grab his bony finger and break it off.

"Of course you know that you and Elli can leave here at any time, if you're willing to use what little spirit is left of Solara. I feel confident that you won't."

"Really?" I asked defiantly. "Why's that?"

Saint Dane kicked aside the green blanket that had been covering an unconscious Mark.

"My good friend Mark Dimond. Strangely enough, I've spent more time with him than anyone else in Halla. Even more than you, Pendragon. I've grown quite fond of Mark. Such a pity that I'll have to execute him."

"What!" I screamed.

I went for Saint Dane, but only got two steps closer before I felt strong hands holding me back. Two Ravinian guards had slipped into the room without my realizing it.

"He is part of an annoying group of guerrillas here on Third Earth," Saint Dane explained. "They've stolen weapons, food, even helicopters. Any one of those offenses is punishable by death."

"You can't kill him!" I shouted. I stopped worrying about appearing cool and in control.

Saint Dane looked at me with wide, innocent eyes. "And why not?"

"Because it's murder," I shot back. "And . . . and he was your friend! You may have been using him, but that didn't mean you didn't like each other. I know he liked you. Or Andy Mitchell."

I was out of my mind. I was willing to pretend that Mark's friendship with Andy Mitchell had positive sides to it, that's how desperate I was to save Mark.

I looked to Nevva. "Nevva? Tell me you don't have feelings for Mark. He's a good guy. Hell, he even fits the

Ravinian profile. He's exceptional, isn't he? Geez, he's the father of the dados! He doesn't deserve to die."

Nevva looked at the unconscious Mark on the floor. I saw her soften. She did like Mark. I knew it. Who didn't?

"It isn't right," she said softly to Saint Dane. "Hasn't he suffered enough?"

Saint Dane walked to Nevva. He towered over her. She couldn't look him in the eye. Suddenly Saint Dane snapped out with his right hand and grabbed Nevva roughly by the neck.

Elli gasped. "Stop that!"

He didn't. She had pushed his buttons one too many times. Saint Dane held her tight, lifting her chin so that their eyes met. He spoke in a low growl. "You either believe in the vision or you are no better than the dirt we've worked so hard to wash away. The choice is yours."

"Let her go!" Elli commanded, her voice cracking.

I saw the intensity of the look between Saint Dane and Nevva. They held it for a good long time. I was actually afraid he'd choke the life out of her, that's how long they stayed in that position. Finally Nevva blinked, and nodded in acceptance. Saint Dane let her go. Nevva tried hard not to gasp for breath. She was too proud to show that he had hurt her.

"I believe in the vision," she gasped. "I always have and always will. But I do have opinions and would appreciate the right to voice them."

"As do I," Saint Dane said, back in command. "And my opinion is that Mark Dimond is a rebel enemy of Ravinia and will be put to death."

Nevva shot him a look, but said nothing.

"Do you have a problem with that?" Saint Dane asked.

Nevva shook her head.

"Good. Then you will be pleased to know that the honor of carrying out the execution will be yours, Nevva."

Elli gasped.

Nevva barely reacted, but I saw her eyes go steely.

"Tell me your opinion of that," Saint Dane demanded, taunting.

Nevva answered through clenched teeth. "It is my duty. I only ask that it happen as soon as possible so that he will not suffer."

Saint Dane scoffed, "And before you lose your nerve."

Nevva shot him a steely look. She was definitely back on her game. "Say what you will about me, but I have never lost my nerve."

They held eye contact a moment more. I could tell that Saint Dane was debating about how to respond.

"As you wish," he finally said, dismissing her remark.

He looked down at Mark and gave him a nudge with his foot. Mark stirred and grumbled.

Saint Dane smirked. "Good. I was beginning to think he was already dead." He turned to me and added, "Now, Pendragon. Will you be leaving us?"

I wanted to tear the guy's heart out, and I might have. If he had one.

Saint Dane laughed. "Of course you won't! You will remain here, hoping to find some way to save your friend." He motioned to the door.

Two more Ravinian guards entered.

"Take the rebel," he ordered, gesturing to Mark.

The guards lifted a barely conscious Mark to his feet and dragged him out of the room. Saint Dane glanced around as if looking to see if he'd forgotten anything.

"And so it will be," he said. "Make yourselves comfortable. We will reconvene at the execution."

"Which one?" I asked.

Saint Dane didn't know what I meant at first. He then smiled and wagged his finger at me. "Very good. I'm going to miss you, Pendragon."

He strode for the door, then stopped and turned to Nevva. "Come," he commanded, as if speaking to a dog.

Nevva straightened. The hard look was back. There was no hint of sympathy. Whatever second thoughts we had given her were gone. Nevva Winter was back to her old, cold self.

"I regret this," she said. "But I will not allow my personal feelings to prevent the creation of a new Halla. It is for the greater good. You of all people must understand that concept, Pendragon. Sacrifices must always be made."

"I do understand," I replied. "I just don't believe that Saint Dane's Halla will be good for anybody but himself."

"So you've told me," Nevva replied, sounding tired. She looked to Elli and offered her a quick, curt, "Good-bye, Mother."

She didn't wait for a response and strode for the door where Saint Dane waited.

"I love you, Nevva," Elli called after her.

Nevva hesitated for the shortest of moments, but didn't stop or turn back. She strode past Saint Dane and out the door.

Saint Dane snickered and gestured to the remaining dados. The two guards let go of me and followed Saint Dane out. The door was slammed behind them. I heard the sound of the lock being thrown. The two of us stood there, dazed. I put my arm around Elli. She buried her face in my shoulder and cried.

"I'm sorry I brought you back," I said, trying to console her. "It was a mistake."

"What are we going to do?" she asked.

"Exactly what Saint Dane expects us to do. We're going to save Mark."

24

Saint Dane knew what he was doing. As usual.

He knew I wouldn't leave if Mark was in trouble. In spite of what Nevva had asked for, I was sure he would play out this execution for as long as possible in order to keep us there. That was pretty clear. What wasn't clear was when he planned on launching his dado attack on the exiles. Or where. I figured the exiles had to be on Third Earth, because the flumes were destroyed and Saint Dane had no way of sending his army to any other territory. So then, where were they? Somewhere in the destroyed New York City?

The logistics made sense, but I tried to make sense of the exchange that Saint Dane and Nevva had about her "little experiment" and her wanting to leave the territory where the exiles landed "unspoiled." Third Earth had definitely been touched and wasn't even close to unspoiled. Did that mean the exiles were somewhere else? And what was Nevva's experiment? Even if we knew the answers to those questions, I had no idea how we could stop an army of dados. We could always go back to Solara and rally the rest of the Travelers, but even with the warriors among us, there was no way we could stop an army.

On top of everything else, my plan to have Elli try and get Nevva to see reason had backfired. All it did was upset Elli and put Mark in danger. I guess it's an understatement to say that things were looking bleak.

"I'm sorry," I said to Elli. "I've messed this up pretty badly."

Elli gently touched my cheek. "Your only fault is that you put too much faith in the power of someone's better nature to triumph. That is who you are, and it is exactly what you should have done. Unfortunately, Nevva's better nature is not what we hoped it would be. For that, I am the one who should be sorry."

"We all make our choices," I said quickly. "Nevva made hers."

Elli nodded, but I didn't think she bought it. "What has happened to Nevva is a reflection of what Saint Dane did to all of Halla. He took something good, and twisted it into something evil by appealing to a darker nature."

"And we couldn't untwist her," I added. "Which makes me question if Halla is too far gone to save."

"Don't think that way," Elli said quickly. "We may be near the end, but there is still hope. There is always hope."

"Is there?" I shot back. "Even if we figured out a way to destroy every last one of those dados, what would stop Saint Dane from building more? And more after that? It's not looking good."

Elli deflated. "Then what should we do? Give up?" she asked softly.

I laughed. "Give up?" I exclaimed, overly enthusiastic.

"Who said anything about giving up? This is just starting to get interesting!"

She knew I was making light of a very dark situation, but she appreciated it just the same and gave me a hug.

"I hope you know that you have done everything possible to put an end to this madness. I am so very proud of you."

I wished I could have taken more comfort from that, but as nice as it was to hear, truth was that I had failed horribly. Many times over. You don't get points for effort. But in spite of my gloomy assessment, Elli was right. As long as the Travelers were around, there was hope. The trick was to figure out what to do next. I gave her a squeeze of thanks, then pulled away and scanned the room. We had to find a way out.

"Saint Dane took Mark because he wants us to stay here," I said, thinking out loud. "That's good. It means he still thinks we can do some damage."

I strolled around the large, empty room. The windows were up near the ceiling. No way to climb up there. The only way in or out of that room was the door—the solid wooden door with the heavy handle. I grabbed the handle and pressed the lever. It was locked. I looked to Elli and shrugged. "What the heck, it was worth a try."

I stepped back from the door, debating about how hard it would be to knock down. I wasn't sure if that was a good idea or not, seeing as there were probably dados outside guarding us.

"It may be time," Elli offered.

"Time for what?"

"To use the power of Solara."

I hadn't even thought about that. I'd put that option out

of my mind because every time the Travelers used the spirit, we were pushing Solara closer to extinction. How much more power was left? Was there a way to measure it? Was Uncle Press looking nervously at some big cartoonlike gas gauge that was creeping toward "empty"? Each time we traveled, I cringed, expecting something horrible to happen. So far we were okay, but how much longer would that last? How much traveling were the other Travelers doing? It wasn't just me and Elli, after all. There were eight other Travelers flying around, searching for the exiles.

"It's supposed to be a last resort," I said.

"I know," Elli said with finality. "I believe we're there."

Glancing around that room, that prison cell, I knew she was right. We could choose to sit there and do nothing while Mark was executed and the dados marched. Or we could do something. But what?

"I guess I could go back to Solara," I said. "Then come back here and hope that the spirit sends me somewhere else. Like the other side of the door. But that seems a little like overkill to move three feet."

"Why don't you just go under the door?" she asked, as if it were the most obvious answer in the world.

"Go under the—" I looked at the floor. It was an old door. Really old. It wasn't airtight by any means. I thought back to when Saint Dane and I were fighting. He swung his electric wand at me, and I willed myself to become smoke. I don't know exactly what happened, but his weapon passed through me with no effect. I had definitely changed my physical self. Was it possible to transform myself so completely that I could just float under the door?

"Yeah," I said thoughtfully. "Under the door. Sure. Why not?"

I took a step back and stared at the wooden door.

Nothing happened.

I looked harder.

Didn't help.

"Feeling silly," I announced.

"Don't. It would be silly not to try."

I shrugged and looked at the door again. How did this work? It was easy enough to move between territories. All I did was think about where I wanted to go and there I was. Compared to that, going under a door should be like, nothing. Right? I closed my eyes and visualized what I wanted to do. I wanted to float. I imagined what it would be like to move with the air. I pictured myself descending to the ground.

I didn't feel any different. Disappointed and feeling like an idiot, I opened my eyes to discover . . . I was different.

It was like my eyes had become a moving camera. I didn't feel like I had changed, but I had. I traveled down, toward the floor, in complete control. Looking around, I didn't see myself. Had I become invisible? My eyes reached floor level, and I looked ahead to see the crack beneath the door. Was I small now? Could I sail right under? I imagined moving forward, and I did. I floated across the surface of the stone floor until I reached the bottom of the door.

I held my breath. At least, I think I did. Did I have breath to hold? I moved forward and passed underneath, seeing the width of the door passing over my head as if I were traveling under a bridge. I have to say, it was the coolest experience ever. If the whole thing wasn't so alien, I probably would have enjoyed it. As it was, I was more worried about how to get back to normal than in taking the time to appreciate the fact that I had turned myself into some other kind of matter.

When I came out from under the door, I imagined myself returning to normal. I floated up. My eyes (or whatever it was I was seeing through) were on the door. I followed the lines of the deep, brown grain of the wood as I moved higher. The ascent took only a few seconds. I stopped. Was it over? Was I back to normal? I was still staring at the door when I sensed movement. I turned quickly to see a Ravinian dado coming for me, his silver wand high, ready to strike.

I was back to normal.

I dove to the ground to avoid the attack. If it hit me, I would be smoke again, and not the good kind. I side-kicked the knee of the dado. It was off balance from its attack and crumpled quickly. But it wasn't in pain. Dados didn't feel pain. As it fell, it was already swinging the weapon back at me. I thrust my hands out and grabbed its wrist. The thing was strong, but I had adrenaline on my side. There was no way I wanted that wand to hit me. I'd already wasted enough power to get out of that room. The other advantage I had was leverage. The dado was off balance, so it couldn't use its legs. After I kicked out its knee, I was already getting my feet under me. It was using its arms to push the wand at me. I was using my arms . . . and my legs.

I won. I twisted the hands of the dado around, breaking its grip. The wand clattered to the floor. I swept it up instantly and hit the dado square in the chest as it was turning to reach around. I felt a sharp jolt through my hands as the power of the weapon unloaded. Instantly the dado went stiff. It was creepy. Like switching off a light. Its eyes went blank. Its body went rigid. With a quick little shove I knocked it backward, and it fell to the floor. Dead. Fried. Whatever.

It had been an interesting thirty seconds.

"Pendragon?" came Elli's voice from the other side of the door.

"I'm okay," I said, breathless. "There was a dado. Now there isn't."

"You turned to smoke," she said, her voice sounding a little shaky.

Oh. Right. That.

"Really?"

"Yes. It was like you melted and floated under the door. Are you all right?"

"I guess" was all I could say. I was too numb for anything more insightful than that.

"Can you open the door?" she asked.

I went for the door, but there was no way to unlock it. I quickly checked the dado to find out he didn't have keys.

"No," I announced.

Elli asked, "Should I try to get out the way you did?"

I had to think about that for a second. Finding Mark was going to be tough enough. Having Elli with me would have made it that much harder.

"No," I replied. "I'm sorry, Elli. Stay here for now. I'll be able to get around faster on my own."

She didn't respond. I'm sure she wasn't thrilled.

"Elli? You all right?"

She answered with conviction. She was trying to be strong. "Yes. I understand."

"If I'm not back in a few hours, go back to Solara. Tell Uncle Press what we've seen."

"And what will you do?"

"I'm going to find Mark."

"And then what?"

I laughed. "Then I'll figure something else out."

"I know you will."

"I'm sorry, Elli, but I think it's better that I do this on my own."

"I do too."

It was an awkward moment, especially because we couldn't see each other.

"Bobby?" she said. "If you get the chance, tell Nevva that I hope we can speak again someday. I want her to understand why I did the things I did."

"I will," I assured her. "Good-bye, Elli."

I had to pull myself away from the door. It killed me to leave her behind, even though I knew she'd be okay. She could always return to Solara. My heart ached for her. I put her through torture by bringing her to see Nevva. All it did was cause her pain. There are a lot of things I would have done differently if I'd had another chance. Add that one to the list.

But I couldn't look back. Not just then, anyway. By using the spirit of Solara to get out of that cell, I'd given myself the chance to do something positive. I didn't want to waste it. It was time to get moving. It was time to find Mark. I started to run and nearly tripped over the dead dado. Seeing the inanimate thing gave me an idea. I dragged the broken device down the corridor until I found another empty room that was much like the one where Elli and I had been kept prisoner. I pulled the dado inside, and took off its clothes.

I was going to become a dado. Or at least try to look like one. Since I had no idea where I would have to go to find Mark, I figured that blending in would be a good thing. I had been wearing my Second Earth clothes for a while now.

Not only were they pretty gamey, I was afraid that I looked more like one of the roughed-up rebels who lived outside the conclave than a clean and tidy Ravinian. Hopefully, I thought, by wearing the red uniform of a Ravinian guard, I might not draw curious looks. It was risky, but I hoped it might give me a slight advantage.

The dado was more or less my size, though a little smaller around the chest and shoulders, which made his uniform fit pretty snug. I felt like I could easily bust out of it, Incredible Hulk–style. I'd have to be careful. I kept my own boxers on. Socks too. The one's I'd been wearing belonged to Courtney's dad. There were some things I wasn't willing to part with. Best of all, the boots fit almost perfectly. From the neck down I figured I looked the part. The problem was from the neck up. My hair was well over my ears and my beard stubble was dark—definitely un-dadolike. All I could do was push my hair behind my ears and pull the red Ravinian guard cap down low. It would have to do. I didn't bother putting my own clothes on the dead dado. It wasn't like he was going to get a chill. I pulled the machine behind the open door and tossed my clothes on top of it. If anybody glanced in from the corridor, they wouldn't see it. If they stepped inside, well, alarms would go off. Nothing I could do about that. The last thing I did was pick up the long silver weapon.

I was ready. I stepped out into the corridor, not knowing which way to go. It stretched out to both sides, with many doors along the way. If I'd had a coin, I'd have tossed it. I chose to go right and jogged down the long, tile-covered hallway. I had absolutely no plan. How could I? I didn't know where I was or where they might have taken Mark. The best I could do was walk around, pretending to be on guard patrol. Or whatever it was the dados did. I decided that the best place to begin my search would be the Taj Mahal. That's where Saint Dane and Nevva hung out. Chances were good that was where they would take Mark.

At the end of the corridor were stairs leading up. I took two at a time, winding around, climbing higher to the next floor. The stairs brought me to a wide-open area that I recognized. I suppose the tile work down below should have given it away, but I hadn't made the connection. I wasn't going to have to go far to get to the Taj Mahal. I was already in it. We had been in Saint Dane's basement all along. I glanced around, wondering where I should begin my search, when I registered an odd sound. I thought I'd heard it earlier, but it was so faint that it hadn't registered. Now that I had climbed out of the dungeon, it was louder. I guess you could call it a "tone." Three tones actually. Like notes. They played over and over again. The same three notes. I couldn't tell where they were coming from, but it definitely wasn't from inside the Taj Mahal. It was like nothing I'd heard during the time I'd spent inside the conclave, so I figured it was worth investigating.

I worked my way through the tall pillars, looking for a way out of the building. The closer I got to the doorway, the louder the tones became. There was definitely something happening outside. I found a set of double wooden doors and pushed my way out into the bright sun. Instantly the three tones grew loud. Really loud. They weren't annoying, but you couldn't miss them. They didn't sound urgent, like a fire warning or anything. It reminded me of the tones they used to play at Stony Brook Junior High to announce that it was time for classes to pass. There was no question these tones had a purpose, and I wanted to know what it was.

I made my way across the wide, marble expanse that

led to the edge of the giant pedestal-like base that the Taj Mahal sat on. Now that I was outside, I saw that other people were around. If I didn't want to draw attention, I was going to have to act like a dado. I'd seen thousands of them, but never really studied how they behaved . . . other than when they were trying to beat my head in, that is. They didn't walk like robots or anything, but their movements were precise. And they had good posture. Why not? They were robots. You don't program a slouch into a robot. So I stood up tall, lifted my chin, and tried to walk perfectly. It was actually easier than I thought. Just being self-conscious about walking makes you a little stiff. My biggest challenge was to not forget that I had to be walking that way.

I gripped the long weapon. There was a small red button in the handle that I figured was the on-off switch. I took a chance, hit it, and felt the wand hum. I hit the button again and it stopped. I decided to leave it off. I didn't want to accidentally brush it against my leg and vaporize myself like an idiot. I thought back to when I had seen the dados walking around and remembered that they held the weapons down at their sides. That's what I did. In all, I thought I was going to pull it off. So long as nobody noticed my hair or beard, I'd be cool.

The tones continued. As I marched closer to the edge of the foundation, I sensed something else. Another unique sound. I reached the perimeter and looked down onto the gardens that surrounded the Taj Mahal to see that the sound was coming from a large crowd of people who were slowly moving toward the front of the building. There had to be hundreds of them. They weren't in a hurry, but I sensed excitement. Little kids sprinted through the crowd, as if they couldn't wait to get where they were going. These weren't dados. They were the Ravinians who lived in this conclave. I saw all types. All ages. All races. These were the chosen of Third Earth. The tones now made sense. It was a signal. Or a notice of some kind. When the tones sounded, people came. I wondered if this was a normal thing, or something special.

I made my way forward in the direction the crowd was moving. As I walked, I joined more people who were on the same level with me, all moving in the same direction as those below. There were dados mixed into the crowd who looked to be scanning for trouble. I didn't want to be spotted, so I did the same, though I guarantee we were looking for different kinds of trouble. I did my best to stay away from them. I didn't want to be recognized. Or *not* recognized. Invisible was good. As I walked closer to the front of the Taj Mahal, it became easier to blend in because the crowd grew dense.

When I reached the front of the building, I realized that this was everyone's destination. Thousands of people crowded around the long reflecting pool that stretched out in front of the Taj Mahal. It was a staggering sight. Behind me loomed the massive onion-shaped dome. In front of me were thousands of people looking toward the building. I no longer felt in danger of being discovered. I was one in thousands. I meant nothing. This was a spectacle. Nobody was going to notice one dado who needed a shave.

The question then became, what the heck were they doing here? This was Saint Dane's house, so whatever it was, it couldn't be good. They had been summoned and I didn't think it was for a barbeque. Looking up at the Taj Mahal, I saw that a platform had been erected. Had that been there before? I didn't remember it. It didn't look to have come from ancient India, either. It looked high-tech modern. It was a wide silver tube that rose about thirty feet into the air. Etched into the surface was a huge Ravinian star. Erected on top were two, thick uprights and a cross bar. They were also made of metal and looked heavy, but with style. Like a modern sculpture. It was this frame, on top of the circular, silver tube, that had everyone's attention.

The tones continued as the people gathered. It was getting crowded. I now noticed that several dados had arrived on ground level. They marched in carrying red Ravinian star flags. The procession moved around the fountain until there was a line of flags stretching along either side of its considerable length. The flags sickened me. They represented everything that Saint Dane stood for. They symbolized the movement that had brought Halla to its knees. The sight reminded me of those old movies I'd seen of Nazi rallies before World War II. I guess people didn't learn from the mistakes of the past.

The tones stopped. I sensed the anticipation of the crowd. Everyone focused their attention on the strange sculpture on top of the silver tube. The show was about to begin.

A loud gong rang out. The huge crowd instantly became silent. It was eerie. A lone figure appeared on the platform on top of the tube. I wasn't sure how he'd gotten up there. Maybe there were stairs that I couldn't see. But he was there, and it didn't surprise me at all.

It was Saint Dane. He held his arms out as if to embrace the masses. No sooner did his arms go up, than the crowd applauded. Like crazy. They loved the guy. Or maybe they were afraid that if they didn't give him a big hand, they'd be in trouble. The dados holding the flags waved them furiously. It was impressive, in a sickening sort of way.

Saint Dane lifted his hands. It was a subtle gesture, but the crowd understood. They fell silent again. Creepy. They were like puppets. I was standing in a crowd of people more than twenty yards away from the platform, but even from that distance I could see that Saint Dane was loving this. He had grown to enjoy his power. He was living the dream.

"Ravinians!" he bellowed, his amplified voice booming from unseen speakers. "Thank you for joining me here today."

I snickered. Like they had a choice. My guess was that if anybody didn't come running whenever the horn sounded, they'd regret it.

"I am asking you to play a role in what I believe is a critical moment in the continuing evolution of Ravinia. You are not here as mere bystanders. You are participants. The decision you make today will help shape the future of our grand experiment. As the chosen, the course of Ravinia has been and always will be in your hands. I am asking you today to once again help me chart the course that will make the vision a reality."

The crowd went nuts. Cheering and applauding. I don't think they had any idea what they were cheering about, but Saint Dane was being all dramatic and firing them up, and they were going right along with it. Did they really think that they were making their own decisions? I guess people believe what they want to believe. When they quieted down, Saint Dane continued.

"Throughout Halla the elite have risen. The pariahs have been marginalized. Look around you. This is the glory of Ravinia. Conclaves such as this exist throughout all worlds. We have been rewarded, and this is only the beginning."

Again, big applause. Watching this crowd brought back memories of other similar scenes on other territories. I thought of the crowds on Quillan, who would do anything, even risk their children, to get ahead. And the quig battles in the Bedoowan castle on Denduron. And the crowds of Ravinians on Second Earth. All those people bought into Saint Dane's vision. As I watched the people here on Third Earth, it struck me again how this was exactly what Saint Dane had been working for. If Solara was created and powered by the spirit of all people, Saint Dane drew strength from the people who only thought the way he did. He weeded out those who didn't fit his plan and would soon be left with only those who bought into his ideal.

It also struck me that Saint Dane hadn't assumed a new identity here on Third Earth. There was no more pretense. No more weaseling into a society and influencing events to go his way. The gloves were off. What I said to Nevva was true. Saint Dane loved the power. He no longer had to work through anybody else. It was all about him now. He had assumed the role of ruler. Or king. Or god. Or whatever it was he envisioned himself to be.

"We are nearing the end of a journey that began thousands of years ago here on Earth with the birth of Alexander Naymeer and the rise of Ravinia. Throughout Halla, the elite have triumphed. Like you, they are the chosen. The entitled. Look around. See the wonderful existence we share. We are spreading this utopian ideal throughout Halla. When we no longer need protection from the evils of the dissenters, the walls that surround us will no longer be needed, and they . . . will . . . come . . . down!"

The crowd went nuts. Again. I guess that was the deal. The Ravinians lived in their own special little paradise, but they were like prisoners. It seemed like Saint Dane promised that the whole world would become as perfect as this conclave, just as soon as all those annoying people on the outside could be eliminated.

When the crowd stopped chanting, Saint Dane continued. "There is still work to be done. There are pockets of resistance. There are people who are no better than hungry, predatory rats, and they are determined to bring down our way of life. They want to live as we do, yet they aren't willing to make sacrifices to achieve it. My question to you is, are you ready to eliminate the threat once and for all? Should we allow these people to continue to eat away at the fabric of our perfect society? That is the choice we are now faced with. Do we tolerate? Or purge? Tolerate? Or purge?"

The chant started slowly, as if they weren't exactly sure of the answer. But once it began, it quickly grew.

"Purge! Purge! Purge!"

It was chilling. These people were worked up, enthusiastically showing their support for a final massacre—all so they could continue to live in a nice parklike home. Even the kids were chanting with intensity. It was bloodlust. Saint Dane held out his hands, smiling, letting the chant wash over him. I was watching his power grow, literally. He was feeding on their spirit. I was certain that whatever darker Solara he had created was feeding on it too. He held up his hands again and the chanting stopped. Looking out over the crowd, and to the people around me, I saw fire in their eyes. People were breathing heavily. Saint Dane had them in his spell.

"Of course that is the way!" Saint Dane proclaimed. "You and your ancestors have always been willing to make the difficult choices for the greater good. The same has been happening all over Halla. The strong have chosen to survive. The weak have been ground under our boots."

Another huge cheer. Yikes. They were ruthless.

"Now we are faced with a decision. As much as I have become your spiritual advisor, every decision I make comes from you."

Yeah, right.

"I have summoned you here to make another such decision. You will determine how we proceed. You all are aware of the growing number of rebels who live outside these walls. It is the same with every conclave that has been built on Earth. There are many who manage to hang on, threatening our lives and forcing us to live behind these walls. Once they are eliminated, these walls will come down. I am here today to tell you that we have captured a leader of these miscreants. He defiled the sanctity of this conclave, crept in like a cockroach searching for crumbs, with the intent of causing malicious harm to anyone who stood in his way."

Okay, not true, but . . . whatever.

He continued, "My question to you is, do we show him mercy? Or do we send a message to all those who oppose us? A message that states beyond any shadow of a doubt that their cause is futile and their true destiny . . . is to perish!"

As the crowd erupted with another cheer, three more people stepped up onto the platform. There were two Ravinian guards and a guy they held tight. He was a prisoner, with a black cloth bag over his head.

Saint Dane reached out and pulled the bag off.

My stomach clenched when I saw his face.

Yeah. It was Mark.

At the same time, from the crossbeam over Mark's head, a noose was lowered. It was all happening much quicker than I imagined.

This crowd had been gathered to witness the execution of Mark Dimond.

25

A fourth person stepped onto the platform. Nevva Winter. Saint Dane wanted her to carry out the execution, and there she was. Ready to go.

"People of Ravinia," Saint Dane's voice boomed. "Give me your decision. Do we show mercy? Or begin the process that will crush our enemies once and for all?"

I wasn't expecting any other response than the one they gave. The chant began quickly, the sound echoing off the Taj Mahal.

"Crush! Crush! Crush! Crush!"

The sentence had been handed down. Saint Dane had done it again. He had already decided to execute Mark, but he first drew these people into the process, making them part of the decision. Putting blood on their hands. He could still claim that the people made their own choice, though in reality he was stoking the evil spirit that gave him the power to re-create Halla.

I looked at the faces of those around me. They seemed like ordinary people. Nobody had three eyes or sharp fangs or looked any different from the rebels who lived outside the conclave. In fact, they weren't any different. They all wanted the same thing, which was to live their lives in peace. Trouble was, the people of Ravinia felt they deserved more and weren't above crushing those who got in their way.

Not all monsters had fangs.

And not all of the Ravinians were chanting. I actually saw a few people who weren't caught up in the furor. It might have been wishful thinking, but to me it seemed as if they were looking around in dismay, the same as I was. Was it possible? Were there some Ravinians who actually had a conscience? It gave me a brief bit of hope, but no more than that. There were plenty of others who wanted Mark's blood.

I pushed my way through the crowd, desperate to get to the silver tower that had become a gallows. I didn't know what I could do, but I wasn't going to let Mark die without a fight. I kept the electric wand to my side, turned off. As badly as I needed to get through the crowd, I wasn't about to kill anybody to do it. That would have made me no better than the bloodthirsty Ravinians who were calling for Mark's head. I kept my eyes on the stage. Mark stood bravely, looking out at the crowd. They had cleaned him up a little for the show. His beard stubble was gone and his long hair was cut short. He stood staring out at the thousands of judges who wanted him dead, showing no fear. He didn't fight. I'm sure he didn't want to give anybody the satisfaction of knowing that he was anything less than a proud, formidable guy.

Saint Dane stalked along the front of the platform, soaking up the energy. He was loving this. After letting the emotion roll over him for a few seconds, he turned toward the Taj Mahal and waved. A quick look showed me who it was meant for.

Elli Winter had arrived. She was being held by two Ravinian guards, who dragged her out the front door of the ancient building. They forced her forward and stopped at the top of a wide set of stairs that led down to the bottom of the silver tube. The level I was on. Being up high like that meant she was roughly on the same level as the top of the platform where her daughter was about to murder my friend. Saint Dane gestured for Nevva to look back. Nevva didn't. I think she knew who was there. It was a cruel move. Saint Dane wanted Nevva to know her mother was watching. Was it a further test of her resolve? Or was it punishment for having questioned him earlier? Either way, Saint Dane proved yet again how vicious he could be.

Having Elli there also meant that the Ravinians knew I was on the loose. It didn't worry me at all. In a few seconds they were going to know exactly where I was.

The intensity of the chanting grew. It became a steady, incessant, "*Crush them! Crush them! Crush them!*"

I pushed my way forward, knocking over anyone and everyone in my path. I saw that beyond the tube were stairs that led up to the platform. That was my goal. I had to get to those stairs.

Up on the platform Nevva moved without expression. I wondered what was going through her mind. She knew Mark. She liked Mark. It didn't seem to matter. Not when it came to showing her blind dedication to Saint Dane. She reached for the dangling noose and slipped it around Mark's neck. Mark didn't make eye contact with her. Seeing the noose around his neck made the chanting grow louder. They knew the end was near. It was a vicious, bloodthirsty lynch mob.

I had only a few seconds to act. I hoped that Saint Dane

would give Mark some last words. Or make a final, grand statement to the crowd before sending him plunging to his death. For once I *wanted* Saint Dane to be his usual, arrogant self. I needed the time. As I drew closer to the platform, I saw that the number of dados had grown. It would only be a matter of time before they realized that somebody was making trouble and try to stop me. I couldn't afford to be cautious anymore.

It was time to get dangerous.

I raised the silver weapon and hit the button. I felt the power surge as it kicked on. I started flashing the powerful wand at the dados in my way. Most never knew what hit them. They were too busy scanning the crowd to realize that one of their own was on a rampage. I flashed the weapon left and right, nailing dados with each swing, knocking their lights out. I guess you could say I was charged with bloodlust as well, or whatever it is that runs through dado veins. I wanted to mow down as many as I could, as fast as I could.

I kept glancing up at the platform, hoping for more time. The stairs were within reach. Two dados were stationed at the bottom. They barely had time to raise and activate their own weapons before I sliced them both, knocking them to the ground. I was on the stairs, flying up three at a time.

The crowd continued chanting. Mark was still alive. I knew what I had to do. Nevva was my quarry. If she was the executioner, she would have her finger on the switch. If I was to save Mark, I would have to stop Nevva.

I couldn't hear anything but the fevered screaming of the crowd. My wand was up and ready. When my head cleared the platform, I saw exactly what I'd hoped to find. Saint Dane was out in front, facing the crowd. Mark stood with a dado on either side of him, keeping him still. Nevva was to the far right of the platform, near one of the uprights of the gallows. There was a small plate on the back side of that upright. On it was a series of switches.

Nevva's hand was on them.

Saint Dane turned to Nevva and nodded.

It was Mark's death sentence.

Nevva put her finger on the center switch.

I wasn't going to make it in time.

"Nevva!" I screamed, hoping to throw her off long enough for me to reach her and knock her into eternity.

Nevva turned toward me. I saw the surprise on her face. It wasn't enough to stop her. Nevva threw the switch. The door beneath Mark's feet swung away. He started to fall. I dropped the weapon and dove for him, hoping to catch him before he disappeared beneath the floor. I hit the deck on my belly and slid toward the opening with my arms outstretched.

Time seemed to slow down. I felt the fabric of Mark's shirt fall past the tips of my fingers. I tried to grab on to something, but got only air. The next second felt as if it took an eternity to pass. My eyes were on the slack rope . . . that suddenly went taught. The gallows shuddered briefly. Not a sound came from below. Though he had fallen into the enclosed tube and could not be seen by the crowd, they knew what had happened. Their reaction told the story. A huge, triumphant cheer erupted. I barely heard it. The only sound that cut through to me was the slow, steady *creak* that came from a rope that had been pulled tight, straining to hold the weight of my best friend.

Mark was dead. Nevva had killed him. Ravinia had killed him. Saint Dane had killed him. I focused past the swinging rope at the thousands of people who shouted and cheered at the death of a hero.

And I snapped.

I rolled and swept up the electric wand. Somebody was going to suffer for what had happened. The two best candidates were up there with me on that platform. The dados ran for me. One got there first and paid the price for his efficiency. I skewered him with the wand and pushed him off the edge of the platform.

The other dado held back. It was the first time I had seen a dado actually make a smart move. It saved his life, at least for a little while. Fine by me. It wasn't the dado I cared about. I wanted Nevva. She stood frozen near the controls she had just used to kill Mark. It didn't seem like she was going to put up a fight. I didn't care. She could defend herself or not. She was going to die.

I reached my arm back, ready to lance her with the wand, when I was tackled from behind. The second dado had regrouped and made its move. I had been so blinded by anger, I didn't expect the attack. I hit the deck, hard. The weight of the dado knocked the wind out of me. Nevva finally made her move. She went for my outstretched arm and grabbed the wand. It all played out so quickly and violently that I couldn't believe what had happened. I struggled to get away from the dado. To get at Nevva. Too late. More dados had arrived on the platform and grabbed me.

"I'll kill you!" I screamed at Nevva, totally out of my mind. "I swear, I'll kill you!"

I was blinded by rage. Tears streamed down my cheeks. Mark was hanging on the end of a rope. All he ever did was try to help me and others who needed it. This was his final reward. I wanted to be dead myself. I wanted to explode.

I wanted to feel my hands around Nevva Winter's throat. I'm not proud of these insane, violent feelings, but I have to write down exactly what happened. In those few seconds up on that platform, I believe I had lost my mind. The dados kept me down, my cheek jammed onto the platform floor. Through the tears, I saw Saint Dane lean down to me.

"If only you had accepted the inevitable," he said. "But I suppose that was not the way it was meant to be. For the last time, Pendragon, good-bye."

I screamed. It wasn't a word or a sentence or anything that was understandable. It was an outpouring of raw emotion, frustration, and grief.

Saint Dane left the platform. Nevva gave me a quick glance. She didn't say a word. At least she had the decency not to make this nightmare any worse than it was. I was left alone on the platform with the dados, and the swinging rope that was a reminder that my best friend was hanging below. Dead.

Once Saint Dane left, the crowd had had enough. The chanting died. Whatever need they had to experience a murder had been filled. They were already dispersing. Many followed the line of dados as they marched out with their red flags snapping in the breeze. There was nothing more for them to see. They didn't have a view of the hanging body of my friend. He was inside the circular base of the gallows. Maybe Saint Dane was afraid that if his followers actually saw the result of their decision, they'd start having second thoughts. As it was, all they knew was that the prisoner had been executed. They didn't have to witness anything gruesome.

My heart continued to race. I was breathing hard. It was surreal. None of what had happened seemed possible.

I must have gone into shock. Fighting against the dados seemed useless. If I wanted to, I could have gone to any territory I chose. But I didn't. My mind was too far gone for that. Thinking straight wasn't a possibility. The dados must have sensed that I was no longer resisting, because they lifted me to my feet. Two held my hands twisted behind my back. Another held a silver weapon in front of my face as a warning. In other words, "Don't try anything or *zap!*" I didn't react. I didn't plan on trying anything. The dado with the weapon turned and started down the stairs. I was led after him. The final dado followed behind. We hit the bottom of the stairs just as a door in the silver tube swung open. It was a section of the steel skin at the bottom of the stairs. Two Ravinian guards stepped out from inside and marched off. They left the door open wide.

I looked inside . . . and wished I hadn't.

It was as hideous a sight as I imagined. My friend hung by the neck at the end of the rope. His head was cocked at an impossible angle. His body swayed slightly. All I could hope for was that his death had been quick. I began to shake uncontrollably. I don't know what it was. Maybe some kind of outpouring of emotion. I guess it was my version of crying. I felt as if I were walking through a dream. A violent, impossible dream.

The Ravinian guards pulled me away from the door and brought me back toward the stairs that led up and into the Taj Mahal. We climbed. I didn't resist. What was the point? When we reached the top of the stairs, Elli was there, being held by two dados. She was in tears. She didn't say anything, and that was good. I wouldn't have known how to respond. Nothing she could have said would make this better. I'd lost my best friend, and the person who pulled the switch was her daughter. We each had to deal with our own private agony.

The dado escorts moved us both toward the Taj Mahal. Elli didn't put up a fight either. The next thing I registered was a small patrol of Ravinian guards walking toward us. Six in all. They marched in tight formation, two by two, holding silver weapons to their sides. As dazed as I was, something felt off to me. This team of dados was headed directly at us. Quickly. I sensed the hesitation on the part of the dados who were holding me. It seemed some odd game of chicken was about to be played out. I expected the oncoming dados to walk around us—after all, we were the ones who were being towed, so to speak. They didn't. They came right for us.

The single dado who was leading us stopped. He didn't know what was happening either. We all stopped, expecting the oncoming dados to skirt by. The lead dado raised his hand and motioned for the oncoming group to go around.

It was the last move he made.

The oncoming dados came within a few feet, and attacked. The first two nailed the dado out in front with their weapons. He fell instantly. I was pulled to the side by one of the two dados that were holding me. He didn't join in the fight. He was all about keeping me under control. He threw me to the ground and sat on my back to keep me from moving. I had to struggle just to see what was happening. The two dados that had been holding Elli let her go and went for their weapons. Too late. All six of the attacking dados had their weapons drawn and mowed them down. They were fast and efficient. The attack took only a few seconds. Five dados went down. When it was done, the team of six regrouped and marched toward me.

I figured this was the end. It was an execution squad sent to take us out.

Elli ran to me and crouched down behind the one dado that hadn't been wiped out. I expected him to jump up and make some final stand. Instead, he stayed on top of me. He was carrying out his mission until the end. The other six dados were nearly on us. They stood shoulder to shoulder, their weapons out and ready. I had no doubt that in moments, Elli and I would be back on Solara. Elli grabbed my hand and squeezed, bracing for an attack. . . .

That never came. When the hit squad got to within a few yards of us, they stopped. Just like that. All six stood there staring at us silently. What the heck was going on? We stayed that way for a few seconds. The only sound I heard was my own heavy breathing. I twisted my head around to look up at the dado who was sitting on me. I figured the next move was his.

What I saw didn't add up. It was the first time I took a close look at the robot. He was one of the dados that had been holding Mark up on the gallows platform. Now that I was close to him, I saw that he had the stubble of a beard. He sat staring at the line of dados. There was a long, silent moment.

Then the dado spoke. "Wow," he said, breathless. "It actually w-worked." He looked down, gave me a big smile and said, "Can we get out of here now?"

Yeah. It was Mark.

26

My best friend was alive.

He wasn't hanging by his neck inside that silver tube. You'd think I would be hit with an overwhelming sense of relief and joy. Don't get me wrong. I was. But at that moment, the overriding feeling was more one of total confusion.

"Wha——" was pretty much all I managed to gasp.

Mark shrugged. "This is the first time I'm okay with those dados looking like me."

Elli gasped. "They executed a dado?"

"Yeah. He's probably not even hurt."

I glanced at the line of dados who had arrived to wipe out our escort party. They stood together, holding their weapons up, waiting for a command.

"They were ordered to protect me," Mark explained. "Dados are handy to have around, so long as they're on your side."

I was still in a state of shock. "But . . . how?"

"Nevva," Mark said.

"Nevva Winter?" I gasped.

Mark actually laughed. "You know anybody else named Nevva?"

I glanced over at Elli. Judging by the way she looked and the way I felt, we were both pretty stunned by that revelation.

"The plan was hers," Mark continued. "Nevva saved me."

The impossible truths kept getting more impossible. I couldn't think fast enough to keep up.

"But why?" I croaked out. "What did she say?"

"Only that she wasn't going to let me die. These dados will protect us until we get to the tunnel out of here, which we should do right now."

I turned to Elli, thinking she would be even more thrilled by this news than I was. But Elli was gone. I looked around quickly to see that she was several yards away from us, running. She was headed into the Taj Mahal.

"Hey!" Mark shouted to her. Then to me he said, "What is she doing?"

I got to my feet. "She must be going after Nevva."

"She can't!" Mark went to run after her, but I stopped him.

"No, you gotta get out of here."

"What? No! You can't go after her. I don't think Nevva's going to protect you too."

"It doesn't matter. We'll be okay. Elli and I can leave whenever we want. But not with you here. I hate to say it, Mark, but you're a liability."

"Uh . . . what?"

"I told you, we don't need flumes to travel anymore. We can just leave. But you can't. If these dados are going to get you to safety, you've got to go."

Mark weighed my words. I knew he didn't understand, but he wasn't about to ask for an explanation. At least not then. There wasn't time. We were still surrounded by a world of dados that *weren't* programmed to protect him.

"Go back to your people," I continued. "Keep searching for the exiles. If we want to help them, we have to find them."

"And what'll you do?" he asked.

"Get Elli and get out of here. After that, I don't know. We've got to come up with a plan to stop that army of dados."

I walked to one of the downed dados and picked up his weapon. He wouldn't be needing it anymore.

"So this is it," Mark said. "The turning point of Third Earth is also the final battle for Halla."

"It's sure looking like it," I replied.

I hated to say good-bye. I'd already lost Mark once that day, I didn't want to go through something like that again. "Go," I said. "We'll find you."

Mark threw his arms around me. "I wish Courtney were here," he said, his voice cracking.

I didn't agree, but I didn't say anything. This was actually the *last* place I wanted Courtney to be.

"Get back safe," I said. "Don't do anything dumb."

"Dumb? Me? You forget who you're talking to."

Mark pulled back. There were tears in his eyes. I knew what he was thinking. It felt as if this might be the last time we would ever see each other.

"We'll probably get back before you do," I said, trying to be light.

Mark nodded, but he didn't believe that any more than I did. "Bobby, I d-don't regret a thing."

Hearing his stutter made my heart break. This was still Mark Dimond.

"I know, Mark."

"And I'm proud of you, man."

"Thanks. And thanks for being my friend."

Mark shrugged.

"Now go," I commanded.

Mark nodded and looked at the line of dados. He stood up straight and fixed his Ravinian cap on his head. His new, confident self was back. "C'mon, boys, let's go knock some roboheads."

The dados turned in a group and followed Mark. He took a few steps backward, gave me a smile, then turned and jogged off. I watched him for a few seconds, hoping I wasn't seeing my best friend for the last time.

I had to pull myself away. Standing there feeling all forlorn wasn't doing anybody any good. I sprinted after Elli. I suppose I should have acted more dadolike, but I didn't care about blending in anymore. I wanted to grab Elli and get the heck out of there. What I told Mark wasn't entirely true. Eventually I planned on joining him, but I didn't want to do it alone. I had to go back to Solara and get Uncle Press. Hopefully the rest of the Travelers would be there as well. If everything was going to play out the way I expected, our final stand was going to be on Third Earth. We had to stop the army of dados before it could march on the exiles, wherever they were. For that, we needed to be together. But first I had to get Elli.

I entered the Taj Mahal on full alert. The place seemed deserted, but I knew it couldn't be. I didn't start yelling out Elli's name. That would have been the quickest way to get some dados landing on my head. As it turned out, the search didn't take long. I made my way through the forest of fancy columns that led to the center of the Taj Mahal, and heard the soft sound of someone crying. I followed the sound until I came upon a sight that took my breath away. Sitting on a bench between two huge columns was Nevva. She was in the arms of her mother, Elli. Her head was buried in Elli's shoulder. It was Nevva who was crying. Since I had known Elli, dating back to when we first met on Quillan, she had been a troubled woman. Her history was a sad one. She wore every moment of it on her face. She was a beautiful woman, but the many tragedies she had lived through had taken their toll. Her expression rarely varied. I think it was the only way she could keep going. It was as if she had turned off her emotions because none of them were good. As I watched her sitting there, cradling her daughter, I saw a different woman. Her eyes were closed. Her entire being had softened. She was at peace.

I didn't want to disturb the moment. I think Elli must have sensed my presence, because she opened her eyes and saw me. She smiled. Elli actually smiled. She looked alive in a way that I hadn't seen before. I'd been through a lot in these past few years. There were more triumphs and tragedies than I could count. But looking back on it all, I think that simple moment of seeing Elli at peace is the most beautiful thing I ever experienced.

Nevva turned and saw me. She instantly stiffened and stood up. "What are you doing here?" she demanded.

"I've come for Elli," I explained. "And to thank you."

"What I did was for Mark," Nevva said, trying to regain her composure. "Things haven't changed."

"But they have," I said. "Your mother was right, Nevva. You do have a heart."

Elli watched us, not saying a word. I got the feeling that it didn't matter to her one way or the other how things would play out from that moment on. The fact that Nevva showed that one small ounce of compassion toward Mark was enough for her to know that her daughter wasn't a monster.

"I still believe in the vision, Pendragon," she announced.

"But you don't," I argued. "What you did for Mark proves it. You say that controlling people's lives and rewarding excellence at the expense of those less fortunate is how Halla should be run, but then you show compassion. Real compassion. That's totally against what Saint Dane has been preaching. You care about Mark. Even though he's working against everything Ravinia stands for, you saved his life. That alone proves you believe there's more than one side to a story."

Nevva wanted to argue, but she knew my logic was sound.

"It wasn't supposed to be like this," she said, her voice wavering. "I saw all that was wrong with Halla. Saint Dane had the answer. The vision. It was about encouraging people to strive for the absolute best. Nothing less would be tolerated. It's such a simple concept."

"But Halla isn't a simple place," I said with passion. "Neither are the people who live there simple. You're one of them, Nevva. You're a Traveler, but you're also a physical being of Halla, with all its flaws."

Nevva wandered away from her mother. She seemed dazed, as if she couldn't get her thoughts straight.

"Everything that happened is what the people wanted," she argued.

"But it wasn't!" I countered. "Saint Dane targeted a certain type of person and influenced them. Then he systematically destroyed all those he couldn't persuade. There's no other way of putting it. What he's left with are people all over Halla who are concerned with only one thing—themselves. Is Halla a better place now? Sure, this conclave is great. I'll bet all the conclaves around Halla are just swell. But that's only a small part of Halla. There are people suffering, Nevva. Everywhere. Does that feel right to you?"

She didn't answer. She didn't have to.

I added, "And now he's going to destroy the last group of people who are keeping the spirit of Solara alive. He's not influencing anybody to do it. He's not using people who believe in his vision. He's created an army of emotionless dados to commit genocide. Is that part of the grand vision?"

Nevva shook her head. I sensed she was trying to find an argument, but couldn't.

"That wasn't supposed to happen," she said, confused. "The territory was to be left alone. That was the plan."

"Looks like the plan changed," I said.

Elli finally spoke. "You put your faith in Saint Dane, and he betrayed you."

Nevva snapped a look to her mother. If there was one thing I could always say about Nevva, it was that she was confident in her beliefs.

Not anymore.

"I lured them to that stadium," Nevva said, pained. "Every last one. I made sure they were sent into that flume. But not to die. I didn't know about the dado army, I truly didn't. If I had known, I wouldn't have—"

"You wouldn't have what?" I pressed. "You wouldn't have exiled those people if you knew they were all going to die eventually?"

"No," Nevva cried. "That's not how it was."

I kept at her. "What about the rest of Halla? Those exiles

aren't Saint Dane's only victims. You may not have had a direct hand in destroying each and every civilization, but you played a pretty big part. Why is that any different from what happened to the exiles?"

"It was . . . it was all for the greater good," she said, grasping. I wasn't so sure she understood what that meant anymore.

"There's still time," Elli said calmly. "The exiles aren't dead yet. Help us stop Saint Dane."

An idea came to me. Something I hadn't dared to think about for a long time. The possibility seemed remote at best. Maybe impossible. But suddenly, with Nevva opening up, it felt as if there might be a chance. She knew more about Saint Dane than any of us.

"Nevva, can he be stopped?" I asked.

Nevva looked to me with confusion.

"What do you mean?" she asked.

"You know what I mean," I said bluntly. "Can he be destroyed?"

Nevva faltered. She knew something. My instincts were right. My pulse started to race.

"Tell us," I pushed. "Make this right. Tell us how to beat Saint Dane."

She opened her mouth to speak, but instead she let out a gasp and fell to her knees.

Behind her, Saint Dane stood with a silver weapon.

"You simply will not give up, will you?" he said, sounding more than a little annoyed.

Nevva fell to the ground, shaking. Was she dead? Was that possible? Had Saint Dane killed her? She wasn't turned to ash, but the weapon had definitely hurt her.

Elli screamed in agony and dove for her daughter.

I, on the other hand, dove for Saint Dane. I wanted to hurt him. I raised my weapon, leaped over Nevva, and attacked. Saint Dane lifted his own wand to defend himself, but I don't think he was ready for the emotion-charged barrage I threw at him. I hammered at the guy, using the wand like an ax. Saint Dane backed off, doing all he could to ward off my blows. He didn't even try to fight back. He couldn't. I didn't give him the chance. Anger took control of me. There was nothing cagey about my attack. The lessons of Mooraj didn't come into play. I channeled all my pent-up emotion into using that silver wand to hammer the guy. I wasn't even sure if the weapon had been activated. It didn't matter. I would have bludgeoned him. In fact, I would have preferred it.

He parried my blows, but he wasn't casual about it. He knew I was serious. I was going to hurt him.

"All you've managed to do," he said in between the ringing sound of metal hitting metal, "is to kill another Traveler."

His words charged me up to slash even harder. He was growing tired. His physical self wasn't as strong as mine. For a moment I actually thought I was going to hurt him. I should have known better. Saint Dane threw his wand to the side. I was so surprised by that move, I stopped my attack. The demon stood there with his arms out, as if giving himself up to me.

"Nevva's death is on your conscience, Pendragon," he said. "It was all for nothing."

I wound up to finish the guy, and he disappeared. Just like that. He took a step back and was gone. I was thrown for a second, but shouldn't have been. He was a Traveler, after all. Why would he stand there and let me pummel him? I stood there alone, breathing hard. My pent-up emotion had no outlet. I let out a scream and flung the wand as far as I could. It clattered to the ground somewhere deep within the Taj Mahal. I screamed again. I couldn't keep the frustration and anger inside.

"Pendragon!" Elli called.

I forced myself to get back some kind of control and ran to her. She was on her knees, holding Nevva's head in her lap. Elli was crying. Her brief moment of bliss was already forgotten. The agony had returned.

Nevva wasn't dead. Yet. She stared up with glazed, unseeing eyes.

"It's okay," I said. "You can't die."

I put my hand on her chest, ready to will her back to health. She grabbed my wrist and held it tight.

"No," she said. "There's nothing you can do."

"I can! I can heal you!"

"No," she insisted. "Don't waste your spirit. It isn't possible. He won't allow it."

I didn't know what she meant by that, but I took her word for it. "Go to Solara," I said. "You'll be safe there."

"I can't, Pendragon," she whispered. "I'm controlled by a different spirit now."

"But your spirit can go to Solara. Right?"

"Not anymore" was her answer.

Elli wiped her tears while stroking her daughter's cheek soothingly.

"It's not only my body that's dying. My spirit is ending. There will be no existence for me beyond this one."

"You don't know that," Elli said desperately.

Nevva looked up to her mother and focused. I saw the affection she had for Elli. That they had for each other.

She took her mother's hand. "I'm sorry, Mother," she said. "None of this was your doing."

Elli looked at me with pleading eyes. "Pendragon, do something."

"How can I save you, Nevva?" I asked.

"You can't. Saint Dane controls the dark power of Solara. He will not allow it to save me. Not anymore."

Nevva started to flicker. Her physical being was fading out.

"What's happening?" Elli asked in a panic.

"I'm ending, Mother," Nevva answered with a weak voice. "My spirit is ending."

Elli wept. Her daughter was about to disappear forever. Literally.

Nevva focused on me. "Pendragon, you must do to him what he has done to Solara. His power will not be fully realized until the light of Solara is destroyed. Make him use his power. It is the only way to weaken him and end his spirit."

"I . . . I don't understand," I said. Nevva was giving me the answers, but I didn't know what they meant.

"Saint Dane has split Solara. He draws his power from the dark spirit he has created. Make him use it . . . and save the exiles. He fears their spirit more than he fears even you, Pendragon."

Nevva's image winked. She wouldn't be there much longer.

"Stay with us," Elli begged.

"Where are the exiles, Nevva? They must be here on Third Earth, right? Where are they?"

Nevva looked at me with glazed eyes. "They aren't on Third Earth," she whispered.

I was rocked. Everything I had seen up to that point

led me to believe this was where the final battle would take place.

"But they must be!" I blurted out. "Saint Dane can't attack another territory without the flumes!"

Nevva struggled to stay focused. She didn't have much time left. "You saw what happened on Second Earth. You were there. He has the power. Make him use it again. Weaken him."

My mind was flying in a million directions. What did I see on Second Earth? Was she talking about Yankee Stadium? The Bronx Massacre? Naymeer created a flume that drew in all those victims. It suddenly came clear to me.

"He's going to create another flume," I stated with finality, realizing the truth as I said the words.

Nevva looked up at her mother. She was in pain. Her imaged winked out, then came back . . . faintly.

"I love you, Mother," she said. "Tell Father I've missed him more than he could know."

"He already knows, Nevva. We both love you and always will."

Nevva smiled. In spite of the pain, and her imminent death, she was at peace.

But I wasn't.

"Where are they, Nevva?" I begged.

Nevva looked to me and said two words. Two words that I had been hunting for. Two words that could hold the salvation of Halla, or lead to its final destruction.

She looked me right in the eye, grabbed my hand, and whispered, "Black Water."

A moment later Nevva Winter was gone. She disappeared. Her spirit had ended along with her physical self. There was nothing left for Elli to hold, or to grieve over.

Her hands were still outstretched, holding nothing. Elli was strong. She barely whimpered. I reached out and held her.

"I'm sorry" was all I managed to say.

We sat that way for several minutes. Elli didn't cry, but she accepted whatever small comfort I could offer. I was ready to stay that way for as long as she needed.

It wasn't long. The troubled woman pulled away and looked at me with weary eyes. Through the tears, came a smile. "She came back to me."

"Yes, she did," I said, trying not to cry myself.

Elli wiped her tears, straightened up, and in a voice that was far stronger than I could have imagined, gave me an order. "Don't let her death be for nothing."

It was exactly what I wanted to hear.

I stood up and backed away from her.

"Go to Solara," I said. "Tell them what we've learned."

"And what will you do?"

We'd had so much thrown at us in the last few moments. The implications were huge. There was so much to digest. So much to try and understand. As confusing as it all may have been, I knew that we were a big step closer to finding the answers we needed.

The next step was clear.

After having been denied access for years by the tragic destruction of a flume, it was time to go back to the jungle. To the klees. To the gars.

To the tangs.

"I'm going to Eelong," I said.

And stepped off Third Earth.

27

The jungles of Eelong.

Yikes.

I never thought I'd see them again. Not after what happened the last time I'd been there. The flume collapsed, killing Kasha and trapping Gunny and Spader on that twisted territory where cats called klees were the dominant species. The destruction of the flume happened because non-Travelers weren't supposed to use them. But they did. Mark and Courtney went to Eelong and brought along the critical piece of information that allowed us to defeat Saint Dane there. But each time they traveled, they weakened the flume, until it crumbled on us. Mark, Courtney, and I got out just in time. Kasha didn't. She was killed by the tumbling gray rocks.

Of course, that was ancient history. As Saint Dane's dark spirit grew, the flumes became open highways. Anybody was able to use them. That is, of course, until they all exploded. Once again, the rules changed. After the destruction, Spader and Gunny left Eelong and moved on to Solara with the rest of the Travelers. Including Kasha. Her body died on Eelong but her spirit lived on.

Now Kasha was back in the game. As with all the Travelers, she was sent to her home territory in order to search for the exiles. My first task on returning to Eelong was to find her. Actually, that was my second task. My first task was to stay alive and not get sent back to Solara. That wasn't going to be easy.

There was no way of knowing *when* I had been sent there and how much time had passed since I'd been there the last time. I found myself standing in a section of jungle that was so thick the overhead canopy of foliage blocked out most of the light. It could have been night for all I knew. That's how dark it was. There wasn't a regular sun that gave Eelong light. It was a distinct band that spread from horizon to horizon and traveled across the sky each day. It gave off heat, too. Lots of it. Eelong was a hot, humid place. It was that intense heat that told me it was daytime, in spite of the lack-o-light. It didn't help that I was still wearing the dark red Ravinian guard uniform. It was pretty heavy and I started sweating right away. In seconds the uniform was sticking to me like a wet suit.

I had no idea which way to go. I hoped to land near Black Water, but if I remembered correctly, there were miles of open, barren land leading to the mountains where the gar stronghold was hidden. The dense jungle I landed in was much more like the area that surrounded the klee village of Leeandra. I did a three-sixty and saw nothing but jungle. I wasn't even on a path. For whatever reason, the spirits of Solara had plunked me down in no-man's-land. Or no-gar's-land. Or whatever.

I picked an arbitrary direction and was about to walk when I heard a rustle coming from the undergrowth not far away, followed by the faint crack of a branch. I snapped to attention. All it took was that one little sound to instantly bring back another memory of Eelong.

Tangs. They were raptorlike dinosaur creatures that roamed the jungles in search of meat. Any meat. The last thing I needed was to square off against one of those bad boys. I listened. Had I heard a creature scrambling in the bushes? Or was it the natural rustle of the jungle? Just in case, I backed away from where the sound had come from. I tried to move quietly, which isn't easy when you're walking on thick snarls of roots and vines.

I sensed movement. Ten yards to my right. It was fleeting, but it was there. Something in the bush had definitely made the noise. Was it a tang? Or a monkey or any other creature that didn't look at me and immediately think "snack"? As much as dying wouldn't be the end of it all for me, getting shredded by a tang's three-pronged talons or chewed by its razor teeth would not have been a pleasant way to get shipped back to Solara. I could blast off of Eelong before that happened, but then I'd be wasting more spirit.

I saw another flash of movement, quicker this time. Whatever it was, was hiding from me. That meant it wasn't a friend. I hoped it was just as scared as I was and was hoping I'd go away and leave it alone. I took another step . . . and heard a low grumble. Grumbling was bad. Klees didn't grumble. I suppose a gar would grumble . . . if it was trying to sound like a freakin' tang! As much as I wanted to step off Eelong and be anywhere else, I knew there had to be a reason why I was dumped in that particular spot. I was going to have to gut it out for as long as possible.

Ooh, gut it out. Bad choice of words. I forced myself to relax. After all, odds were that it wasn't a tang and I was totally safe. With renewed confidence I boldly walked in the other direction. . . .

And was immediately attacked by the tang. So much for playing the odds. The beast leaped from the bushes with its mouth open and its claws up. I had no way to defend myself. All I could do was run. I took off through the jungle, crashing through dense foliage that pulled at my legs, trying to slow me down. I felt as if I were clearing a path for the tang, making it a lot easier for it to follow me than for me to get away. I didn't look back to see how close it was, that would have slowed me down. I had to judge distance from the sound of its breathing and the sharp crunching that came each time its taloned feet hit the ground. I dodged around a few small trees, taking a winding route that I hoped would be hard to follow. Tangs weren't all that agile. If we'd been out in the open, it would have gotten me for sure. The one hope I had was to duck and dodge through the undergrowth until I lost it.

The plan wasn't working. I was being all cagey by changing direction every few feet, depending on how dense the foliage was. The tang didn't care. It blasted straight ahead, tearing through any vines in its way. I didn't have that particular ability. Though I was able to stay ahead of the monster by confusing it, I soon realized that losing it wasn't going to happen. This was his jungle. He knew how to navigate it much better than I did. I was going to run out of gas long before the tang did. Worse, I was stumbling more than running. The footing wasn't exactly solid. At any second I expected to catch my ankle on a vine, take a header, and it would be lunchtime. I didn't want to give up and leave though. At least, not right away. But it was beginning to look as if I would have to step off Eelong before the tang stepped on *me*.

I spotted a gnarled tree about thirty yards ahead. It had a thick vinelike root wrapped around the trunk that would make for easy climbing. For me, that is. Tangs didn't climb. I thought that if I could get enough distance between me and the beast, it would give me the few seconds I'd need to scramble up the tree and be out of reach. I had to go for it. Though I was almost out of gas, I dug down and poured on speed. The tang howled. They weren't exactly smart lizards, but I got the feeling that this one knew exactly what I was going to do. Which meant it was going to do all it could to munch me before I got the chance. Which meant it started crashing through the jungle faster. Which meant I had to pick up the pace. Which meant I had to stop analyzing things, put my head down, and motor. It was time for a full-on sprint. I lifted my knees, hoping not to trip on the undergrowth. The jungle grew less dense, which is probably why I could see the tree. It stood in the center of a small clearing. So close.

I stopped worrying about the tang and locked my eyes on the tree to figure out the quickest climbing route. I knew I'd only have a few seconds to climb high enough to be out of reach. Most tangs were about seven feet tall. They stood on two legs, but their arms weren't all that long. I figured I needed to climb at least ten feet before I'd be out of snapping distance.

Only a few more yards to go. I knew I'd get to the tree before the tang got to me, but could I climb fast enough? There was no room for caution. I had to pick a route and more or less run up the tree. If I stopped to search for the next best hand- or foothold, I'd be done. I had to climb without thinking. With one last burst of energy, I jumped the last few feet and landed with my right foot on one of the curls of vine. It was thick and already had a shell of bark. That was good—it meant that it was solid and wouldn't give way. I scrambled up the tree, climbing the swirling vine like a living ladder.

The tang bellowed. Angrily. I kept expecting to feel the sting of its jaws as they clamped on to my foot. I wondered if I should imagine my feet turning to smoke the way I had when Saint Dane attacked me with the silver weapon. How would that work? If my feet disappeared, would I tumble down into tang teeth? Then again, if I waited too long, the tang might chew off my feet anyway. In the end, I stopped thinking and kept climbing. The tree shook as the tang hit it. I nearly lost my grip, but that didn't stop me from groping my way higher. I heard the scratch of claws on bark. I figured the tang must be desperately raking at the tree. I had the fleeting thought that maybe tangs had learned how to climb since I'd been there. But since I felt no pain from an attack, I was confident that its feet were still on the ground . . . and mine were safe.

I finally got to a horizontal branch where I could stop safely. Clutching the trunk, I looked down to see the enraged tang jumping and swiping its talons, trying to get me. It was futile. I was out of reach. Strings of slobber flew from its mouth as it whipped its head back and forth angrily. Poor guy must have had his heart all set on some Bobby-burger. I stood on that branch, spent, trying to catch my breath. I had dodged being eviscerated, but to what end? I was stuck up in a tree. If the tang thought it through for a couple of seconds, he'd realize that all he had to do was relax and hang out. I'd have to come down eventually. I felt I had done the right thing, but if I couldn't get down from that tree, it was all for nothing. I looked higher, hoping to see some way of crawling along branches to another tree. I remembered the elaborate, intertwining tree system that I'd seen in other parts of Eelong, but this tree wasn't part of that. As I said, it was in the middle of a clearing. The only place to go from there was down. Down wasn't a good option. Not with Toothy waiting for me.

As I looked at the monster, wondering how the heck I was going to get past that thing, another creature emerged from the jungle. I expected to see another tang or two showing up for the picnic. That would have clinched it. I would have to leave the territory and hope that when I came back, I wouldn't land in the middle of team tang again. But it wasn't another tang. It was a gar. A human-looking guy. His hair was long, and he was dressed in roughly cut leathers. I'm not exactly sure how to describe this, but as much as he looked rough around the edges, he wasn't as primitive looking as the gars I had seen in the jungle on my last visit. The leather clothes he wore seemed to be made better than that. And though his hair was long, it wasn't all crazy like some wild jungle guy.

Still, he was a gar. Tangs ate gars. I wasn't sure what to do. I didn't want to let the tang know that he had another option for lunch. The gar had come out of the jungle on the opposite side of the tree from the tang and was walking straight for it. He had no clue what was on the other side. I figured I had to take the chance.

"Hey!" I called out. "Run! There's a tang down there!"

The guy looked up at me and jumped with surprise. I guess he didn't expect to see a gar up in the tree, wearing a red outfit. But I wasn't his problem. He had a lot more to worry about on the ground.

"There's a tang down there!" I called.

The guy stared at me like I was some freak giant red bird.

"Don't you understand?" I called. "There's a tang! Get out of here!"

The guy didn't seem worried at all. While keeping his eyes on me, he reached to his neck and grabbed something that was on a leather strap. He raised it to his lips and blew. A high-pitched, almost inaudible whistle followed. What was this guy doing? If anything, he was only going to let the tang know that somebody was around. I had the brief hope that the tang would react to the whistle the same way the quigs did on Denduron, and fall over in brain-drilling pain. A quick look back to the tang showed me something else entirely.

The beast wasn't in pain. Far from it. A second before, it had been leaping and grabbing at the air, desperate to get at me. Now it was totally relaxed and sitting down on its bottom like an obedient dog. Its entire attitude had changed. It went from sixty to zero in the time it took for the sound of the whistle to reach its ears. Or whatever it was it heard through.

The gar put away the whistle and rounded the tree toward the tang. I thought that as soon as the tang caught sight of the guy, he'd get all slobbered and bothered again.

"Look out!" I screamed at the guy.

He ignored me and walked around the tree. I cringed, waiting for the bloodbath. But the gar walked right up to the tang and petted him on its long snout . . . like a dog. I knew that when I came back to Eelong I was going to see changes, but I never imagined this one. Tangs were the scourge of the jungle. They were feared by both the klees and the gars. They were mindless, predatory beasts. But here a gar was petting a tang as casually as if it were, well, a pet. I half expected the gar to give him a "Good boy!" and throw him a treat. Of course, the only treat a tang would like is somebody's foot, so I didn't think that would happen. At least, I hoped it wouldn't.

As I stood there with my mouth open in shock, the gar looked up to me and called, "Who are you?"

I didn't get the chance to answer. A loud snarl echoed through the jungle. There was a klee around. The gar didn't wait for my answer. No sooner did he hear the snarl than he took off running. As he went, he blew on his whistle again. The tang trotted after him obediently. What the hell? Things had definitely changed since I had been to Eelong.

I was now faced with another challenge. Klees ate gars too. I was a gar. I knew they had upheld Edict Forty-six, which forbids klees to hunt and eat gars, but after seeing the change in the whole tang and gar relationship, I didn't want to assume anything about what the relationship between klees and gars had become. But what was I supposed to do? I was stuck up in a freakin' tree. I could have climbed down, but there was no way I could outrun a cat. I stood there, frozen, hoping that the klee was more interested in the gar on the ground than the gar in the tree. Me.

I felt the tree shake, as if something had jumped onto a branch above me. Something big. I heard the sound of claws skittering across the bark, gouging into the tree as it made its way along. That was it. I couldn't take it anymore. I was out of there. I pictured Solara in my head and was about to take a step when . . .

"Pendragon?" came a voice from above.

I stopped and looked up. Standing on a thick branch not five feet from my head was a huge black cat. A panther. A klee. Kasha.

"What are you doing in this tree?" she asked in such a surprised voice that I actually felt kind of foolish standing there.

"Avoiding a tang. Did you know tangs can be tamed?" I asked.

"Not until I came back to Eelong. A lot has changed since we left."

Kasha wore the same dark tunic that she always wore. She was a forager. When I knew her, she and her team would scour the jungle floor for food. Her job was to protect the others from tangs. From what I'd just seen, that wasn't so important anymore.

"How long have you been back?" I asked. She could have landed back there fifteen minutes ago, or fifteen years. Time was becoming increasingly irrelevant.

"Only a day, but I've seen a lot."

I stared at her, waiting for what I hoped would be good news. She knew exactly what I was thinking and added soberly, "I haven't found the exiles."

"It's okay," I said. "I have. At least I know where they are."

Kasha's eyes widened. "That's wonderful! Have you come to bring me back to Solara?"

"Uh, no. They're here, Kasha. They're in Black Water."

Kasha stared at me, stunned. Yes, she was a klee, but I could tell that she was stunned.

"But . . . how?" she asked.

"Can we get out of this tree first?"

"Yes, yes of course."

The two of us climbed down. Kasha was much more agile than I was, naturally. I felt a lot more safe with Kasha there.

"Where are we?" I asked. "I mean, where on Eelong?"

"Not far from Leeandra. I was headed there when I

heard the tang attack. I didn't expect to see you here."

"I guess that's why I landed where I did," I said. "To find you."

"Probably, and also because I believe it's important that you see Leeandra."

"Why? Has it changed?" I asked.

Kasha nodded. "You must see it for yourself."

"But we need to get to Black Water," I argued.

"Agreed. But you need to understand the new Eelong. If the exiles are in Black Water, what has happened to Leeandra will affect them."

I was convinced. We would head back to the klee city in the trees. As Kasha led me through the jungle, I filled her in on all that had happened, right up to Nevva's death and her dying words.

Kasha shook her head in dismay. "Black Water. I had no idea."

"What am I gonna see in Leeandra?" I asked. I wanted to be a *little* prepared at least.

"It's a dangerous place for gars. Far more than when you were here."

Oh. Swell.

"More dangerous than being treated like a slave and being put on the menu?" I asked.

"Yes. Gars no longer live in Leeandra" was her answer. "They were banished."

"But . . . no," I argued. "There was a whole new cooperation going on between the two races. Gunny and Spader were part of it."

"That was long ago," Kasha answered. "Whatever truce was established was later torn apart."

I couldn't imagine what had happened that could turn

things so far the other way. Before I could ask, I had my answer. We were indeed very close to Leeandra. Kasha and I stepped to the edge of the dense jungle to see the giant, wooden wall that protected the city in the trees. It had been erected to keep the tangs away from the klees. That hadn't changed, but there was one distinct difference. I could see up to the top edge of the city wall, high above. Every ten feet or so was a long pole, from which flew a flag. A red flag with a star on it. The Ravinian star.

"The Ravinians control Eelong," Kasha said.

"I should have guessed," I said softly.

"It's been difficult for me," Kasha continued. "They no longer know who I am, so I'm not trusted. In the short time I've been back, I haven't learned much, but there are rumors. Something is about to happen, and I fear it won't go well for the gars."

"We have to find out what it is," I said. "On Eelong the exiles are all gars."

"That's why we must go inside. The answers will be there."

28

In order for us to get inside the walls of Leeandra, I had to die. Sort of.

"Gars are no longer allowed inside the city walls," Kasha explained. "At least, not by their own choice."

"What does that mean?" I asked.

Kasha didn't answer. She was nervous. That wasn't like her. At least, it wasn't like the confident Kasha I knew. The two of us crouched in the jungle, just before the clearing that surrounded Leeandra. I'd guess there was a stretch of about fifty yards from where the jungle ended until the big wall that protected the tree city of Leeandra.

"Forgive me, Pendragon," she said. "I've seen things since my return that have been quite disturbing. I'm having trouble understanding it all."

"Tell me," I said.

"When I returned, I arrived inside the walls of Leeandra. But the village had changed so drastically, it took me a while to realize it. The structure of the city had been altered dramatically. I tried to find Boon, but had no luck. I even tried to contact him through my Traveler ring. After all, he was my acolyte. But the ring no longer functions."

"I hadn't even thought about the rings," I said. "They probably went dead when the flumes exploded."

"That's my guess. I asked anyone who would listen if they knew him, but got nowhere. Finally, I found someone who said that Boon had gone on an expedition to one of the outlying farms. That's why I was on the outside. To look for Boon."

"Did you find him?"

"No. The farms are no longer where they used to be. I came back, for fear of getting lost. That's when I stumbled on the tang attack, and you."

I nodded. "What else did you find in the city?"

"I roamed about, trying to get my bearings. It was nearly impossible. That's when I realized that I had been sent to a time that was further in the future than when I had lived here. It was the only explanation as to why the city could have changed so."

"You said something is about to happen to the gars. That must be why we are here now."

"I believe it is."

"So? What is it?" I asked.

Kasha fell silent. Something was obviously bothering her.

"You discovered something, didn't you?" I asked.

"I saw something. Something I never thought would happen, yet it has. I walked to the part of the city that the foragers used as their base, hoping to find someone I might know. It is still there. Mostly as I remembered it. The foragers still function. They still leave the city to gather food. But . . ."

She couldn't continue. Whatever she'd seen had really disturbed her. I didn't push her, because I knew she'd eventually open up. Though she was a klee, I could read her expressions as clearly as if she were human. Her dark fur glistened, as if she were sweating. Kasha was definitely off balance.

"There was a group of foragers inside the barracks. They were eating and talking, and laughing about how their jobs would soon be so much easier. They said there would be no more lurking through the jungle. No more worrying about tangs. No more guarding those who harvested fruits and vegetables at the farms. It was a celebration of sorts. It was all about how their lives would soon change because they would no longer have to forage in the jungle."

"So then, what are they going to do for food?" I asked.

"They didn't say," Kasha said. "They didn't have to. I saw." She swallowed. Hard. The memory was a tough one. "One of the foragers was chewing on a bone. He finished and threw it onto a pile that had been building near the door."

I felt as if I knew where this was headed, but I still had to hear.

"What was he eating, Kasha?"

"It was a leg bone. A gar leg bone. All of the bones were gar bones. It's happened, Pendragon. Gars have become food. They're on the verge of repealing Edict Forty-six. It's going to be legal to eat intelligent creatures! The foragers' jobs will no longer be about finding food in the jungle. I believe they now will be in charge of gathering the gars for . . . for . . ." Kasha had to work hard to hold back her emotions. "It's a step away from cannibalism."

I looked toward the high walls of Leeandra, with its flapping Ravinian flags. Knowing the truth, the fantastic village in the trees took on a whole new feeling for me. It was no longer a wondrous village of talking cats. It was a slaughterhouse.

"Kinda makes me not want to go inside," I said.

"I do not believe the issue has been decided yet," Kasha said. "They spoke as if it were something that was about to happen, but had not yet occurred."

"But they were eating gars!" I shot back.

"Foragers always lived above the law," Kasha explained. "They feel the rules of the common klee do not apply to them. There is arrogance among the foragers. I know. I was one of them. One of the worst."

"But you never ate gars."

"No. It was something my father instilled in me. I suppose at one time it would have been acceptable, but since we discovered that the gars were intelligent, it could no longer be justified. How is it possible that after such great strides were made, the klee took such a giant step backward?"

I pointed up to the flapping Ravinian flags.

"Ravinia" was my answer. "Fueled by Saint Dane's vision. Power to the powerful at the expense of the weak. That's pretty much what he's spread throughout Halla. It doesn't surprise me at all."

"I'm devastated," Kasha said, her head down.

"Don't be," I said quickly. "We're not done yet. We're here to protect the exiles, and given all that you told me, I think I know what the Ravinian klees have in mind for them."

The thought was sickening.

"That's why we need to get inside Leeandra," Kasha offered. "We need to learn when the edict will be repealed. That will tell us how much time we have before the exiles are in danger."

I looked at the tall wall again. I didn't want to go in there. I *really* didn't want to go in there. But Kasha was right. We needed to know when Edict Forty-six would fall. Once that happened, it would be open season on all gars.

And exiles.

"There's no way I can get through those gates the way I did last time," I said. "Not if gars are banned from Leeandra."

Kasha gave me an uneasy look. "Some gars are allowed inside."

"Which ones?"

"Dead ones."

I stared at the cat for a good long time, trying to figure out what the heck she meant by that. I soon found out. A few minutes later I found myself lying on the bottom of a four-wheeled forager wheelbarrow. Kasha was pushing. A dirty tarp was over me. The plan was simple. As far as anybody would know, she was wheeling in a dead gar to be eaten by her fellow foragers. Yeah, how sick is that? I lay there, trying my best to act dead. I had taken off my Ravinian shirt and dirtied up my pants, so that it wouldn't be obvious I was wearing the uniform of a Ravinian guard. I didn't think that would go over too well if I were discovered by a klee Ravinian guard. They might think that I had stolen it from one of their guards and, well, I figured their revenge might be messy. I kept the boots, though. Kasha pointed out that klee boots were very different from what gars wore, so nobody would suspect that I had gotten them from a Ravinian guard. So that's how I was wheeled toward Leeandra—naked from the waist up and covered in mud to make me look like lunch.

I looked out through a fold in the tarp that gave me a

narrow view ahead. Kasha quickly pushed me along the base of the wall until we came upon one of the huge gates that led into the village of Leeandra. Guarding the entrance were two large, scary-looking klees wearing red Ravinian guard uniforms. They each had spears strapped to their backs. As scary as it was entering Leeandra the last time I had been there, it didn't compare to this. I was food. Simple as that. I hoped that the klees inside were civilized enough that they wouldn't all pounce on me and start chowing. To say it was an uneasy feeling is a pretty big understatement.

"What is in there?" one guard asked Kasha gruffly.

"None of your concern," Kasha answered just as sharply. She tried to move forward, but the guard stopped her.

"Stop," he commanded. "It is our duty to inspect all items entering the city."

"I'm a forager," Kasha said impatiently. "I'm not governed by the same pedestrian laws as the other klees."

From under the tarp I got a good view of the guard. He was a red-furred cat, with sharp, green eyes. Bad kitty. He stared at Kasha, as if deciding whether or not to make an issue out of it.

"You foragers are all alike," he snarled. "You think you are above the law. Those days are past. Everyone is beholden to Ravinia. And Ravinian law says that we are empowered to inspect anything and everything that passes through these gates. If you would like to take this up with the circle, I would be more than happy to detain you until the next meeting."

It was a standoff. Who was going to blink? An instant later I felt the tarp being pulled off me. I went into dead mode, whatever that is. I definitely held my breath. I had the fleeting thought that it was a good move to have dumped my Ravinian uniform. There was a long moment of silence. It killed me not to be able to open my eyes to see what the guards were doing.

"For my fellow foragers," Kasha said. "Or would you rather we chose not to bring food back for the likes of you anymore?"

For a second I feared that the guy would grab my arm and take a bite. I had all I could do to keep still.

I heard the klee growl, as if trying to maintain some kind of dignity. "You are all alike," he snarled. "Move on!"

Kasha threw the tarp back over my head, and we started moving again. We were in. Kasha and the corpse.

"Stay still," she half whispered. "I'll say when you can move."

I was only too happy to play dead. The idea that we were surrounded by vicious cats, who could pounce on me and start chewing any second, was terrifying. I wondered if they were like dogs. Could they smell fear? If so, I must have smelled pretty rank. As much as I wanted to see the transformed Leeandra, I didn't take the chance to try and peek out through the folds in the tarp.

"Where are we going?" I whispered.

"Shhh," Kasha scolded.

I shushed. A talking corpse would arouse suspicion. And after all, cats had pretty good hearing. I tried to relax and be dead. Kasha wheeled me along for several minutes. After a few bumps we stopped, and I sensed that we were rising up, which meant we were in one of the elevators that brought klees from the ground into the village buildings that were built at all different levels in the giant trees. The elevator bumped to a stop and Kasha wheeled me off. We moved along for a few minutes more, the wheels of the cart chattering over what I figured were the wooden boards of the bridges that soared between trees. With one final bump, we stopped.

"It's safe here," Kasha said. "We can't be seen."

I cautiously pushed the tarp aside. Since I was on my back, I found myself staring up into the thick canopy of foliage. I saw that we were on a large platform built around a tree. This was exactly like the Leeandra I knew. When I stood up, I got a view of a Leeandra I didn't.

I walked to the railing to look out over a changed city. It was still built within impossibly massive trees, but the structures themselves were totally different. Gone were the huts that were erected on sturdy limbs. Now Leeandra was a city of buildings. They were wooden buildings, but modern looking. The wood planks were obviously milled. The designs were varied. Some were round. Others soared high into the sky, rivaling the trees they were built next to. The roped walkways that had connected the trees and buildings were replaced by solid-looking bridges.

When I was there before, very few buildings were on the ground. That was a precaution against tang attacks. Now buildings were everywhere. Hundreds were still in the trees, but many rose from the jungle floor as well. Powered vehicles passed below us on wide streets. There were wooden sidewalks, traffic lights, and even giant billboards that didn't advertise products, but instead displayed interesting works of art.

As different as it was from the Leeandra I remembered, it made total sense. This was the Eelong version of the Conclave of Ravinia on Third Earth. This was Utopia for the privileged.

Kasha said, "It is like looking into the future of my own time."

"It *is* the future of your own time," I corrected.

"With no gars whatsoever," she added.

With that in mind, I looked around to try and spot one. Of course klees were everywhere. Leeandra had become a busy city. I saw them walking along the streets—some on two feet, some on all four. Elevators rose on the outside of buildings, loaded with klees. Klees were even driving the powered vehicles. Not a single gar was in sight. Though they had been treated as slaves and pets, my memory of Leeandra was that there were almost as many gars as klees. They may have been on leashes, or forced into performing the worst menial labor, but they were very much a part of Leeandra. Not anymore.

I also saw several klees, dressed in the red uniform of the Ravinian guards, stationed on street corners. Ravinia was a part of life in Leeandra now. I wondered if they were living klees, or dado klees that had been built on Third Earth.

"Do not move!" came a harsh voice from behind us.

Uh-oh. We weren't alone after all. I tensed up, ready for a fight. I looked to Kasha. She looked surprisingly relaxed. No, it was stranger than that. Kasha was smiling.

"Who are you?" the voice asked. "What are you doing in my home with that gar?"

I figured I should let Kasha handle this. After all, who would listen to a talking dinner?

"Is that any way to welcome back a tired Traveler?"

Huh? Kasha knew this guy?

"Kasha?" the voice gasped in disbelief.

Kasha turned and faced the klee.

"Hello, Boon," she said. "I can't tell you how happy I am to see you."

The light brown klee stood there for a moment, stunned.

He then ran to Kasha and threw his paws/arms/hands/ whatever around her. The two hugged like long-lost friends, which was exactly what they were.

"I—I don't understand," Boon mumbled. He was in tears. "I saw you die. In that tunnel."

Kasha glanced to me. I wondered how deep an explanation she was going to offer her friend.

"Obviously, I didn't. I was able to escape and was nursed back to health."

Smart move.

"Do you remember Pendragon?"

Boon looked at me and his eyes grew even wider.

"Pendragon!" he screamed, and leaped at me.

It was kind of scary. After all, klees ate us tasty gars now. But Boon wrapped his furry arms around me and gave me just as big a hug as he'd given to Kasha.

"You shouldn't be here, Pendragon!" he exclaimed. "It's too dangerous!"

"I know, Boon, it's okay."

Boon was just as full of energy and enthusiasm as I'd remembered. He pulled back from me and held me at arm's length to size me up.

"You've grown," he declared. "You are stronger."

I shrugged. He was right.

"What about Spader and Gunny?" he asked. "I haven't heard from them since . . . since . . ."

"Since the klees kicked out the gars?" I asked.

Boon nodded. "Yes. Are they all right? Are they still in Black Water?"

"No," I said.

He relaxed. "That's a good thing."

Alarms went off in my head.

"Why's that? Has something happened to Black Water?"

"No," he answered. "Not yet."

Kasha and I exchanged looks.

"Tell us what's happening," she said to Boon.

Boon took a quick look around, as if to make sure nobody was watching.

"Come," he said. "Into my home. It would not be good to be seen by a Ravinian guard."

Ravinian guard. Unbelievable. It didn't matter what territory or what race or even what species was on a world, the Ravinians' control of Halla was complete.

As it turned out, Kasha had brought us to the platform that led into the tree where Boon lived. It was a small, old-school Leeandra apartment structure built into the hollow tree. There were old, crumbling chairs and threadbare rugs on the floor. Boon didn't live in luxury. We made ourselves comfortable, and Boon gave us some sweet drink that re-energized me. He also gave me one of his old cloth shirts, so I didn't have to walk around half naked.

"So much has happened since you two left," Boon told us. "I don't know where to begin."

I wanted to learn it all, but I was much more concerned about the future. About Edict Forty-six and what it would mean to the gars and the exiles in Black Water.

"Let me guess," I said. "Things were going really well between the klees and the gars. Once the klees understood that the gars were intelligent, they began to accept them, and a new society began to emerge. But then came Ravinia."

Boon sat down on the floor next to me.

"How could you know?" he asked.

"The same kind of thing has been happening all over Halla. The Ravinians promise a better way of life, but in order to achieve it, they only reward those who provide something they consider valuable to society. Those who don't make the cut are cast aside or reduced to slavery. I'm guessing that Ravinia was the beginning of the end for the gars here in Leeandra."

"That was exactly it!" Boon exclaimed. "The Circle of Klee had become just 'the Circle,' to allow the gars to be part of it. Now it is called 'the Circle of Ravinia.'"

"Of course it is," I said with a sarcastic huff.

"The rights of the gars were reduced instantly. They barely had time to get used to being equals when the Ravinians began tossing them out into the jungle."

"Why weren't they kept around to perform the menial jobs?" Kasha asked. "Like before?"

"Because there were plenty of klees to do that," Boon answered. "Ravinia separated those klees they considered special from those who did not contribute. The chosen were given incredible houses and positions of power, while everyone else was forced into building the new city."

"And I'm guessing the gars were considered beneath even them, so they were cast out. Right?"

Boon nodded.

"What happened to you, Boon?" Kasha asked.

Boon dropped his head. He looked ashamed. "I was just a lowly forager, and not a very good one at that. I thought the part I played in bringing the gars from Black Water would allow me to be part of the elite. I was wrong. Actually, I think it hurt me. They saw me as a gar sympathizer. I'm no longer a forager. My job is to clean the sewage lines that carry waste from the new buildings. I am easily replaceable, as they tell me each day. Look at this apartment. I'm lucky to still have it. Soon this will be taken over by the Circle of Ravinia and knocked down, and another mansion will be erected. I'll have to live in the outskirts of the city, at a place they call the Horizon Compound. I hear that klees live four to a room there, with little food and even less comfort." Boon sighed. "The future for Eelong seemed so bright."

"Until Ravinia," I said.

"Yes, until Ravinia."

Kasha added, "And now Edict Forty-six is about to be repealed. It sickens me."

Boon shook his head. "Oh, no. Edict Forty-six was rescinded long ago. Gars are regularly killed and eaten for food."

Kasha shot me a surprised look. Then to Boon she said, "But I overheard some foragers say that something important was about to happen that would make the hunt for food so much easier. I assumed they meant the repeal of Edict Forty-six."

Boon's expression turned even darker. "Something *is* about to happen to make the hunt for food easier," he explained. "But it isn't the repeal of Edict Forty-six."

"Then what is it?" I asked.

"It's why I asked about Gunny and Spader," Boon answered. "The klee army has been massing and training for a long time now. They play their maneuvers out on the old wippen fields. I have never seen so many soldiers assemble in one place."

"What are they training for?" I asked nervously.

"I am not supposed to know, but as a worker, I turn up in many places that most would never expect. I have heard the plans."

"What, Boon?" I demanded.

"The army is going to march on Black Water," he stated

flatly. "Whatever gars are not killed in the strike will be captured and kept alive—"

"For food," I said, numb.

Boon nodded. "The army is immense. The gars won't stand a chance."

"Do you think they know of the exiles?" Kasha asked.

"What exiles?" was Boon's answer.

"Doesn't matter," I said. "The klees won't know the difference between a gar or a human. Or care."

"What's a human?" Boon asked, confused.

"Show me, Boon," I demanded. "I need to see this army."

"Can you do that?" Kasha asked Boon.

Boon thought a moment, then nodded. "Yes. I know a trail through the trees, along a route that is off-limits to most, but I have the combinations to the locks, since I clean everywhere. I can show you the entire klee army."

"Now," I said. "I want to see them now."

"Why?" Boon asked. "They train the same way in the same location every day."

"I want to know what we're up against" was my simple answer.

"Up against!" Boon said, aghast. "You cannot stop this army!"

"Let me be the judge of that," I said boldly.

Kasha stood up. "I'm sorry if this is difficult for you, Boon, but it's important."

Boon pounced to his feet. "You don't have to convince me. I'm happy to be back in action!"

I took the tarp from the forager wheelbarrow and draped it over my head in case we were spotted by a Ravinian guard. Or any other hungry klee, for that matter. Since Edict Forty-six had already been repealed, there were no restrictions on

Bobby-chow. Boon led us on a journey along the catwalk pathways that snaked across the treetops of Leeandra.

"Most klees don't come up here," Boon explained. "Only the workers. We're able to move equipment and supplies without having to bother the klees below."

"Typical Ravinians," I scoffed. "They want everybody to do their dirty work, but don't want to see how it's done."

"That's pretty much it," Boon agreed.

Every so often we'd hit a doorway that had a complex lock made from twisted bamboo. They were primitive combination locks, and Boon knew all the combinations.

"I'd get lost up here," Kasha said.

"I have. More than once." Boon chuckled. "How do you think I learned my way around?"

We traveled for at least twenty minutes, moving from bridge to bridge, level to level, until we drew near the large, grassy wippen fields.

"Just past this last tree," Boon explained. "That's where you'll see them. Be careful; once we're over their heads, we can be seen."

"Don't worry, I don't want to be eaten," I said.

"That would be the least of your problems," Boon said somberly. "This army is training to invade the gar stronghold. If they saw a gar spying on them from above, I don't think there'd be enough of you left to eat."

Oh. Thanks for that.

We cautiously approached a thick tree. The pathway continued through the center of it. All three of us entered into the dark of the tunnel. Boon stopped us before we could exit out the other side.

"Now be careful, and quiet. No sudden moves. When you pass through that opening, look down. We're directly above the wippen fields. The armies are below. Hopefully they'll be in the middle of one of their mock battles and won't notice us. You still want to risk going out there?"

"I have to, Boon. We have to know what the gars are up against, because we're going to have to try and stop them."

"Oh," Boon said. "Then I suppose you really are a spy."

"Absolutely."

"Good. I will go first and signal for you to come if it is safe."

Boon padded quietly (which was easy for him since he was a cat) out and onto the bridge that continued beyond the wide tree. Cautiously he peered down over the edge. Kasha and I watched nervously, waiting for his signal.

It didn't come.

"What is he waiting for?" Kasha whispered nervously.

Boon stood on the bridge, looking down. His body language changed. He no longer kept low to make himself less visible. He stood up straight on his back two feet.

"What is it?" Kasha called to him.

Boon looked back to us. There was no expression on his face. He slowly lifted his paw and motioned for us to join him. Kasha and I crept forward quickly. We stayed low and quietly stepped out onto the bridge. I held my breath. We were about to see the enemy. The army below was gathered, organized, and trained to march on Black Water. It was a gruesome hunt for food that could end up wiping out the last hope for the salvation of Halla. Did Saint Dane know that? Was this his doing? If the invasion succeeded, he wouldn't need the dado army on Third Earth. He wouldn't need to use any of his dark power to create another flume. Halla would be his.

I prepared myself for the worst. Would the army be

mechanized? How would they be armed? Would this be a primitive army of cats? Or had Ravinia somehow developed more deadly weapons? Maybe most important, would we find that the army was filled with dados? As we crept out onto that bridge and looked below, I expected all of those questions to be answered.

They weren't. What I saw below was far worse than anything I could have imagined.

"I don't understand," Boon said, sounding as dumb as I felt.

What we saw below was . . . nothing. The wippen fields were empty. The armies were gone.

"I do," I gasped. "They're on their way. They've already left for Black Water."

29

How long?" I asked.

"How long what?" Boon replied.

"Since you saw them the last time!" I shouted. My heart was pounding. I had the sick feeling that we were too late.

"Yesterday. Maybe the day before. I don't remember."

"It's a long day's ride to the mountains that surround Black Water," Kasha reasoned. "I believe an army the size that Boon described would take at least twice as long to get there."

"So if they left two days ago, we're too late," I snarled.

"Let's hope they left yesterday" was Kasha's reasoned answer.

"We've got to get there," I said. "Before they do."

"There's only one way to do that," Kasha offered.

I knew exactly what she meant, and it wasn't about going back to Solara and hoping that the spirit would send us back to Black Water.

"You think you can still fly?" I asked.

"No!" Boon shouted in protest. "You want to steal a gig?"

I shrugged. "We've done it before."

"Things have changed, Pendragon," Boon argued. "The Ravinian security is much tighter. Leeandra is on a war footing."

"Good," I said. "Then they won't be surprised when we bring the war to them."

"You do not have to help us, Boon," Kasha said sincerely. "You have already done far more than I should ever have asked for."

Boon looked back and forth between the two of us. "Wait," he said. "Do you think for one second that I would *not* come with you? I am your acolyte, Kasha. And in case you did not understand, I have no love for the Ravinians. Trust me, I want to do everything I can to stop them. If that means trying to steal a gig and landing in the middle of Black Water, so be it. I just want you to know the risks."

Kasha smiled. "Thank you, Boon. We understand the risks."

"Then when do we leave?" he asked.

"How about yesterday?" was my obnoxious answer.

The three of us made our way quickly across the sky bridges, headed for the tree that housed the hangar where the gigs were stored. Kasha and I had flown one of the small, two-seater helicopters to Black Water once before, and ended up in a dogfight over the jungle with other, more-experienced gig pilots. We won. I hoped that she was just as sharp with her flying skills as she'd been back then. No, what I really hoped for was that she wouldn't have to use those skills again. An uneventful flight would be just fine. But first we had to get a gig.

The trip back was easy. I kept the tarp over my head and couldn't see much. Kasha and Boon more or less led me along. I'm sure we got plenty of strange glances, but nobody stopped us. The gig hangar was in the same spot as I remembered, but as with the rest of Leeandra, it had changed. My memory of the place was that it was a massive space hollowed out from one of the monster trees, high in the air. One whole side of the tree was open, under which a launch platform was built out over the city. Launching a gig meant wheeling it out from inside the tree and onto the platform, and taking off from there. All of that was the same . . . but there was more. The first change I noticed was that when we reached the doorway that led into the back of the hangar, there were no guards.

"What happened to the increased security?" I asked.

Boon shrugged. "I don't know, Pendragon. I clean sewers. They don't discuss those details with me."

"Oh. Right. Sorry."

"Perhaps they don't need security anymore," Kasha said soberly. "The gigs may all be gone to support the army."

"Let's find out," I said, and dropped the tarp for the last time. I hoped.

I boldly went for the wooden door that led into the hangar. Opening it cautiously, I was met with darkness.

"I don't get it," I said softly, for fear there were Ravinians inside. "Are we in the right place?"

"Yes," Boon answered. "There is no other hangar."

"Then why is it dark? The opening where they launch the gigs is huge."

Kasha didn't wait for the answer that Boon didn't have. She pushed past me and into the hangar.

It was definitely the same hangar, but with one big difference. The opening through which the gigs were launched now had massive doors that looked to be made from bamboo. They were closed. I waited for my eyes to adjust, which was something Kasha and Boon didn't have to worry about. After all, they were cats.

"The gigs are here," Kasha whispered.

My eyes hadn't adjusted enough to make out any detail, but I could sense that the room was full. That was a relief. At least the klees weren't planning another aerial attack on Black Water. The gigs were there for the taking. But it wouldn't be easy. Not only were the giant doors shut, the helicopters were powered by crystals fueled by light from the sunbelt. Good news was that it was daytime, without a cloud in the sky. Bad news was that it wouldn't matter how much light there was outside if we couldn't open those doors to get at it.

"Look," Kasha said, pointing high above.

I saw a room two stories up, built out from the hangar wall. It looked like a control room with an open balcony surrounding it. My guess was that it was a flight tower where they coordinated the gig launches. A light was on inside the room. I clearly saw a klee sitting inside.

Kasha continued, "I would guess the hangar doors are controlled from up there."

My eyes had adjusted enough to see that there was a set of open stairs built against the wall that led up to the control room. The way to go seemed obvious.

"Find a gig," I said to Kasha. "Boon and I will go up there and open the doors. As soon as the light comes in, power up."

"You cannot fight a klee," Kasha warned.

I grabbed Kasha's forager weapon that she always had strapped to her back. It was a long wooden stick much like the ones Loor and the Batu warriors used.

"I can fight one klee," I said.

"And I'll be with him," Boon added.

"Even so, we can't fight a bunch of klees," I cautioned. "Once things start getting nasty, we've got to get out of here fast."

Kasha nodded. There wasn't any more to be discussed. I tapped Boon on the back and motioned for him to head for the stairs. We wound our way through the gigs, trying to hide from the eyes of the klee up above in the control room. If there was one thing we needed, it was surprise. If that klee thought he was being attacked, I'd bet anything that there was an alarm he could sound and bring others running. We had to be quiet and fast and out of there before he knew what hit him, which hopefully would be the end of Kasha's stick.

At the bottom of the stairs I stopped Boon to strategize.

"Get him to come outside onto the balcony," I instructed.

"Are you sure?" Boon asked, uncertain. "I know you're brave, Pendragon, but you're not a warrior."

I almost laughed. I probably would have if I hadn't been afraid of alerting the klee.

"Boon," I whispered. "A lot has changed since we were together. Just get him outside."

I think he sensed my confidence and didn't question me again. The klee pounced up the stairs on all fours. Though he moved quietly, the stairs rattled under his weight. The klee in the control room would know pretty quickly that somebody was coming up. Hopefully, when he saw another klee, he wouldn't think anything bad was about to happen to him . . . because something bad was about to happen to him. The stairs twisted and turned as we climbed. I kept one section of stairs between us, thinking that if the klee came out to see who was coming up, he'd see Boon and not me.

When Boon was almost to the top, he gave me a quick look. I waved as if to say, "Go for it." He continued on up to the balcony, where a closed door led into the room. He didn't open it. Instead, he walked around on the balcony to the front of the room, where there were two large windows that looked out from the control room onto the hangar floor. I could lean out, look up, and see Boon as he rapped on the glass. I couldn't see the klee inside, but I saw Boon gesture for him to come outside.

This was it. I crouched low on the stairs. Directly above me was the door into the room. As soon as the klee came out and turned to round toward Boon, I'd have my chance to spring from behind and knock him into next week.

The door opened. The klee came storming out, looking angry. I guess he didn't like having surprise visitors knocking on his window. I was close enough to see that he wore a red Ravinian guard uniform. I stayed low, hoping he wouldn't see me on the stairs. He walked around the balcony to the front, where Boon waited for him.

"Who are you?" the klee demanded to know. "This is a restricted area. You are not authorized to be—"

Before he could finish the sentence, I jumped up onto the balcony and clocked him on the side of the head. Hard. My plan had worked. Everything went perfectly, except that the klee barely reacted, other than to stop talking. Uh-oh. The klee slowly turned around to see what had hit him, so I hit him again. *Whack*. Right on the side of his cat head. The klee's head snapped to the side, but he wasn't hurt. My first thought was that it was impossible. I had nailed the guy with two blows that should have crushed him. The truth hit back a second later.

"Dado," I gasped.

The cat jumped at me, paws up, claws out. I was so stunned that I barely moved. By all rights the thing should have torn me apart, but Boon jumped at the klee and tackled him from behind. The dado klee hit the floor of the balcony with Boon on top of him.

"The hangar door!" Boon yelled.

Right. The reason we were there. I backed away and went for the control room. Inside I saw that besides the door that led to the balcony, there was another door in the back wall of the room that must have led inside the tree. I feared there might be klees beyond that door, so I jammed Kasha's weapon against it, hoping it might give us an extra few seconds.

On the balcony, Boon and the klee were wrestling. I didn't know what kind of fighter Boon was, but there was no way he'd be able to battle a dado for long. I had to get the hangar doors open so that Kasha could power up a gig, then get back out to help my friend.

There was a long control panel with dozens of toggle switches. I really wished there was one that read: HANGAR DOORS. There wasn't. Luckily, most of the switches were the same size, which meant they must have more or less done the same thing. Whatever that was. To the far right of the panel was a large toggle switch. It looked just as good as any, so I threw it.

The overhead lights went on, bringing the hangar to life. The hangar doors didn't budge though. On the far left of the panel was another large toggle. I quickly went for it and threw it. Two things happened. With a jolt and a screech, the giant doors at the front of the hangar began to slide open. They separated in the middle and slowly moved to either side, like a curtain on a stage, opening up our escape route. Sunlight streamed in, which meant Kasha would have power. That was all great except for the second thing that happened.

Alarms blared. There must have been a special security process required to properly open those doors. Unfortunately, I didn't know it. I had no doubt that we would soon be flooded with Ravinian guards, because you didn't need to have the acute hearing of a cat to hear the harsh, jangling horn that honked incessantly. I ran for the door to help Boon as the back door into the control room blew open. The bad guys had arrived sooner than expected. Kasha's weapon did nothing to keep the door closed. A Ravinian klee burst into the room, picked me up, and threw me against the far wall of the control room, opposite the door to the balcony. I was trapped. A Ravinian klee was between me and the way out. There was nothing good that could come of this scenario. I figured I could battle the klee for a while, but his claws would make for a short fight. I was all set to step out of there and go back to Solara when I saw something leaning against the control panel that made perfect sense. These were dados. Dados that were built on Third Earth. There was no more pretense about not mixing territories. Saint Dane had seen to that. So it made perfect sense that if dados were on Eelong, they would also have dado weapons. Leaning against the control panel was a long, silver wand exactly like the Ravinian dados used on Third Earth.

The klee went for me.

I went for the weapon.

I snagged it just as the klee swiped at me with its claws out. I ducked, feeling the whistle as he barely missed my head. My hands were on the weapon, but I didn't have time to turn it on. Instead, I jammed the handle back into the dado's gut. Or whatever it is that area is called on a standing-up cat. The dado didn't flinch. Its instinct was to take another swipe at me. I didn't bother trying to block it. I just pushed away from the klee and fell down on my butt. It swiped nothing but air, then set its eyes on me and pounced.

I fumbled with the red power button. I didn't know if I'd have the chance to power it up and defend myself at the same time. It was more important to use it to ward off the attack than to damage the dado. I stopped worrying about the power and held up the silver wand. The cat did the rest. It leaped with all four paws in the air. Its eyes were locked on mine. It landed square on the point of the wand and seemingly perched there for a second, though I know that was impossible. I pushed, and the cat fell on the floor right next to me. Its lifeless eyes staring at the ceiling.

Dead cat.

I guess I'd gotten the power on.

There wasn't time to celebrate. Where there was one klee, there would be more. I jumped to my feet and ran for the door to the balcony. Outside, Boon was struggling with the first klee. He was holding his own, too. I think if Boon had known it was a robot, he wouldn't have been so bold. The klee kept swiping at Boon. Boon kept warding off the blows. He didn't bother to go in to attack the Ravinian, and I knew why. He wanted to keep it occupied long enough so that I could get the hangar doors open.

"Back here!" I shouted.

The klee stopped swinging at Boon and whipped around toward me. It was the last move he made. I nailed him in the chest with the electric wand and pushed him to the side. It hit the rail of the balcony and toppled over, falling to the floor far below, where it landed on the overhead rotor of a gig. It flipped like a rag doll, and settled on the ground with a sickening thud.

Two dead cats.

Boon was exhausted, but he was okay.

"What is that thing?" he asked through gasps of air, pointing at the weapon.

"Not a toy. Don't touch it."

"Don't worry!"

The two of us scrambled for the stairs and quickly ran down. As we got closer to the floor, I glanced out over the hangar. The doors were continuing to open, but slowly. Too slowly. I wondered where Kasha was. Hopefully, she had picked a gig that would be hit with light, to give it power sooner rather than later. But none of the gigs were powering up.

I also saw that the gigs themselves had changed. When I was there before, they had been small vehicles that reminded me of bumper cars in an amusement park. They had two seats with an overhead rotor for lift and smaller side rotors for maneuverability. These gigs looked more or less the same, except that they were much bigger than the old two-seater jobs. Most of them were ten times that size, which said only one thing to me: troop transports. They were lined up near the hangar doors, ready to lift off. I had the sinking feeling that Kasha didn't know how to fly one of those big boys, and that's why none of the rotors were turning.

The alarm horn continued to shriek. Flashing red lights painted the room. There was no question that we would soon be flooded with cats, and there was nothing that a single electric wand could do against them.

We hit the floor and both sprinted toward the opening doors, because that's where we both hoped that Kasha would be. We got to the front line of gigs, but there was no Kasha in sight.

"There!" Boon called out.

To the far side of the first line was one small red gig. It was still larger than the two-seater gig we had flown before, but it was a fraction of the size of the troop carriers. At the controls behind the clear windscreen was Kasha. The light from the opening doorway hadn't hit that gig yet. A quick look around told me that this gig was the only small one, which I figured was the only one she could fly. That was okay, so long as the sunlight hit it before other klees showed up to start hitting *us*!

"Get on board!" I shouted.

Boon ran toward Kasha. I ran for the opening door and sprinted outside, where the launch platform continued on for another forty feet out over Leeandra. I ran to the edge and looked around to see if we were causing a disturbance. We were. On the ground, dozens of Ravinian guards sprinted for the tree. Above us on the sky bridges, I saw more Ravinians headed our way. It would only be a matter of minutes before we were swarmed.

I ran back to the gig, where Kasha was nervously waiting for the light.

"It was the only choice I had," she complained.

"Don't worry. Boon, push."

Boon and I got behind the red gig and pushed. We needed to get it out of line and into the light from the sunbelt, so the crystal in the nose could be hit and give us power. The door was not yet open wide enough for us to get the gig through to outside, and the light was still several yards away. Boon and I grunted and pushed and cajoled the little chopper forward until we finally joined sunbelt light with gig.

"Clear away!" Kasha shouted.

Boon and I backed off as Kasha toggled the engine switches. The whining sound of the crystal-driven rotors coming to life was like music.

"Get in!" I shouted to Boon.

As he jumped in, I sprinted back out through the opening doors. I ran to the platform edge to see that the klees below had reached our tree. How much time did we have? Seconds? It was then that I heard another sound. Actually, what I heard was a sound that had stopped. I spun around to see that the hangar doors weren't moving anymore. A second later, with a grinding of gears, they began to close! I sprinted back inside and looked up at the control room to see two more klees at the panel. They didn't need to hurry after us. They knew what we were trying to do. So long as they got those doors closed, we wouldn't be able to get the gig out, and they'd have us.

I ran for the open-cockpit gig and jumped in. There were four seats. Two in front, two in back. Boon was already in back. Kasha was in the left-hand pilot's seat.

"This is going to be close," I said as I buckled in.

"We are going to have to lift off inside the hangar," she said. "Very dangerous."

"It's going to be a lot more dangerous if those doors close much more," I pointed out.

The overhead rotor was now humming. I saw Kasha glance ahead to the closing doors.

"We won't have time to get the side rotors up to speed," she said soberly.

"Can we still fly?" I asked.

"Yes, but only straight ahead. I will not be able to maneuver much. Either we are lined up properly in the opening, or not."

I looked back up to the control room to see that more klees had arrived. Many more. Dozens of red-shirted Ravinian guards had come through the back door to the control room and were flooding down the stairs.

"The longer we wait the smaller that opening gets," I said.

Kasha's response was to pull back on the control stick. With a lurch the gig lifted off the deck. I winced, as if that would have done anything if we crashed into another gig. Or flew too high. Or slammed into the hangar door. I winced anyway.

The ground-floor door burst open at the rear of the hangar. More klees were on the way in.

"Now, Kasha," Boon said calmly.

Kasha pushed the joystick forward. The nose of the gig dipped a few degrees, and we floated forward. Without lateral control, the gig felt like a puppet on a string. We swayed left, then right. Kasha couldn't compensate. We spun a few degrees clockwise and found ourselves moving sideways toward the rapidly diminishing opening.

"We gonna make this?" I asked skeptically.

"We'll know soon" was her obvious answer.

I felt the gig lurch. A klee had jumped up and was hanging from the skid below.

"Take him for a ride," I ordered.

Kasha coaxed the gig forward. We got closer to the

opening. I tried to gauge how much time we had and if the space was big enough, as if my calculations had any impact whatsoever on what was happening. We were in Kasha's hands. Or her paws. The gig slid to the right. It was no longer a case of whether or not we could make it through the opening, because we weren't headed for the opening anymore. It must have been the weight of the klee hanger-on that threw us off.

"Uh, Kasha," I said, as if she didn't see the exact same thing.

We were seconds from slamming into the door when Kasha said, "I have lateral control."

The rotors to the sides had finally gotten up to speed. Kasha jammed the stick to her left. The gig swung back, maybe a little too far. I held my breath. It was like we were going around a speedway race track, making banked turns. We hung up to the left for a second, then shot down to our right and forward. I was still holding my breath when we slipped through the opening.

"Woooohhhhh!" Boon shouted with joy.

We cleared the platform and were high in the air over Leeandra. Kasha took us up very high, very fast. So fast that the g-force slammed me down into the hard seat. That was okay. I wanted to be out of range of anything the Ravinians might throw at us. I also feared that they might come after us again with the other gigs. The slow-moving hangar doors had suddenly become our friends, because by the time they opened them again, we'd be long gone. I relaxed. We had made it.

Suddenly the gig lurched and bounced.

"What was that?" I asked nervously. "Are we losing power?"

"No," Kasha answered calmly. "I believe that was the klee falling off from below."

Oh. Yeah. Right. That guy. I hoped it was a dado.

"You remember where we're going?" I asked.

"Like it was yesterday," she replied.

Kasha took us up high over Leeandra into the beautiful blue skies of Eelong. Looking out of the open cockpit gave us a three-sixty view of the territory. It was just as stunning as I'd remembered it. The jungle canopy that was now below us looked like a sea of green clouds. I let myself enjoy the view. There wasn't anything I could do just then, except to catch my breath and wonder what we would find when we hit Black Water.

Seeing the familiar jungles of Eelong made me think back to something Nevva had said. When she heard that Saint Dane was going to launch a dado attack on the exiles, she was genuinely upset. Besides not wanting to harm the exiles, she said something to the effect of "that territory was to remain untouched." I didn't know what she meant at the time, but thinking about it and seeing that Eelong was pretty much the same Eelong as before, I wondered if Saint Dane had told Nevva that Eelong would evolve without much interference. Earth had been devastated. The other territories were in different stages of decay and destruction. But not Eelong. I could tell that by looking over the side of the gig as we sailed overhead. Leeandra had become more modernized, but the jungles below were unspoiled. Was it possible that Nevva held on to the hope that not all of Halla would be crushed by Saint Dane in order to fulfill his vision?

Nevva bought into Saint Dane's philosophy. That much was for sure. But I don't believe she was evil. Misguided, maybe. A little too willing to achieve her goals at the expense of others, definitely. But she wasn't an evil person. If Saint Dane promised not to harm Eelong, then he had broken his promise to her. Who knows? Was that one act enough to make Nevva realize that Saint Dane's way of thinking was wrong? She was fiercely loyal, but how loyal can you be to someone who betrays you? In the end, Nevva chose to help us. To help her mother. Her natural mother. For that, she paid with her life. I still didn't know if her help would make a difference, but if there's some small ray of light that came from this whole mess, it's that Nevva Winter became the person her mother always wanted her to be. She became a Traveler who tried to defend Halla. Wherever she is, assuming she is anywhere, I hope she knows that she made the right choice.

"Look there!" Boon called out.

We had been flying for a few hours. I was daydreaming, lost in my thoughts. Or maybe I was dreaming for real. Whatever. While I was out, we had left the jungle and reached the miles of wasteland that separated the vegetated regions and the majestic, rocky mountains where Black Water was hidden. Looking over the side of the gig, I was met with a frightening sight.

We had caught up with the Ravinian army. They marched below us, moving toward the mountains. It was a formidable force. There had to be thousands of klees, all marching in formation. Half the force wore the uniforms of the Ravinians guards. Many carried the red flags of Ravinia. I wondered if they were all dados. The other half wore dark green, lightweight armor. These were soldiers from Leeandra. On their backs they carried their weapons. They had staves, lassos, and bolas.

Most walked, but there were many, probably officers, who rode on zenzens. The large horses with the multijointed legs bucked and bridled as they were coaxed along the rocky path toward their meeting with the gars. There were also small, mechanized vehicles that carried equipment of some kind, but I couldn't tell what it might be. Were they weapons? Provisions? From that high up in the air, I couldn't tell.

Most disturbing of all was the line of covered transport trucks that followed at the rear. I figured there were even more klees inside, but had no doubt what they would be used for after the battle. These would be the transports that would bring the captured gars back to Leeandra. These gars weren't going to be prisoners of war. They were to be food for the Ravinians. The sight of those trucks turned my stomach for so many reasons. Not only because of the gruesome cargo they were meant to carry, but because of the vicious philosophy that drove the klees to be hunting gars in the first place.

There was only one thing I was happy about while looking down on this army. They had not reached Black Water yet. I had no idea what we could do to stop them, but at least we wouldn't be too late.

Kasha said, "They have another half day's journey. Then they must make their way over the mountains to enter the valley before reaching Black Water. We have time, Pendragon."

I nodded, but didn't say what I was thinking: Sure, but time for what?

We flew on, headed for the mountain range and Black Water. I remembered hiking up the narrow, rocky path that led to a narrow cleft in the mountains and a long, winding path that eventually opened up onto a beautiful, green valley. I remembered the large lake in the center of that valley, and the forest, and the seven waterfalls, one of which protected the entrance to Black Water. It was only when the sunbelt hit that waterfall at a certain angle that it cast a shadow that blocked all light, making its water seem black. That was the only way into the second valley, which was the home of the gars. It was surrounded on all sides by impassable mountains. The only way in was through that cave tunnel behind the waterfall. Or you could fly. Obviously, our plan was to fly.

"It might get a little bumpy over the mountains with updrafts," Kasha explained. "Make sure your belts are tight."

Boon and I buckled down. As fun as it was to fly in an open cockpit, it wouldn't have been wise to get ejected by sudden turbulence. Soon we were sailing over the rocky spires of the first range of mountains. Kasha was right. It was bumpy.

"Do not worry, this is normal," Kasha assured us.

In no time we had cleared the front range, and I could look down onto that amazing, green valley that was so out of place among the gray, dry mountains.

"Nothing has changed," Boon called out above the whine of the rotors.

It reminded me again of what Nevva said to Saint Dane. The valley was as spectacular as I remembered. Nevva expected it to stay that way. I wondered if it would.

We had gotten maybe halfway across when we were hit with sudden turbulence. The gig must have dropped several yards, then suddenly rocketed higher. I looked to Kasha, waiting for her assurance that we were okay.

She didn't give it.

"That was not normal," she announced.

The craft was suddenly thrown again. It was like we where hit with something that knocked us sideways. Were we under attack? I couldn't tell. The gig wasn't damaged and we definitely didn't hear anything being fired from the ground.

"Are those updrafts?" I asked, hoping that she would give me a simple, "Yes."

She didn't. Kasha looked worried. That was something I hadn't seen in her before.

"Whatever it is, it is not natural."

We were hit again, and again. Each time, the little gig was buffeted. First one way, then the other.

"I cannot maintain control," Kasha announced with a voice that was way too calm for the circumstances.

"Get us down!" I shouted. "Whatever it is, we're better off not flying in it."

We were hit again. The gig began to spin.

"Kasha?" Boon called nervously.

I looked over the side to see that the ground was coming up fast.

"There's a clearing beyond the lake," I announced.

"I'll try to keep us in the air long enough to reach it," Kasha replied.

The gig was rocked again. We nearly went over sideways, but Kasha was able to right us. It was amazing that she was as skillful as she was, considering she hadn't flown in a long while.

"Brace yourselves," she called out. "I don't know how hard we'll hit."

She held on to the control stick with both paws, fighting

gravity and the rotors and whatever force was knocking us out of the sky.

"Thirty feet!" I called out as a warning. "Move forward! We were still over the water. It wouldn't have been good to land on wet.

We were hit again; this time we were knocked forward, as if we had gotten a huge kick from behind.

"Whatever it is, it's coming at us from all angles!" I shouted.

"Losing control," Kasha announced calmly, as if she were actually not losing control.

"Twenty feet. We're over land."

"Put it down!" Boon called.

Kasha dropped the bottom out. We half fell, half descended under control. I grabbed on to anything I could find to brace for the impact. We were hit one last time. The force knocked the gig onto its side. We were so low, the overhead rotor hit the ground and tore apart.

"Cover up!" I shouted.

Boon and I huddled down into the cockpit, desperate to protect ourselves from flying shrapnel. Kasha didn't flinch. She maintained control until the end. The gig hit the ground with a violent thud that felt as if it shook my teeth loose. We were down. Dazed, but down. What followed was a jumble of hands and feet and paws and fur. The crystal engines whined louder for a few seconds more, then calmed down. We weren't moving anymore. I took mental and physical inventory. Was I alive? Yes. Was anything broken? I didn't think so. What about the others?

"Kasha? Boon?"

"I'm all right," Kasha answered.

"I can't move my arms," Boon announced, scared. "I'm trapped."

The gig was on its side. The rotor was gone. The side rotors were winding down. The fuselage walls were crushed in around us. We were all still in our seats, held in by seat belts.

"We gotta get out of this," I said.

No sooner did we start to pull ourselves out of the wreck, than the scene turned chaotic. The attack came from everywhere. We were descended upon by a group of gars that screamed and yelled to intimidate and confuse us. They didn't have to bother. I was plenty confused as it was. I have no idea how many there were. Ten? A hundred? They wore hoods, much like the gars I had first encountered on my original visit to Black Water.

"Friends! We're friends!" I shouted, but I didn't think they heard me. Or understood. Or cared. They were too caught up in their attack. They moved quickly, as if not wanting to let us get our wits back. As chaotic as it seemed, I got the feeling that it was being orchestrated. I guess you'd call it organized chaos.

They first went after Boon. They violently pulled out the chunk of fuselage that had pinned him inside and dragged him out of the gig. He didn't fight back.

"We're here to help you," he called in desperation. "Listen to me!"

They didn't. Boon was a klee. Klees were bad. That's all they cared about. Kasha was yanked from her pilot seat and pulled away the same as Boon. She didn't try to speak. She knew it was futile. As the gars hauled her out, they cheered at having bagged another klee.

Finally they came for me. I felt hands reaching in to grab

at me, and I was rudely pulled from the wreck. They dragged me out and threw me on the ground next to the destroyed gig. I think it wasn't until then that somebody realized they weren't dealing just with klees. I heard somebody shout, "It's a gar!"

The chaotic screaming suddenly stopped. A confused rumble followed, as word spread that a gar had been pulled from the wreckage. Nobody made a move for me. Instead, they formed a protective circle, staring in at me like I was some kind of freak. My cheek was on the dirt, which meant a lot of dirt was in my eyes, which meant I couldn't see all that well. I made out the fact that all the gars wore brown cloaks with hoods that covered their faces. It was a frightening sight. I wasn't sure if they were going to welcome me as a friend . . . or tear me apart.

"Leave the klees alone," I coughed. "They've come as friends."

Someone pushed through the crowd. He was a tall guy with his head completely covered by the hood. He stood over me, looking down. It seemed like whoever it was, he was in charge, because nobody pulled him back. He stuck the tip of his boot under my chin and lifted it to get a better look.

I squinted up, but saw nothing more than a shadow, because the sunbelt was high in the sky behind his head.

I squinted and croaked out, "Sorry for dropping in like this, but you're all in danger."

I sensed the guy stiffen, as if I had said something earth shattering. Or Eelong shattering. As it turned out, I had. But it wasn't what I expected. I had rocked him all right, but it wasn't because of what I said. It was because of who I was.

He knelt down by my head and said, "Tell me something I don't know."

I knew that voice. It wasn't a he, either. It was a she. The hood came off and I was faced with a vision. It was a girl with long, brown hair and amazing gray eyes.

"Cutting it kind of close, aren't you, Bobby?"

Yeah. I found Courtney.

30

If I were a crying kind of guy, I would have cried.

Okay, maybe I did anyway. A little. But I'm not admitting to anything for certain. Courtney held out her hand and helped me to my feet. I wrapped my arms around her and held her so close I was afraid she might break. Oddly, I thought of a line from a Marx Brothers movie I had seen on First Earth. "If I held you any closer, I'd be in back of you." If I could have squeezed her any tighter, I would have. Seeing her was not only a complete surprise, it triggered a feeling that I never would have expected.

It gave me hope. The last time I'd seen her, she and Mark were being herded into the flume on Second Earth. I feared they had both been killed. But Mark turned up alive. And now, so had Courtney. Knowing that my two oldest and best friends in Halla were okay re-energized me. After all I had learned about my true origins, holding Courtney reminded me that I had another life. A much more familiar, comfortable, and yes, understandable one. I was Bobby Pendragon from Stony Brook, Connecticut. As much as I believed all that I learned on Solara, I couldn't imagine turning my back on the person I had always been. Being with Courtney centered me. It brought back my base. For those few seconds I didn't think about how impossible the battle was that we were about to face.

I thought about how I wanted to win it more than ever.

"I've been waiting for you," she whispered.

"Sorry it took so long."

"Doesn't matter. I always knew you would come," she said, breathless.

"I was afraid you were killed."

"I came close. A couple of times. I still don't know what happened to Mark."

"He's okay. He's on Third Earth."

I felt Courtney shudder. I wasn't sure if it was a laugh or the physical release of tension she'd been holding for a long time. She pulled away from me and looked me right in the eye. Like Mark, Courtney was older. By how much, I couldn't tell. A few years maybe. She had been through a lot. I could see that just by looking into her eyes. They were hard. They had seen things. Courtney had always been intense. When she played, she wanted to win. But the look she had in her eyes just then showed more than that. The stakes were higher in this particular game.

And she was more beautiful than ever.

"They're coming, aren't they?" she asked straight out. The joyous reunion was over.

I nodded and looked at the sky. "They won't reach the mountains before dark. I'm guessing the earliest they would attack is sunrise."

"How many?"

I took a breath before answering. She wasn't going to like what I had to say.

"It's an army."

She shrugged and sighed. "We've been expecting this. We're ready."

"You are?" I asked, surprised. "How?"

"Come with me," she said, and started to walk off.

I reached out and stopped her. "Wait. Are they here?"

"Who?"

"The rest of the people from Second Earth who were pulled into the flume. The exiles."

She looked at me for a moment, as if trying to understand exactly what I had asked. I held my breath. Her answer was going to determine the future of all that ever was or would be. Whatever she had to say would be kind of important.

"I don't know what happened to the people who went in with Mark and me," she finally said. "We somehow scattered. That's why I lost touch with Mark. I haven't seen him since that day."

"But the others," I asked, getting anxious. "From Yankee Stadium. There were thousands. Tens of thousands. Do you know what happened to them?"

Courtney looked me square in the eye and said, "You should see something."

I wanted to scream out, "Just tell me!" But I was on Courtney's turf now. However she wanted to play this was fine by me. Sort of. She turned to look at the gars that surrounded us. I'd almost forgotten that we weren't alone. There were around a dozen of the little people. None of them were much taller than five feet, but that didn't mean they weren't dangerous. Boon and Kasha were being held tight by several of the small gars. After all the excitement, and the sudden appearance of klees from the sky, it probably didn't make sense to them that Courtney and I would have hugged each other like that. You could see the confusion on their faces.

Courtney stood up tall and announced to them in a bold voice, "They are friends."

The gars stared back at her, dumbfounded.

Courtney walked up to the gars who were holding Kasha and Boon.

"Let them go," she ordered.

They didn't. Courtney added with more authority, "I said let them go; they are my friends."

The gars finally followed orders and released the two klees, though reluctantly. It was strange. Courtney acted like she was in charge. She had always been bold and confident, but now it seemed she was the leader of this band of gars. The image was completed by the fact that she stood nearly a foot taller than most of them.

"Hello, Kasha," Courtney said awkwardly. Unlike the confidence she had shown to the gars, with Kasha she seemed tentative. "I don't know what to say about what happened to the flume. I'm sorry."

"Do not apologize. You could not have known. You came here to help us, to help Pendragon, that is all that matters."

Courtney added, "It's a relief to see you. I thought you were, I mean, Bobby wrote that you had been, you know. . . ."

"Killed?" Kasha asked. "I was."

Courtney started at her blankly. "Uh . . . what?"

"My body died. My spirit didn't" was Kasha's answer.

Courtney shot me a questioning look, as if to ask, "What the hell is she talking about?"

I shrugged and said, "Long story."

"Hi, Courtney," Boon said.

"Hey, Boon. Sorry for shooting you all out of the sky. I thought you were klees. The bad kind, I mean."

I jumped in and asked, "You shot us out of the sky? How?"

Courtney gave me a sly look and said, "I told you we were ready."

My hopes were raised even higher. Was it possible? Could the gars have really found a way to defend themselves?

"Is anybody hurt?" Courtney asked. "Can you walk?"

A quick look around told her that we were all good to go.

"Then let's get to Black Water."

We left the wreckage of the gig and began the long walk to the waterfall that shielded the tunnel through the mountains that led to Black Water. The home of the gars. And I hoped, the home of the exiles from Second Earth.

Courtney and I walked first, followed closely by Kasha and Boon. I noticed that the rest of the gars hovered closely around the klees. In spite of what Courtney had said, they weren't trusted.

The trip was a familiar one. We hiked through the dense forest and up to the series of majestic waterfalls. A short walk through shallow runoff led us to the waterfall that protected the entrance to the tunnel.

The whole way I filled Courtney in on what had happened since we had been with each other on the floating docks near her parents' sailboat on Second Earth. When I was with Mark, I held back explaining about the whole Solara-spirit thing. We had been on the run, and I was afraid that laying all of that on him would only confuse issues. But now, here, when we were so close to finding the exiles, I felt as if Courtney should know. So I told her everything. I told her about Solara and finding my family. I explained how the flumes were destroyed, but that it didn't matter anymore. At least not to the Travelers. I laid out the most important aspect of all, which was how the spirit of mankind helps guide Halla and gives the Travelers their abilities. Courtney listened without saying a word. She kept her eyes on the ground, taking it all in. I had no way of knowing if she accepted and believed it all, or if she would turn to me with her typical sarcasm and say, "Okay, yeah, funny. Now what *really* happened?"

Kasha and Boon walked behind us. Of course, Kasha knew it all already, but Boon didn't. Every so often I heard him gasp. Boon was a trusting klee. I knew he believed. The question was, did Courtney?

We all rounded the waterfall and entered the dark cave tunnel through the mountain. I continued my story as we made our way along the rocky path that I hoped would bring us to the end of our journey, and the prize we had been seeking for so long. I didn't even want to think ahead to what we would do once we got there. I just wanted the truth. I wanted to see the exiles. By the time I saw the spec of light ahead that marked the end of the tunnel and the entrance to Black Water, I had told Courtney everything. Whether she accepted it or not was another matter. We had nearly reached the end when I stopped, and stopped Courtney.

"That's it," I said. "I know it's incredible, but it's the truth. The exiles are now the last remaining source of positive spirit that is keeping Solara alive. At least, the Solara that has been guiding existence for so long. If anything happens to the exiles, the Travelers will be done, Solara will be done, and the split that Saint Dane has created will be complete. The dark spirit of Solara will control Halla. So you can see why we're a little bit anxious about knowing whether or not the exiles are here."

Courtney nodded thoughtfully and said, "You probably think I'm having trouble accepting all this."

"Well, yeah. It's not exactly the kind of thing you hear about every day."

She chuckled. "No, it isn't. But the thing is, I already knew. At least, I knew some of it."

I glanced to Kasha. She looked just as stunned as I felt.

"Wh—how?" I asked.

Courtney smiled and motioned for us to follow her to the end of the tunnel.

Kasha whispered, "I wish she would just tell us what she knows and eliminate the dramatics."

"Yeah, well, that's Courtney."

We walked to the end of the tunnel and looked out onto the valley surrounded by mountains that was home to the gar colony of Black Water. Much of what I saw was the exact same. It was a pretty valley with a waterfall on the far end that fed a narrow river that wound its way through the farmland and eventually through the town itself. The buildings were wooden, like log cabins. They were built as concentric rings that grew larger as they moved away from the hub. I had seen all this before.

What I hadn't seen was that the village had grown much larger than when I had been there before. There were many more rings. If I were to guess, I'd say that the number of buildings had tripled. And grown in size. From the high perch we were on, I could see that the streets were full of people. More people than I remembered. Lots more.

Even from our faraway vantage point, I could tell many of them weren't gars. At least, they were much taller than the average gar.

My heart leaped.

Courtney could tell. "They're here, Bobby," she said with a smile. "All of them. More than all, actually. It's been a couple of years, you know. Some babies were born."

I grabbed Courtney and held her again. My relief was complete. I flashed back to that horrible moment when the giant flume was created in Yankee Stadium that sucked thousands of innocent, terrified people into the void. It was known as the Bronx Massacre, and at the time I had no reason to doubt that I was watching a mass execution. But that wasn't the case. They were here. Alive. Healthy. And safe. Sort of. For a fleeting moment I felt as if we had completed our mission. We had found the exiles. Truth was, our mission was only beginning. But at that very moment, all I felt was joy. They were here. They were alive. We were looking down on the people whose spirit was keeping Halla alive. It was a staggering thought. We were still here, Halla still had hope, because of them. Or more to the point, because of the powerful spirit they possessed. The spirit to survive and to thrive. These were the people who were keeping us in the battle to defeat Saint Dane. I didn't know a single one of them, but I loved them all.

I even thought I saw a tear in Kasha's eye, and that's saying something. "They do not know how precious they are," she said, once again reading my mind.

"No, they don't," Courtney agreed.

"So then, how do *you* know?" I asked. "I mean, about Solara and the spirit and all?"

Courtney shrugged. "I didn't believe it at first. I didn't understand. But everything you told me confirms it. So I guess it's true. Wow."

She started walking down the slope toward the village.

"But how did you hear about it?" I called to her.

"From Nevva Winter," she said, and continued walking.

31

⎡⎤ow I was the one who needed answers.

I ran after Courtney. Boon and Kasha were right behind me, with the other gars keeping pace.

"Nevva told you about Solara?" I asked, incredulous. "How? When?"

"Wait until we get to my house," she cautioned. "I have a lot to tell you."

She had *that* right. I couldn't imagine any situation, or possibility, or opportunity, or reason that could have explained how Nevva Winter told Courtney about Solara. That was impossible. Yet Courtney knew, and she wasn't one to make something like that up. She may have grown up a little, but she was still Courtney. I had all that I could do to stay calm and wait until we had the chance to talk.

We descended along the slope that led down to the village. It was a route I had taken before and was familiar with, only this time we reached the first ring of structures much sooner. As I said, the size of the village had tripled to accommodate the exiles. The first ring of houses weren't houses at all. They were larger than the other log-cabin homes and had no personal touches of any kind.

"Defensive structures," Courtney explained. "Like I said, we're ready."

I didn't know what kind of defense these wooden huts offered. I didn't think they would do much against a dado-klee army, but it wasn't the time to point that out. That would come soon enough. As we walked toward the center of the village, the structures became smaller and looked more like homes. I saw kids in the street playing catch, riding skateboards on paved roads, and generally running around. I could almost imagine this to be a suburban street back on Second Earth. The lineup of homes with front yards looked right out of suburbia. The idea that this quiet, hypernormal community was about to be under siege was almost too much to comprehend.

"These outer rings are where the Yanks settled and made their homes," Courtney explained.

"Yanks?" I asked.

"That's what they call themselves. I was more of a Mets fan myself, but considering how they got here, I guess the name fits. They've become an important part of the Black Water community. There are people here with all sorts of skills. Carpenters, teachers, plumbers, farmers. This isn't the Black Water you remember."

I looked around at the new structures. Though the general style was the same as when I had last been to Black Water, there were subtle differences that showed the hands of skilled craftsmen. Black Water had improved. You could even say it evolved. I had mixed feelings about it.

"I know what you're thinking," Courtney said. "We're not supposed to mix the territories. Get over it. That ship sailed a long time ago, thanks to our demon friend."

She was right. Halla was in shambles. It was no longer what it should have been, thanks to Saint Dane's Convergence. I figured that at this point, any positive move was a good one, even if it meant mixing technology and know-how from one territory with another's.

Many people called out a friendly "Hi!" to Courtney. She was well-known and liked. Of course, that was quickly followed by a sudden change in attitude when they saw two klees walking with us. It's not like they ran into their homes and slammed the doors or anything. But I could read the confusion on their faces. Klees had become the hated enemy once again.

We arrived at one of the small cabins in the outer ring of what was the old village. The huts beyond seemed older and crude. This was the dividing line between the old Black Water and the ring of new cabins that the exiles helped build. The Yanks. Incredible.

"Wait here," Courtney ordered.

Boon, Kasha, and I did as we were told as she went to talk with the gars who had been escorting us. After a few words they cast us dark, worried looks, then reluctantly backed away and left us alone.

Courtney returned and spoke to Boon and Kasha. "Don't take it personally. They just don't want to be eaten."

"Understood," Kasha said.

Courtney opened the front door and motioned for us to enter. "This is my home. It's small, but it's strange."

We entered to find a two-room home. The first room had a living area with some rough chairs and tables. Across from it was a sink and a fireplace. The door beyond led to a small bedroom.

"Not exactly like what you'd find in Stony Brook,"

Courtney said. "But it's all I need. Who's hungry?"

As much as I wanted to eat, I had other more pressing things to worry about. "Uh, you do get that the klee army is on the way, right?" I asked.

"I told you, we're ready," she answered. "How do you think you were shot out of the sky?"

"Yes, how did you do that?" Boon asked.

"We developed a weapon that fires a short, intense burst of radio waves," she explained. "Some of the Yank geeks used the link radio technology that the gars developed and found a way to direct and control it. Don't ask me to get more technical than that. It doesn't affect living things, only mechanical devices."

"So it'll shoot a gig out of the sky, but it won't stop a living klee?" I asked.

"Pretty much," Courtney answered.

"What about a dado klee?"

Courtney gave me a dark look. I had finally given her a bit of information she didn't already know. "You're kidding, right? Dados?"

"I wish."

"You mean that klee army on the way here might be dados?"

"Sorry to give you the bad news," I said.

"Bad news? That's the best news I've gotten in forever!"

"Uh, it is?"

"Eat first, business later."

Courtney set out a meal of fresh fruit that was harvested from the farms that circled the village. She even grilled some fish from the stream. Boon and Kasha preferred to eat their fish raw, which was kind of disgusting, but who am

I to judge? I'm not a cat. Or a sushi guy. Courtney was all sorts of bubbly as she worked. Giving her the news about the dados seemed to energize her. How weird was that? I couldn't speak for my klee friends, but I was starving. I was dying to hear Courtney's story, but after all that had happened, I didn't think it would hurt to eat a little. Or a lot. We didn't speak much while Courtney busied herself cooking, but once we sat down to enjoy the meal, I couldn't take it anymore.

"You're killing me here, you know," I said.

Courtney put her food down and looked off to nowhere in particular. It felt like she was winding her thoughts back. From the hard look in her eyes, it was clear that she wasn't bringing up happy memories. Her light attitude was gone. When she spoke, she rarely made eye contact with us, as if she weren't really in the room, but drifting through the past.

"When the Ravinians threw us into the flume, I wasn't scared. Not at first, anyway. I'd been through the flume before. The only thing strange about it was that I was flying along with other people."

"Were they the people Naymeer chose from outside the conclave?" I asked.

"I guess. They were terrified. That much was for sure. I tried to calm them down and tell them that everything was going to be okay, though I wasn't so sure about that myself. I figured the flume would send us to some territory that I knew about through your journals. That's what I kept telling myself. It was going to be okay. I spent most of the journey trying to refresh my memory about all the various territories I'd read about."

"Did you see Mark?" I asked.

Courtney shook her head. "The last I saw him was when he was trying to reach me in the crowd outside of the flume." She sighed and continued. "We flew for a long time. Longer than the other flume journies I'd taken. Slowly the people I was traveling with separated. Some shot ahead faster. Others lagged behind. It wasn't like we had a choice. We were totally at the mercy of the flume. It wasn't long before I was alone. That's when things started getting scary. Outside the crystal walls, the images of Halla were everywhere. It was like the entire universe was out there, jumbled together, looking at me. I saw a light far ahead in the flume. I thought I was nearing the end, but realized that the light was moving. Toward me. It seemed as if we were going to collide and that would be the end of the trip, and me. I covered my head, but the thing streaked by me in a blur of light and music. I looked back to see it disappear behind me. It was followed by another, then another. Some came from ahead of me, others caught up with me from behind and shot past. After a while I got used to it. No, I looked forward to it. Those streaks of light were the only things that kept me company and broke up the monotony."

"What do you think they were?" Kasha asked.

Courtney shrugged. "All I can figure is that they were other people traveling through the flumes."

"They might have been," I offered. "The Ravinians were sending people all over Halla."

"I lost track of time," Courtney continued. "I know this sounds weird, but I can't say how long I was in there. It could have been hours or months. I truly don't know. It was like I was suspended in time and space. I'd never experienced that kind of loneliness before. I kept expecting to be dumped at a gate, but it never happened."

"But it did, when you arrived here," Boon offered.

"Well, sort of. When things started happening, it was dramatic. The flume started to shake. It was definitely a new sensation, and it didn't feel right. I heard this deep rumble, like an earthquake. The tunnel must have moved, because I was thrown against the side wall and spun around. It didn't hurt, but I was sent tumbling. I was terrified. It felt like the flume was falling apart, almost like what happened here on Eelong."

Courtney threw a pained look to Kasha. Kasha knew what she was talking about all too well. We all did.

"I had no control. Up until that moment the ride through the flume was like floating on a warm cushion of air. Suddenly it felt like I was being tumbled inside of a washing machine. I kept getting glimpses out beyond the crystal walls and began to see stars, which meant the images of Halla were disappearing. I won't lie. I thought it was the end of Halla right then and there. It felt like everything was coming apart."

I knew what Courtney was experiencing. I had witnessed the destruction of the flumes myself. As horrifying a sight as that was, I never thought that there might have been people traveling inside them when it happened.

"Then everything went white, and I was floating again," Courtney continued. "I thought I had been killed. I really did. I even thought I heard the voice of an angel. It was a voice I recognized. A woman. My mind was still flying fast, and it took a while for me to focus on her words. I heard her trying to calm me down by saying things like 'relax' and 'you're going to be okay.' I kind of hoped she'd say 'welcome to heaven,' but that didn't happen. Then I saw her face."

Courtney looked right at me and said, "It was Nevva Winter."

I didn't react. How could I? I had no clue as to how that could have happened.

"Where were you?" Kasha asked.

"I didn't know. At least not at first. I felt the pull of gravity again, so I knew I was no longer moving through the flume. I think I was lying on my back. All I saw was Nevva's face looking down at me. Under any other circumstances I would have jumped up and slugged her, but I couldn't move. And besides, hers was the first face I'd seen since I was separated from those people in the flume. As much as I hated her, I was happy to see her. I would have been happy to see anybody."

"Did she say anything else?" I asked.

"Oh yeah. She said that she had given us a gift. All of us. I didn't know who the heck she was talking about. She promised that the territory wouldn't be touched. As much as she believed in the new vision for Halla, she also believed that there was good in the old way. And for that, she was protecting Eelong."

"Protecting Eelong," Kasha repeated.

Courtney nodded. "She said we should build a new life and make the best of what we had. She also asked that we not judge her too harshly. That was it. She was gone. I lay there for a while, trying to understand what had happened. Slowly my physical senses returned. I realized that I wasn't surrounded by white; I had been staring up into the sky. The first thing I recognized was the sunbelt. I knew then that I was definitely on Eelong."

I hadn't touched a bite of food while Courtney told us her story. After hearing about Nevva, my hunger was gone for good. I stood up. My mind was racing too fast to let me sit still. What had Nevva done? And when had she done it?

Did this happen before I brought Elli to Third Earth? Was it possible that Nevva had always questioned Saint Dane and his quest?

"What are you thinking, Pendragon?" Kasha asked.

"On Third Earth, Nevva panicked when I told her that Saint Dane was going to attack the exiles with an army of dados."

It was Courtney's turn to jump to her feet.

"Whoa! I thought that was a klee army headed this way. I didn't know Saint Dane was behind it."

"I'm not sure he is," I replied. "At least, not directly. The Ravinians brought dados here, so it's not like Saint Dane had nothing to do with it. But I don't think he planned this attack."

Courtney frowned. "But you said Saint Dane was going to attack with a dado army."

"He is. I saw thousands of dados on Third Earth that Saint Dane said would be used against the exiles. Nevva said he was going to create a flume to move them. But he didn't know that the exiles were here until recently. So I don't think the army that's on the way here has anything to do with the dados from Third Earth. I think this attack would have happened anyway."

"Oh. Swell. That means there's going to be another attack after this one?" Courtney cried.

"Unless the klee army does Saint Dane's dirty work for him. However it happens, Saint Dane wants the exiles dead."

"But Nevva didn't," Kasha said.

I said, "Strange as it may seem, it's looking like Nevva did what she could to try and preserve one of the original territories of Halla. Why she picked Eelong, I have no idea, but that was her plan, and it looks like she somehow directed the exiles to be sent here to help keep the territory alive."

Kasha added, "And it cost her her life."

We all let that sink in for a moment, then Courtney said softly, "So if not for Nevva Winter, the battle for Halla would already be over."

I smiled. "For what it's worth, in the end, she did her job as a Traveler."

"What about the exiles?" Boon asked. "When did they get here?"

We all looked to Courtney. She sat down and turned her thoughts back to the day she had arrived on Eelong.

"Once Nevva left, I collected my thoughts and realized I had to figure out exactly where I was on Eelong. I sat up, hoping to see something familiar. What I saw instead seemed impossible."

She stopped talking, letting her mind drift back. Whatever it was that Courtney had seen, she was seeing it again in her mind's eye and judging by the look on her face, it wasn't a happy memory.

"I saw that I was lying in a huge, open area . . . along with thousands of other people."

"What!" I blurted out.

"It's true," she continued. "I couldn't breathe. There were bodies everywhere. All lying down. Some had their faces turned to the sunbelt, others were facedown. Many were in the fetal position. They all looked like they were sleeping, or dead. Right next to me was an old guy in jeans and a plaid shirt. On my other side were two kids. Twins. A woman who was probably their mother was at my feet. It was a sea of people. I can't even describe the numb feeling it gave me. The sight of this many people was staggering, but the idea that they might all be dead put me into brain lock."

"The exiles?" Kasha asked.

Courtney nodded. "Of course, I didn't know that at the time. I sat there for a few seconds, dumbfounded. I didn't know what to do. I truly thought I was going to lose my mind. That's when the guy in the flannel shirt moved. I was so surprised that I yelped. But I saw him reach for his eyes and rub them. That little, natural movement was enough to calm me down. This guy was coming around the exact same way I had. Then the twins moved. All around me I saw the beginnings of this giant mass of humanity come to life like some giant creature. I hadn't yet heard about what happened at Yankee Stadium, so the idea of this many people suddenly dropping in on Eelong still didn't make sense, but I was glad to know I wasn't in corpseworld."

"It must have been an incredible relief," Kasha said.

Courtney's expression turned dark. "It didn't last. I was lying near one edge of the mass of people. I'd guess I was about fifty people away from the outer edge. Being there saved my life."

The klees and I exchanged nervous looks.

"How?" Boon asked, hanging on her every word.

"We were being stalked. I think when the people started to move, it was like a cue. As soon as the mass of humanity began to stir, the attack began."

"Klees?" I asked.

"Tangs. They must have been stalking through the jungle, growing closer. When they saw that their prey was coming alive—"

Courtney closed her eyes. The memory was a bad one.

"The screams came first. I jumped up and saw three

tangs pounce on the people who were closest to the edge of the clearing. Not far from me. If I had been lying a little bit closer to the edge . . ." She didn't finish that sentence. "Those poor people didn't have a chance. It was brutal. More tangs jumped from cover and picked off the first people they came to. Those closest could see what was going on and panicked. The fear spread like a wave. The screaming was unbearable. I didn't know which screams came from fear, and which came from the people being mauled by those monsters."

I couldn't imagine the horror.

"Some people jumped in and tried to pull the tangs off. They paid for it. The beasts were on a bloody rampage. With all the people jostling me, I could only make out fleeting images. Maybe that was a good thing. I kept seeing talons flashing and the horror and pain on the faces of the poor people. I could even smell the tangs. And the blood. It was a frenzy feed. I kept getting knocked around by people who were desperate to escape. At first I went with the crowd, but I was afraid I'd get crushed. I looked around for any other way to go. That's when I saw the waterfalls and realized that we were in the valley that led into Black Water. As soon as I saw those falls, I knew what I had to do. I had to get into Black Water and find Gunny and Spader. I pushed my way through the crowd, going against the flow. It wasn't easy, but eventually I broke out of the stampede. Now it was just me and the group of tangs about twenty yards away who were bent down over their prey." She closed her eyes and added, "Feeding."

I tried not to imagine it.

"I ran for the falls and didn't look back. I couldn't. I don't know how many people were killed that day. When I talked to people about it later, they told me the tangs simply disappeared into the jungle . . . once they had gotten their fill."

I winced.

"I kept running, heading for the waterfall. I hit the runoff and splashed through, not daring to stop. When I got into the tunnel, I kept going, sprinting the whole way. I didn't stop to rest until I reached the far side. Looking down the slope, I saw that the village in Black Water was just as I remembered it. It wasn't the village you see here today. It was the same village that we saved from the klee attack five years ago."

"Five years," I echoed. "Black Water has grown this much in five years?"

"Pretty amazing, isn't it?" she said. "I found Aron, the gar leader, and begged him to take me to Gunny and Spader. But he said they had disappeared. Nobody knew where they had gone."

"I'm sure they went to Solara when the flumes exploded, just as I did," I offered.

"I told Aron about the people outside. I said they were gars. What else was I supposed to say? And they were, sort of. Aron immediately gathered a team of gars with weapons and set out to bring the people back."

"That wasn't a small job," I said.

Courtney snickered. "Tell me about it. Do you know how hard it is to gather seventy thousand people? Especially people who are confused and scared that they might be eaten by hungry dinosaurs?"

"Can't say that I do," I answered.

"I'm not going to bore you with all the details of what followed, because you see the results all around you. It was awkward and confusing and impossible, but the gars accepted the newcomers and gave them a home. In return, the Yanks helped Black Water to grow and prosper. It's been a perfect partnership."

"What about language?" I asked. "How did the gars understand the Yanks?"

"Good question. It was never an issue," Courtney answered. "Like when Mark and I first came here. For whatever strange reason, the two groups could understand each other from the get-go. As far as I can tell, everybody's speaking English, but that makes no sense."

"It must have to do with the boundaries between territories breaking down. It's like Veego and LaBerge. They're from Veelox, yet they understood everyone on Quillan. And vice versa. Something must happen to people when they go through the flume. It's like they become part of the combined Halla. Or something like that. I don't know."

"It doesn't seem right, but it is kind of convenient," Courtney said sheepishly.

"A fringe benefit of letting Ravinia run the universe. Kind of a big price to pay for not having to learn a new language."

"Ravinia. Yeah. By the time I got here those guys had already gotten a toehold on the territory. I guess Nevva couldn't stop that. Or didn't want to. I found out that whatever cooperation had existed between the klees and the gars was gone."

"You know the klees finally repealed Edict Forty-six?" I asked.

"Yeah. Great, huh? We're officially food. But the gars saw it coming. That's why they developed weapons and worked to create defenses around Black Water. The Yanks had a lot to do with that."

"They accepted and understood the fact that they were on a different territory?" I asked.

"They didn't have a choice" was Courtney's answer. "And it didn't happen overnight. I was the one person who knew it all, so I kind of became the ambassador between the gars and the Yanks. They're my people, after all. I gotta tell you, I'm proud of them. They became teachers and mentors to the gars. Now there are times when I'm talking to somebody that I don't think of them as being a gar or a Yank. They're just . . . a person. Maybe that's what Nevva hoped would happen."

"It makes sense. If Nevva dropped seventy thousand people anywhere else in Halla, they would have been crushed by the Ravinians along with whatever culture they found themselves in. But here on Eelong, the gars were considered a lower form of life. They lived in isolation, protected by the mountains. The Ravinians first had to weed through the klees to determine who was worthy of joining them. They didn't bother much with the gars in Black Water."

"Until now," Kasha said softly.

"Yeah, until now," I repeated.

Kasha asked, "Do you really think they will be able to repel a klee attack?"

Courtney smiled. "No guarantees, but I can tell you, they've been training. Lots of the Yanks were former military on Second Earth. We're organized, and we're smart. I think the klees are going to be in for a surprise if they attack."

"*When* they attack," I corrected.

With that grim reality put out there, we went back to eating. I wasn't hungry, but we needed fuel. As we silently devoured the food Courtney had prepared, I thought to the challenges ahead. Were the gars and exiles of Black Water capable of defending themselves against the klee army? Courtney seemed confident, but I wasn't so sure. Worse than that, even if they somehow managed to repel the klees, would they be able to do the same against Saint Dane's army of dados? The future was looking dark, which didn't do much for my appetite.

"They won't attack at night," Courtney announced. "We should rest."

"What if you're wrong?" Boon asked.

"We'll know long before they get close to the valley" was Courtney's answer. "We have eyes everywhere. Get some sleep. Before the sunbelt rises, I'll get us all up, and I'll show you why I think the klees are in trouble."

I didn't doubt her.

Courtney told us to make ourselves at home. She left to meet with the gar defenders to tell them of the possibility that the oncoming army might be partly mechanical. She promised to be back shortly.

Kasha and Boon made themselves comfortable in the outer room next to the fireplace. There was a large chair in Courtney's bedroom that I claimed. Soon after I settled in, Courtney returned and crawled into her own bed.

"How did it go?" I asked.

"It took a while to convince them that the klees might be mechanical, but they were willing to listen. If our radio cannons work on the dados, it'll give us one more little advantage. Obviously, we need all we can get."

I didn't argue.

Before long I heard the steady breathing of Kasha and Boon as they slept. It was almost like purring. Or maybe it was exactly like purring. They were out and I was glad. The next day was going to be a tough one for them. If all went the way we expected, they would witness their own people—klees—going to war. Though I suspected that the majority of the advancing army was made up of dado klees, I had to believe that there were also plenty of living klees on the way. Somebody had to tell the dados what to do. I knew which side Kasha was on, but it would be tough for her to see the klees going to battle. I trusted Boon as well, but it was going to be hard for him, too. I made my mind up that I would ask Boon to stay away. It would be unfair to ask him to fight his own kind, no matter how right or important it was.

I was so incredibly proud of Courtney. From all that I heard, she was the one who held the exiles together and helped create a community with the gars. When she first became my acolyte so long ago, I knew that I could rely on her. I had no idea that she would be pushed to such extremes, but wasn't surprised that she had risen to every challenge. As did Mark. I loved those guys.

"Bobby?" Courtney called from her bed. "You awake?"

"What do you think?" I replied.

She snickered. "Can I ask you something?"

"Sure."

"What do you think is the way it was meant to be?"

"That's, like, a huge question," I answered. "Where do I begin to answer that?"

"Begin with us."

I froze. I wasn't sure what she meant.

"Do you remember the night you first left home?" she asked.

"How could I forget?"

"Do you remember what I said to you when I came to your house that night?"

I debated about being cool, or telling the truth. I chose the truth.

"You said that you had this feeling about me, and that if you didn't tell me that night, you were afraid that you'd never get the chance again. Then you kissed me."

"I guess that would be a yes. You remember."

"Every second of it."

"So do you ever wonder what would have happened if not for the whole Traveler thing?"

"You mean that night?"

"No," she laughed. "I mean with us. If we'd had the chance to live our lives out the way they were supposed to be lived."

"Who says what happened isn't the way it was supposed to be?" I said, ducking the question.

"I do," Courtney said flatly.

That shut me up.

She continued, "Do you think we would have gotten together and, like, had a life?"

"Courtney," I said, "believe it or not, I've wondered that same thing more times than I can count."

"And what did you come up with?" she asked.

"You mean what did I think would happen, or what do I wish would have happened?"

Courtney hesitated a moment, debating about the answer.

"What do you wish?" she finally asked.

This was it. The big answer.

"I wish we could have had the chance to find out."

"Yeah, me too."

I don't know why I did what I did, but it would have been wrong not to. I got out of the chair and lay down on the bed next to Courtney. I got down on my side behind her and put my arm around her. She hugged my arm around her waist. It wasn't uncomfortable. Or awkward. It was just . . . right. I could smell her hair. Whatever she used to wash it on that primitive territory made it smell like flowers from home. Lying there with her made me feel vulnerable, because I was letting my guard down. Not my physical guard, my emotional guard. I had become a badass. I was a warrior. If I hadn't, I wouldn't have survived. Holding Courtney like that was like admitting I needed the touch of another human. I'd put any thoughts of companionship out of my head, because I knew it wasn't possible. I had once opened myself up to Loor, and she pointed out that letting down our guard and allowing ourselves normal emotions would be dangerous. She was right. But at that moment, lying with Courtney, I didn't care.

"I don't regret anything that happened, Bobby," she whispered. "If I had to do it over again, I would."

"I can't believe I'm saying this," I said. "But I think I would too. Except that I wouldn't involve you and Mark. It's the only regret I have."

"And that would have been a mistake, because without us you wouldn't have gotten this far."

I laughed. "You're right."

"Just promise me one thing," she said.

"What?"

"When this is over, remember me."

It seemed like such a simple request. A dumb one, even. How could I ever forget the glorious Courtney Chetwynde? I was about to say something to that effect, but stopped. For a brief moment I had forgotten the truth. I forgot that I wasn't really Bobby Pendragon from Second Earth. I was a spirit from a place called Solara. When this was over, no matter how it came out, where would I end up? What kind of person . . . what kind of *being* would I be? I suppose it was a very real possibility that when it was over, I wouldn't remember Courtney. What she was asking for was a promise I couldn't make. So I did the only thing that made sense. I lied.

"Of course I promise," I said. "What a dumb thing to ask."

I hugged her tighter and kissed her on the back of the head.

"I knew you would," she said. "I just wanted to hear it."

I stopped talking. I wanted to experience the simple joy of holding Courtney Chetwynde without the added baggage of worrying about the future. We fell asleep that way, as close to each other as possible, in every sense of the word.

I can't say how long we rested, but the next thing I knew, I was dreaming about being on board a submarine. Not a submarine from Cloral, either. This was right out of some old World War II movie, complete with sailors. We were diving. I knew that because the steady *whoop* sound of the dive horn was sounding. I'd never actually been aboard that kind of submarine, but I'd seen plenty of movies. This was just like that. It was one of those dreams where you stepped out of yourself and looked back on what was happening, because you knew it was a dream. I was floating somewhere near the periscope as the whooping horn continued, wondering why I was dreaming about movie submarines.

The answer came quickly. I felt Courtney bolt away from me and jump to her feet. It jostled me out of my dream and back to reality, sort of. I figured I was still half in my dream, because I was still hearing the *whoop* of the dive horn.

Of course, it wasn't a dive horn. It wasn't a dream.

Courtney knew that and was on her feet before I could tell the difference between dreamland and Black Water.

"Get up," she commanded.

"Why? What's going on?" I mumbled.

"It's the warning alarm," she answered quickly.

"Warning? Warning for what?"

"Two guesses," she said, and headed for the bedroom door.

I didn't need the second guess. I was finally awake enough to understand what was happening, and it had nothing to do with submarines. Or dreams.

The battle for Black Water was about to begin.

32

Boon should stay here," I announced as I came out of the bedroom, rubbing my eyes, trying to gear myself up.

"What? No!" he protested. "Why?"

"It isn't fair to ask you to take sides," I said. "Better that you sit it out."

"I have already chosen my side, Pendragon," he shot back. "I do not agree with what Ravinia has done to Eelong."

"And you're willing to side with the gars against the klees to prove it?" I asked. "That's too much to ask."

Boon started to argue, but stopped himself. I don't think he had thought it through that far. To side with the gars would mean to take up arms against his own kind. His own species. That would have been hard, if not impossible, no matter what the circumstances.

"I agree with you, Bobby, but Boon can't stay here," Courtney said as she slipped into a lightweight green vest that covered her chest and back. It looked like protective gear.

"Why not?" I asked.

"Because I can't guarantee he'd be safe. Nobody around

here is going to know he's on our side. All they'll see is a klee, and if we aren't here to protect him—"

She didn't finish the thought. She didn't have to.

"All right, I get it," I admitted. "Boon comes."

"Put these on," Courtney instructed, and handed each of us one of the green vests.

"What will they do?" Kasha asked as she slipped hers on.

"The material will protect against arrows and knives and claws. Let's hope it doesn't come to that."

Kasha held her vest in one paw. She flicked out one of her claws and raked it across the material, testing it.

"Strong," she concluded.

"What's the plan?" I asked. "What exactly are you ready for? Hand-to-hand combat? Courtney, these little vests might slow down an angry klee for a second or two, but that's about it."

"You're right. We could never go toe-to-toe with them. These vests are just a precaution. The plan is to not let it get that far. We knew the klees would eventually attack Black Water. Want to see how we're going to welcome them?"

"Absolutely."

Courtney led us out of her cabin into the gray, predawn light of Black Water. The steady *whoop* of the warning horn continued. People were running everywhere, all away from the center of the village. I noticed both short gars and taller exiles from Second Earth. Yanks. It wasn't a frantic rush, but it was fast. Everyone had purpose. They knew what they had to do.

"We're going up top," Courtney announced.

"Up top where?" Boon asked.

Courtney pointed up to the mountains that surrounded Black Water.

My heart sank. "We have to climb all the way up there?"

"Who said anything about climbing?" she answered with a sly smile. "I told you, this isn't the same Black Water you knew."

The four of us jogged away from Courtney's cabin in the general direction of the tunnel that led here from the valley of waterfalls. Nobody seemed to be bothered by Kasha and Boon. Either it was still too dark to notice them, or everyone was so focused on their task that they thought of nothing else. Either way, we weren't bothered.

When we reached the outer ring of structures, I saw what Courtney meant when she said that the larger cabins were there for defense. Men and women entered and came out quickly with what looked like weapons, but they were like nothing I had ever seen before. They were green tubes about eight feet long. They seemed heavy and unwieldy. It took two people to carry each one. There were braces on the tube, so that the weapon could rest on their shoulders, along with hand grips to control it. On the back end there was a large silver box device.

"Radio cannons," Courtney explained. "That's what we used to knock your gig out of the sky. If they come by air again, they won't be up there for long."

The people with the radio cannons took up positions on the back side of each of the defensive structures, looking out. They were ready. I assumed that the same was happening along the entire outer ring of the village. When we ran past the structures, I looked back to see that several gars were positioned inside the large huts, looking out of long, narrow windows along the top of each structure.

"Archers," Courtney explained. "That's our last line of

defense. If a huge number of klees get this far, this will only slow them down. It won't stop them. Still, our finest fighters are here. They will battle to the death before letting a single klee pass." She then looked at Kasha and Boon and added, "Sorry."

Kasha wasn't bothered by this news in the least. "But you are still confident of victory?" Kasha asked skeptically.

"Oh yeah. What you see here is only going to come into play if things get desperate. If things go well, no one inside Black Water will have to face a single klee."

"So what is this incredible scheme you've got going on?" I asked.

Courtney's answer was to pick up the pace. Several other gars ran alongside us, all headed in the same direction. Looking off to either side, I could see that there were gars and Yanks everywhere, all headed for the mountains. Courtney led us to a spot a few hundred feet to the right of the tunnel that led out and into the valley of waterfalls. There, cut into the rock at the base of the mountain, was a man-made tunnel entrance. Above the entrance a symbol was carved into the rock that I didn't recognize. But Courtney did.

"This is my station," she explained.

"You seem to know exactly what you are doing," Kasha commented.

"We all do," Courtney shot back. "We usually drill once a day. We never know when it's going to happen, either. Whatever we're doing, we've been trained to drop everything and get to our stations immediately."

As with Mark, it was hard to believe that this was the Courtney Chetwynde I had grown up with. She was always confident, but with the experience that came with age and conflict, she had become a force. It made me love her even more. Courtney jogged right into the tunnel. It wasn't deep. We ran for about thirty seconds until we hit a set of black double doors. Courtney touched a button to the right and the double doors slid open immediately.

It was an elevator.

"Going up?" she announced. "No dawdling. It's the express."

The four of us hurried inside. There were only two places where this elevator stopped. The bottom and the top. In seconds we were launched up through the center of the mountain, climbing higher and higher toward Courtney's post. Nobody said anything on the ride up, which was pretty much the way it always worked on elevators, no matter where you were. I wonder why that is? I stole a sideways glance at Courtney. She didn't seem nervous, but she was definitely focused. Maybe they had done this drill so many times that it was old hat to her. But this was no drill. If the warning horns were correct, the klees had arrived.

When the elevator stopped and the doors opened, we were hit with a blast of warm air and a breathtaking view of Black Water. It's a good thing I'm not afraid of heights, or I would have lost it. For a second I was worried about Kasha and Boon, but then realized how idiotic that was. They were cats. It wasn't in their DNA to be freaked by heights. According to Courtney she had been up there once a day, so the only person who had wet palms was me.

"This way," Courtney said, and left without waiting. She was on a mission, after all.

She led us out onto a narrow, wooden walkway that had been built along the uppermost ridge of the mountain range. It was like walking along the top of a long triangular prism. The steep mountain fell off to either side of us. On one side was Black Water, on the other was the green valley of waterfalls, where Kasha and Boon and I crashed the gig. My palms were no longer sweaty. They were dripping wet. My knees felt like rubber. The walkway was a ribbon with no handrail. A sudden gust of wind would have blown us off. Compared to this, slipping down the outside of that Lifelight pyramid on Veelox was like monkeying around on a playground slide. It didn't seem to bother Courtney. She walked quickly and confidently, as if she were on a sidewalk. I didn't risk looking back at Kasha and Boon to see if they were okay. I had to focus.

We walked for maybe fifty yards, until we came upon a platform that was built firmly into the rock. There was a rail around the outside that looked solid enough. To me it felt like a safe oasis. When I stepped onto it, I looked back to see that both Kasha and Boon had been walking on all fours. It gave me a little bit of satisfaction to know that they may not have been scared, but they were cautious enough not to be walking on their hind legs.

Courtney went to the edge of the platform that overlooked the green valley and gazed out over the vast expanse. The sunbelt was about to creep up over the horizon directly in front of us. That meant if there was an aerial attack, the klees would be coming out of the light—a typical tactic. Her eyes were trained on the mountain range on the far side of the valley, occasionally looking through a small pair of binoculars. I could still hear the whooping horn below, though it was far away, down in the village. Looking to my right and left, I saw other platforms like ours that were built along the length of the walkway. I'd guess they were a few hundred yards apart. Too far to yell to each other, but close enough to see that there were people on them. Everyone's gaze was locked on the horizon. Toward Leeandra. Toward the direction that the attack would surely come from.

"What's your job up here?" Boon asked.

"We have spotters all through the mountains," Courtney replied while still keeping a keen eye ahead. "If there's an attack, we can view the movement of the klees below and relay it everywhere."

"Who sounded the alarm?" I asked.

"The spotters in the front range. The side facing Leeandra. We figured that if an attack came, it would be from that direction. These stations back here are only manned if there's an attack. The front stations are constantly on alert. They're the first line of defense. My guess is that the spotters up there saw the klee army nearing the pass."

"There is only one path through the mountains," Kasha said. "That does not seem like a practical avenue for attack."

"It isn't," Courtney answered. "We have armed gars stationed all along the route. If the klees are dumb enough to try and march through, they won't make it."

"That means an attack from the air is more likely," I said.

Courtney nodded. "That's what we figured. We have spies, you know. Gars have been cautiously observing Leeandra for years to try and learn of their plans. Many have paid for the information with their lives."

I thought of Mark and his band of rebels outside the conclave on Third Earth. Courtney's life wasn't much different from that. They both lived outside the privileged world of the Ravinians and did what they could to help the rest of the people survive.

"That's why we developed the radio cannons," she

continued. "Black Water is naturally protected by these mountains, which makes a ground assault difficult. If they send in gigs, we punch them out of the sky. I think they know that, which is why they haven't attacked."

"Why do you think they're attacking now?" I asked.

Courtney squinted and continued to scan the far mountain range. "I don't know. It's the one thing that has me worried. I've heard rumblings that they were working on a new plan, but we never could figure out what it might be. It's the one wild card today."

"Maybe it's the dados," I offered hopefully.

"I hope so, because the radio cannons should handle them."

Boon asked, "Suppose large numbers of real klees get through somehow? Not the dados, the living ones. Are the gars able to defend themselves?"

Courtney looked back to us and gave a sly smile. "If any klees get into the valley, we have our own surprise waiting for them."

"What kind of surprise?" Kasha asked.

"If I told you, it wouldn't be a surprise," Courtney answered playfully. "Let's hope it won't come to that."

The sound of an explosion echoed across the green valley. It was huge, and was quickly followed by another, and another. I felt a slight vibration rattle the platform. It was subtle, but unnerving. More unnerving was the surprised look on Courtney's face.

"What?" I asked.

"I don't know" was her shaky answer.

"Is it a weapon?" Kasha asked.

"No," Courtney said quickly. "The klees don't have anything that can deliver a punch like that. I don't think."

Kasha looked to Boon and asked, "Do you know of anything the klees have that could create such a sound?"

Boon shook his head in confusion. "No, but the Ravinians are very secretive about their work. You saw how they put the door on the gig hangar. Everything used to be open. Now there are secrets."

"Secrets like . . . creating powerful weapons?" I asked.

"I'm sorry, Pendragon, I don't know," Boon said, his voice wavering.

Courtney reached into her pocket and took out a small, amber cube that I recognized as one of the link radio devices that the gars had developed. That cube represented the turning point for Eelong—the first radio broadcast on that world. Courtney put a finger to her ear where I saw she had a small earpiece. She touched the cube. It glowed. Courtney was listening. She frowned and closed her eyes.

"Is it a weapon?" I asked.

Courtney dropped her hand holding the radio. I saw the tension on her face.

"I don't know. If it is, they aren't using it to target us. At least, not yet."

"Then what are they shooting at?" I asked.

Courtney turned to me and said, "The mountain. They're blasting open the pass that leads from the outside into the valley. Whatever device is shooting is too far away for the gars to hit with the radio cannons."

The explosions continued. They were incessant. One after the other, each as loud as the last.

Courtney continued, "They're blasting a road through the mountain."

"Can they do that?" Boon asked. "Are those weapons powerful enough?"

As if in answer, the explosions intensified. The sounds tumbled on top of one another; the rumbling echoed across the valley like the finale of some monstrous fireworks show. Only it wasn't the end. It was the beginning.

"The spotters say they are blasting through the mountain like it was made of bread. The gars are fleeing for their lives. If the klees cut a path wide enough, we won't be able to prevent them from marching through."

"Won't that take a long time?" I asked, desperate for some little bit of good news.

I saw the first billow of smoke rise up over the mountain. What seemed so far away suddenly was in sight.

"Apparently not" was Courtney's sober answer.

We watched for a few minutes as the billow of black smoke grew larger and mixed with the dust of pulverized rock. I felt as if we were watching the approach of a monster that was eating through the mountain on a quest to find prey . . . which was exactly what was happening.

"Bobby," Courtney said, suddenly sounding uncertain. "If they can blast through that mountain so easily, they'll be able to do the same on this side of the valley and create a route directly into Black Water. We were prepared for an attack from the air. If they are able to mount a straight ahead attack of klees, we won't stand a chance."

As if to underline the point, we heard the loudest explosion yet, followed by an eruption of rock that spewed from the valley side of the far mountain. Even from as far away as we were, I could make out an avalanche of rock and debris tumbling down on the inside of the valley of waterfalls. In only a few short minutes, they had broken through. If things continued, it wouldn't be long before the very mountain ridge we were standing on would be targeted, and the Ravinian army would be on the threshold of Black Water.

The klee army was only a short distance away from taking on the exiles, and obliterating the last hope for Solara. And Halla.

33

The barrage continued.

Courtney gripped the handrail, staring intently as a wide section of mountain range crumbled. Every so often, through the smoke and dust, I could see light creeping through where there had once been only rock. They were indeed blasting a road through the mountains.

"We had no idea that they had that kind of firepower," she said through gritted teeth. "This is the surprise I feared."

"When we flew in, we saw that they had a load of transport trucks," I offered. "Whatever that weapon is, they must have brought it here in those trucks."

"We could stop trucks with the radio cannons," Courtney said, thinking out loud. "Unless they're out of range. Or if the gars are running for their lives, and right now it looks like we're dealing with both."

Kasha said, "Perhaps it's time to change tactics and prepare for the ground assault."

Courtney kept her binoculars trained on the mountain. I could see her jaw muscle working. Boon, Kasha, and I exchanged looks. This was not going well. The klees had obviously played a wild card that the gars hadn't anticipated. There were thousands of klees on the way. If there was an open highway into the valley, and then into Black Water, the gars would be done. A few archers inside of wooden huts wouldn't stop them, which meant the exiles would be done too. Standing up there on that platform, I felt totally helpless. There was nothing I could do. Nothing any of us could do. I wasn't even sure of what to hope for. Would the klees run out of ammunition before breaking through? Would the radio cannons be able to stop the dado klees? Was there any fallback position? What was the surprise defense Courtney mentioned? I couldn't imagine anything that would put a dent in the oncoming army.

"Wait," Courtney said. Her whole body went tense. She'd seen something. "What is that?"

She handed me the binoculars. I looked out over the valley to the target zone, and saw nothing but smoke and dirt billowing from the point of attack.

"What?" I asked.

"Keep looking," she commanded. "In the sky through the smoke."

I wished for the swirling smoke to blow away to give me a look at whatever it was she thought she saw.

"Something is moving in the air," she said. "Something big."

That's when I saw it. It was only a brief flash as the smoke parted, but there was no mistake.

"It's a gig," I announced. "A big one. It's hovering over the destruction."

"The klees have gigs that large?" she asked, surprised.

"Yes," Kasha answered. "We saw them in the hangar back in Leeandra."

"That's it," she declared, as if realizing something for the first time. "They're firing from gigs."

"So what?" I asked.

"So watch," she answered. She grabbed her link cube and shouted at the amber radio. "Gigs are in the air. They're launching those bombs from the sky." She listened, then added, "Because I can see them from up here. There are definitely gigs up there. Knock 'em down!"

She looked at us and said, "The gigs must have been firing from a distance. Now they're in range."

"But the gars up front are running away!" Boon exclaimed.

Courtney gave him a sly look. "Who said they were the only ones with cannons?"

Of course. There had to have been radio cannons positioned in the valley of waterfalls. That was how Kasha and Boon and I got knocked out of the sky. But using them would mean the gigs had to be inside the valley, and that much closer to Black Water. It was a dangerous tactic, but as I watched the destruction unfold below, it was clear that the gars had no choice.

The explosions continued. There was nothing we could do but watch and hope. The billowing cloud of smoke and dust grew larger. I wondered how much longer it would be before the klees blasted a wide enough path to send their army through.

"Look!" Boon yelled.

A gig blasted out of the clouds, headed our way. It was definitely one of the big helicopters we'd seen in the tree hangar. This thing was armed for bear. There were missiles strapped to either side and beneath. There was no doubt now, the klees had developed missiles and could launch them from gigs. Or maybe they'd been shipped from the helicopter factory on Third Earth. Didn't matter. They were here, and the klees knew how to use them. My heart sank. What possible chance did the gars and the exiles stand against such a sophisticated attack from the air?

I was about to find out.

The gig charged forward, high over the valley.

"Why are the gars not firing on it?" Boon asked nervously.

"Hang on," Courtney said calmly.

A quick look and calculation told me its destination. It was headed for the waterfall that protected the tunnel into Black Water . . . directly beneath us. This killer chopper's mission was clear. It was about to start the second phase of an assault that would open up a highway for the klee army, giving it access to Black Water. I held on to the railing, bracing for the moment that it would launch its missiles. I feared that the faint tremor we felt during the attack on the far mountain range would be nothing compared to what would happen once the missiles starting hitting the rock below our feet. I stole a quick look at the walkway that snaked over the backbone of the mountain and wondered if it would come crashing down, with us and every gar up there along with it. I felt like this was the beginning of the end.

"Patience," Courtney whispered to nobody.

I heard a faint whistling sound. Suddenly the oncoming helicopter spun sideways. More whistling followed. The large gig started twisting, as if it were being hit by stiff winds that came from different directions.

"He's done," Courtney said with total confidence.

Turned out she was a lot less nervous about what was happening than I was. The helicopter spun wildly. It was out of control and headed down. This chopper was being targeted the same way that Kasha and Boon and I were when we first flew in.

"We've got cannons positioned all over the valley," Courtney explained. "This is the kind of attack we've been ready for."

I couldn't tell where the radio cannons were being fired from. The two-person weapons were portable, which meant they could hide anywhere in the trees below. Wherever they were, the shooters knew what they were doing. Their aim was perfect. The helicopter pitched and spun and finally slammed into the ground. This crash was a lot more spectacular than ours was, thanks to the unfired missiles it had on board. As soon as the gig hit the ground, *ka-boom*. Multiple explosions erupted from the point of impact, shooting flames and debris high into the air. As much as the klees were the bad guys here, I hoped that the pilots were dados. Seeing the huge explosion, I realized that there wouldn't be anything left of them to figure it out one way or the other. The gig hit just before it reached the lake in the center of the crater, but the explosion was so huge I could feel the heat from as far away as we were.

"One down," Courtney said. "Bring 'em on."

As if following her orders, two more gigs flew out of the cloud of dust and smoke, headed for the Black Water waterfall. Both were loaded with missiles. Both met the same fate. Two more spectacular crashes followed, creating multiple infernos on the valley floor.

"Listen," Kasha called out. "The explosions have stopped."

I had been concentrating so intently on the gigs that I didn't realize the distant thunder from the explosions on the far mountain had ended.

"What do you think that means?" Boon asked. "Were the other gigs taken down too?"

Courtney put her finger to her ear to listen to her link radio. She smiled.

"Seven gigs down," she reported. "Including the three that made it into the valley. The spotters went back and took them down. Unbelievable. You want to talk about bravery? Those guys had to fire on the gigs while all hell was raining down on them."

"Are there more?" I asked.

Courtney listened, and shook her head. "No. They're done. We got them all. Wait—"

It wasn't time to celebrate. Courtney's dark look told me that much. She listened intently to the report that was coming in over the link radio. As she concentrated, I looked to the far mountain. The smoke was starting to dissipate. It wouldn't be long till we would see how much damage the klees had done before their helicopters were put out of business. Kasha and Boon joined me at the front of the platform. We all gazed across the valley floor, straining for a glimpse of what the gig attack had accomplished.

"Question is," I said, "did they finish the road?"

The wind picked up, blowing away the rest of the debris in the air. What we saw made my mouth go dry. There was a very clear, wide gap cut through the mountain. In the few short minutes that the klees had been targeting the mountain, they had succeeded in blasting out a wide chasm. I now realized why the second wave of gigs had started across the valley. It wasn't to escape the gars who were firing on them from below. It was because their destruction of the first mountain pass was complete.

"They're coming," Courtney declared. "The klee army is

on the march. We don't have enough gar shooters over there to stop them. They can't protect such a wide entryway."

"Is there anything we can do?" I asked lamely.

"Yeah," Courtney answered. "We can hope that the rest of the klees are dados."

How twisted was that? The last, best hope to save Black Water would be if the klees had blundered and sent a dado army to attack. The gar radio cannons could stop them. What they couldn't stop were flesh-and-blood klees. As much as the gars had anticipated and prepared for a battle, they never expected that the klees would be able to flood so many warriors at them at once. They were hoping to pick them off one by one as they came through the narrow pass. But the pass wasn't narrow anymore. It was wide enough for thousands of klees at a time to march through.

"What if they're not dados?" Kasha asked.

Courtney shrugged. She looked grim. "We have one last chance after that to keep them in the valley. If that fails and they break through into Black Water, I know the gars will fight until the end, but I don't think they'll stand a chance. Both the gars and the Yanks are dedicated. Confident, even. They believe that they will be able to stop anything that is thrown at us, but I think that's more bravery speaking than common sense. If the klees get into Black Water, it'll be a bloodbath. We've got to stop them right here."

The wait was killing me. It all came down to this. When the klee army emerged from the newly formed passage into the valley, would they be sending dados or klees? It felt odd to be rooting for dados.

The smoke cleared entirely, giving us an unobstructed view of the valley below. The three gigs burned where they'd crashed. I didn't see a single survivor. I also didn't see any gars on the valley floor. I assumed they were all in hiding, waiting for the klee army to appear. It was tense as all hell. I couldn't imagine how the gars who were waiting below felt. They had no way of knowing this, but they were not only going to fight to protect Black Water, but this battle would determine the future of all existence. It was just as well they didn't know.

I wondered how many of the defenders below were exiles from Second Earth. The Yanks. It didn't surprise me that they had put in with the gars and were all working together to protect Black Water. These were the people who had stood up to Alexander Naymeer and his Ravinians on Second Earth. They paid for their beliefs by being sucked into a flume and banished from their home. They could have landed on Eelong and given up. Instead, they rallied and created a new and better Black Water. It was no surprise to me, knowing the kind of people they were, that they were willing to put their lives on the line to protect it. Uncle Press explained to us that it was their spirit that was keeping Solara alive. Seeing the work they had done, the sacrifices they had made, and the bravery they'd shown here on Eelong made me understand it fully. These people were special. I truly believed they could be the foundation upon which Halla would be rebuilt.

If they survived.

"They're here," Courtney said softly.

She held up her binoculars to get a better look at the wound in the mountain. She didn't have to bother. We could all see it plain enough with the naked eye. At first it seemed like a wave of red blood flowing out of the cleft in the mountain. It took only a few seconds to realize what it really was. Moving forward, filling the width of the gap, was an army of klees carrying red Ravinian flags. There were hundreds of the flags, snapping in the wind, headed into the valley as if in triumph. I was amazed at the bold move. They weren't being defensive. It didn't look as if they even had weapons. Did they seriously think the battle was already won?

The wave continued. Line after line of klees marched forward in lockstep, flags waving as they descended into the crater that was the valley of waterfalls.

"We'll know soon," Courtney announced. "If they're dados, they're walking into a kill zone. If not—" She gave me a grave look.

The mass of flag-bearing klees ended. They were followed by klees wearing the uniform of Leeandran soldiers. These guys carried the weapons I had seen the foragers use. From far away they looked like they were carrying flagpoles with no flags, but I knew they were the wooden staves that would be used to crack heads. They would also have the three-stone bolas that they threw at gars to tie up their legs. The sick thing is that they weren't coming in to obliterate the gars. This was a roundup. Sure, gars would go down, but I believe their mission was to capture as many as possible. Those trucks we saw weren't carrying weapons. They were here to take the gars back to Leeandra for the klees' barbaric feasts. I wondered what their orders were. How aggressive were they going to be? There was no way that the gars or the exiles would go without a fight.

"What have the gars been told?" I asked Courtney. "I mean, if it comes to a close-in fight, what will they do?"

"You mean what's going to happen if it looks like we're losing?" she asked.

I nodded.

"There will be no prisoners," she said with certainty. "One way or the other, this will be a fight to the death."

As fatalistic a thought as that was, it made perfect sense. If I had to choose between dying in battle or being rounded up and put into a cage and held until I was slaughtered for food, I know the decision I'd make. Surrender was worse than suicide.

The four of us stood on that platform, watching as the klee army emerged from the destroyed mountain.

"Is there no end to them?" Kasha said, thinking out loud.

I thought back to the view we'd gotten of the army from the sky when we flew in the day before. There were thousands of them. Multiple thousands. There was no way that a guerrilla force of gars and Yanks would stand a chance against them.

"When you met with the gar defenders last night, did you plan for this possibility?" I asked.

"You mean did we figure out what to do if the klees got in and they turned out to be dados?" she asked. "Yes. We put together a rough plan."

"How rough?" I asked.

"Well, considering we didn't think this would really happen, not a whole lot of thought went into it. But it's not complicated. The plan is to lay back with the radio cannons, wait until the klees enter the kill zone, then give the order to unload on them."

"How precise are the weapons?" Kasha asked. "Does each dado have to be shot separately?"

"Yes," Courtney answered. "The throw of the radio cannons isn't very wide. But we've got the best marksmen in charge. All they need is the order to fire."

"And who gives that order?"

Courtney looked at me and gave me the confident smile that I had seen so often. "That would be me."

Of course it would. She's the one who introduced the concept of dados to the gars. Why shouldn't she be in charge? Courtney trained her binoculars back down into the valley. The hordes of klees continued to pour into the valley. There seemed to be even more than we'd seen from the air, but I think that was because they were more concentrated from having come through the gap.

"Are there enough cannons?" Boon asked nervously. "There are a whole lot of targets down there."

"More than enough," Courtney answered without taking her eyes away from the binoculars. "With plenty of power to fire several charges from each weapon. The trick is to get our shooters close enough to be able to target the klees, but not so close that, if the cannons are ineffective, they would be in the way of our counterattack."

"Counterattack?" Kasha asked.

Courtney didn't answer. She was focused on events down below. The flag-carrying klees were a third of the way through the valley, headed for the waterfalls. They were about to pass by the thick stand of trees that grew along one shore of the lake. I had no doubt that the gar shooters were hidden among those trees. Courtney held the binoculars with one hand and lifted her link radio with the other.

"Stand by," she spoke into the radio.

Her voice didn't betray the tension I knew she was feeling. Were the klees dados? Would the radio weapons be effective against them? We would know in a few short seconds.

"Wait for my command," Courtney said softly, as if she didn't want her words to be overheard by the klees below.

The army marched on. The first line reached the stand of trees. How long would Courtney wait? Was the hurried plan they hatched being put into gear? Were the gar shooters in position?

"On my command," Courtney finally said.

I didn't know what she was waiting for, but this was her show, so I wasn't going to comment.

"Five . . . four . . . three . . . two . . . one . . . *fire!*"

The first line of klees froze in their tracks. That one reaction was all we needed to know.

"Dados," Courtney growled in triumph.

The dado klees dropped their flags. The red stars of Ravinia fell into the dirt. In seconds, multiple hundreds of klees were lying on the ground, lifeless. There was no doubt. They were dados. Wave after wave hit the ground. I heard the faint sound of the whine of radio waves rising from the valley floor as the gar shooters unloaded on them. There must have been hundreds of weapons down there, all firing incessantly. That's how many dados fell.

"They aren't klees!" Boon shouted with joy. "They can be stopped!"

Within a minute the bodies of a thousand dado klees littered the valley of waterfalls. It looked like total victory. At first I thought that the only reason the klees to the rear weren't falling was because they couldn't get past the sea of bodies and enter the kill zone. I figured it was only a matter of time before word got passed back and the remaining dados beat a quick retreat.

That didn't happen.

"Why are they continuing to march forward?" Boon asked. "They must realize they have entered a trap."

The first hint of doubt crept into my head. Every last

klee wearing the red uniform of Ravinia was dead. Or deactivated. Or whatever. They were joined by many more who wore the uniform of soldiers from Leeandra and wound up dead as well. But there were many to the rear who kept moving forward, crawling over the bodies, continuing the assault.

"Something's wrong," Courtney announced.

"Could the gars be out of ammunition?" I asked.

"Maybe," she said ominously. "Or maybe the rest aren't dados."

The truth suddenly seemed obvious. The radio cannons had knocked out the dados, but there was more to this army. Much more. The dados were sent in first, perhaps for this very reason, to draw out the radio-cannon fire. Coming up from the rear were flesh-and-blood klees. Most of the army had been wiped out, but there were still plenty of living klees to bring the battle to Black Water.

Courtney kept her eyes down on the valley. If she was scared, she didn't show it.

Kasha said, "You said something about a surprise?"

"Yeah," Courtney replied. "Now or never."

The klees clambered over the fallen dados effortlessly. After all, they were cats. They dropped to all fours and continued moving forward. It was almost as if they had practiced this maneuver. The first ones over the pile of dead dados advanced several yards and then stopped, waiting for the others to make their way over and assemble. It was hard to tell how many were there. Five hundred? A thousand? More? The army had been cut down considerably, but there were still plenty of living klees left to do some damage.

"What's going to happen?" I asked, my voice cracking.

"This isn't the Black Water you knew, Bobby," Courtney explained, sounding way too calm for the situation. "Much of the change has to do with the Yanks, who helped the gars advance. It was clear that if the klees ever decided to attack, the gars wouldn't stand a chance. So they had to come up with unexpected ways to defend themselves. Creating the radio cannons was one of those ways."

"But there's another, right?" I asked hopefully.

"The theory is there," Courtney answered. "We weren't able to fully test it, for reasons that will become obvious, so I guess you'd call this a 'trial by fire.' It's either going to work, or Black Water is done."

The remaining klees assembled beyond the mass of dado bodies. Several klees on zenzens rode to the front of the pack. I figured these must be the officers. They had been lying back, safely waiting for this moment. Now they were about to lead the charge into Black Water. One officer rode to the front of the klees, raised his arm as a signal, and motioned for the waterfall. Moving as one, the mass of klees began to make their way toward Black Water.

"Are gars guarding the waterfall?" I asked.

"No," Courtney answered. "The tunnel doesn't offer any position to attack from. Gars are waiting on the far side, but we're hoping the klees don't make it that far."

Kasha asked, "So you will try to stop them before they reach the tunnel?"

"That's the idea," Courtney answered.

We all looked down over the edge as the re-formed but smaller klee army marched toward the waterfall. I glanced up into the mountains on our side of the valley. Were there guns up there? Were the gars going to roll rocks down onto the klees? What was going to happen?

Courtney lifted her link cube. The command to launch the counterattack was hers to give. "All units, prepare to release," she ordered.

I watched her scanning the scene below, calculating. I glanced to Kasha. Kasha shrugged. She didn't have any better idea of what was about to happen than I did.

Courtney looked to us and said, "If we're lucky, this is going to get ugly."

She brought the link cube to her mouth and gave the order. "Three . . . two . . . one . . . release!"

"Release what?" I asked.

My answer came in the form of a high, shrill whistle. It was soon joined by another. And another. Soon the piercing whistle sound filled the valley, echoing off the stone face of the surrounding mountains. Looking at the klees, I saw that the sound didn't affect them at all. They continued their march.

"It didn't work," Boon fretted. "They aren't stopping."

"Hang on," Courtney said with patience.

Whatever was supposed to happen wasn't happening. The whistle sound continued, growing in pitch and in volume. I felt bad for any stray dogs that might have been wandering around. Not that there were any dogs on Eelong.

That's when I remembered. I had heard a whistle like that before. On Eelong. There may not have been dogs on this territory, but there were other animals. Was it possible? Was this the final defense that the gars had pinned their hopes on?

A second later they struck. The forest that surrounded the base of the mountains came to life. Leaping from the dark confines of the trees were . . . tangs. Hundreds of them. They had appeared from nowhere, and they looked pissed. The klee officer held up his hand to signal his soldiers, but they already knew. They were surrounded by a ring of angry tangs. The first line of klees stopped, which meant the rest of the army bunched up behind them. In seconds the klee army had gone from a tight, formidable force, to a group of confused cats. Obviously, they hadn't expected this, which is exactly what the gars had been counting on.

Courtney glanced back at me with a sly smile and said, "We stopped battling tangs and learned how to train them."

I thought back to when I had been treed by the tang, when I first got back to Eelong. That thing was just as vicious as any tang I had ever seen, and I had no doubt it would have ripped me apart if it hadn't been for the gar that called him off—with a whistle. The gar had petted the snout of the subdued beast. The carnivorous lizard had become as docile as my dog, Marley. From that one event I had learned that the gars could calm the tangs. From what I saw below, they could also fire them up.

The klees turned outward to defend themselves. They raised their weapons to protect against the rampage. It was too little, too late. The vicious tangs descended on the klees like a swarm of hungry locusts. There was a bloodlust going on that actually turned my stomach. Courtney's prediction came true. It got ugly. I couldn't watch. Looking to Kasha and Boon, I saw that they had to turn away as well. These were their brothers down there. As misguided as they may have been, these soldiers were still klees. Saint Dane's influence put them on a violent path, and that violence was now being turned back on them. They were slaughtered.

There was no other word for it. I heard the tortured screams of the cats as they desperately tried to fend off the tangs, or to flee. The tangs were merciless. I was grateful to be as far away as we were, because I couldn't imagine hearing the sounds of tearing flesh. And chewing. And death.

Some klees escaped. The officers on zenzens were the first to bolt. They galloped back toward the newly cut gap and out of the valley as fast as their zenzens would take them. A few were hunted down before their zenzens got up to speed. The tangs leaped at them and took them down violently. Several stragglers managed to escape. A running klee was faster than a running tang. I can't judge how many got away, but it wasn't many. The rest fell to the teeth and talons.

The battle didn't last long. The event was swift and violent. Within minutes hundreds of klee bodies lay in their own blood, being devoured by tangs. I guess that's justice for you. The klees came to eat the gars, and instead, they found themselves on the menu.

Kasha's voice quivered when she said, "I do not know if I should be repulsed . . . or thrilled."

Another whistle sounded. Different pitch. Different frequency. The trained tangs instantly gathered together and trotted back into the forest from where they'd come, looking suddenly docile . . . and satiated. In minutes, all that was left of the massive klee assault on Black Water was a gap blown into the mountains, seven destroyed gigs, a pile of fried dados, and the bodies of hundreds of half-eaten klees.

The attack had been an absolute and total failure.

Courtney pulled the earpiece from her ear and turned to me. The relief on her face was obvious. "Guess it worked."

It was over. The klees had come knocking and the gars

shut the door. The four of us hurried back for the elevator and descended quickly into Black Water. When we exited the elevator tunnel, we witnessed a scene of total joy. It was pandemonium. This was a war they had been preparing for for a long time. It had ended in complete victory. The four of us stood at the mouth of the tunnel, looking down the slope into the village. We didn't join the celebration. That would have been tricky, considering Boon and Kasha were klees. We had to make do with witnessing it from afar.

The village was in an uproar. People cheered. Music played over loudspeakers. Gars hugged Yanks. People were kissing. The radio cannons that minutes before had been set to protect the first ring of buildings were laid down, and their shooters were dancing joyously. It was an outpouring of positive emotion like I had never seen before. It reminded me of when we had prevented the klees from poisoning Black Water so many years before . . . times twenty.

I could only imagine the positive spirit that was flooding into Solara.

The gars had been living under the threat of the klees for a long time. I had no doubt that with this battle, the klees would think twice before attacking again. For the Yanks, the exiles, this was a moment of victory for them as well. They had to know the connection between Ravinia and the klees. They saw the flags and the uniforms as clearly as I did. It didn't matter that they were being worn by cats. It was Ravinia, the people who had banished them from their own home. I hoped they got some satisfaction in having struck a blow back at them.

Courtney put her arms around me. The two of us stood there, holding each other, enjoying the celebration.

"Unbelievable," I said.

"No, it isn't," she replied. "It's proof that Ravinia isn't all-powerful."

There was something about those words that struck a note with me. It was a thought I couldn't fully grab on to, but it started me thinking. The gars and the Yanks had proven that Ravinia wasn't all-powerful. Interesting.

"Shorty?" came a familiar voice.

We all turned quickly to see a tall, dark-skinned man standing near the mouth of the cave. It was Gunny. He was still wearing the dark suit, white shirt, and tie that was his normal outfit on First Earth. He seemed totally out of place here on Eelong. The tall, soft-spoken man walked over to us, and in his usual calm, soft voice said, "Morning, Kasha. Boon. Hello there, young lady." He said this last to Courtney. "You're growing up more beautiful than I imagined."

"Good to see you, Gunny."

Gunny looked down at the celebration and asked, "What happened?"

"The klees attacked and the gars turned them back," I answered. "It was incredible."

"Seems so," Gunny said as he viewed the celebration with a smile. "And the exiles? Elli said they were here."

"They are," Courtney answered. "They helped save Black Water."

Gunny nodded knowingly. "That explains a lot."

"What do you mean?" I asked.

Gunny turned to us and said, "Bobby, Kasha, it's time you came back to Solara."

"Why? What's happened?" Kasha asked.

"You've got to see it for yourself. Solara has changed. I'm

guessing it has something to do with what just happened here. I don't know how to describe it, but you two better get back."

I couldn't imagine what Gunny was talking about, but I knew that if he came looking for us, it was important. It was time to go.

I looked to Courtney and said, "You just kicked some serious ass."

"Pretty cool, aye?" Courtney wasn't one for false modesty. She turned serious and added, "But this was just the warm-up, wasn't it?"

I hadn't wanted to kill the celebration by reminding everyone of Saint Dane's plan. There were several thousand dados on Third Earth waiting to get their own shot at Black Water.

"Try not to think about it right now," I answered. "Enjoy this."

Courtney nodded. She knew their victory was going to be short-lived.

Kasha gave Boon a hug. "Thank you."

"I'm not sure what I should do now," Boon said. "I'm not going back to Leeandra, and I can't stay here. I'm the enemy, remember?"

"Stay," Courtney said quickly. "You aren't one of them. This is your home now. Nothing's going to happen to you. I'll make sure of it."

Boon looked sick. I felt bad for the guy. He was caught between two lives.

"I'm serious, Boon. You'll be okay," Courtney assured him.

Boon nodded, but still looked nervous.

"What are we going to see, Gunny?" I asked. I wanted a little bit of a preview before being hit with another surprise.

"I can't exactly say for sure," the old man said. "What I'm hoping is that you're going to see the future."

With that mysterious comment, Gunny, Kasha, and I took a step back.

And returned to Solara.

34

Solara had changed.

Dramatically. At first I thought we were in the wrong place. Had we somehow taken a wrong turn through time and space?

Kasha was just as confused.

"Pendragon?" was all she said, but I knew what she meant. Where the heck were we?

I looked at Gunny.

My tall friend gave me a warm smile. "Amazing, isn't it?"

It's hard to explain this, since Solara wasn't like any other place I'd ever been. There weren't buildings or roads or much else that you'd think of to define a location. Solara was the beginning of Halla. It was the crossroads for the spirit of man, and the spirit of man didn't exactly need a normal house to live in. When we were all there before, right after the destruction of the flumes, Solara was a vast wasteland of dark matter. Though I sensed the spirits around me, it felt dead. Or dying. What we learned was that the last of the positive spirit in Halla was being kept alive by the exiles. When the Travelers had gathered there earlier, it wasn't looking so hot for the good guys.

Now I saw life. Actual life. Kasha, Gunny, and I stepped into a pretty meadow covered with green grass. We were surrounded by rolling hills. I wondered if the grass had grown out of the gray rock that we had all seen before, or if the rock had actually transformed. The meadow was dotted with flowers. Solara had become a bright, beautiful place.

The only thing I recognized from our previous visit was overhead. The sky was still dark and filled with stars. Bright, colorful clouds continued to roll by. Maybe it was wishful thinking, but it seemed like there were more brilliant clouds than we had seen before. Since there was no sun, it felt as though light from these brilliant clouds was what made Solara so bright.

As positive as this all seemed, there was also something odd about it. Looking off in the distance, the meadow seemed to go out of focus. The view wasn't infinite. It ended. We could only see so far, and then the view became blurred. It was as if we were surrounded by a wall of water. There was no way to judge how large this green meadow was, but it didn't go on forever.

I looked to Gunny and asked the obvious question: "What happened?"

"Not sure" was his answer. "Looks pretty good though, doesn't it?"

A fourth person joined the party. Uncle Press walked up from the edges of reality. "What happened on Eelong?" he asked with excitement in his voice.

I was used to Uncle Press having all the answers. It was strange to be the one getting him up to speed. As we spoke, one by one the other Travelers appeared and joined us. First Elli, then Siry, Spader, Patrick, Aja, Alder, and finally Loor.

"An army of klee attacked Black Water," I explained. "Most of them were dados, which meant that Saint Dane had a hand in it. Bottom line? The gars kicked butt."

"And the exiles?" he asked cautiously.

"Safe," Kasha answered. "If not for their help, the gars would have been wiped out."

Siry asked, "So it's true? The exiles are on Eelong?"

"Every one of 'em" was my answer. I walked to Elli and held her hands. "Because of Nevva. She sent them there. She wanted Eelong to survive and sent those people there to help keep it alive. She saved their lives, Elli. As much as she agreed with Saint Dane, she didn't buy into his vision entirely."

I looked back to the group and added, "Saint Dane made a mistake, but it wasn't that he chose to exile the people from Second Earth. He wanted them killed from the beginning."

Siry asked, "So what did he do wrong?"

"He believed that Nevva was as evil as he was."

I saw tears well up in Elli's eyes. "You didn't lose your daughter," I said softly. "She just took a bad detour."

Elli gave me a rare smile. It was a beautiful thing.

Uncle Press looked around, still trying to piece together what it all meant.

"This is a rejuvenation," he said, thinking out loud. "No question. There was an infusion of positive spirit into Solara like I haven't seen in a long while."

Loor asked, "Is this what Solara normally looks like?"

"Yes and no," he answered. "Solara is seen differently through the eyes of every spirit. I think this meadow is an appealing place for all of us, so that's what we're seeing."

I took a closer look at our surroundings. The feeling
life and spirit was almost electric. I sensed more images c
the corners of my vision. Lights moved about. Other image.
seemed to be actual people. Did I see my parents? I thought
so, but it was fleeting. The sky crackled with light and
energy and color. Where before Solara felt as if it were out
of gas, it now looked alive. I can only speak for myself, but
looking around at the other Travelers, I thought they all
felt the same as I did. We had new life. And with it, maybe
some hope.

"So is that it?" Aja asked. "Was that Saint Dane's last
attack?"

"It might be," Patrick offered somewhat sheepishly.
"The tide may have turned."

"Is that possible?" Alder said hopefully. "Has Solara
been reborn?"

"No," Uncle Press said flatly. That single, definitive
word echoed across the strange meadow. It was like the air
had come out of a very big balloon.

Aja countered, "But you said that—"

"I said that Solara was rejuvenated, I didn't say it was
complete. Look around. How far can you see?"

"Not very," Spader admitted.

"This is one tiny speck of Solara," Uncle Press continued.
"Beyond this, nothing has changed. Think of it this way—
the gas tank was almost empty and a few ounces were
pumped in. It won't be long before that gas is burned, and
we're back where we started."

"What's a gas tank?" Siry asked.

I stepped away from the group to gaze out at what Solara
had become. Or at least, what this tiny section of Solara
had become. I tried to focus on the blurred edges of this

all oasis, imagining what was beyond the veil. What had happened to Solara was positive. No doubt. It was due to the victory on Eelong. I didn't doubt that, either. An idea had been tickling the edges of my brain for a while. At first it seemed like fantasy, but as each new event unfolded, the possibility of it becoming a reality grew stronger. I had been afraid to share it with the others, because the time never seemed right. As we stood together in that rejuvenated spot of Solara, after all I had seen, I realized that my fantasy idea might just be the only chance we had at making this small victory permanent.

"We've taken a huge step forward," Uncle Press declared. "We may not have reclaimed Solara, but we have slowed the slide, thanks to the exiles. They experienced an incredible victory. You see the result. This is what Solara can be. Positive energy is flowing once again. Not just from the exiles, but from the gars as well. This is the triumph of positive spirit."

"Sounds good," Gunny said cautiously. "How can we build on that?"

"We focus all our energy on protecting the exiles" was Uncle Press's answer. "They are the seeds of a new Halla. If they flourish, Solara will once again grow the way it was meant to." He gestured around him and added, "This is the proof. Nevva Winter gave us a gift. We have to nurture it."

"No," I called out.

Everyone snapped a look to me. The surprise was obvious on all their faces, most of all Uncle Press's.

"What's the problem, Bobby?" Uncle Press asked.

"It won't add up," I answered.

"What won't?" Aja asked, always skeptical of anything I had to offer.

"We had a victory. The gars and the exiles had a victory. Great. But it's not over. Did Elli tell you about the army of dados on Third Earth?"

"She did," Uncle Press replied. He was totally focused on me. He wasn't skeptical. He didn't argue. He wanted to hear what I was thinking.

"This isn't done yet," I declared. "Third Earth is still in play, and Saint Dane has an army that's ready and waiting to finish off the exiles on Eelong."

Aja jumped in again. "Is he really capable of creating a flume to send that army to Black Water?"

All eyes went right to Uncle Press. He didn't look happy.

"He could" was his simple, direct answer.

"He may not even need to!" I added.

It was my turn to get everybody's attention.

"The gars sent the klees off with their tails between their legs. Yay, big victory. But I guarantee you, the klees aren't done. Not as long as Ravinia controls them. They'll regroup and try again. And again. Protecting Black Water and the exiles will get more difficult, even if Saint Dane *doesn't* unleash his army of dados. If we think all we have to do to save Halla is circle the wagons around Black Water and hope that the exiles grow into a new civilization, we're kidding ourselves. Even if we're able to protect Black Water, that's only one territory. What about all the others that are controlled by Ravinia? Maybe keeping the exiles alive will help Solara sputter along for a while, but the numbers aren't on our side. How long can we hold out? Years? Decades? A century? We're talking about the future of all civilization. All mankind. Forever. A century is a blip of time when we're talking about eternity. If we're going to stop Saint Dane for ood, we're going to have to do more than pat ourselves on the back over a single victory."

I looked around to see that everyone's expression of hope and optimism was long gone. I hated being the buzz killer, but I was speaking the truth, and they knew it.

"I think there's only one way to end this, and that's to take the battle to him," I declared. "If we don't, the only question will be how long we can hold out, because eventually he'll wear us down and win it all."

Nobody argued.

The first one to speak was Uncle Press. "You say this like you have a plan," he said with caution.

I smiled. "I always have a plan," I said with confidence. "Well, usually I do."

I could feel the anticipation grow within the group of friends. I had just laid out a pretty nasty scenario. After getting hit with a cold splash of reality, I think they were desperate to hear that there was still hope. I didn't jump into it quickly. I knew it would take some convincing. Heck, I wasn't entirely sure it was the right thing to do myself. I took a few moments to look around at Solara. The meadows. The colorful vapors in the sky. The stars. The feeling of life and spirit that was all around us.

"Look what happened here when the gars and the exiles defeated the klees," I began. "What was the word you used, Uncle Press? 'Rejuvenation.' The positive spirit and energy of those people on Eelong proved that Uncle Press is right. They are the future. Their spirit was so strong, it brought new life to Solara."

Aja scoffed, "Didn't you just say that it's only temporary?"

"It is," I agreed. "If all we do now is focus on keeping the exiles alive for a while, it will only prolong the inevitable."

"You're contradicting yourself, Pendragon," Aja said firmly.

"But I'm not," I argued. "I saw what those exiles are capable of. They were willing to sacrifice it all to protect Black Water. Question is, would they be willing to do it again to save Halla?"

I saw plenty of confused looks being thrown around. The only person who stayed focused on me was Uncle Press. I didn't want to disappoint him.

"Keep going," he said thoughtfully.

"Just before she died, Nevva told me that Saint Dane split Solara in two. I think where we are, here, is the Solara that has always been. But Saint Dane has somehow splintered it, or made a wall or something, to create a Solara that is being fed by the negative spirit that he's created throughout Halla. It's like he's draining the positive spirit and weakening us, while building the dark spirit of his own Solara. That's the source of his power, and it's growing all the time. It's why he threw Halla into chaos, to feed the spirit of his own Solara."

"I've sensed that," Uncle Press agreed. "Spirits are not only diminishing, they are fleeing. The spirit of Solara has been about all mankind, the good and the bad. The positive and the negative."

Loor offered, "Does that mean Saint Dane has been collecting the negative, aggressive spirits to create his own base of power?"

Uncle Press thought, and nodded. "It makes sense."

Gunny whistled in awe. "So if the spirit of the exiles is the only thing keeping the proper Solara alive, the rest of Halla is pretty much feeding Saint Dane's side."

"Exactly!" I declared. "But Nevva said he won't have

full control until the light from the proper Solara is snuffed. Forget the little blip that just happened because of the Black Water victory. Solara is dangerously close to extinction."

Alder said, "Perhaps there is some way to diminish the power of this dark Solara."

"Now we're talking!" I shouted. "It's what Nevva said. To defeat him we have to weaken him. I think there's only one way of doing that. We have to force him into using his own power to defend himself. Let's snuff his light before he snuffs ours."

Siry said, "Uh, how?"

"By attacking him in the Conclave of Ravinia," I said flat out.

I don't know if I actually heard gasps, or imagined it because I was expecting them. I definitely got a lot of shocked, openmouthed looks.

"How?" was the simple, stunned question that came from Aja.

"With an army that is seventy thousand strong" was my answer.

There was another moment of stunned silence.

"The exiles?" Kasha said with confusion. "That isn't possible. They are on Eelong."

"They are," I admitted. "I might be totally wrong about this, and if I am, I'll back off, but if we have the power of Solara at our disposal, why can't we use it the same way Saint Dane does?"

The Travelers exchanged confused looks. Nobody had any idea what I was talking about.

Except for Loor.

"Is it possible?" she asked tentatively. "Could we do it too?"

"Do what?" Aja snapped at her.

Uncle Press was next to join the party. "I can't think of a riskier move, on many levels."

"But is it possible?" I asked him.

Uncle Press thought for a moment, then nodded. "It may be, especially in light of what happened here after the victory on Eelong."

"Exactly what I was thinking," I added.

Aja was getting frustrated. She didn't like being behind the curve on ideas. "Would someone please explain this to me?"

"Solara has been rejuvenated," I said. "Positive spirit has flooded back in. We could use that power to continue being Travelers and jumping around Halla and trying to protect the exiles, or we could make one grand move and try to end this once and for all."

Elli gasped when she realized what I was proposing. "You want to create a flume to move the exiles."

"Exactly," I answered.

I sensed everybody stiffen. What I was proposing was nothing short of desperation. No argument there. I looked to Aja. She stared back at me. I was waiting for her to say how crazy I was. How dumb a move it would be. How it would drain every last bit of spirit from Solara, and that if we failed, it would mean Saint Dane would be free to create his own universe. She would have been right on every count.

"It's brilliant," she declared.

Gotta love Aja Killian.

"Can we really do this, Press?" Gunny asked with concern. "It's quite the tall order."

"Not long ago my answer would have been no," Uncle

Press said. "But we've been handed an opportunity. The victory on Eelong gave it to us. The exiles gave it to us." He looked to Elli and added, "Nevva gave it to us."

Elli beamed.

Uncle Press continued, "What we're talking about here would deplete the spirit of Solara, but if what happened on Eelong is any indication, defeating Saint Dane where he lives, controlling the heart of Ravinia, and taking back Third Earth might just turn things around."

"Then let's do it!" Siry shouted enthusiastically. Siry never needed much convincing when it came to taking action.

Uncle Press cut him off. "Hang on. If this is going to work, two things have to happen."

He walked up to me and spoke with dead seriousness. "This is still about the exiles. Do you think they can be convinced to go on the offense like this?"

"I don't know" was my honest answer. "All I can do is ask. They could turn me down cold, but I don't think so. I've seen them in action, and they have a score to settle."

"What is the second thing?" Alder asked.

Uncle Press looked around at the group and said, "Defeating Saint Dane on Third Earth cannot be our entire goal."

"What else is there?" Kasha asked.

"This is not about a battle. Or a territory. This is about taking the positive spirit that exists inside each and every one of those exiles and using it to take back Halla. It's not about a place. Or destroying an army. Or even revenge. It's about free will triumphing over oppression. For that victory to be complete, the exiles must triumph . . . and Saint Dane's spirit must end."

"Hobey," Spader gasped. "You think that in order win this battle, we have to destroy Saint Dane?"

"I do," Uncle Press said sadly. "Bobby's right. He controls the worlds of Halla. If he were to continue, I have no doubt that he would simply regroup somewhere else. This battle must not only rebuild the spirit of Solara, it must end the dark spirit that Saint Dane has been nurturing—the spirit that he embodies."

Uncle Press looked at me and added, "If you think that's possible, then you have my blessing, and the blessing of each and every spirit of Solara."

Yikes. Putting it that way, I kind of had second thoughts. Could we really do it? Could we not only beat Saint Dane, but *end* him as well?

Uncle Press added, "I can't see the future. I have no idea how this might come out. I only know the way things were meant to be. It's clear to me now, more so than ever before. I believe the conflict has been leading to this moment from the beginning. This is why you're here. This is why you're *all* here. To do anything less than take all that Solara has left and use it to defeat Saint Dane would be denying our destiny. You're right, Bobby, this is our moment. Let's seize it, and end this once and for all."

35

I knew it was the end.

I felt it in the core of my being. There have been many times over the past few years that I felt we might be nearing the end, only to have another wrinkle appear. Another surprise. Another door opening that we didn't even know existed. Each time, the struggle continued. This time would be different. There would be no second chances. No do-overs. No hope of salvaging victory from defeat. We were gambling it all, which meant there could be only one of two outcomes: We would either vanquish Saint Dane and begin to rebuild Halla, or Solara would be destroyed along with the Travelers. There would be no in between.

Uncle Press was right. It had all been leading to this moment. Every battle, every territory in jeopardy, every twist had been nothing more than prelude. As I looked back on it all, it seemed impossible that it could have been any other way. Saint Dane had brought out the darker nature of mankind, promising Utopia in exchange for freedom. In the end it proved too tempting for too many people.

I wondered if the Ravinians, those who benefited from

his evil quest, felt that it had been worthwhile. Would t. have made the same choices if they could have seen t. future? We'd never know.

Now the last hope rested with those who did not accept that vision of Utopia. Would the spirit of mankind, the spirit of free will and compassion, be strong enough to triumph over the dark power of repression and persecution? That's what this battle would be about, and it would start with the exiles. If they backed down, the battle would be lost right then and there, for it would mean they no longer were willing to fight for what they believed in. Their spirit was keeping Solara alive. I feared that if they did not accept the challenge, it would be a sign that that spirit had already diminished. If they accepted it, I believed that act alone would help to reinvigorate Solara. I felt certain that if the exiles accepted the challenge, Solara would be able to provide us with the means to fight one last battle.

As to who would win, I had no idea.

Being there, at that moment, felt right. For me, that is. In the beginning I had been frustrated that I didn't know every truth. Uncle Press told me that I needed to learn through experience, and he was right. I had to go through it all to become the person I was. If not for all that I had learned, all that I had seen and suffered and lost, I would not have had the strength or conviction to fight the battle before us. I had truly become the lead Traveler. The others looked to me for strength and guidance. I didn't have all the answers, but I had grown confident enough to make choices. And I chose to fight. I believed that this was the way it was meant to be.

I was ready.

My first stop was not Eelong. For this battle to work, we needed to lay the groundwork. Instead of going right to Eelong, Patrick and I went to Third Earth. I needed to see Mark.

"Something's happening," Mark told me.

He was on edge. Much more so than when I had seen him the last time. I wouldn't have been surprised if he began stuttering again. The three of us were together in the Manhattan warehouse where his band of rebels made their base. We sat in front of one of the stolen Ravinian helicopters while many of his friends watched us from a distance, trying to hear our conversation. I didn't want them to be part of this. We needed Mark's sole attention.

"The dados are being moved out of the factory," he continued.

"To where?" Patrick asked, surprised.

"They're gathering outside the walls of the conclave. They're activating them long enough to bring them out, then shutting them down again. Bobby, I think they're making room so they can build more."

That was a sobering thought, but I didn't think it was correct. There were already thousands of those robots.

Mark continued, "If they march on Manhattan, they'll wipe us out."

"They're not going to march on Manhattan," I said with confidence. "That's why we're here."

I had Mark's full attention.

"I need you to be my eyes, Mark," I said. "We need to know exactly what's happening with those dados. Patrick will stay with you. If something happens, he can blast out of here and let us know instantly. Can you do that?"

Mark shrugged. "Sure. I can have eyes in every one of

those tunnels around the conclave. We're organized, B
If somebody so much as farts, we'll know it."

"You can keep that to yourself," I said with a chuck.
"Anything else, let Patrick know immediately."

"And I'll let the Travelers know," Patrick added.

"What's going on?" Mark asked. "If they're not going to march on Third Earth, what's the point?"

I told him flat out. "The exiles are on Eelong. In Black Water. Saint Dane is going to create a flume and send the dado army to attack them there."

Mark squinted, thinking, working to get his head around the idea.

"Okay. Not good," he concluded.

"No, and we've come up with a plan to stop them."

Mark sat silently, anxiously waiting for my next words. It was time to drop the bomb on him.

"We're going to attack the Ravinian conclave."

He stared at me with a blank look, as if he didn't understand what I'd said. He didn't move for a solid ten seconds.

"Mark? You there?"

He shook his head and said, "Yeah. Wow. For a second I thought you said you wanted to attack the Ravinian conclave."

"I did."

He blinked once. And again. "L-Listen, Bobby," he stuttered, and instantly reacted to it. "Damn! I hate that."

"It's okay. You should be nervous."

"I'm not nervous. I'm stunned. And you're crazy. We've got rebels hiding all over the area. We've built up a pretty decent armory of stolen weapons, too. But to defend ourselves. We don't have the manpower to attack that fort. I admire your guts, Bobby, but it's suicide."

'm not asking you or your rebels to join in the attack,"
.d.

Mark frowned. "Then who the heck is going to do it?
ou? The Travelers? It might be different if we could enlist
those seventy thousand exiles, but short of that, no way."

My answer was to smile at him. It took about five seconds
until I saw the look of realization change his expression.

"Are you serious?" he asked with a mixture of hope and
disbelief.

"Deadly."

"They agreed to attack the conclave?"

Patrick and I shared looks.

"Not yet," I admitted. "That's my next stop."

Mark winced. My boast of leading an overwhelming
attack force suddenly appeared not only crazy, but hollow. I
figured it was time to let him know exactly where we stood.
With everything.

I had briefly explained it before, but this time I laid it all
out in detail. For the next hour Patrick and I told him about
Solara and the force of spirit that helped guide mankind. We
explained how Saint Dane corrupted that spirit into giving him
the power to create a new universe. I even explained our plan
to create a flume that would bring the exiles to Third Earth.
We told him everything. Mark didn't question a word. I think
that as incredible a story as it was, we were filling in the blanks
that had been confounding him since he was fourteen years
old. He had been just as involved with this war as I had. He
understood. He accepted. Mark Dimond was up to speed.

When I finished, the first thing he said was, "So whatever
chance we have, we owe to Nevva Winter."

"Without her, the exiles would be dead and so would
Halla."

He shook his head in dismay. "That may be the most incredible thing you've told me. Nevva Winter. Geez."

"Kinda makes you think there might still be hope for mankind, doesn't it?"

Patrick added, "But we still have to convince the exiles. Without them, none of this works."

We let Mark work the information over in his head. I knew him. He was calculating possibilities.

"How long?" he asked.

"No idea. But I'm thinking that if they're moving dados, Saint Dane is getting ready to make that flume and move on Eelong."

"Doing recon is cake," he said. "If something happens, you'll know it."

"That's all I'm asking," I said.

"It's not all you're going to get," Mark added.

"Excuse me?" Patrick asked.

"You see how we live. Hiding, running, wondering when a helicopter might show up to blow us away. We live like rats waiting to be exterminated. Up until now we've only thought about survival. I can tell you, if given the chance to strike back, we're going to take it."

"We're not asking you to put your friends or any of the rebels on the line," I said. "Your weapons will be welcome, but I can't ask you to risk your lives."

Mark laughed. "Risk our lives? This is no life! Bobby, you're looking at a bunch of people who've lost hope. Hearing what you're saying is the first ray of light we've seen in a very long time. Do you think for one second that if there's a chance to fight for ourselves, no matter how impossible it may seem, we wouldn't go for it?"

I felt like I was being watched. Looking around, I

saw that several of Mark's grungy rebel friends had been hanging around, eavesdropping. At least twenty men and women stood to the rear of one of the helicopters, staring at us. They heard every word we were saying.

"Is it true?" I called to them. "Are you willing to attack the conclave?"

They exchanged tentative looks. At first I thought it was because they weren't sure how to answer. I quickly realized it was more about deciding who would be the one to speak. Finally a girl stepped forward. It was Maddie, the crazy cabdriver. Her eyes blazed.

"Say when" was her simple answer.

Patrick smiled. "Looking better all the time."

Mark was all business. "We can offer more than reconnaissance. We've been making plans to cause some trouble on our own. Maybe they can fit in with yours."

I looked around at the eager faces of the rebels and answered, "At the risk of losing any faith you might have in us, there is no real attack plan. We're figuring this out as we go along. So if you've got any ideas . . ."

Mark looked at his friends. I expected to see disappointment all around. Just the opposite happened. They seemed even more charged up than before.

Mark said, "Maybe I should tell you what we've been planning."

He went ahead and detailed a series of guerrilla attacks they had planned to carry out on the conclave. They didn't expect them to be any more than a nuisance to the Ravinians, but coupled with the addition of an able-bodied army, these small-scale attacks suddenly felt like they could be the foundation of a very large-scale invasion.

We shared our own ideas on how we might be able to

pull off the impossible. After batting around all the ideas, we came up with a plan.

"It could work," Mark said. "It relies on a lot, but it could work."

"It has to work," I added.

"I'll call in every last able-bodied person within a fifty-mile radius and start the wheels in motion," Mark explained. "We have weapons stored all over Manhattan. Will the exiles be armed?"

"They have portable weapons that neutralize dados" was my answer.

Mark's eyes lit up. He looked at his friends. They were just as impressed.

"Those would be handy," he said, understating the obvious. "Not worried about mixing territories?"

"Not anymore," I answered. "The Convergence has made Halla one under Saint Dane's thumb."

Patrick asked Mark, "Where should we gather? Seventy thousand people need a lot of room."

Mark thought for a moment, then said, "Most of our weapons are stored downtown. I think the best rallying spot is Washington Square Park."

"Done," I said. "That's where we'll create this end of the flume."

"Assuming you can," Mark said, letting a bit of skepticism show. "And that you can convince the exiles to join up."

"We can," Patrick said with supreme confidence. "And we will."

Patrick Mac had come a long way from being the tentative teacher who lived the perfect life on Third Earth. Maybe more so than any of us, his world had been turned upside down. While all of us witnessed the social upheavals caused by Ravinia on our homes, Patrick's territory had gone through the most dramatic change. There were times when I worried that he could keep it together. But he always met each challenge head-on. Being able to work through his fears proved that, in many ways, Patrick was the bravest of us all.

Patrick and I left Mark and his people to begin making preparations. We stepped outside for one moment alone.

"Looks like you were right," I said to him.

"About what?" Patrick asked.

"It's come down to Third Earth. The last territory. It really is your turn."

Patrick got a faraway look in his eye. I believe that for those few moments, his head went back to what Third Earth was before. His true home. The way it was meant to be. He came back to reality with a look in his eye that was as determined as I'd ever seen from him.

"Then I guess I'd better make the most of it," he said, almost cocky.

The Traveler from Third Earth was ready to go.

I had one more moment with Mark. My friend and I had been through so much, together and apart, even *before* I had become a Traveler. He was my oldest friend. He was my brother.

"So . . . she's okay?" he asked.

"Yeah, she's good. Better than good. You can ask her yourself pretty soon."

"You think she'll come here with the exiles?" he asked, daring to hope.

I laughed. "Are you serious? We're talking about Courtney, right?"

Mark laughed too. "Yeah, dumb question. She'll probably lead the way."

The two of us looked at each other. Neither knew what to say. Instead, we hugged.

"You know something," he said softly. "The memory of our life back at home is the only thing that's kept me going."

"I know. I think that goes for everybody."

"I miss it."

"Me too."

"Are we going to win this one?" he whispered, so none of the others could hear.

"We have to" was the only answer I could give.

He pulled away from me. His eyes were watery. "We better. I want to go home."

"I do too," I said.

It was the first time I had been less than honest with Mark. Of course I wanted to go home. To Second Earth. To Stony Brook. To my old life. But win or lose, that wasn't possible. I wasn't from Second Earth. Not really. I was only a visitor. My life back there had been fabricated. It tore me up to accept that. There was no way I'd say that to Mark. At least, not then. Our friendship meant too much to me.

Patrick joined us. It was time to get going.

"Be alert," I said to them. "And be ready."

"Good luck," Patrick said.

I gave one last look to Patrick, then to Mark, then stepped off the territory to begin the most important mission I'd ever undertaken as a Traveler. I had to convince a multitude of civilians that they had one more battle to fight.

Whether they wanted it or not, they were the final hope for Halla.

36

Gunny met me on the outskirts of the village of Black Water.

He had been waiting for me. That was the plan. In the time Gunny had spent with the gars on Eelong, they had come to trust him. Spader too. But I didn't think it would be smart to bring Spader along on this diplomatic mission. This wasn't the time for enthusiasm and "Hobey! Let's go get 'em!" We needed a steady, guiding hand if we were to convince the exiles to come on board. Gunny was that guy. He sat on a rock, overlooking the village, waiting.

"How'd it go, shorty?" Gunny said as casually as if he were asking about the weather.

"Mark and his people are with us. Patrick will let us know if things start happening on Third Earth."

Gunny shook his head. He looked tired. "Such a thing," he said wistfully, as he gazed down at the village of Black Water. He wiped the sweat off his forehead. "This all just keeps getting more complicated."

Gunny was the oldest Traveler. He'd seen so much more in his life than the rest of us. His *real* life, that is. As tough as it was to accept the fact that we all originally came from Solara, it must have been the hardest on Gunny. He had lived pretty close to a full life on Earth before learning he was a Traveler. He had a different perspective than most of the rest of us.

"You okay, Gunny?" I asked. "I mean, we've been hit with a lot of things lately."

"You know, shorty, I'm near sixty-five years old. At least, I think I am. I've kind of lost track of the years. I seen a lot of things, even before I learned about the Travelers. It's not easy for an old duffer like me to accept new things, and I'm not so sure I would have believed this business about us being spirits from some other dimension, 'cept for one thing."

"What's that?"

Gunny held his hands up. Both of them. I don't know why I hadn't noticed before, but Gunny had two hands again. I blinked. How could that have happened? His left hand had been chewed off by a tang on Eelong years before. Now it was back, as good as new. He flexed it and made a fist to show me how real it was.

"How?" was all I could get out.

"Don't really know" was his answer. "When Spader and I got swept out of here, wouldn't you know it, but my old hand came right along with me. Like nothin' ever happened. I guess I should be happy about it, and I am. But what it tells me, more than anything, is that we really aren't natural to Earth. We're made-up beings, and that's why those spirit folks were able to make me up a new hand. Heck of a thing."

"But a good thing, right?"

"Sure, 'cept it makes me a might sad. I liked the life I was living."

"I hear you."

"Makes me realize something else, too. I was poor most of my life. Had to teach myself to read and write. Never wore a single piece of clothing that didn't first belong to somebody else, till I joined the army. But I made something of myself. I was the bell captain of the Manhattan Tower Hotel and proud of it. I might not have been setting the world on fire, but I was good at what I did. People appreciated it, and I was happy."

"Can't ask for much more than that."

"My point exactly. Thing is, a guy like me wouldn't make it in this new setup. There's no room for regular folks in this world of Ravinia. There's the few people who have it all, and everybody else. There's always been those who have more than others, but now, the regular folks don't even have the chance to build a life they can be proud of. With all the philosophizing and theorizing and threats and highfalutin goals, it all comes down to one thing: Saint Dane is killing the chance for people to be happy."

Gunny had pretty much summed up what this was all about. Saint Dane was taking away the chance for people to be happy. It sounds so simple, but being happy is probably the number one goal for everyone, no matter what world they come from. Talk about basic rights. What was that phrase from the Declaration of Independence? Life, liberty, and the pursuit of happiness? Except for a chosen few, Saint Dane was taking away those rights. It took a sixty-five-year-old guy who had lived most of his life not knowing anything about Travelers or Halla or guiding spirits to put it into such clear perspective.

"And that's why I'm glad you're here right now," I said to my friend. "You and I have to convince those people down there that this is their chance to take back those rights and have another shot at being happy."

Gunny took a deep breath and stood up. His energy was renewed. "Then let's get it done," he declared.

It wasn't long before Gunny and I were sitting in the chambers of the gar leaders in the dead center of the ring of buildings that made up the village of Black Water. It wasn't hard to get an audience. Aron was still one of the village elders. Most of the others remembered Gunny and were grateful for all he had done to help educate the gars while he was trapped there with Spader. Some of them remembered me, too. We were friends. We were trusted.

Also in the meeting were ten leaders of the Yanks. Years before, they had divided the group up into ten distinct units, to help manage and organize their lives. Each group elected a leader that reported to the gar elders. The liaison between the gars and the Yank leaders was none other than Courtney. She was in the meeting too. Courtney had a foot in both camps. She knew Black Water, and she was from Second Earth. She could speak intelligently to both groups. It seemed to be a pretty smart way to quickly organize a village that had suddenly tripled in size. The proof was not only in the fact that the village ran smoothly, but also that they were able to work together and organize a solid defense against the klees. Everybody was feeling pretty good about themselves.

I hated to have to burst their bubble.

I won't detail all the arguments we put before the group. I've already written most of them earlier in this journal. Bottom line was that Gunny and I tried to impress upon them that they may have defeated the klees once, but they'd be back again. And again. More important than that, we warned them that an attack was coming that was far more threatening than anything the klees could throw at them. We warned them that an army like they had never seen was preparing to march on Black Water with the single goal of wiping out the Yanks. The gars weren't necessarily the target, but with the kind of attack that was being planned, it would be wrong to believe the gars would be spared.

"The question isn't *if* the attack will come," I said. "It's *when*. I believe it's going to be soon."

Both the gar leaders and the exile leaders exchanged uneasy looks. It was a lot to accept.

"What is your proposal, Pendragon?" Aron asked.

I outlined the bare bones of our plan. I knew it wouldn't be an easy sell. It not only involved getting multiple thousands of people to jump into a flume—again—but when they reached the other side, they would be faced with a seemingly unbeatable foe. How unbeatable depended on a number of things, none of which we had control over. As I said the words out loud, and listened to myself speak, the whole idea sounded impossible. Maybe even insane. What was I thinking? The more I spoke, the more I realized that these people wouldn't go for it in a million years. Heck, if I were in their position, I wouldn't go for it either. It was suicide. I finished on a whimper, ready to get tossed out of there.

Before anyone had a chance to respond, Gunny stood up. "I can only imagine what you're thinking," he began. "Believe me, we feel the same way. The odds we face are long indeed. There is no guarantee of victory. People will die. Perhaps by the thousands. To that, I have two things to say. You are faced with a dire situation. Black Water will come under attack again. Soon. By a force much larger and more deadly than you have just defeated. Your weapons may stop some of theirs, but the numbers are not on your side. Their army is immense. They will keep coming, and attacking, until every last one of the people who came here from Second Earth is killed. That is a simple, sad fact. After they are finished, it's anybody's guess as to what shape you will be in when the klees decide to come calling again. Make no mistake. Whether you choose to follow our plan, or decide to stay and defend yourselves, you will have to fight this army. The choice you have is to fight them here, or take the battle to them. We wish there was a third choice. There isn't."

Everyone shifted in their seats uneasily.

"There's something else," Gunny continued. "To those who came from Earth, you must understand that this attack is going to be launched by the very same people who tore you from your home. The truth is, they wanted you dead back then. If not for the work of one woman, you would be. The Ravinians eliminated you because you posed a threat to their plans. You still pose a threat, and that is why they are coming after you. To the gars of Black Water, you are in much the same situation. You've seen how Ravinia changed Eelong. There was peace with the klees. I know. I helped forge it. But Ravinia has thrown out every bit of progress we made and declared you to be fair game. To be hunted as food. This is the kind of world that Ravinia has created all over Halla. In one way or another, they are eating their enemies. You gars haven't seen these other worlds, but you Yanks have. You know about the flumes. You've already traveled through one. You know there are other societies out there. Other worlds. Other lives. Ravinia is controlling it all, and it began when they exiled you from your home. This is your chance to take back your lives. To stop the people who have wronged so many. This is the last chance to try and make things right."

Gunny sat down, winded, but his eyes were clear and focused. He had made an impassioned plea that was hard to argue with. At least, I hoped it was hard to argue with.

One of the Yank leaders stood and said, "Perhaps there *is* a third choice. What if we Yanks picked up and left Black Water? If the Ravinians are targeting us, we shouldn't stay and endanger the gars."

Aron said, "That's a noble gesture, but without the Yanks, I do not believe we will have the strength to fend off the klees again. I think I am speaking for all the gars here, who say that whatever we decide to do, we must do it together. Gars and Yanks."

One of the gar leaders asked, "If this army you speak of is made up of creatures like the ones that attacked Black Water, we have weapons that will stop them."

"Do you?" I asked. "How many of those radio cannons do you have? How much power do they have? Is it limitless? We're talking about multiple thousands of dados. You could wipe out half of them and still be overrun by thousands more. Are your weapons that powerful?"

Their dark looks told me that they weren't.

Courtney stood and said, "If I can add one thing. I haven't seen this Ravinian army on Third Earth, but I've seen what their leader is capable of. We here, all of us, gars and Yanks, represent the last hurdle in his plan to conquer Halla. I believe that. And I believe that Ravinia's leader, Saint Dane, will do everything in his power to wipe us out of his way. He is close now. He won't back down. We're in danger one way or the other. I say we should agree to Pendragon's plan. If I have to die, I want it to be while I'm fighting for what is right."

She sat back down and gave me a quick, sheepish smile.

The leaders looked at one another, not sure who should speak. It was Aron who took command.

"Do you have any idea when this attack might come?" he asked.

"The last I heard was that their army was being mobilized. I don't know if that means an attack is imminent, or will take several days. Either way, I think we've got to move quickly."

Aron nodded thoughtfully. "If you do not mind, we need to discuss this among ourselves."

Gunny, Courtney, and I stood up to leave.

"Courtney, you should remain," Aron said quickly. "You are one of us now."

"Thank you," she said, and sat back down while giving me a reassuring smile.

It was odd to think of Courtney as one of them, but if her sticking around meant a strong voice who would try to convince them to follow our plan, I was all for it.

"Whatever your decision is, we will respect it," I said. Then added, "But please, don't take long."

Gunny and I were given a hut to rest and relax in. Rest and relax. Yeah, right. They brought us some food, which I was grateful for. I hadn't eaten in centuries.

"What do you think?" I asked Gunny.

"About what? Our plan, or if they're going to join us?"

"Both."

"I don't know if they'll join us," he answered. "I wouldn't be surprised either way. As for our plan, well . . ." He finished the thought with a shrug. He didn't want to say the words, but it was clear that his confidence wasn't high.

I didn't blame him for thinking that way. My confidence wasn't exactly soaring either. We had cobbled together a plan that not only involved timing, but moving multiple thousands of people across time and space. Oh yeah, and it all hinged on our ability to create a giant flume. It was beginning to seem like fantasy. But it was the only fantasy we had. There was no Plan B.

Hours went by with no answer. I tried to sleep, but that was impossible. It was like having an alarm clock close by that you know will go off any second. You can't sleep with that hanging over your head. There was no way to know how long it would take for them to make a decision. Worse, we didn't know how long we had before the dados began to move from Third Earth. With each passing second, my anxiety grew.

Gunny wasn't doing much better. He was lying on his back with his eyes closed, but he didn't fool me. He wasn't sleeping. His steadily tapping shoe gave him away. Finally, after what seemed like a lifetime, the door opened, and Courtney hurried in. Gunny and I were both on our feet before she was halfway into the room.

"It's looking bad," she said. "Most of the Yanks want to join, but the one thing they decided was that it had to be unanimous. It isn't."

"What about Aron?" Gunny asked.

Courtney looked to the floor. "He's against the idea."

I punched the wall in frustration. "They're going to be in there arguing while the dados come knocking on their door."

Courtney added, "They've brought in several people from the community to get their opinions. Both Yanks and gars."

"Swell," I said sarcastically. "Add more opinions. That'll help."

"They're doing the right thing, Bobby," Gunny said calmly. "We've asked a lot of them."

"I know, I'm just venting. Can we get outta here and get some air?"

The three of us left the building. Night had fallen. That was one consolation. I didn't think that Saint Dane's army would attack at night.

"Eight hours till dawn," Courtney said, reading my mind. "Do you think they'll come then?"

"I have no idea," I replied.

"I do," came an unfamiliar voice.

The three of us turned to see the last person in Halla that I wanted to see just then. Okay, maybe there were a few others, but the fact that Patrick had arrived on Eelong was not a good sign.

"They're moving, Pendragon," he said, his voice quivering. "Every last dado has been marched onto the expanse between the Ravinian compound and the river."

"Perfect spot for a big flume," I said.

"I believe we're out of time," Gunny said with a sigh.

We had to do something. But what? Going back into that meeting and screaming about the army on the way wouldn't help. It's not like they'd suddenly say, "Oh? Really? In that case, we're with you!" No way.

"Should I go back in there?" Courtney asked.

I made a decision. It was a desperate move, but it was the only one I could think of.

"Yeah. Tell them to stop talking and get ready to defend themselves, because the dados are on the way."

"And what are you going to do?"

"I don't know."

Courtney wanted to challenge me, but knew better. She took off, sprinting through the village.

"What do we do, shorty?" Gunny asked.

"We go back to Solara," I said.

Gunny, Patrick, and I were greeted by the rest of the Travelers, including Uncle Press. They came to us quickly, eager to hear the news.

"It's not good," I said. "Mark and his people are with us on Third Earth. But the exiles and the gars are still debating about what to do."

Patrick added, "And the dados on Third Earth are gathering. They're ready to move."

Gunny said, "It's looking like they'll make their flume and attack Black Water at first light. We're out of time."

Nobody knew what to say. It was beginning to seem as if the battle were over before it could begin.

Elli asked, "Is there any chance that they can defend Black Water?"

I shook my head. "For a while maybe. They can use their radio cannons, but those weapons are limited. With so many dados thrown at them, they'll be overwhelmed."

"So that's it?" Siry shouted. "We just sit here and wait for Solara to fall apart?"

"No," I said quickly. "I say we make the flume anyway."

Most of the Travelers erupted with "What?" "No!" "What's the point?"

Uncle Press quieted everyone down and said, "Explain, Bobby."

"The dados are going to attack, we know that. The gars

and the exiles won't be able to defend themselves for long. When the radio cannons are spent, Black Water's done. We know that, too. Their only hope for survival is with a new flume. Two things can happen. Either we rally the exiles and convince them to fight on Third Earth, or worst case scenario is it becomes an escape route when Black Water falls."

Uncle Press thought quickly, calculating the possibilities.

Aja asked, "If we make this flume, what will happen to Solara?"

"The same thing that'll happen if we *don't* make it," I argued. "Either we use whatever spirit is left to keep this going, or wait until the dados snuff out the exiles. Then Solara is done anyway. At least this way we go down fighting."

Uncle Press looked unsure . . . as did everyone else.

"If anybody's got a better idea," I added, "now's the time to bring it."

I looked into the eyes of each Traveler, one at a time, waiting for an answer. Elli, Gunny, Siry, Alder. Nobody blinked. Kasha, Patrick, Aja, and then Loor all stared back, silent.

Finally I looked to Spader. "What do you say, mate?" I asked him.

"I say we build the bloody tunnel," he declared with conviction. "What have we got to lose?"

I looked to Uncle Press and said, "Good question. What have we got to lose?"

Night had fallen on Black Water. The only light came from the stars overhead.

We all stood in a circle. All eleven of us. We were on the

edge of the farmland that was beyond the village. It was on the exact opposite side of the valley from the tunnel that led to the waterfalls. It seemed as good a place as any to build a flume. We stood shoulder to shoulder in a tight circle, close enough to feel each other's heartbeats. Let me tell you, they were all beating fast.

"I can't say for sure if this will work," Uncle Press warned. "Certainly it will deplete whatever positive spirit is left of Solara."

"Does that mean Solara ends?" Elli asked.

"I don't know," Uncle Press answered honestly.

"Isn't that exactly what Saint Dane wants?" Aja asked.

"It is, but the exiles will still exist. Hopefully, their spirit will keep Solara from being destroyed entirely."

"So it's more important than ever to keep them safe," Gunny said.

There was a general murmur of understanding. We all got it.

"There's one other thing," Press said. "The spirit of Solara is what has given us the ability to function as Travelers. Once that power is depleted, I don't know what that will mean for us."

"You mean we might not be able to travel anymore?" Patrick asked.

"That might be the least of it" was Uncle Press's somber answer. "There's a chance we may not exist anymore."

Nobody commented. What could we say?

"What we're doing here has never been done before," Uncle Press continued. "By anyone other than Saint Dane, that is. We're in uncharted waters. Once we start, there's no turning back."

We all nodded. We understood.

Uncle Press looked around at us. "Second thoughts?"

We shared looks. Nobody was backing out.

"What do we do?" Spader asked.

Uncle Press said, "The power of Solara flows through us all. We have to focus it here, in much the same way that enables our moving between territories. I don't think any one of us would be able to channel enough of the spirit on our own, so it's critical that we all do this together."

He took off his Traveler ring and threw it into the center of the circle. "The dark matter," he said. "It will act as a prism to focus the spirit."

One by one, we each took off our Traveler rings and tossed them into the circle. It was a strange feeling. It smacked of finality. One way or another, it would all soon be over, and we wouldn't need them anymore. Still, it was a hollow feeling to have given up my ring. By the sober looks on the faces of the other Travelers, I knew they felt the same way.

"Now," Uncle Press continued, "concentrate. Visualize. Like stepping from one territory to the next, imagine the tunnel we've all traveled through so many times."

I stared down at the pile of eleven rings lying in the dirt. I didn't allow myself to think of how silly this felt. Ordinarily, I'd be the guy making fun of a bunch of people out in a field trying to channel cosmic energy. Not this night. I had to believe it was possible. I sensed the presence of all my Traveler friends. It was as if I were part of them. We weren't holding hands or anything goofy like that, yet it felt as if we had formed a continuous, unbroken circle. My heart beat with theirs. We took the same breaths. Uncle Press was still talking, but I couldn't hear him anymore. It was the closest thing to an "out of body" experience I ever had. Though it wasn't truly out of body. It was the creation of one body. It seemed as if I weren't in my physical self anymore. I rose up and looked down at the ring of people who were forever bound by destiny.

I felt a warm tingle. It wasn't unpleasant. If anything, it felt . . . electric. I wondered if anyone else was feeling the same thing, but didn't dare look around. I stayed focused on the rings. The Traveler rings. Eleven in all. Together.

One by one, the stones in the rings began to glow. They were activating. Something was really happening. This wasn't just a bunch of new-age hocus-pocus. The rings glowed bright. Far brighter than when they were getting ready to deliver a journal. The light from each spread and enveloped the rings around it. It soon became a single mass of light. The light spread across the ground, radiating out from the center. I sensed, more than felt, that we all had stepped backward, making the circle larger. Though we weren't physically touching each other, I felt as if we were still connected. We were one. We moved back, farther and farther, until the circle was probably twenty yards across.

The light from the center followed us, like water bubbling up from a spring. It lit up the ground, growing brighter as it got larger. I heard a sound. What was it? Yes! It was the music I had heard so many times while flying through the flumes. There was no tune. No melody. Just a mixed-up series of sweet notes that made me smile. It was familiar. It was exhilarating. We were doing it. We were channeling the spirit of Solara.

The circle of light grew until it nearly reached the ring of Travelers. The music grew louder. The light became so bright it obliterated everything else. It was then that I heard Uncle Press's voice cut through. He said two simple words—two words that made absolute sense.

"Third Earth."

The circle of light responded instantly. It began to drop below ground level. It wasn't as dramatic as the spinning Ravinian star that had cut the giant flume into the turf of Yankee Stadium, but the result was the same. The intense, glowing light sank deeper and deeper into the earth. The power that surged through me felt stronger than ever. I felt as if I were shaking, but I knew that wasn't the case. It was such an intense feeling that as I looked around at the other Travelers, I half expected them to be glowing. In fact, just the opposite was happening. For brief moments some of the other Travelers seemed to fade out, becoming momentarily transparent. A second later their images would return, but then other Travelers would fade. And return. I fought panic. Was this the end? Had we gone too far in trying to create this impossible phenomenon? Had we sucked all the life out of Solara, and now all that was left was for us to wink out along with it?

Below the far edge of the circle, I caught sight of the first line of gray rocks that I knew would be continuing down until it became a tunnel to infinity. The light grew dim as it sank deeper. I looked up at the other Travelers, fearing that they would fade out along with it. Everyone was there. Rock solid.

A moment later the music ended. The light below went dark. I looked up to make sure that all the Travelers were there. I counted ten. Plus me. All eleven of us stood in the circle, dazed. I looked to the ground to see a large, round hole, maybe twenty yards across. We had done it.

We had made a new flume.

And we were all still there to see it.

"Well," I said casually, "that's something you don't see every day."

Spader laughed first, followed by Uncle Press, then Patrick. Soon everyone was laughing. Not because of my casual understatement, but out of relief. We had done it and we were all there. Uncle Press came over and put his arm around my shoulders.

"To be honest, I didn't think it would work," he said.

"Oh great, now you tell me."

The moment of triumph passed. Creating the flume was only the beginning. We stood staring at one another, not sure what to do next.

It was Aja who stepped up. "I think Patrick should go to Third Earth to see where the attack stands."

"I can't," Patrick declared.

"Why not?" she asked.

"Because I just tried. Nothing happened."

"You tried to travel to Third Earth?" I asked quickly. "Just now? And you're still here?"

"I think Press was right," Patrick said, glum. "Whatever powers we had as Travelers are gone."

"But we are still here," Alder said. "We still exist."

"What happened, Uncle Press?" I asked.

Uncle Press sighed. "I guess I can be positive and say that you are now the people you always thought you were. Your physical selves are all that is left."

Gunny said, "So no more healing? No more traveling? What happens to our spirits if we die?"

Uncle Press shrugged and said, "Don't."

"So then, what do we do now?" Siry asked.

"This doesn't change a thing," I called out. "The dados

are still headed this way. I'm going to find Courtney and take one last shot with the exiles. You all should go to Third Earth. Find Mark and be ready."

"Did you forget, Pendragon?" Siry said. "We can't travel."

I looked at the young Jakill from Ibara. He was a brave, dedicated kid. But he didn't always think things through. I walked to the edge of the new flume and gestured to it with open arms.

"Oh," he said, embarrassed. "Right."

"Third Earth!" I called.

The tunnel came to life. The music was back. The lights were back. We were in business.

"I'll be right behind you," I said, and jogged toward the village.

My goal was to get back to the council meeting and give them one last warning about the army that was about to arrive on their doorstep. I hoped that maybe by showing them the flume, I'd have a little more credibility. Worst case, if they insisted on staying to defend Black Water, knowing about the flume might help set up an evacuation, if things started going badly. No, that would be *when* things started going badly. I ran over all the arguments and options in my mind. I had to be positive. I had to convince them.

It wasn't until I reached the village and almost to the center building that I realized something was wrong. There was no sound. No activity. No gars walking around. No signs of life anywhere. It was eerie. Where had everybody gone? I hoped that it was actually very late at night, and everyone was in bed asleep. I expected to have to track these people down in their homes and wake them up . . .

When the warning horn sounded. The steady *whoop*

whoop filled the oddly quiet village with ear-numbing sound. The wrong kind of sound. I didn't think for a second that it was a drill. I ran to the far side of the village, toward the mountains and the tunnel into the valley of waterfalls. I expected to see gars and Yanks running to their posts to man their positions.

I didn't. I was alone. Where was everybody? Maybe, I thought, they were already at their posts. It was the only explanation. But when I reached the outer ring of the village, I saw that the defensive huts were empty. There were no gars manning the radio cannons, or peering out of windows with arrows at the ready. The huts were dark and quiet.

What was going on?

My eye finally caught movement, but it only added to my confusion. I saw what looked like a pin spot of light glowing on the side of the mountain. It was maybe twenty yards up from the walkable slope, where the rock face turned sheer. It was like nothing I had seen before. Was it some new technology that was brought by the exiles? Was it a visual alarm to go with the horn? Was it an emergency beacon? I stood still, watching. Fascinated. The pin light grew. A beam shot out from the glowing spot and flashed across the sky, casting a line of light over the empty huts of Black Water. All I could do was stare in wonder. The pin spot continued to grow, spilling light onto the face of the mountain. The light became a growing circle. That's when I realized the truth. I didn't need to hear the musical notes that soon followed.

I was witnessing the birth of another flume.

Light blasted out of the circle, eating away at the rock, creating the new opening. The music arrived next, quickly growing loud and jangly. I looked back to the village to see if any gars had come out from wherever they were to see what was going on. The village was empty. I was alone. Within a minute the hole of light had grown to thirty yards across. That's when it stopped. The enormous tunnel was complete. Even from as far away as I was, I recognized the walls of gray stone.

The highway was open.

I knew what was going to happen next.

Saint Dane wasn't going to wait until morning.

Enough light glowed from the flume so that I could see what was coming in. This tunnel stretched to another world. From deep inside, marching in step, came the first line of invaders, carrying red Ravinian flags. They marched to the mouth of the new tunnel and continued down the slope toward the village. There were more. Many more. Looking beyond them into the flume, I saw no end to them. Like a swarm of red locusts, the Ravinian army poured from the depths of infinity, bent on their deadly mission.

Saint Dane had sent his entire force to march on Black Water.

The final battle for Halla had begun.

37

Wave after wave of dados marched out of the flume, headed toward the village of Black Water.

Some wore the uniform of the Ravinian soldiers. Others were dressed in the green uniform and gold helmet of the security dados from Quillan. There were even hundreds of dado klees that came pouring out. All were armed with the silver prods that could extinguish life with a single shot. Unlike the attack on Black Water by the klees, these dados weren't interested in capturing anybody for food. This was an army of execution. As far as I could tell, every dado we had seen in the factory on Third Earth had made the journey. It meant that Saint Dane was pulling out all the stops. This was his final assault. He wanted to complete his quest by destroying every last one of the exiles.

But where were they?

I watched the massive show of force pouring into Black Water from behind the safety of one of the defensive huts in the first ring of structures. Seeing so many dados confirmed my fear that there was no way the gars and Yanks would be able to hold them off for long. Depending on how long the radio cannons had power, they could knock out a thousand, or a few thousand. But there would be a thousand more to take their place. And a thousand more after that. It was small consolation that my fears were correct. I was mesmerized by the sight of such an overwhelming force pouring from the flume.

It wasn't until I felt the hair on my arms crackle with energy that I was snapped back into the moment. One of the invaders must have seen me and fired his weapon. What the heck was I still doing there? Alone. Facing an army of thousands. With weapons. It was time to be somewhere else.

I ran back into the heart of the village, not sure if I should look for Courtney and the council, or just get back to the flume and jump to Third Earth. I ran past house after empty house. All the lights were still on, but nobody was home.

Paf! Paf! I felt the surge of two blasts of power fly past. The dados were after me. I made a quick turn down a narrow street and was faced with two red-shirt Ravinian dados. Their weapons were up and pointed. At me. I jumped off the street as *paf*. Another shot flew by. Too close. I couldn't let myself get hit. No way. If the spirit of Solara was as good as gone, my own spirit wouldn't survive my body's death and end up back on Solara. If I got shot now, it would be over. For good. There was no more safety net. I was now running for my life.

I heard dados everywhere, yelling orders and knocking down doors in their search for the exiles. Running through the rings of structures was like sprinting through a maze. I kept changing direction, making it difficult to be tracked. Unfortunately, I outsmarted myself and got turned around. I wanted to end up at the flume, but I was dangerously close to being lost, or accidentally circling back and ending up surrounded by dados. I kept looking up at the mountains that surrounded Black Water, trying to get my bearings. It was impossible. The mountains formed a continuous ridge. There were no particular peaks that stood out. It was like running around inside of a bowl. With every turn I kept hoping that I'd run into a gar, but the village was empty. Totally empty.

Except for one lone creature.

I rounded a corner and was met by a klee. A dado klee. The Ravinian uniform was the tip-off. The cat seemed just as surprised as I was. I froze. The klee raised its weapon. I had nowhere to run. No place for protection.

"I'm Pendragon," I called out, hoping that it would mean something. Maybe Saint Dane wanted me taken alive. It was a desperate move . . . that didn't work. The klee raised its silver weapon and took aim. I dove to the ground and rolled. I wanted to make a tough target. Maybe I would get lucky. The klee brought the weapon to its eye . . .

And was attacked by another snarling klee. The big brown cat leaped from a window and knocked the Ravinian to the ground.

"Boon!" I called out.

I jumped to my feet and ran for the two wrestling klees.

"Don't let that thing touch you!" I warned, knowing that one touch of that silver wand and Boon would be vapor.

Boon clamped his powerful jaws on the Ravinian's neck. The klee didn't react, of course. It was a dado. But as it fought to get loose, I was able to jump forward and kick the wand out of its paw. The weapon clattered away. The klee tried to fight off Boon while reaching for it. He didn't have a chance. I grabbed the wand and screamed, "Let it go!"

Boon jumped back, and I jabbed the business end of the silver wand at the dado. It instantly stopped moving.

Boon was out of breath and wide eyed. "What's happening?" he shouted. "Where is everybody?"

"You don't know?"

Boon shook his head. "I was sleeping on the outskirts of the village. They know I'm not a threat, but I'm still a klee. So I decided to stay clear of everybody. When the alarm went off, I came back looking to see what was happening, but everybody's gone!"

"And the dados are attacking from Third Earth. We've got to get out of here."

Boon and I took off running, but it seemed as though every way we turned, there were more dados. With nobody to stop them, the city was quickly becoming infested.

"There's another flume," I told him. "Far to the south on the edge of the farm. But we're cut off."

Boon grabbed my arm and yanked me in another direction. "I've got a way."

We continued our twisting route until we got to the very center of the village and the large building that was Gar Central. Boon led me inside.

"Is there a tunnel or something?" I asked.

"No. Just the opposite."

We hit stairs. Boon sprinted up on all fours. I had all I could do to keep up with the cat. I trusted Boon but didn't like that we were climbing up. It wouldn't be good to be trapped on the roof, with no escape route.

He said, "In the brief time that there was a truce between the gars and the klees, technology was exchanged. Things were going well, until Ravinia."

"What kind of technology?"

We made it to the top stairs. Boon opened a door that led out onto the roof. "*That* kind," he announced.

Sitting there, square in the middle of the roof of the large building, were three yellow gigs.

"Tell me you know how to fly," I demanded.

"Kasha would never admit it, but I'm a better pilot than she is."

I didn't need convincing. I pushed past him, headed for the small helicopters. Boon jumped in the pilot seat of one, while I strapped into the passenger side. Boon immediately toggled the ignition switches. The overhead rotor whined to life.

"Wait," I exclaimed. "There's no sun. What's powering this?"

"Like I said, it's new technology," he explained. "This is something the gars came up with. They didn't even have one back in Leeandra. The gars added a device for storing the energy. We'll have about an hour of flight time."

That news actually made me angry. It was more proof that the gars weren't animals. The merger of the two tribes, the two species, had been a huge benefit for all the beings on Eelong. Until Ravinia.

Boon added, "Let's hope the dados don't know how to use the radio cannons."

Oh. Right. Those things.

Boon pulled the control stick back, and we lifted off . . . just in time. The door leading to the roof burst open, and three Ravinian dados ran out, their weapons up and firing. I felt the ping of energy as the underside of the gig was hit. They weren't radio cannons. They couldn't stop us.

"Take us up high over the village," I called to Boon. "I want to see what's happening."

Boon lifted the small gig high into the night sky, directly over the dead center of the village. From there we had a perfect view of the entire valley. It was like looking down on a football game from a blimp. I saw the flume that had burned into the mountainside. Light continued to spew out, along with more dados. The numbers were incredible. The dados had pretty much filled up the entire space between the flume and the outer ring of the village. They stood poised to completely overrun the place.

Several dados ran through the streets. They must have been the advance troops. They were fast and mobile, searching for signs of life. They weren't having any luck. The village was totally empty. Boon circled around so we could scout the entire place. I wondered if the gars had built a shelter in the mountains, where they could retreat in case of an attack. That seemed like the most logical answer. Maybe Courtney had finally convinced them that the attack was inevitable, so they decided to hide instead of joining us. If that was the case, how long could they hold out? Not all the gars and exiles were candidates for fighting a war. There were kids. And babies. And older people. Would they be able to stay hidden until the dados gave up and left? It seemed like a temporary solution, at best.

"Now what?" Boon asked. "We don't have enough power to stay up here forever."

I looked to the south and the farm. Even from as far away as we were, I could make out the dark, round shadow that I knew was the mouth of the Travelers' flume.

The gig lurched. I knew the feeling. Boon did too.

"I guess they figured out how to use the radio cannons," I said.

"We've got to fly out of here," Boon said, and pushed the gig forward.

The craft rocked two more times. Boon fought for control.

"That way!" I shouted, pointing toward the farm.

Boon struggled to keep the gig in the air. We spun to the right. He fought to keep us headed south.

"I've got to put it down," he declared.

"No!" I shouted. "Keep headed south!"

"But we'll crash!"

We got hit again. The gig spun the opposite way, snapping my head to the side.

"We're going to find out just how good a pilot you are," I called out. "Head for that hole."

"Hole?" Boon screamed, terrified. "What hole?"

"Trust me."

We were losing altitude fast. If we crashed, there was no guarantee we'd walk away from it. I knew we only had one chance. We had to fly the gig into the flume.

Boon spotted the flume and directed the gig toward the gaping hole. "I don't think I can put it in there without clipping the side," he cried.

"Yes, you can. Concentrate."

The dark hole of the flume grew larger as we got closer. We were dropping fast. The mouth of the tunnel was big enough for the gig, but Boon would have to drop it in the dead center.

"Pendragon!" he cried out.

"Do it!" I screamed.

Boon eased back on the throttle, and we dropped down. I winced, waiting for the rotor to catch the rim of the tunnel. I didn't know whether Boon was in control or we were falling.

"Third Earth!" I screamed out over the whine of the engine.

The tunnel lit up beneath us.

"Pendragon!" Boon screamed again, this time in terror.

"Just get us close," I called back to him.

"I've lost control!" Boon shouted.

"It's okay," I said calmly. "You don't need it anymore."

The rock walls around us melted into crystal. The gig twisted. Instead of falling down, we found ourselves flying forward. We were in the gig, in the flume, flying to Third Earth.

I glanced at Boon. He was looking forward, fixed on the tunnel with huge cat eyes.

"You did it," I said.

"Did what?" he gasped. "What is this?"

"You're taking your first flume trip."

His paw was wrapped around the control stick in a death grip. I put my hand on it and coaxed him to let go. He did reluctantly. The gig stayed upright and charged through the flume. It turned when the tunnel turned, dropping and rising with every curve. The rotors still spun, dangerously close to the edges of the tunnel. I didn't worry. I felt sure we would make it. We were surrounded by stars beyond the crystal walls. The multiple images of Halla were no longer there.

"It's beautiful," Boon declared, finally relaxed.

"It better be. We paid a steep price for this little construction job."

Boon gave me a puzzled look, but I didn't bother to explain.

Up ahead I saw light. We were nearing the end.

"Grab the stick," I ordered. "When we come out, you're back in control."

I had no way of knowing where the flume opened up on Third Earth. A sick thought hit me that if it opened in a subterranean cavern, we were in trouble. I had assumed that it would be out in the open, like the other larger flumes. But we wouldn't know until we emerged.

"Get ready," I said. For what, I didn't know.

The light grew brighter. I held my breath. The gig flew into the light. I felt gravity take over as I was pressed back into my seat. A few seconds passed. We didn't crash into anything. That meant we were outside . . . and climbing fast.

"Level out!" I commanded.

We had flown out of the flume, nose first, headed skyward like a rocket. Boon took control and pressed forward. For a moment I felt weightless as we blasted over the arc and finally went level. It was a hell of a ride. My stomach was in my throat and my head felt twisted. The disorientation was complete.

"Try to hover," I said, though it wasn't easy, because my brain was scrambled. "We need to see where we are."

Boon wasn't suffering the same effects that I was. He masterfully kept control of the gig, stopping our forward movement. I closed my eyes, hoping that my brain would stop spinning around inside my skull.

Boon laughed.

"Don't laugh," I said. "I feel like puking."

"I'm not laughing at you," Boon said. "You gotta see this."

I cautiously opened my eyes. The first thing I realized was that it was daytime. Gray clouds traveled overhead. It looked like we were back on Third Earth.

"What am I supposed to see?" I asked.

"Down there!" he shouted.

I shifted my weight and peered over the side of the g The derelict buildings were proof that we were hoverir over the city. We had made it. We were on Third Earth Directly below us was a large, cleared, square space. Many of the buildings surrounding it had been laid to rubble. One structure stood out because it was in the cleared square, untouched. It was a large, marble archway. I recognized it. It was the arch in Washington Square Park.

"Can you believe it?" Boon laughed.

He wasn't talking about the buildings. Or the archway. Or the fact that we had made it to Third Earth in one piece. He was laughing giddily about something else that was down in that park. Actually, it wasn't just in the park. It also spilled out along adjoining streets. The sight made me laugh too. What we saw below were people. Thousands of them.

The exiles had come home.

With them looked to be every last gar from Black Water. I'd never seen so many people in one place before. They filled the park and the sidewalks and most of the streets. In the dead center of the square was the flume we had just flown out of. The mystery of where the gars and exiles had gone was solved. They had made it to Third Earth. They had escaped.

They were safe.

I hoped they were ready for a war.

38

Boon put the gig down right next to the flume.

A large area was cleared near the arch. People were pushed back to make room. We touched down in the center of a group of thousands . . . who were all cheering. Seriously. All eyes were on us for as far as I could see. They were applauding for us, though I wasn't sure why.

I looked to Boon and said, "I guess they liked your flying."

Boon didn't know what to make of it either. His cat eyes were wide with wonder.

Uncle Press was the first to reach us.

"What's going on?" I asked.

"Can you feel it?" he exclaimed with a big, broad smile.

"I don't know what I feel, except a little airsick," I said as I crawled out of the gig.

"Their spirit. It's already re-energizing Solara."

I looked around at the cheering crowd. I saw both exiles from Earth and gars from Eelong. Their excitement and enthusiasm was overwhelming. I couldn't imagine what was

going through their heads. I didn't even know how the
ended up here.

I suddenly felt arms around me, squeezing me in a big hug

"We did it!" Courtney exclaimed.

Yes, Courtney was there too. As we spoke, the rest of the
Travelers gathered around us.

"What happened?" I shouted to her. "I don't get it."

"The gars and Yanks had voted to join us even before I
got back to them!" she shouted above the cheering. "They'd
already begun to mobilize when you returned to Solara to
create the flume. They completely evacuated Black Water.
When they saw the flume you made, every last doubt was
erased. Isn't it amazing? They're with us, Bobby. They're
with *you*."

I took another look around at the cheering mass of
humanity. Their enthusiasm had nothing to do with our
trick gig flying. It was a show of support. For us, and for
the chance to strike back at Ravinia. It was more than we
could have hoped for. No, I take that back. I also hoped
that these people would be just as happy when the sun
set on that fateful day. On Eelong I had barely missed the
evacuation. The entire population must have been moving
to the outskirts of the village as I was running into the
center. Incredible. I wanted to revel in the moment, and the
applause, but we weren't even close to being done. Our plan
was working, but barely.

As the applause died down, I said to Uncle Press, "We
dodged a bullet. Saint Dane has made his move. He created
a flume. The entire dado army is in Black Water."

The Travelers exchanged nervous looks.

"Hobey," Spader gasped. "That was cutting things a
might close."

"Where is the flume?" Uncle Press asked.

"On Eelong it's on the exact opposite side of Black Water :om ours. Here, I don't know."

"I do," came a familiar voice. Mark Dimond stepped up through the crowd. He had an earth-style walkie-talkie pressed to his ear. "It's directly in front of the Ravinian conclave . . . just as we thought."

So far things were working out the way we expected. More or less.

"The clock's ticking," Mark cautioned.

There was no time to second-guess and fine-tune. Now that the dados had moved, we had to put our plan into action.

"You ready?" I asked Mark.

"Waiting on your word," he answered with a clear, strong voice.

Courtney put her arm around him and beamed. "Can you believe how this guy turned out?"

It was an awesome moment. We were back together again. The three of us. We'd been through this entire adventure together in spirit; it was fitting that we were together, for real, at the end.

"We've got to go," Uncle Press said, all business.

"Is Aron here?" I called out.

"Here, Pendragon," the gar leader replied as he made his way toward us.

Aron and all the gars wore their dark brown clothing. Here on Earth they looked like dwarfs. He joined us, along with the Yank leaders we'd met with earlier.

"I shouldn't have doubted you, Pendragon," Aron said. "Forgive me."

"No, I should be thanking you," I said. "I wish you

could understand the importance of what your people are going to attempt today."

"We do," Aron assured me.

Courtney said, "Between the Yanks and the gars, there are roughly forty-five thousand who are able to fight. They've been positioned front and center. The young, the sick, and the elderly have been moved to the side streets."

I looked around at the crowd. The task suddenly seemed overwhelming. Impossible, even. How could we mobilize so many people and get them all moving in the right direction, let alone wage a war? For a second my brain froze at the enormity and, yes, idiocy of what we were about to undertake.

"You look worried, Pendragon," Aron said. "Do not be. Our fighting force is trained. It does not matter what the battlefield is. We are organized and we are disciplined. There are twenty smaller units, each with its own leader. They in turn have their own subdivisions." Aron held up a link cube. "We are all in contact. I will remain with you. When an order is given, it will be relayed instantly."

Gunny asked, "Gars and Yanks? Together?"

Aron said, "We are one. The Yanks have protected our home. Now they have returned to reclaim theirs. The gars will be by their side. There is no other way."

I couldn't come up with the words to express to Aron how incredibly brave and selfless his people were. I wanted to tell them that they embodied the spirit of Solara, but he wouldn't have understood. Or maybe he already did without realizing it.

The gar leader could see that I was overwhelmed. He smiled. "You needed an army to defeat Ravinia? Pendragon, you came to the right place."

I glanced to Uncle Press. He smiled. He knew. Maybe he always knew.

Mark added, "I assigned five of my guys to each of their groups. They'll all have somebody with them who has knowledge of the city. And the target."

"What about the radio cannons?" I asked.

Aron answered, "The evacuation was quick. We weren't able to bring as many as we'd hoped, but we are armed. Just as you asked."

Mark added, "We've got transportation waiting to bring equipment to the site. But that's it. I'm afraid the people have to walk."

I looked to Aron. "You'll have to move out right away."

He nodded and said, "We are ready and waiting."

My mind raced. Had we thought of everything? No, that was impossible. The plan we concocted was incredibly complicated. Anything could go wrong, and if it did, we would fail. But it was the only plan we had. All we could do was move quickly, and hope.

"Maybe you should say something," I said to Uncle Press. "To these people. Most have no idea what they're getting into."

"You're right," he replied. "Something should be said. But not by me."

All eyes were on me. Oops. I suddenly wished I hadn't come up with such a brilliant idea. Still, I couldn't argue. This was my show. I had to take responsibility. The job of addressing this army would have to be mine.

"We don't have loudspeakers, Bobby," Mark said. "You can't talk to this many people."

Aron said, "But you can." He held out a link radio cube. "Most all of us have a link. Whoever doesn't, can listen to another's."

I wasn't sure of what to say. Many of these brave people would not live to see another day. They deserved something, if only to hear that whatever the outcome, they had made the right choice. I reached for the cube. My hand was shaking. Aron placed it in my palm. I looked to him and nodded. He activated the link. The amber material glowed.

"Does this work?" I said. "Can you hear me?"

A cheer went up from the crowd. They heard me. It was such a surprise that I nearly dropped the cube.

"Easy there, cowboy," Courtney said. "You want me to hold it for you?"

I shook my head, gathered my thoughts, and spoke. "You don't know me. My name is Bobby Pendragon."

The crowd erupted in cheers again. Maybe some of them *did* know me. I waited for them to quiet down and continued.

"For many years now, my friends and I have been battling a force I think you are all familiar with. Ravinia."

The crowd booed. They knew. All too well. I looked up at the group of Travelers who surrounded me. They all gave me nods of encouragement.

"You know of Halla and the worlds that exist around us. What happened on Eelong has happened on each of those other worlds. Look around you. This is the home of the Yanks. It's not the world they knew. Ravinia has destroyed a once-mighty city. A once-mighty world. We here, today, are the last hope. Not only for this world called Earth. But for Denduron. Zadaa. Quillan. Veelox. Cloral. And for Eelong."

I kind of expected a cheer after I said Eelong, but the crowed remained silent. Eerily so. There were tens of thousands of people, yet it sounded like the streets were empty. It was a reminder that they all knew exactly what we were up against. This was not a game. It was deadly serious business.

"The future of all those worlds will be determined by our actions here today. A few miles from here is the Conclave of Ravinia. It is the center of Ravinia on this world, and for all of Halla. Our goal is to seize it and make it our own."

This time the cheers came. I glanced around at the Travelers. They too applauded. It made my confidence grow and my words come easier.

"Our battle today is not about taking back a piece of land. Or hurting those who have chosen to side with Ravinia. Or even revenge. It is about fighting for what is right. Those of you who were sent through the flume in Yankee Stadium were there because you saw the truth. You knew the dangers of Ravinia and dared to speak out against it. For that you were punished. Exiled. It is your spirit that has kept the hope alive. You being here today, along with the gars, proves that there are those who want sanity restored. I have to believe that we cannot lose. Just by fighting back, we will lay the foundation for generations to come. Our battle today, no matter what the outcome, will begin the process of making Halla right again. The way it was. This is the beginning of a new history . . . the way it was meant to be. Good luck to us all."

The ovation was instant and thunderous. I was overwhelmed by the show of enthusiasm. Courtney leaned on Mark. I saw tears in her eyes. The Travelers stood together as one. They too were ready. I handed the cube back to Aron, who patted me warmly on the shoulder.

Uncle Press leaned down to whisper in my ear so he could be heard through the cheering. "I told you a long time ago that some people needed your help. This is what I meant. You've carried the burden of every last soul in Halla and could not have done a finer job. I'm proud of you, Bobby."

He put his hand on my shoulder and added, "One other thing."

"What's that?"

"Saint Dane thinks he's won."

"I know," I said with a smile.

I looked to Mark. He stood up straight and said with total confidence, "Give me the word, Bibs."

He used my sister's pet name for me, which he hadn't done since we were little. It was perfect. It made me think of my family, and my past life. We all had families. We all had better lives. Every last person there. It was time to fight for them. It was time to get dangerous. I took a breath. It was the last moment before the final battle. I wanted it to last, because I knew that once I pulled the trigger, nothing would be the same. Anywhere. Ever again. Time would tell if that was a good thing. I took one last look around at all the Travelers, drawing strength from their looks of confidence.

"Okay," I announced. "Bring 'em in."

Mark instantly lifted his walkie-talkie and barked, "Let's go."

The wheels were set in motion. There would be no turning back. I looked at the Travelers and said, "Elli. Aja. Gunny. Patrick. I want you to stay back."

They all made grumbles of protest, but they knew it was futile. They weren't prepared for a fight. Their roles were critical just the same.

"Help evacuate this area. We don't want anybody near this flume once the dados discover the other end on Eelong."

Mark stepped up to say, "There's sanctuary all over

Manhattan for those who are staying back. We need all the help we can get to divide them up and get them moving."

The Travelers nodded in understanding, and acceptance.

"We'll do everything we can," Gunny assured me. It wasn't necessary. I knew they would.

"Do me a favor?" Aja asked.

"What?"

"Think of us when you take him down."

I nodded.

Uncle Press said, "The rest of us will make the journey on foot with the exiles and gars."

"Boon!" I called. "You up for this?"

"Do you have to ask?" the klee replied.

"Good. Stay with the Travelers," I commanded.

"Understood," he answered enthusiastically.

I was glad he was there. We needed all the help we could get.

"What about me?" Courtney asked.

"Courtney and Mark are with me. Kasha, I need you with us too."

Kasha bristled. I actually saw the fur go up on her back. "What? No. That is not the plan. I am to be with the others."

"Sorry," I said. "No arguments."

Kasha fumed but didn't fight it. The train was on the tracks, and she knew enough not to get in the way.

I turned to Uncle Press. Beside him stood Siry, Alder, Spader, and Loor. Unlike the other Travelers, this group *was* prepared to fight.

"This day has been a long time coming," Alder said.

"You are ready, Pendragon," Loor said. "We all are."

"You know something?" I said. "We *are* ready."

"Then let's go!" Siry called out impatiently.

"We'll be right behind you," Uncle Press said to me.

I gave them one last look, wondering for a fleeting instant if I'd see any of them ever again. Anywhere. "See you inside the conclave," I said.

With that, we separated.

I led Kasha, Mark, and Courtney back through the park. As we moved, four black helicopters appeared over the tops of the buildings to the south. They had been lying back, waiting for Mark's call. Just as planned.

"We need to clear a landing space," Mark said.

"No, we don't," I replied without stopping. "Keep 'em all in the air."

Mark scowled. This wasn't part of the plan. But he didn't question. He had no idea why I was changing things up . . . until I led them to the gig that Boon and I had flown in from Eelong.

Mark laughed and raised his walkie to contact the incoming helicopters. "Hold formation. We've got another ride." He then looked to me and added, "Nice."

Kasha gave me a sly look. "I didn't think you'd keep me out of the fight," she said, relieved.

"Zero chance of that," I answered. "You're leading the assault."

She pounced into the pilot seat.

"Take shotgun," I said to Mark.

He climbed in next to Kasha as Courtney and I hopped in back. The crowd cleared as the rotors began to spin.

"You will direct me?" Kasha asked Mark.

"Right to the target" was his reply.

As soon as the rotors hit speed, we lifted off the ground and climbed straight up. I looked down to see those who would soon assault the conclave making their way up Fifth Avenue. It reminded me of the start of a world-class marathon. This journey would only last ten miles . . . the distance to the Conclave of Ravinia.

"Look," I said.

Arriving at the park from all directions were dozens of yellow taxicabs.

"That's how we're moving those cannon things and the shooters," Mark explained. "They'll arrive on site before the crowd does."

"Long before, I hope" was my response.

"We'll get them there," Mark said with confidence.

"Perfect. You did an incredible job, Mark."

"Don't go praising me yet," he cautioned. "We're just getting started."

We hovered in the air over the park. Behind us the four helicopters settled in and hovered at the same altitude—one by one they came into formation. Mark watched to make sure they were all there. I took another look down to see the crowd moving farther up Fifth Avenue. It was an inspiring sight. In front, leading the way, was Uncle Press. Along with Loor, Alder, Spader, and Siry. Aron and Boon, the gar and the klee, were right behind them. This army had a long walk in front of them. That was okay. We had other business to attend to first.

Mark put the walkie-talkie to his lips. "Are we go?" he barked into it.

He got back four replies. "Go one." "Go two." "Go three." "Go four."

"Follow us, kids," Mark replied. He clicked off his walkie and motioned for Kasha to kick it.

The gig shot forward, flying straight up Fifth Avenue. I looked down to see that the exiles and gars were waving and cheering us on. We flew over them with our gig in the lead, the point of an arrow, followed by the four black helicopters.

Attack helicopters.

The soldiers of Halla were on the move.

So far everything had gone according to plan, but it all felt so tenuous. Each new step was critical to the success of the following step. Right now, the next step was ours. If we were successful, the attack had a chance. If not, it could turn into a bloodbath before we even got close to the Conclave of Ravinia.

As we flew north, Courtney held my hand. We didn't speak. What was there to say? Our heads were in the game. There would be time for talk later. I hoped.

We flew through the gray fog and swirling dust that was now a familiar aspect of Third Earth. I hoped that Mark could find his way through the muck. It was hard to see the ground, and the only thing in front of us was nothing. I trusted him, just as I had trusted him so many times before. Kasha dutifully followed his every instruction and made slight course adjustments when asked.

It was about ten miles from the park to the conclave. Not far in a helicopter. There wasn't much time to kick back and get psyched for the challenges ahead. It seemed as if we had been flying for only a few minutes when Mark said to Kasha, "The bridge is our marker. When we clear the top, drop down fast. Like *real* fast. The fog will clear. As soon as we spot the target, break left and ascend. We don't want to be in the way. That would hurt."

Kasha nodded. She got it.

I hoped that the fog wasn't covering the top of the bridge structure. It wouldn't be smart to hit that thing.

"We're close," Mark announced.

I felt the tension in his voice. He was focused. He leaned forward, as if those extra few inches would help him to see a little better. Courtney squeezed my hand. Where was that bridge? All we saw was swirling gray.

Mark couldn't take it anymore. "We've gotta be close," he said to nobody, and toggled his walkie-talkie. "Go hot," he barked.

The replies came back in seconds.

"One is armed." "Two is armed." "Three is armed."

That was it. Ten seconds passed. I saw a bead of sweat slip down Mark's temple. His jaw muscle worked furiously. He pulled the walkie back to his lips and was about to speak when . . .

"Four is armed. Sorry, Mark."

"You're killing me here, Tony. You ready?"

"Yes."

"You sure?"

"Show us the way, boss."

"There!" Kasha announced.

The top of the bridge came into view, barely visible through the swirling fog.

"Got it," Mark said, obviously relieved. "Little to the right . . . little more . . ."

We sailed by the left of the bridge with only a few yards to spare.

Mark lifted his walkie. "Stand by. This is it," he announced.

He waited another two seconds, then shouted to Kasha, "Down! Now!"

Kasha pushed the stick forward. We dove to the deck. The four choppers were right on our tail. Suddenly the fog cleared, and the massive front wall of the conclave appeared before us.

"Oh, man," Courtney gasped. It was her first view of th imposing structure.

I was more concerned about seeing something else. It was the next piece in the puzzle. If it wasn't there, we'd be in trouble.

It was. Exactly where it had to be.

"On the money," Mark called over the walkie. "Take it out!"

He motioned for Kasha to break off our run. "Go! Get outta here!" She throttled up and broke hard to the left. The choppers behind us didn't. They stayed on line, headed right for the target.

Saint Dane's flume.

Kasha pulled up and circled around so we could get a view of the attack. The stolen helicopters were armed with the same type of rocket that we had seen used to blast the zoo building. The first two choppers let them fly. Multiple white streaks shot from their bellies, headed for the mouth of the flume. They hit. Hard. The explosions were deafening. Right on target. The first two choppers broke off, left and right, barely missing the wall of the conclave. The way was clear for the second two choppers to make their attack run. They launched, again hitting the flume dead-on. Debris from the concussions flew high into the air. Smoke was everywhere. It was hard to see exactly what damage they had done. The second set of helicopters broke off. The first two had already come around for a second run. They launched again, pulverizing the ground around the flume.

"Hang on," Mark ordered into the walkie. "Let's see what we've got."

All four choppers circled away. We watched the ground, waiting for the smoke to clear. The plan we had devised to attle Saint Dane and his dado army was tricky. It relied totally on timing. Our success or failure in destroying this flume could easily mean the difference between victory and defeat. We knew that Saint Dane would send his army to Eelong, so we used that. We wanted him to use his power to build a flume. We wanted the dados to go. *All* of the dados. We just didn't want him to be able to bring them back. At least, not quickly.

"They're going to find the other flume," Courtney said soberly.

"Eventually," I said. "Hopefully, too late."

"Why don't we destroy the other one too?" Kasha asked.

Mark kept his eyes on the clearing smoke as he answered. "We put everything we had into this attack. There are no more rockets."

We knew that from the beginning. We only had enough firepower to destroy one flume. Whether we liked it or not, we were going to have to face the army of dados. Our hope was that we would stand a better chance against them from behind the walls of the fortress. That was the thinking, anyway. There was still a very big hurdle to jump over before we got that far. We had to invade and control the fortress.

Right. That.

"I can see it," Kasha exclaimed.

The smoke cleared, revealing a huge expanse of shattered rocks, dirt, and debris. The flume was sealed.

"I'm thinking they know we're here," I said.

"Yeah," Mark concurred. "Now it gets scary."

39

We had come up with a bold plot for the conquest of Ravinia.

The exiles and gars had accepted the battle. We had successfully evacuated Black Water and brought them to Third Earth. Saint Dane had created a flume and used his dark spirit to send his dado army to Eelong, just as Nevva said he would.

Then we destroyed their flume, trapping the dados on Eelong.

That is, they were trapped until they discovered the second flume. I had no doubt that as soon as they realized they were on the wrong territory, the dados would leap into the second flume and return to Third Earth. The wild card would be how long it would take the dado army to change gears and deal with the unexpected. I hoped the size of that army would actually help us. It wouldn't be easy to reassemble so many and quickly march them into the second flume. At least, that's what we were counting on.

Surprise had been on our side. Not anymore. With the firing of those missiles and the destruction of Saint

Dane's flume, we had announced our arrival. The clock was definitely ticking. Our goal was to control the Conclave of Ravinia before the dados returned. We stood a much better chance against that immense army from behind the protective walls of the conclave. That was the immediate goal. We needed to get into the conclave. Quickly.

"Here they come," Mark announced.

Rising up from the factory beyond the gates of the conclave were helicopters. I counted a dozen. Just as we expected.

"Get us on the ground," I ordered Kasha.

She quickly dropped the gig to the edge of the river that separated Manhattan from the Bronx. We landed on the conclave side. It wouldn't be good to be in the air, because we knew what was coming. The rebels who had blasted the flume were long gone. They knew what was coming too.

Mark ordered a simple, sharp command into his walkie. "Take 'em down."

We all looked to the Manhattan side of the river. There, lined up along the far bank, stretching out for several hundred yards, were dozens of yellow taxicabs. Crouched down in front of each cab were two gars.

With radio cannons.

The green tubes were on their shoulders, pointed to the sky. The trap was set.

The Ravinian copters rose in attack formation. It was an imposing sight. Even from where we were, I could see their rocket launchers beneath. I had no doubt that they were fully loaded. They hovered together until the formation tightened up, then moved forward as one, headed toward Manhattan and the oncoming army of exiles and gars.

Toward our radio cannons.

"Tell me those things really work," Mark said softly.

"Watch" was my answer.

Courtney leaned in to me. One way or another, this was going to get ugly.

The wave of choppers cleared the fortress wall and passed over the destroyed flume. I heard their engines revving harder. They were ready to do some damage. They were about to cross the river when the trap was sprung.

There was no sound. No explosion. No rocket trails. The only way we knew that the radio cannons had begun firing was that the helicopters started to gyrate. It was as if they were hit by an invisible force. The gars hit dead-on-target. The choppers kept moving forward, but they had lost control. Each spun in a different direction. Two went down immediately. They slammed into the ground, their rockets exploding on impact.

"Wow," Mark gasped. That said it all.

Two more helicopters collided. The explosion ate up another that flew into them from behind. I don't think the dado pilots had any idea what was happening. One moment they were in tight formation, moving forward. The next it was chaos. And destruction.

Three more choppers bought it, slamming into the ground. The area in front of the conclave had become a mass of twisted steel and fire. I was happy to see that at least two of them had crashed into the flume grave. If it wasn't sealed before, it definitely was after that.

The few helicopters that had escaped the initial barrage fought back. They must have been far enough behind to see the strange lineup of taxicabs on the other side of the river and realized where the attack was coming from. They fired their rockets. Instantly two taxicabs were hit. I couldn't watch. The Ravinians had drawn blood. We had gotten this far without a single casualty. I knew that wouldn't last, and it didn't. I don't know how many gars and rebel drivers died in the helicopter attack, but I do know that none of them left their positions. Every last one of those sharpshooters continued to fire at the helicopters until the end.

"Such brave souls," Kasha whispered.

They were heroes. I had no doubt that their spirits would find themselves on Solara.

More taxicabs were targeted. Rockets slammed the ground around them, but the gars didn't flinch. They moved their radio cannons in concert with the movements of the choppers, keeping them in their sights. The last wave of Ravinian copters had reached the river. It had all happened so fast that none of them thought to peel off and avoid the barrage. It wasn't something they anticipated, and they weren't prepared to react. For that, they all went down. The final wave of choppers twisted out of control. Their rockets fired aimlessly. Harmlessly. The last four helicopters splashed down in the river to either side of the rickety bridge. It had only taken a few minutes, but every last Ravinian helicopter had been shot out of the sky.

The remaining gars on the far bank stood and cheered. Mark gave me a smile, then barked into his walkie. "Stay tight, there might be more."

The celebration on the ground ended quickly. We could see that the gars, with the help of the rebels and exiles, were repositioning themselves in case another wave of helicopters arrived.

My mind was already on to the next phase of the plan. Much of what we were about to do had already been planned by the rebels. They had spent years living in the shadows, doing what they could to give the Ravinians trouble. They hijacked the helicopters. They stole weapons and defense shields. They confounded the Ravinians—who were constantly trying to smoke them out and eliminate them—by sinking safely back into the city like ghosts. What the rebels lacked was manpower. They didn't have the numbers to be anything more than a nuisance to Ravinia. They always had big plans, but were never able to carry them out.

Until now.

Mark changed the frequency on his walkie and called out, "Float 'em in."

The reply came back, "On the way."

I looked beyond the sea of burning helicopter wrecks to the Conclave of Ravinia. The wall looked more imposing than ever. The giant steel doors were shut tight. A line of people appeared along the top. Defenders. Though the sight of them paled in comparison to the image of the massive army of dados, or the attack helicopters, I knew that the defenders now lining the wall of the conclave would cause us the most trouble. That is, if the next phase of the plan was successful.

I said to Mark, "Please, tell me we caught the express."

Mark changed the walkie frequency again and called, "Give me good news."

The reply came back, "Say the word."

Mark looked to me and winked. "All aboard."

I took one more look at the conclave wall. In spite of the carnage that surrounded us, there was a strange calm. At least I thought so, because I knew what was going to happen. The battle was about to escalate far beyond the downing of a few helicopters.

"Do it," I said.

Mark immediately hit the send button. "Bring it," he ordered.

The reply: "We're on the move. You might want to stand back."

The ground in front of us began to shake. The sound of machinery could be heard above the crackle of the fires that were consuming the helicopters. Just as I had seen it happen before, a crack appeared that led from the river's edge right up to the large, red rectangular door of the conclave. The ground parted, revealing the single train track beneath. At the same time, the water of the river boiled, followed by the large, long tube of a tunnel that rose up from beneath and connected with the rail.

Mark shook his head in awe. "We've been planning this forever. Never thought we'd actually do it."

I said, "Nothing like a good old-fashioned train hijack, pardner."

A whistle shrieked from inside the tunnel. Once, twice. It issued a harsh warning. *Get out of the way.* Looking up at the track that led to the conclave, I saw that it ran beneath one of the burning helicopters. Mark saw it too.

"Shouldn't be a problem," he said. "So long as there's no unexploded rockets in that wreck."

It was too late to worry about it. A second later the golden train engine blasted out of the tunnel. It charged out at full speed, far faster than the train Patrick and I had hitched a ride on. They must have started back far enough to get up a full head of steam. That was wise. They were going to need it.

As soon as the train cleared the tunnel, three men jumped off. Actually, two jumped. One was pushed. Two were Mark's guys, the third was the engineer. The plan was to hijack the train at Penn Station and force the engineer to drive it here. There was no reason to leave him on board for this unscheduled, one-way trip, so they pushed him off. They all rolled away from the accelerating train, hopefully unhurt.

There was only an engine. No other cars. They were cut loose because they would have slowed the engine down. I felt Courtney tense next to me, as the engine bore down on the burning wreck of the helicopter. The golden engine slammed into the fiery mass, knocking the hulk away as easily as if it were batting away a fly. The chopper carcass bounced and rolled as the train engine charged on, headed for the giant red door that protected the conclave.

"Here we go," Mark said.

I winced. It was going to be a spectacular crash. The engine hit the door at full speed. The sound was horrifying. Metal clashed with metal. The engine roared angrily as it slammed full-speed into the solid mass. The door gave way from the bottom. The train forced the immense hunk of metal inward, which broke the top loose. The engine paid for the mayhem it caused. The golden train jumped the tracks, but kept moving forward. There was too much inertia. Too much hurtling weight. Part of the stone frame around the door crumbled. The giant red door slammed the ground where the train had just been.

I only caught glimpses through the smoke and dust, but that was enough. Through the destroyed doorway I saw that the train had flipped and rolled. It may have been huge, but it was spinning like a toy. When it finally came to rest, it was at least thirty yards inside the conclave.

I hoped it had missed the statue of David.

Courtney said, "Well, I guess *that* worked."

The wreck had blasted a massive wound into the wall that protected the Conclave of Ravinia.

"Now comes the hard part," Mark said, dead serious.

We had blazed the path. The Conclave of Ravinia was wide open. There was nothing clever or surprising about what was to happen next. When the exiles and the gars arrived, we would storm the walls. Nothing fancy. Nothing crafty. We would use our numbers to overpower whatever force was left behind to protect the conclave. People would die. The strength of the remaining dado force would determine how many. The exiles knew it. The gars knew it. The rebels knew it. And of course, the Travelers knew it. But we were all willing to risk our lives for what we believed in.

"It will be a while before they arrive," Kasha said.

"That's okay," Mark replied. "We need time to get ready."

Mark led us to the edge of the river, where down below on the water we saw two massive barges headed our way. We had been able to move thousands of people across time and space, but if they couldn't get across this narrow river, it would all have been for nothing. Mark's solution was for the rebels to come in with two barges, creating a makeshift bridge. Side by side they would span the width of the river. The trick was to secure them. Rebel barge pilots were in command of the vessels. They carefully maneuvered the two crafts into position so that they could be wedged together, forming a solid surface. It was an arduous process that made me crazy. I didn't know how much time we had before the dado army returned. Or the Ravinians threw something unexpected at us. I kept glancing south, wondering when the Travelers would arrive with our army. Standing by the river, waiting, wishing it would all happen faster, was torture.

"Will it be ready?" I asked nervously. "I mean, by the time they get here?"

"It will," he assured me.

Mark had already pulled off the impossible. Five times over. Maneuvering a couple of barges was cake compared to the other miracles he had worked this day. Still, I was sweating it out.

Finally, with a grinding of metal against metal, the barges stopped moving. The rebel pilots on board each gave us a thumbs-up. The bridge was in place.

"You want to be the first over?" Mark asked.

"We'll all go," I said, and ran down the steep bank of the river's edge. I jumped onto the wooden-decked barge. It felt solid. Kasha, Mark, and Courtney followed. It seemed safe enough, but we were only four people. There could be four hundred at a time on this thing. I put all doubts out of my mind and continued across. When I got to the far side and climbed up the bank, I was greeted with a welcome sight.

Directly in front of us were the taxicabs and gars with their cannons. They were still in firing position, ready for whatever the Ravinians threw at us. Seeing them wasn't a surprise. My focus was on what lay beyond. Maybe four blocks behind the line of cabs, moving toward us, was Uncle Press . . . along with about forty thousand other welcome faces.

"Yikes," Courtney gasped.

Yikes was a good word to describe it. Uncle Press led the way, along with Aron and Boon and the other Travelers. They were followed by such a huge mass of people that it took my breath away. Many carried silver shields that looked like riot-police gear. Those shields, along with some short rifle-looking weapons, had been distributed by the rebels.

Or should I say, they were courtesy of Ravinia and stolen by the rebels. As much as we needed every weapon we could find, the shields looked pitiful compared to what we would be facing on the far side of the river.

Uncle Press led the army up to the line of taxicabs, where a signal was given and quickly passed back through the link cubes. In no time the mass of humanity was halted. Aron was right. Commands moved quickly.

"It's done," I exclaimed. "The door is down, the bridge is in place."

"What about the choppers?" Uncle Press asked.

"What choppers?" Mark asked. "Oh, you mean those flaming wrecks?"

Uncle Press smiled.

"There are guards stationed along the top of the wall," Courtney said. "Waiting."

"We can't let them wait long," I pointed out.

Uncle Press looked ahead to the target, then back to the army that he had led all the way from Eelong.

"What we do here today is for the people of Halla," he said. "We can hope for a lot of things to happen from this point on, but most important, we have to hope that this will never, ever happen again."

With those words, the assault on Ravinia began.

40

The first move was to cross the river.

It would take a while to get everyone across the barge bridge. Or, at least enough people to begin the assault. Alder, Loor, Spader, and Siry took charge, directing the movement. It was kind of eerie. Nobody spoke. The tension was obvious. They knew that their time had come.

I went across first with Mark, Courtney, and Uncle Press. We walked a short way toward the conclave and stopped, motioning that that was as far as the first line should come. First over the bridge were several gars with radio cannons. They would be critical in knocking out any dados on top of the wall. They were followed by several exiles and gars, who carried either the silver shields or stolen weapons. These were the same weapons that we had used to fend off the dados when Mark, Elli, and I were in the dado factory. They were like rifles, but with wide barrels. They worked. I walked back to the river and looked down to see that the barges weren't as stable as I would have liked, but they were holding. At any one time I'd say there were several hundred people on top. They swayed and tipped, but the weight was divided evenly, so there were no disasters.

I went back up front to join Uncle Press and the others. A formidable force was gathering. I could only imagine what the Ravinians were thinking. I hoped they were scared.

I wondered where Saint Dane was. He had to know that a storm was brewing. Was he ready? Or was he on Eelong, frantically trying to rally the dado army? Had he envisioned something like this happening? Saint Dane always thought four steps ahead. There was every possibility that he had something planned for us once we got inside. That was the scariest thought of all.

Our mission from this point on was straightforward. Control the Conclave of Ravinia. To do that, we had to eliminate every last dado. Once that was accomplished, we would gather every resource possible and defend the conclave against the dado army that was sure to return. I was confident that we outnumbered the Ravinian security force a hundred times over. My fear was what the human Ravinians might do. If they got into the fight, it would be a bloodbath. On both sides.

Looking back at our gathering forces, I felt as if we had waited long enough. Aron came forward and explained to me the logistics of the assault they had worked out during their march from downtown.

"We have four waves," he explained. "The first will bring the radio cannons to neutralize the dados. They'll also have shields and rifles. Their job is to pave the way for the following waves to enter the conclave."

"They're going to take the brunt of it," Uncle Press said gravely.

The concept made sense. The job of the first wave was critical. They would be charging into the strength of the

Ravinians' defense. The grim reality was that these brave people would take the heaviest losses.

Uncle Press continued, "I think the Travelers, Aron, and Boon should be in the second wave. We will need them once we get inside."

"I will attack with the first wave," Loor said. It was a flat-out statement. There was no arguing with her. She wasn't going to hide behind anybody.

"As will I," Alder said.

"What about me?" Spader chimed in. "I think I'd like first crack at these wogglies. We earned it, didn't we?"

"Me too," Siry chimed in.

"And me," Boon said.

Uncle Press looked to Aron. Aron shrugged. "It is not the time to be cautious."

Uncle Press shook his head and sighed. "Fine. Who picked you people anyway?"

"That would be you, mate," Spader said. "And you made some fine choices, I have to say."

I said, "Mark, you've got to hang back."

"Not a chance!" he shouted.

"You have to. You're the only one who can coordinate the rebels. We have no idea what's going to get thrown at us. If you go down, we're done."

He wanted to argue. Instead he offered a compromise. "I'll be in the second wave."

I didn't fight him. "Courtney, stay with him."

"I'll watch his back," she said in her typical bold way. "Just watch your own."

"I've got plenty of people watching my back," I assured her.

"You're not going," Uncle Press said to me.

I snapped a surprised look to him. "The hell I'm not!"

"It can't end for you here, Bobby. Not like this."

"No way. I'm not asking anybody to do anything I wouldn't do myself."

"You have to. There's more to this battle than claiming the Ravinian conclave. We could get inside and take over the fortress and even turn back the dado army, but that isn't what this is about. It's about the return of the spirit of Halla. It's about taking back what was meant to be and ending the dark cloud that has altered events throughout time and space. Like I said, there's only one way that can happen. For that, we will look to you."

I didn't understand what he meant at first. What kind of double-talk was this? There was no way he was talking me out of this fight. I looked to the other Travelers for support, but they seemed to know what Uncle Press meant.

Alder was the one who put it into words. "What Press means is, you have a bigger task ahead."

My anger slipped away as the realization hit me. It was true. I couldn't risk falling during the attack. My destiny went beyond the storming of the conclave. If we were to triumph, once and forever, Saint Dane had to be ended.

That job was mine.

"I want to be there with you all," I said.

"You will be," Alder said.

"You have always been with us," Loor added. "Your spirit was our guide from the beginning. Today is no different."

I believe that was the highest compliment I'd ever been paid. I hoped it was true. I hoped I could live up to it.

"Boon, stay back with me," I said. "We'll fly in over the top."

"Yes, sir!" Boon said eagerly, and jumped to my side.

I took one last look at my Traveler friends. Alder, Spader, Siry, Kasha, and my uncle. Press Tilton. The Traveler from Second Earth before me. Each carried a silver shield, except for Loor, who had her wooden stave out and ready.

"And so we go," I said.

Uncle Press nodded to Aron. Aron brought out his link radio cube.

"First wave at the ready," he said into the glowing cube.

Instantly the first line of warriors tensed up. Boon, Mark, Courtney, and I got out of the way. We quickly made our way through the mass of people, headed for the gig that was waiting near the river.

Suddenly I heard what I thought was a huge cheer. It wasn't. It was a battle cry. I turned back to see the first wave of exiles and gars running for the conclave. The assault was under way. Just like that. My stomach turned over. Such brave people, all willing to give their lives for a better world. Or rather, for the better world that used to be. They charged across the open field with nothing to protect them but those tiny shields. There were thousands in that first wave. I wondered how many would be left standing when it was complete.

I wondered what would happen to the Travelers.

The dados didn't wait for the assault to get too close before they began shooting. The steady *paf paf paf* of their weapons echoed across the battlefield. Several of our people were hit, and turned to ash instantly. The result of getting hit by a charge from one of those weapons had the same effect as what we'd seen when the Ravinian guards had executed that poor guy inside the conclave. Instant incineration. I hoped it wasn't painful. Adding to the sound of the weapons firing was a constant metallic pinging sound.

"What is that?" I asked.

"Those silver shields repel the charge from those guns," Mark explained. "We stole them from the Ravinians a long time ago. Never thought we'd have to use them."

It gave me a little bit of hope that at least they had some protection. But there looked to be hundreds of dados on top of the wall, the high ground, firing down. No matter where they shot, they were sure to hit one of our people. That's how many of us there were. A couple of gars dropped to their knees with their radio cannons and started firing back. One by one, dados were knocked backward off the wall, never to be seen again. It looked like a shooting gallery.

Boon ran for the gig and started powering up.

"I gotta go," I said to Mark and Courtney.

"We'll see you inside," Courtney replied.

There was a quick group hug.

"Get us home, Bobby," Mark whispered.

I pulled away and looked into the faces of my two best friends. We were no longer the little kids who'd grown up together in Stony Brook. Yet we were. Who could have foreseen the people we would become? I was proud of who we were and what we had done, but this was not the way it was meant to be. It made me sad, and a little angry.

"I love you guys" was all I said, and ran for the gig. I had to get out of there. I didn't want to let my emotions take over by even thinking of the possibility that I would never see them again.

The gig's rotors were up to speed. I jumped in next to Boon and strapped in.

"We going straight in?" he asked.

"No. We should hover above until they break through."

We lifted off smoothly. After a quick wave down to Mark and Courtney, we shot skyward and got a bird's-eye view of the battle below. It looked like one of those battlefield attacks from the American Civil War or World War I. Thousands of people charged for the fortress, while the Ravinians fired back to keep them away. This was old-school warfare with some new-school weapons. The only difference was that there weren't any bodies on the battlefield. That's because they had been obliterated. There were no remains. At least, not yet.

Leading the way were Uncle Press and the Travelers. They dodged around the smoking hulks of the downed choppers, using them for protection when possible. Wisely, they were not running in a straight line. They wanted to be difficult targets.

"Uh-oh," Boon said.

Looking forward, I saw that two more helicopters had lifted off from beside the conclave and were headed for the battlefield. My fear was that they were going to start firing rockets into the crowd. Those little silver shields would have no effect against that kind of barrage.

"Buzz 'em!" I said.

"What?"

"Distract them. Anything!" I shouted.

Boon pushed the gig forward, and we shot toward the choppers.

The first helicopter fired a rocket into the crowd. When it hit, the explosion was violent. And sickening. I hated to think how many people had been killed in that one short second. A second rocket was fired, making another direct hit into the charging army. The explosion ripped the ground, tearing up cement. Bodies were launched like rag dolls.

"Do it!" I screamed at Boon.

The klee cut across the nose of the first chopper, barely missing it. The pilot pulled out of his attack run and turned his chopper to come after us. Boon buzzed the second chopper, doing a figure eight between the two. Okay, maybe I was wrong. Maybe Boon *was* a better pilot than Kasha. Our aerobatics seemed to confuse the pilots, which was the best we could have hoped for. All I wanted was for them to stop firing long enough for . . .

Suddenly both helicopters started to rotate wildly. They were out of control, and I thought I knew why. They kept firing rockets but had no way of directing them. Several hit the conclave wall. None hit our people.

"Pull up!" I shouted.

Boon shot skyward to get away from the doomed helicopters. There was no telling which way they would fly as they struggled to stay airborne. The hunters had become hunted. The gars were firing their radio cannons at them from the ground, which meant the marauders wouldn't be in the air for long. I didn't know if the weapons from Black Water were disrupting the choppers, or had damaged their dado pilots. Didn't matter. Either way, they were going down. I feared for a moment that they might crash onto the battlefield . . . with tragic results for those below. I held my breath, watching the helicopters dodge about like crazed butterflies. They crashed within seconds of each other . . . but not on the battlefield. Both hit square onto the roof of the dado factory.

"Woohaa!" I screamed in victory, surprise . . . and relief.

Explosions erupted that tore through the factory's roof. More explosions followed from below . . . far more than made sense for the number of rockets they were carrying.

"That's where they build the helicopters," I told Boon. "They must store the rockets—"

I was cut off by the sound of an immense explosion that came from inside the factory. A huge mushroom cloud of fire and black smoke blasted into the air, blowing out the roof. The wave of heat buffeted our little gig. Boon had to fight to keep control.

"I guess they store their fuel there too," I added.

We both laughed. It was an incredible stroke of luck. I hoped the explosions carried through to the dado side of the factory.

I heard several smaller explosions coming from the ground. Besides the rifles that the rebels provided, there were also a few weapons that packed a little more punch. I saw people dropping to their knees and bracing another type of rifle against the ground. When they fired, a burst of flame erupted from each muzzle. It must have packed a heck of a kick. Seconds later explosions erupted near the destroyed door of the fortress.

"They're like grenade launchers," I said to Boon, not that he knew what a grenade launcher was. "They're getting closer."

Dados gathered inside the destroyed doorway to defend the obvious point of attack. There were dozens of them, all with the silver weapons. They fired wildly into the crowd that was growing ever closer. Every one up front held a shield. The constant metallic pings told me that they were warding off the charges fired by the Ravinians.

More grenades were launched, blowing dados away, throwing them back into the fortress. Several people formed a wall of shields to protect the gars that were moving forward with their radio cannons. When they got to within forty yards of the door, the sharp-shooting gars planted and fired. Dados fell like paper dolls in the wind.

The first wave of the attack was nearly at the fortress.

Looking back, I saw that the second wave had begun their charge. I hoped that the first wave would get into the conclave soon and neutralize the dados, because none of the people in the second wave had shields.

The dados along the top of the wall had grown sparse. Either they had been blown away by the gars, or had gone to the ground to make the final stand at the door.

"They're going to make it," Boon declared.

Sure enough, the first of the attacking force had reached the door and fought their way inside. I couldn't tell if any Travelers were among them.

"Now!" I shouted. "Get us over the top."

Boon throttled up and flew the gig over the giant wall. We were in, and got our first view of the action behind enemy lines. Below, our people poured in through the destroyed door, past the wreck of the golden engine. There were still a lot of Ravinian guards on the ground, fighting back, but far more were laid out on the ground. Finished. As the exiles and gars pushed inside, anyone who didn't have a weapon to begin with picked up a silver wand from a fallen dado. We were gaining firepower.

That proved to be the last straw for the defense of the conclave. The dados didn't retreat. They weren't programmed to retreat. They didn't know fear. They fought till the end, but the end came quickly. In minutes the grassy park below was filled with the remains of hundreds of dados.

I looked farther into the conclave, fearing that there might be a counterattack, either from more dados or from human Ravinians. As I wrote before, that is what I truly feared. If the human Ravinians engaged this army, they would lose and they would die. That wasn't why we were there. This wasn't meant to be a slaughter. From our vantage point flying high over the compound, I saw no counterattack. In fact, I saw very few Ravinians at all. I caught glimpses of a few who were deeper in the compound, but they were fleeing. They wanted no part of this fight. They expected the dados to protect them.

The dados failed.

"Put us down," I said to Boon.

We dropped quickly and landed softly on the grass. We had done it. We were in. More and more exiles and gars flooded in through the destroyed door. Many grabbed weapons and began climbing up to the top of the wall. They all knew the score. This was only the first half of the battle. The attackers would soon become defenders, and it would be our turn to hold off a huge army bent on taking over the conclave.

I ran toward the destroyed door, looking for Uncle Press and the Travelers. There was a moment of panic. Had any of them been hit? People ran past me, running deeper into the conclave. They knew their mission. Seek out and destroy every last dado. They would move in patrols of twenty, searching everywhere. The destruction of the dados had to be complete. Another group would be headed for the factory to root out any last dados there, but I was pretty sure all they'd find was burning wreckage. The assault had been a complete success.

But where were the Travelers?

I stepped over a fallen dado . . . and the robot grabbed my leg. He was down, but he wasn't dead. I was so surprised that I didn't defend myself. The dado tossed me down. I hit the grass and spun back, expecting an attack. The dado still had his silver weapon. He raised it to fire at me . . . and got clocked in the head by a wooden stave. The dado fell to its knee and got clocked again. It may have been a robot, but it couldn't stand up to the vicious onslaught. It dropped the weapon, reached for it, grabbed the wrong end . . . and instantly went dead.

"I prefer doing things the old way," Loor said, spinning her stave triumphantly.

"You didn't kill it, it was the weapon," I shot back, kidding.

"It was as good as dead already," she argued.

"Yeah, whatever. Thank you."

Loor gave me a small smile, which for her was huge. "Will I ever have to stop protecting you, Pendragon?"

"Man, I hope so."

"Bobby!" Uncle Press called.

He ran up, out of breath. Behind him were Alder, Spader, Kasha, and Siry. Boon joined us as well. We all stood there looking at one another. Spader began to laugh. Alder followed. Then Siry and Uncle Press and even Kasha and Loor. It was a moment of pure exhilaration. We had done it. We had gotten a toehold in the Conclave of Ravinia. There was nothing funny going on; it was more a laugh of pure joy.

"Where's Aron?" I asked.

Uncle Press stopped laughing. The others did as well. The mood instantly turned dark.

"He almost made it," Uncle Press answered. "He was near the door. But he took a hit from a dado that we thought was finished."

It was a shocking, hollow feeling. Aron was the leader of the gars, and had been since my first visit to Black Water. He was the visionary who helped civilize the gars and earn them respect. It was hard to believe that he was gone. His spirit had surely became part of Solara, and Solara was all the better for it.

"Hey!" came a familiar voice.

Mark and Courtney came running up to join us.

"Can you believe this?" I said. "We did it."

"Not yet, we didn't," Mark said, dead serious.

His tone didn't fit the moment of victory. I looked over his shoulder to see hundreds upon hundreds of our people streaming into the conclave. I didn't get it. From what I could see, we had most definitely done it.

"What do you mean?" I asked.

Mark held up his walkie-talkie. "They found it."

We all knew what he meant.

"When?" I asked.

Courtney answered, "The flume downtown came to life five minutes ago. Dados are pouring out in droves. They're headed this way."

We stood there in stunned silence. Our celebration was a short one. Though it was something we expected, knowing it was actually happening was still a shock.

Mark said, "I'd say we have two hours at best before we get swarmed."

Uncle Press looked around and said, "We know what to do. Bring all the radio cannons inside. Call back the choppers. Find every weapon and get it into the hands of a gar or a Yank."

The Travelers scattered to carry out the commands. I was left with Mark and Courtney and Uncle Press.

"Two hours," Uncle Press said, looking at me.

"We can do it," Mark said. "We *will* do it."

Uncle Press didn't respond to Mark. He was focused on me.

"Two hours," he repeated.

His grave look said it all. I nodded in understanding.

He stood straight, looked me square in the eye, and said, "Go get him."

41

He was there.

I knew it. I felt it. I knew where to find him. For the first time I understood how he always seemed to know where I was and what I was doing. I could sense him. I don't know how else to say it.

Our success in taking over the Conclave of Ravinia had far greater meaning than the conquering of a fortress. We were gaining strength. The spirit of Solara was returning. It came from the selfless efforts of a group of people who, in storming the walls of Ravinia, had seized control of their own destiny. It's hard to describe this feeling, but it came from the core of my being. I felt stronger. I felt hope. I didn't think for a second that the battle was over, but as I ran through the conclave, for the first time in a very long while, I thought that there was a chance we might actually turn the tide. We were no longer fighting a losing battle.

As I sprinted through the parklike grounds of the conclave, I saw very few Ravinians. Those who made an appearance looked terrified. Their perfect world was threatened, so they ran and hid inside their opulent homes and peered out of their windows in fear. I realized that my concern that they might step up to defend themselves was unfounded. They didn't have it in them. It made my confidence grow. This was the true legacy of Ravinia. They were cowards who hid behind the power of their mentor.

Saint Dane.

This wouldn't be over until Saint Dane's influence ended. For that, his spirit had to end. I was racing toward a showdown. I had suspected it would come to this for a long time. I feared it. I tried to ignore it. I hoped there would be some other way.

I was kidding myself.

This day had to come. It was inevitable. From the very beginning, this conflict was about a battle between two forces. Two ways of thinking. Two spirits. Saint Dane . . . and me.

It was time to end it.

I ran to the center of the conclave and to the spot where I knew he would be. The Taj Mahal. When I got my first view of the majestic building, I noticed a change. There were no Ravinian guards. They must all have been sent to the front wall to defend the conclave. Which meant they were history. I sprinted along the fountains, through the manicured grounds and up the steps, near where I had seen Mark executed. Or his dado double executed. Either way, it wasn't a happy memory, and it only got me more fired up for what was to come. I strode boldly inside. There was nothing secretive about my visit. I wanted him to know I was there. I went straight to the center of the building, where I knew the red-carpeted stairs would lead up to the platform that held his golden throne. The throne of a king who was losing his kingdom.

There he sat. Alone. As much as I knew I would find

him there, I was surprised when I actually saw him. He had changed. Gone was the long, dark hair and youthful appearance. Saint Dane now looked as he did the very first day I met him. His long hair had gone gray. His face had aged. He still wore the rich, red clothing of a Ravinian king, but he looked small inside the elaborate robe. He sat slumped in the chair, looking like an old man. Looking beaten. Not that I needed more proof, but it confirmed that the spirit of Solara was rising. And Saint Dane's was waning.

"You shouldn't be hanging around inside on such a nice day," I called to him. "You're missing a hell of a show."

He didn't react. I wasn't sure if he even heard me. His eyes stared straight ahead, vacant. It didn't matter. He could have looked as if he were dead, and I still wouldn't have let my guard down. If Saint Dane was anything, he was unpredictable. Like they say about wild animals, they're the most dangerous when they feel trapped and threatened.

"We know the dado army is coming back," I said, taunting. "We're ready for them. That must have taken a heck of a lot of spirit out of you to be moving so many of them around Halla like that. Is that why you look like hell? Is your dark power almost gone? Hmmm?"

His eyes moved a fraction to focus on me. In spite of the fact that he looked old and tired, his blue-white eyes still burned. He wasn't done. Not by a long shot.

"Is that what Nevva told you?" he said with a low growl. "The way to defeat me was to deplete the spirit we worked so hard to build?"

"More or less," I answered casually. "Pretty good advice, don't you think?"

"She betrayed me," he said with a barely perceptible whisper.

"You betrayed yourself," I shot back.

His eyes flared. He didn't budge, but his eyes sparkled with rage.

"It took me a while to realize this, but you know what? You never had a chance."

"I control Halla," he hissed.

"*Controlled*. Past tense. Big difference."

"There are millions throughout Halla who would dispute that," he muttered.

"For now. It won't last. It can't last."

I definitely had his attention. The fact was, I wasn't bluffing. I believed what I was saying. It took me a very long time to come to the truth, but now that I had it, I was confident. As I spoke, I stayed at the bottom of the stairs. I didn't want to get any closer to him than I had to. Just in case.

"From the beginning this has been a battle about destiny. Free will versus control. Domination versus tolerance. How many times have you told me that all you've done is give the people of Halla what they want? You said they were selfish and shortsighted and couldn't be trusted to guide their own future. So you stepped in to show them the way. You elevated the elite and crushed the weak—all in the name of creating Utopia. Or, your idea of Utopia."

"And they followed me like lambs because that's what they are," he spat at me. "Stupid lambs. Everything they did, they did to themselves."

"But they didn't!" I shot back. "And you knew they wouldn't. You didn't hold true to your own vision."

He cocked his head like a curious dog.

"Whether you can admit it or not, even to yourself, you didn't believe that the people of Halla were truly weak. You didn't trust in your own philosophy. Sure, it sounded good to say they were only getting what they wanted, but when it came down to it, you didn't think that would be enough for you to deplete their spirit, did you?"

"I don't know what you're talking about," he snarled.

"Sure you do. If you truly believed in your vision—if you thought that all you needed to do was influence a little here, push a little there, play to people's worst instincts and all of Halla would crumble at your feet—why did you need to create the dados?"

"I didn't," he snickered. "They were the creation of your friend. Of a being from Halla."

"Give me a break!" I shouted. "Getting Mark to create the dados was your plan from the start. Why else would you have done that if you didn't need help? I think you knew that, in spite of all you did to influence and tempt the people of Halla to make wrong choices, eventually they would bounce back, because that's what they've always done. People make mistakes all the time, big and small, but they're resilient. They survive. They cope. They correct their mistakes. But you didn't want them to bounce back this time, and for that you needed insurance. So you created an army to intimidate those who didn't follow you."

"You're grasping," he chuckled.

"Really? I've seen it all over Halla. Blok used the dados on Quillan to enforce their rule. Ibara was nearly destroyed by dados once, and now Veego has brought them back. The Ravinians rose to power on Second Earth and Eelong by using dados as intimidation. Dados are now on Cloral and Denduron. They are your power. You can't make clear choices when you're being threatened with violence. Who are you trying to kid? I've seen it all. Do you think for a second if you took the dados out of the equation that Ravinia would have risen to power so easily?"

"The dados are a tool, nothing more," he said, his eyes flickering away from me nervously.

"A tool for what?" I cried. "You know what I think? All this talk about guiding the people of Halla may have been how this began. Maybe you actually had noble intentions at one time, but they gave way to your own ego. Saying you wanted to guide destiny and save the people from themselves was just an excuse. You were a spirit from Solara, and what has your noble quest led to? A palace! A throne! You've surrounded yourself with the greatest artwork and architecture from this world. I'll bet you've got palaces like this on every territory, don't you?"

He didn't answer. He didn't have to.

"You're no longer satisfied with pulling strings from behind the scenes. No more disguises. No more role-playing. Look at you! You've put yourself out there front and center, wearing king's clothes and playing to the masses. I think the truth is that you envy the people of Halla. You want to be their king. You want to be their god. But you know what? Even with the dados, it wasn't meant to be. The positive spirit of Solara is returning. It was inevitable. If it wasn't the exiles and the gars, it would have been someone else. The Batu from Zadaa or the poverty-stricken from Quillan. People somewhere would rise up and fight back, just as they have here. What you don't understand is that the true power of Halla rests with its people. The spirit of the people created Solara. Guess what? They're about to *un*create you."

Saint Dane leaped without warning. He sprang from the throne and launched himself at me. I didn't have time to react, that's how sudden the move was. He hit me dead-on, knocking me backward. I braced myself for what was sure to be a violent fall. When I hit the floor, I looked up to realize that I was no longer in the Taj Mahal. The sky had gone dark. Wind howled. Saint Dane had literally knocked me out of Third Earth to a place I had never seen before.

"You think you know me?" he shouted angrily. "I have eons on you!"

He hauled off and kicked me square in the ribs. I was right. He wasn't done. I rolled away and tried to get to my feet, but he tackled me from behind. I went crashing down onto what looked like a rocky surface. Whatever it was, it was hard and it hurt. I barely had the chance to see where we were. It was so dark, though the sky was alive with lightning. I sensed huge, dark shapes all around us that could have been buildings or rocks. I couldn't tell. I had my hands full.

I whipped my elbow back and felt a satisfying crunch as I nailed Saint Dane in the nose. I landed a solid shot. That meant he wasn't using his power to transform himself. Was he able to do that anymore? Or was he choosing to fight me like a human? I pulled away from him. He sprang to his feet, blood spurting from what looked like a broken nose. I had no sympathy. I ran at him and tackled him dead-on. He grunted and fell back. When we hit the ground . . .

We were back in the Taj Mahal. Saint Dane jumped to his feet and grabbed a silver weapon that was lying at the foot of his stairs. He waved it at me, swiping the air back and forth, laughing. Taunting.

"You're just pathetic," I snarled. "You still need help to fight your fights."

He screamed in anger, dropped the wand, and lunged at

me. I danced out of the way, but he reared back and lifted a kick right to my chest. He drilled me good. I fell back. . . .

Into the dark, ominous territory. Lightning flashed, illuminating some of the shapes around us. I thought I saw a Lifelight pyramid and a templelike structure that could have come from Faar. In that one moment I realized where we were. This was Solara. Saint Dane's Solara. This was where he was gathering his dark spirit. From the looks of things, the place was in turmoil.

Saint Dane wasn't there, and then he was. He appeared out of nowhere and threw a punch that nailed me right in the head. I reeled back. He threw another punch to my gut. He was beating the crap out of me. With each punch it seemed as if a lightning bolt flashed. Or maybe it was just that I was seeing stars . . . the kind you see when you're getting pummeled. Images jumped out at me from everywhere. I saw the stairs of the New York Public Library with the lions on either side; the massive *Hindenburg* sailed by overhead; in the distance I saw the shadow of a giant pyramid from Zadaa. It was like seeing those images that floated in space outside the flume as the Convergence drew nearer. Only this time, the images seemed real. With substance. Saint Dane had created a world that was a dark reflection of Halla. These were all twisted, nightmare visions of the originals.

I kept stumbling backward until my back hit a wall. I pushed off as Saint Dane threw another punch. I ducked under it and found myself back in the Taj Mahal. I looked around, desperate to find something to defend myself with. I felt a kick to my back and jerked forward.

I was back in the dark Solara. I saw darting images all around me. Circling. A giant snake slithered across the ground, larger than any snake I'd ever seen . . . except on

Zadaa. It was a quig. It wasn't alone. A pack of snarling, yellow-eyed dogs darted behind a broken wall. A hollow growl shot my attention to the right, where a quig-bear from Denduron reared up on its hind legs, ready to pounce. I backed away and turned to see Saint Dane's blue eyes flashing out from the dark, focused on me. He was coming again. I had to start fighting. He threw a punch. I ducked and nailed him in the chest.

We were back in the Taj Mahal. He shot a knee to my chest.

I saw the image of an oversize tang from Eelong dart behind a building in the dark of Solara. I fell and kicked out Saint Dane's knees.

We were back in the Taj Mahal. He grabbed at my shirt, pulling me forward. We both tumbled onto a pile of brilliant blue glaze stones from Denduron. Their sharp edges cut into my ribs. Saint Dane wrapped his hands around my throat. I grabbed his wrists, desperate to break his grip. I was looking up at the dome of the Taj Mahal. Third Earth. He squeezed tighter. Lightning flashed. The dome became a crystal tunnel that flew to infinity. The hatred in his brilliant eyes was beyond anything I could imagine. I couldn't breathe. The flume tunnel transformed into the open, gaping mouth of a sharp-toothed quig-shark. With a flash of lightning it turned into a laughing Dr. Zetlin from Veelox. I was seconds from blacking out. I wasn't sure if any of this was really happening or if it was some horrifying dream. Lightning flashed again. Behind Saint Dane's head I saw the most jarring image of all. It was my house, from Second Earth. It was a sight I hadn't seen since I'd climbed on the back of Uncle Press's motorcycle and left to become a Traveler. The house was right there. I felt as if I could touch it . . . until it exploded in flames. Rather than send me totally out of my mind, the image gave me one last burst of energy. I let go of Saint Dane's wrists, brought my two hands up between his, and used every ounce of force I could muster to knock his hands away from my throat.

I quickly rolled, gasping for air. He was on me again. He jumped onto my back, driving both feet into me, forcing me to the ground. I shifted my weight quickly, throwing him off balance. As soon as I felt him move, I jumped up. My adrenaline was spiked. I knew that I needed to take control. I went after Saint Dane with a fury I didn't know existed inside me. He may have had eons on me, but I knew how to fight. I threw punches as if I were drilling a speed bag. He blocked some, but I was relentless and kept hammering him with short, controlled bursts. No big roundhouses. I knew that every strike had to count. Each time I hit him, the world changed. Dark to light. Reality to insanity. Solid to chaos. I sensed it more than felt it, because I didn't take my eyes off him. This was it. I had to end it. I channeled the years of hatred I had built up into my fists. I was out of control, but totally focused. I pummeled the guy. The worlds kept changing, but I barely noticed. Putrid creatures flew around me, daring me to look. Pulling at my sanity. I wasn't even tempted to look. My focus was unshakable. I had only one goal—to take Saint Dane apart.

He grew tired. He stopped blocking punches, then stopped throwing his own. That didn't stop me. I kept up the barrage until he tumbled backward, fell onto the floor, and didn't move.

He was done, and so was I.

I was out of breath and in pain. My fists were numb. I stood over him and tried to focus. We were in the Taj Mahal.

That was good. I never wanted to set foot in that other place ever again. Saint Dane lay at my feet. A broken, old man. But it wasn't the end. His body had been crushed, but his spirit still lived.

The last battle had yet to be fought.

I reached down, grabbed his robe, and lifted him up. He wasn't unconscious, but he was close. I grabbed the back of his neck and pushed him toward the door. He stumbled forward. The fight was out of him. His spirit was depleted. I felt that. He didn't try to change shape. Or escape. We walked to the front of the Taj Mahal. I only had to give him a couple of shoves to keep him moving. My only goal was to get him to the front of the conclave before the dado army arrived. I wanted us both there as witnesses. When we reached the front door, I shoved him right into it. He hit it with his head. I didn't care. He backed off and pushed the door open.

We stepped out into bright sunlight. I had to squint at first, before my eyes adjusted. When they did, I stopped short. We weren't alone. Standing in front of the Taj Mahal were people. Thousands of people.

I had found the Ravinians.

42

The mass of people stood silently, looking at us. Or at the Taj Mahal. I couldn't tell. Nobody said a word. It was eerie. Saint Dane and I stood on the top step, looking down at them.

Saint Dane laughed. He was bleeding, he was beaten, he could barely breathe, but he laughed. He gave me a sideways look and said, "Now we'll see which spirit is in control of Halla."

I said, "The spirit doesn't control Halla, the people of Halla control the spirit."

The smile dropped from his face.

A shout came from the crowd, "What have you done? What have you brought down upon us?"

Saint Dane raised his hands and said, "I am protecting you. Even now our army is returning to wipe away the vermin that has dared to invade our—"

"No!" someone shouted. "They have no quarrel with us. They have only destroyed the guards. They seek refuge."

"Refuge? This is Ravinia! We don't provide refuge!"

"And why not?" someone shouted.

The crowd started shouting. Saint Dane didn't know

how to react. They were no longer on his side, and he didn't have any Ravinian dado guards to keep them in line. He held up his hands, trying to quiet them, but that only made them shout louder.

It was awesome.

Somebody stepped out of the crowd and walked up the steps. It was Siry. He climbed directly toward Saint Dane, stopping a few stairs below us. He turned to the crowd and raised his hand. The crowd became quiet. Siry looked at me and asked, "You okay?"

"I am now," I said.

"You have to see something," he said.

Siry turned to the crowd and shouted out, "Please, let us pass. He must see."

The crowd obeyed. At the base of the stairs, the people parted, forming an alleyway for us to walk through. I couldn't believe it.

"What is it?" I asked, dumbfounded.

Siry smiled. "Nah, you should see it." He looked at Saint Dane and snapped, "You too."

We both grabbed one of Saint Dane's arms and pulled him down the stairs. We hit the bottom and walked through the passageway the people had formed. Nobody spoke. Nobody made a sound. It was eerie. They stood silently, staring at Saint Dane as we passed. I saw the hatred in their eyes.

I thought back to the moment when Mark was supposed to have been executed. As much as Saint Dane had whipped the crowd into a lynch mob, there were many who weren't swept up in the emotion. They had questions and doubts. It gave me hope that some small seed of humanity still existed in the hearts of the Ravinians. What we saw as we passed by them outside the Taj Mahal confirmed it.

I wondered if Saint Dane realized it. If he did, he didn't show it. He held his head up proudly, staring ahead, making eye contact with nobody.

As we walked, I realized that the crowd wasn't made up of just Ravinians. The farther we walked, the more I saw others seeded into the group. We went from clean-looking Ravinians to scruffy-looking exiles and gars. I even recognized some of the rebels. The people were jammed together, shoulder to shoulder, all the way to the front wall of the conclave. Nobody spoke. All eyes were on Saint Dane as he passed.

I looked at Siry and shrugged, as if to ask, "What the hell is going on?"

"Wait," he replied.

I didn't know what to think. The dados were sure to attack at any moment. What were all the exiles doing inside like this? They should have been getting ready to defend the conclave. We were nearly at the front wall. Up ahead I saw the Travelers, waiting at the bottom of the stairs that led to the top of the wall. All of them. Gunny, Patrick, Aja, and Elli were there as well.

We walked Saint Dane right up to Uncle Press. The two stood there, toe to toe, glaring at one another. They were two old friends. Two enemies. Two warriors who had reached the end of the battle.

"I made a huge mistake," Uncle Press said.

"Only one?" Saint Dane replied.

Uncle Press nodded. "Yes, only one. I should have had more faith in the people of Halla, because in the end, the battle was won by the people. And that's the way it was meant to be."

Saint Dane frowned. He had no idea what Uncle Press

meant. Neither did I, for that matter. Uncle Press motioned for us to take Saint Dane up the stairs. I was totally confused. What the heck were we doing? Siry and I pushed Saint Dane ahead of us. We were followed by Uncle Press and the rest of the Travelers. On top of the steps was a large platform. Twenty feet away was the edge of the conclave wall. It was low enough to be able to look over, but high enough so you wouldn't fall. Siry and I stopped Saint Dane on top and waited for the others to join us. We were all there. All eleven Travelers, along with Boon.

Last up were Mark and Courtney. Courtney came over to me and touched my cheek. I winced. It hurt.

"You look like hell," Courtney said.

I shrugged.

She looked at Saint Dane, then back at me. "He looks worse." She smiled. "Awesome."

The whole way from the Taj Mahal, I wondered why Saint Dane hadn't tried to get away by turning into a bird or smoke or something. It was Uncle Press who had the answer to that. He walked over to the edge and looked out. Then turned back to Saint Dane.

"The spirit of Solara is well on the way to being restored," he began. "Thanks to what happened here today. Just as important, the dark spirit of Solara has diminished."

That had to be it. Saint Dane no longer had the power.

"The final victory here was not decided by the Travelers. Or by the exiles from Second Earth or the gars from Eelong. It was decided by the Ravinians."

For the first time since we'd left the Taj Mahal, I saw Saint Dane react. He stiffened.

"What do you mean?" he growled.

"This has been a prison for them. An attractive prison,

but a prison. They knew they were being controlled, but they had no hope of freedom, until today. Until we arrived. Until your guards were eliminated. For the first time in a long time, these people understand that they have the freedom to choose their own destiny, not the one that you impose on them."

Saint Dane looked shaken.

"But . . . they live in luxury. They are the chosen."

"They were slaves to your vision, as much as anyone else in Halla. Today we brought them their freedom."

"I don't believe it," Saint Dane said. "I am their bene-factor. I protect them. I reward them."

"All they wanted was the freedom to choose their own destiny, and today they did that," Uncle Press said.

"How?" Saint Dane shot back.

Uncle Press gestured for us to look over the edge. Saint Dane and I slowly walked forward. As the scene below revealed itself, I thought I was looking at a painting. I'm serious. That's how impossible the image was. Saint Dane gave a little gasp. He was just as surprised as I was.

Down on the ground, for as far as I could see, were dados. Thousands of them. Multiple thousands of them. It was the army that marched on Eelong. I saw red Ravinians, the green uniforms and golden helmets of the Quillan guards, thousands of Mark-looking dados, and just as many klees. They had made it back through the flume downtown and marched along the same route that the exiles and gars had taken to get to the conclave. That's where their journey ended.

These dados were no longer functioning.

They were frozen. Deactivated. Dead. Whatever you want to call it. It was an impossible sea of dados that stood frozen. They filled the expanse between the conclave and the river, continued across the double-barge bridge, and stretched out on the far side of the river, back toward the city. There was no end to them.

Uncle Press said, "This was the work of your Ravinians. They entered the dado control center and deactivated every last one. They ended the war. You're looking at a sea of worthless junk."

Now I knew why there were so few Ravinians around during the attack. I had thought they were cowards, when in reality, they had seen their chance. The dados weren't magic. They were mechanical. They had to be controlled from somewhere, and the Ravinians knew where. In the end the positive spirit of Solara had triumphed over the darker motives of man. Saint Dane's chosen had chosen the right path.

Saint Dane pulled back from the wall, his eyes darting left and right. He looked panicked.

"I don't believe it," he cried. "It cannot be."

He ran across the platform to look down inside the conclave and the multitude that was inside, staring up at him.

"People of Ravinia!" he shouted. "It isn't too late! The choice is still yours! You are the elite! The perfect! The future of Halla!"

The people glared at him blankly, unmoved, silent.

"Take back what is rightfully yours! You have earned it by proving your own excellence. You don't want to live like animals! You have chosen to excel. To thrive. You aren't shackled by the common trials of those less deserving than you!"

The Travelers stood silently. Saint Dane turned to them.

What he expected any of us to say, I didn't know. He was breathing hard. He looked desperate. He looked . . . older. Was that possible? Saint Dane's face had changed yet again. He was deteriorating.

"Listen to me!" he called out to the crowd. "You cannot give up in mere moments what your ancestors have worked centuries to achieve! You are better than that. Far better. Together we will rebuild this world. Ravinia will spread beyond these walls. But that cannot happen until we eliminate those who are not deserving."

Every last person in the conclave stared up at Saint Dane silently. It was eerie.

Courtney stepped up next to me and grabbed my arm. "Did you see that?" she whispered.

I did. For a brief moment Saint Dane had seemed transparent.

"Look at those around you," Saint Dane bellowed. "The interlopers who have invaded our sanctuary. Is that what you want? Are these the kind of people you want to share your lives with?"

It happened again. Saint Dane momentarily faded, then came back. I looked to Uncle Press. He nodded in understanding. He knew.

Saint Dane pulled himself away from the edge. He was losing it. His blue eyes had turned from fierce to frightened. He reached out to the other Travelers. "There is still hope," he cried. "Still time. Perhaps I have been too resolute. Yes, too arrogant. I can admit that. There is a better way. We can build a better Halla. All of us. Together. That was always my goal."

The Travelers didn't react. He went to each in turn, looking for some kind of confirmation. Some hope. They all stood silently, with no expression. Saint Dane's face was aging. He seemed shorter. He was stooped, no longer standing erect.

He ran to Uncle Press. "We have been friends. You know I only meant well."

"Perhaps," Uncle Press said with no emotion. "At one time."

"We can bring that back!" Saint Dane exclaimed. "That spirit! It can be as it once was. It can! I was only trying to help the people of Halla. You know that."

Uncle Press didn't say another word. Saint Dane then came to me. We stood eye-to-eye. Both of our faces were battered from the beating we had taken, and given. He clutched at my shirt.

"Pendragon," he gasped, his voice getting raspy. "My adversary. We are not so different, you and I."

Saint Dane's image blinked again. For a moment I saw right through him. Literally.

"We both want what is best for Halla; we just come at it from different perspectives. Think. Think, Bobby. Together, you and I embody exactly what Solara is about. There is no right and wrong, there is only balance. Together, you and I, we can restore that balance and heal the wounds."

"You mean the wounds that you inflicted?" I said.

Saint Dane was losing strength. He started to cry. He fell to one knee while still clutching at me.

"It wasn't supposed to happen this way," he sobbed. "I made mistakes. I was weak. I was seduced by my own vision. You of all people should understand that. You know that Halla is imperfect, and I am the embodiment of Halla. Forgive me. Please. Save me."

"I can't," I said.

"Why?" he cried. "Why can't you?"

Saint Dane was sobbing. His image winked out again, then returned, but not fully. He raised his chin, and I looked into those blue-white eyes for the last time.

"Because this is the way it was meant to be."

Saint Dane dropped his head, let out a guttural cry, and disappeared.

The demon was dead. His spirit had ended. It was only fitting that, in the end, I wasn't the one who destroyed Saint Dane. His final undoing came at the hands of the very people he'd set out to dominate. The people of Halla finished Saint Dane. In doing so, they took back control of their own destiny.

THE END

A few weeks have passed since that incredible day that saw the end of Saint Dane and his bid to create a new Halla. I've been walking around in kind of a dream state. It's hard to believe that it is over. Truly over. The quest to stop Saint Dane consumed my every thought for nearly five years. It changed my life. No, it revealed to me a life that I never imagined existed. I know this is going to sound strange, but now that reality has sunk in, I'm feeling kind of sad. Don't get me wrong, defeating Saint Dane was a glorious thing. It was the right thing. I'm still having trouble getting my head around the fact that by ending his spirit, we have put Halla back on the proper course. I know that it's true, but come on . . . it's a lot to accept.

The other Travelers are in much the same state of dis-belief. We all took up residence here in the Taj Mahal. This is where I'm writing my final journals. We all are. Uncle Press asked that we all take the time to reflect on events and write them down. I'm not sure why that's so important, other than as a record from ten different points of view. He hasn't said what's going to happen to them, but the way

I look at it is, if there is ever any hint of somebody like Saint Dane making rumblings about causing trouble again, maybe our journals will serve as a warning. Learning from the mistakes of the past is a good thing.

So I'm writing. Everything. I can remember it all in such amazing detail. All of it. From when I kissed Courtney in my home on Second Earth to Saint Dane disappearing before my eyes. Maybe that has something to do with the fact that I'm not really human. Maybe I'm somehow channeling the spirits of Solara into my consciousness to bring back every little fact. I wish I knew I had this ability back in algebra class.

Of course, that raises the question that's on everybody's mind. Nobody has said it yet. Most of the time we spend reflecting on the past, reliving events, filling in the blanks of what happened to each of us when we weren't together. Filling out the story. But there is a very big elephant in the room that nobody has dared mention.

What happens to us now?

In my head I'm still Bobby Pendragon from Second Earth. I understand about Solara and the spirit of mankind. It's true. It's real. I saw it all. The idea that we Travelers are spirits that were taken from Solara and given physical life to battle Saint Dane makes sense to me. More or less. What I can't conceive of is a future. Our future. Nobody has brought it up. I'm not sure we're ready to know. At least, I'm not.

Luckily, there has been enough happening to keep our minds off such cosmic concerns.

The heroic gars returned to Eelong. To Black Water. By joining with the exiles, they exemplified the spirit of Solara and helped save Halla. That was a no-brainer. They belonged on Eelong and were sent back to continue their lives and their fight to gain respect from the klees.

Boon went along with them of course. Eelong was his home. He and Kasha said their good-byes privately. Seeing their tearful farewell made me realize I would soon be in the same position with my own friends. I put it out of my mind. I didn't want to deal with that until I had to.

More difficult was the issue of what to do with the exiles. These were people who originally came from Second Earth. Many of Mark's rebels were also from Second Earth. Should they go back?

The answer was a harsh one. No. Uncle Press was adamant. There were no territories anymore, only the seven worlds of Halla. To send those people back in time would once again disrupt the way things were meant to be. Or had become. He said that Halla should rebuild based on the events that had occurred. On all the worlds. There would be no more traveling. No more interference from Solara. He said that the natural order had been restored, and sending those people to the past of their own world with the knowledge they had of the future would be wrong.

Many discussions took place with the exiles and the leaders they had chosen. They were divided. Some wanted to return, others understood that it would be disruptive. In the end they agreed to start a new life in the future of the world to which they had been born.

Once that decision was made and accepted by all, the flume was destroyed. Using explosives taken from the Ravinian armory, the final tunnel through time and space was buried. Forever. There would be no others.

I'm happy to say that the Ravinians welcomed the exiles with open arms. They had been living in a gilded cage. Few were allowed to leave the conclave, and when they did, it was usually to travel to another conclave. Now the entire world was open to them. It was a thrilling concept. The exiles would be spread among many conclaves that had been built worldwide. From these centers, a new civilization would grow. Like Halla, Earth had been reborn.

There was no way of knowing what was happening on the other territories. At least, not yet. I assumed that once we returned to Solara and became part of the spirit, we'd be able to witness events all over Halla. Not participate in them, but witness them and offer the kind of gentle guidance that was the essence of Solara. I still didn't know exactly how that would work, but I believed we would all know soon enough. I also believed that with Saint Dane's influence gone, the hold that the Ravinians had on all the various societies across Halla would weaken and eventually crumble. The positive spirit of mankind was too strong to allow Ravinia to keep its grip. There was no telling how long it would take on each territory, but after seeing what happened here on Earth, I had no doubt that the days of Ravinia were numbered, and each world would eventually return to its normal path. The way it was meant to be. All these broad-stroke decisions made full sense to me. I accepted them and encouraged them. Where it got difficult was when it became personal.

What was to become of Mark and Courtney?

If our theory about not sending the exiles back in time was correct, the same would have to apply to Mark and Courtney. As much as it killed me, I agreed with the decision. I was so incredibly proud of these guys. From day one they embraced every challenge that was thrown at them. That I had thrown at them. Now that the battle was won, they didn't stop. They had both been working very hard to act as ambassadors. Mark knew the rebels. Courtney knew the exiles. Together they worked to bridge the gap between them and help them become one. Their knowledge of these newcomers put them in the perfect position to do the same with the Ravinians. They were the liaisons. They were incredible. I loved these guys, which made it hard to tell them the truth.

It happened one night after dinner. The Ravinians had prepared a great thank-you feast that was attended by Mark, Courtney, Uncle Press, and me. It was in the Taj Mahal, of all places. It was kind of funny, actually. The Ravinian hosts weren't the greatest cooks. The had always relied on dados to do their grunt work . . . or non-Ravinian slaves. But they were determined to do the right thing and insisted on cooking. Most of the food tasted like shoes, but it didn't matter. The thought was there.

Afterward I sat with Mark and Courtney, just the three of us, on the pedestal that held the throne Saint Dane had built for himself. Mark ran his hand over the elaborate gold carvings and said thoughtfully, "In the end he became the kind of person he had such disdain for. Self-centered. Shortsighted. Selfish."

"He was that way from the start," Courtney offered. "He just didn't see it."

I added, "I really think in the beginning he believed he was doing the right thing. I mean, he was a spirit of Solara. He was created by man."

"Yeah," Courtney shot back. "So was Frankenstein's monster, and we know how *that* turned out."

"I guess," I said. "I just can't help thinking that something went wrong. He should have been stopped early on. Which makes me think, could it happen again?"

"Who knows?" Mark said.

Courtney added, "You will, Bobby. Once you return to Solara."

She had raised the topic I had been avoiding. I hated thinking about it and what it meant.

"And while we're on the issue of what's to come," Courtney said, "what's going to happen to Mark and me?"

Which, of course, was the *other* topic I hated thinking about. Leave it to Courtney to put it right out there. I didn't answer right away. I wanted to choose the right words and have it make sense. I wanted to make it easier on them. They were my friends. They helped save Halla. They deserved every ounce of respect and consideration I could give them.

"We're not going home, are we?" Courtney asked.

Or there was that way.

I still had trouble finding words. How could I possibly tell them that after all they had been through, they had to live the rest of their lives in a strange future, away from their families and the life they loved so much? It wasn't fair.

"No" was the best word I could come up with.

The three of us sat on the top step of the platform.

"It's okay, Bobby," he said soothingly. "We already figured it out."

"Yeah," Courtney added, "blowing up that flume was a dead giveaway."

"The worlds have to remain separate," I said. "There's no more traveling. Saint Dane interfered in the natural evolution of Halla and nearly brought it all down. We have to make the choice now that it can't happen again."

"There's going to be a problem," Courtney said.

"What?"

"I've got a library book that's been overdue for about, oh, three thousand years. Who's going to pay that fine?"

Courtney always made me laugh. She put her arm around me and said, "It's all right. To be honest, I'm not sure if we'd even want to go home. We're different people now, Bobby. What would we do? Go back to Davis Gregory High? Play volleyball? Watch TV? It's kind of hard to go back to that after you've helped alter the course of the universe."

Mark said, "Though I could sure go for some Garden Poultry fries."

"You could always start a volleyball team here," I offered.

"Sure," Courtney said. "That would be a fun break from reconstructing civilization. Nice."

We all laughed again, then fell silent. We were goofing around, but the situation was serious.

"There aren't any words that can express how great I think you guys are," I said. "I want to say that I'm sorry for getting you involved in this, but I'm not. If not for you, we wouldn't be sitting here right now. You guys beat Saint Dane."

"We all beat Saint Dane," Mark corrected.

"But we did help a little," Courtney added.

"All I can say is . . . thank you and I love you."

The three of us shared a group hug. It was a sad and beautiful moment.

"There's another question," Mark said. "What are *you* going to do, Bobby?"

"Really," Courtney said. "Starting a new life here is one thing, but I can't imagine doing it without you."

I had the answer. At least, I *thought* I had the answer. It wasn't one they wanted to hear.

"Truth is, I don't know," I said. "But I can guess, and my guess is that I won't be here much longer."

That was it.

The impossible happened.

Courtney Chetwynde cried.

THE END

We were gathered together for what we expected to be the last time. The ten Travelers and Uncle Press. Our final meeting took place in the same spot where I had said my good-byes to Mark and Courtney. We were in the center rotunda of the Taj Mahal. Uncle Press had called us together, and we knew why.

It was time to move on.

We stood in a circle, much the same way we had come together after the flumes collapsed. Uncle Press stood in the center, walking over the Ravinian star. The feeling was much different than when we had last gathered. Back then, we feared that all was lost. There was still fear present, but now it was the fear of the unknown. Not one of us knew what the future would hold.

"So many things have happened," Uncle Press began. "The most important of which is that the positive spirit of mankind has triumphed. We played a role in that. We had to. Saint Dane gave us no choice. But ultimately, the battle was won by the people. And that is the way it was meant to be."

"What about the other territories?" Gunny asked.

"Not territories, worlds," Uncle Press corrected. "Have faith in the power of the human spirit. Without Saint Dane's influence, they will return to the natural path. They are the masters of their own destiny once again. Change won't happen overnight. Ravinia still exists in many places. But it will happen. I believe that, and once you all return to Solara, you will too."

There it was. He said it. We were going back to Solara. For good. I felt a nervous ripple move through the group, and through my stomach. It was Aja who dared ask the question that was bothering us all.

"So what happens to us?" she asked. "Do we lose our personalities? Am I no longer Aja Killian? Will we even remember who we were?"

"You will," Uncle Press answered. "And you will remember all the other lives you've lived and things you've seen. Please, don't be afraid. I know that you're still looking at this through the eyes of the physical beings you've become. But that will change. Don't lament the loss of this life. Rejoice in the many lives you're going to experience."

"I kind of like this one," Spader said, chuckling nervously. "I'm going to miss it."

"That's just it, you won't," Uncle Press said. "Trust me on this. You're not losing something, you're gaining."

Alder asked, "Will we know one another? Will we be able to communicate?"

"It is a good question," Loor added. "We have forged many strong bonds. To think that those would dissolve is disturbing."

"Those bonds won't be broken," Uncle Press answered. "I promise. You are one. You are part of the spirit of Solara. You will always be with one another."

I think that made everybody feel better. None of us

knew exactly how it was going to work out, but we trusted Uncle Press. If he said we'd still be together, I believed him. The fact that we had all seen our loved ones made it that much more believable. The sense of relief was obvious.

"You have all done well," Uncle Press said. "But your job isn't complete, and never will be. As with all the spirits of Solara, you will continue to guide the physical beings of Halla. You won't walk among them, but you will be with them. It's a wonderful experience. It is why we exist. Don't be afraid, be excited."

I was feeling less apprehensive, but I couldn't shake the sadness. I liked being Bobby Pendragon. I felt I was going to miss him in spite of Uncle Press's assurances.

"It's time," Uncle Press said.

He looked to Elli. She never looked better, and I knew why. In spite of all that her daughter, Nevva, had done to help Saint Dane, in the end she played a major role in the salvation of Halla. For that reason, Elli was at peace. She looked around to each of us, smiled, and vanished.

Uncle Press turned to Siry.

Siry asked, "Will I ever see the Jakills again?"

"Whenever you like."

He was satisfied. He gave me a nod, and disappeared.

Uncle Press looked to Patrick.

"I won't lie," Patrick said. "I'm crushed over what has become of my world. Of all the territories of Halla, it has fallen the farthest. It was so . . . perfect."

Uncle Press said, "There is no such thing as perfection. I have faith that it will rise again, and you should too."

Patrick nodded, and disappeared. I hoped he felt better.

Aja was next. "I'm actually looking forward to this. I like the idea of being all knowing and all seeing."

"Then you're going to the right place," Uncle Press said with a chuckle.

Aja couldn't vanish fast enough.

Kasha took a step forward and said, "I fear for the gars."

"Don't," Uncle Press said quickly. "They came a long way before Saint Dane interfered. They'll find their way again."

I called out, "I'm sorry, Kasha."

"For what?" she replied.

"I promised I'd return your ashes to Eelong."

She shrugged. "I understand, Pendragon. Maybe in another life." With that, she smiled, and was gone.

Next was Spader. "It's been quite the adventure!" he said with a laugh.

"Hey!" I called to him. "Maybe they have sniggers in Solara!"

Spader's eyes widened. He hadn't thought of that.

"Last one there buys!" he exclaimed, and was gone.

Uncle Press turned to Gunny.

"I've lived a long life here," he said. "Longer than any of my young friends. And you know something? I'm looking forward to seeing what's next."

"You won't be disappointed," Uncle Press said.

Gunny looked at me with that warm, knowing smile I had grown to love so much. His eyes seemed to twinkle with excitement.

"I love you all," he said. "Thanks for carrying an old man through."

And he was gone.

Alder came over to me. The two of us hugged.

"I am proud to say that you are my brother," he said. "There have been so many events. So many battles. So many choices. We all played a role. But if not for you, Halla would be lost. That is a simple fact."

I didn't know what to say. I had all I could do to hold back tears. He pulled away from me and said, "I look forward to the next adventure with you, Pendragon."

With that, Alder vanished.

It was down to Loor. She stood on the far side of the star from where I was. Slowly she walked forward and stopped in front of me.

"I had many doubts," she said. "When we first met, I thought you were useless and weak."

"I was," I pointed out.

"No, you were not," she corrected. "You were confused, as we all were. I came to the truth quickly. You were the light, Pendragon. You were the soul. You put aside your fears, which is the most difficult thing of all to do. It is easy to be a warrior. It is far more difficult to inspire. You, Bobby Pendragon, were my inspiration."

We hugged. My feelings for Loor ran deep.

I said, "You challenged and pushed and helped me become the Traveler I needed to be."

"I would do it again without hesitation," she said. "And perhaps if given another chance, I would kiss you that night in the rain."

"Promise?" I said.

Loor gave me a rare smile. She looked at Uncle Press. He winked at her. She took a step back. The warrior girl from Zadaa was gone.

I was alone with Uncle Press. The two of us stood together on the Ravinian star. No, the star that marked the gates to the flumes.

"So!" he said with a crooked smile, suddenly acting

like the Uncle Press I had grown up with and loved so much. "I wasn't lying. I *told* you some people needed our help."

"Yeah, but you didn't mention it was every last person who ever existed or *would* ever exist. You left out that little detail."

He chuckled. "Would you have gone with me if I told you that?"

"Hell, no!" I exclaimed.

The two of us laughed. I was brought back to that night so long ago when Uncle Press came to take me away from home and begin the incredible journey that's about to come to a close.

"I need more time," I said.

"For what?" he asked, puzzled.

"I have to finish my journal. It won't be complete until I write about what happened here, with everyone returning to Solara. Gotta finish the story, right?"

Uncle Press nodded. "Okay. I'll wait."

I started to walk back toward my room when Uncle Press called, "Bobby?"

I turned to him.

"I am in absolute awe of what you've done," he said sincerely.

I shrugged. "Yeah, me too."

We both chuckled at that. I started walking again, but stopped. Something was bugging me. I wasn't planning on talking about it, but I couldn't help myself.

"You know," I said, "I'm okay with things. Mostly. I don't regret having gone with you that night and making the sacrifices and fighting a battle I never asked for. I get it. I understand why we were created the way we were, and were given lives, and became part of our own territories. It all makes sense."

"But?"

"But it doesn't seem fair. We all went to war for what we learned to love on our home territories. That's what drove us. You know that. It's why we were prepared the way we were. We were defined by our lives. We loved our homes. We loved them so much that we were willing to leave it all behind to protect them. And what are we getting in return? We lose the very lives we fought so hard to save." I shrugged sadly. "I get it, but it just doesn't seem fair."

"Bobby Pendragon will always be part of you," he said.

"I guess. But he's a guy whose life ended at fourteen years of age, just before the biggest basketball game of his life. He'll never know how that game would have come out. Or if Courtney really liked him. Or a million other things. Kind of sad, don't you think?"

Uncle Press frowned. He started to speak, but stopped. He was the guy who had all the answers.

But not this one.

"You're right," he said sadly. "It isn't fair."

I nodded, happy that I had at least told him how I felt. "It's weird," I added. "After jumping around through so many centuries, my only wish is that we had a little more time."

I left Uncle Press standing alone on the star.

I had to finish my writing. The journals had been a constant companion throughout my journey. They kept me focused. They helped me analyze things that didn't seem clear at first. They let me blow off steam. Writing them helped me do what I had to do.

They helped me save Halla.

Now I'm writing the final words. I don't know who might read this someday. Maybe nobody. But if you come across my story, please know that what happened to me, to us, was a wonderful thing. We proved that the power of the human spirit is supreme. It will always triumph, no matter what the adversity. There are no simple answers in life. There is good and bad in everyone and everything. No decision is made without consequence. No road is taken that doesn't lead to another. What's important is that those roads always be kept open, for there's no telling what wonder they might lead to.

For the last time, I write the words, "And so we go." It's my way of saying that I'm prepared for the next adventure. The next chapter. The next challenge. Whatever comes my way, I'm ready for it.

Because that truly is the way it was meant to be.

END OF JOURNAL #37

THE FINAL JOURNAL OF BOBBY PENDRAGON

☻ EARTH ☻

The door opened slowly.

Standing there nervously leaning on the frame was Courtney Chetwynde. The glorious Courtney Chetwynde. The girl with the amazing gray eyes that Bobby had known since he was in kindergarten. She never failed to take his breath away.

"Yo," Bobby said, trying to sound cool.

He immediately regretted it. Nobody said "Yo" unless they were trying to impersonate Sylvester Stallone, and nobody tried to impersonate Sylvester Stallone anymore. Nobody even remembered who he was.

"Yo?" Courtney snickered. "What does that mean?"

Courtney always kept Bobby on his toes. It was one of the things he liked about her. One of the many things.

"It means whatever you want it to mean. I'm always saying interesting things, you know that."

"I do, unfortunately."

Courtney stepped into the room. She looked at the overhead light and squinted. "So bright. What are you doing in here? Growing geraniums?"

She clicked off the overhead, dropping the room into shadows cast by the light from a single table lamp.

"What are *you* doing? Trying to get romantic on me?"

"You wish."

Bobby chuckled. "What *are* you doing here?"

"I'm not welcome?"

Bobby didn't have to answer.

"I couldn't sleep," she said.

Courtney was nervous. That wasn't like her. Bobby sensed it instantly.

"What's up?" he asked sincerely.

Courtney had trouble looking Bobby in the eye. She had something to say, that much was obvious. She wanted to choose the right words.

"It's just that," she began hesitantly, "I want to tell you something. I have the odd feeling that if I don't do it now, I might not get another chance."

"Oooh, sounds ominous," Bobby joked.

Courtney frowned.

Bobby backed off. "Sorry. What do you want to tell me?"

Courtney took a deep breath and said, "I just wanted to say . . . I love you."

Bobby waited for something more. It didn't come.

"Yeah, and?" he asked.

"What? That's not enough?" she shot back.

"Well, no, it's fine. I just don't understand why you had such trouble getting it out. It's not like you haven't told me once or twice . . . or a few thousand times."

Courtney reached out and took Bobby's hands. Bobby looked at them. As always, he was surprised by the sight. He was always surprised when he was reminded of things he had deliberately chosen to ignore. Seeing what his hands had become was always a shock.

They were once strong and large enough to palm a basketball. Now he had trouble steadying a cup of tea . . . when he was allowed to have tea. Which wasn't often. His hands had grown smaller. Wine-colored spots appeared on the backs of them with growing regularity. His skin seemed gray, though he knew that wasn't possible. He felt as if he needed some sun, but he didn't spend much time out of doors anymore. It wasn't allowed.

In his mind he was still a young, vital guy who strode boldly through life with confidence and good humor. The confidence and humor were still there, but he was no longer a young man. At least not physically. In his dreams he could still run with the joy of youth. He was never quite sure when he was dreaming anymore. Or sleeping, for that matter. The hours blended together. Time was irrelevant. In his mind he was another person. The person he used to be. Of course, that wasn't really the case. He made a point of not looking into mirrors much. Or ever.

"What's the trouble, Courtney?" Bobby asked softly.

Courtney held his hands lovingly. She tried not to cry. She didn't want to have to let go to wipe away a tear.

"I'm sorry," she sniffed. "I'm being an old fool."

"Well, there's no fool like an old fool," Bobby said, trying to be light.

Courtney smiled. Bobby loved it when she smiled. After so many years, her gray eyes were as bright and alive as always. She still kept her hair long, but it was now silver. A beautiful, sparkling silver. Though random streaks of brown remained. He used to tell her that her hair looked like delicious golden amber. Courtney never really knew what that meant, but it sounded good, so she didn't ask. Though her skin had lost the vitality of youth, and she couldn't walk more than a few yards without the help of a cane, to Bobby she was still the most beautiful girl in the world. For him it was the eyes. It was always the eyes.

"I don't know why I'm being this way," she said, laughing nervously. "I—I just felt as if I needed to see you. Now. Tonight."

"You just saw me this afternoon," Bobby replied, trying not to sound too sarcastic.

Courtney nodded. She sat down next to him on the hospital bed. The same hospital bed where he'd been resting for nearly two weeks. "I know."

"You still have the hots for me, don'tcha?" Bobby winked. "Better be careful, the nurses might start thinking we've got a little something something going on."

Courtney laughed. Bobby always made her laugh. Even when she was in despair. *Especially* when she was in despair.

Though he wouldn't admit it, Bobby knew what she was feeling. He felt it too.

He had been in and out of hospitals for the better part of a year with any number of problems. The tests were never ending. The results were never good. The list of troubles was too long to keep track of. Eventually he stopped listening to the doctors. In his mind, nothing they discovered mattered anymore. He knew what his trouble was. He was old. Really old. When his time came, he knew the doctors would write down some specific reason or failure or condition, but that would be a formality. You had to put something on the paper. It was the law. Under the "cause of death" section, no doctor ever wrote "old age." But that's what Bobby Pendragon was suffering from. Simple as that.

As he looked into Courtney's eyes, he knew what was troubling her.

They weren't going to have much more time together.

Though they were the same age, Courtney was in better health than Bobby. It was a fact she didn't hesitate to point out to him every chance she got. Through the years they never stopped giving each other a hard time. Bobby wouldn't have traded a second of it. He had no regrets. He'd lived a full life that he could look back on and be proud of. Looking back was something he did often. Especially as he got older.

Bobby had lots of promise when he was young, and he made good on it. When he graduated from high school he went to his father's old college, Villanova University, on full scholarship. There, as in high school, he played basketball. Villanova was a big-time basketball school. As good as he was, Bobby wasn't in that league. At least, not as a starter. But he played. He would come in off the bench when the Wildcats were in need of 3s. Bobby was smaller than the rest of the pro-bound players. He didn't have their skill. But he could always hit the 3s. He even got the chance to play in front of a national audience when 'Nova went to the NCAA tournament his senior year. It was one of the most memorable and rewarding experiences of his life.

Bobby had no inclination to play pro basketball. When he graduated, he didn't have much inclination at all. Life was full of opportunities; he just wasn't sure which one appealed to him. He floundered for a while, working odd jobs just to make money. His parents wanted him to go to law school. They thought he could change the world. He didn't want to let them down, but his heart wasn't in it. He knew that he had a calling; the trick was to discover it.

Besides playing basketball, there was one thing that Bobby enjoyed more than anything else. He liked to tell stories. He had a knack for taking complicated concepts and writing them in accessible ways. He thought that nothing could be better than to make a career out of doing something he loved. Writing. But it didn't come easy. At first he couldn't catch a break or make a sale. Of anything. He wrote every kind of story, from epic adventures to online serials. He even stopped going by Bobby and used his full name, Robert Pendragon, just to appear more professional. Nothing seemed to be working. After suffering through one too many rejections, Bobby was ready to give up and, as his father put it, "get a *real* job." Of course, that's when he got his first break. He sold a short story to a magazine about Allied POWs being used as slave labor for private Japanese companies during World War II. His story was fiction, but based on fact. It not only gave him his first sale as a professional writer, but launched a successful, decades-long career as an author.

Bobby may not have become a lawyer as his parents had hoped, but in his own small way, he did change the world. He specialized in writing dramatic fiction based on true incidents. He brought history to life and made it accessible to people who wouldn't ordinarily be interested. Among his many topics he wrote stories of child labor in third-world nations, handling illness without health insurance, and the challenge of combating illiteracy. He always picked topics that had social relevance. He wanted to take his readers beyond the story of his characters and illustrate the larger challenge in compelling ways. He won praise for his thought-provoking portrayals that shed light on so many pressing issues. Many of the books written by Robert Pendragon became required reading in classrooms. He never got rich from his work. At least, he never earned a ton of money. But he had the satisfaction of knowing that his work helped make a difference.

He didn't see much of Courtney right after high school. She went to New York University, where she majored in communications while playing both varsity volleyball and softball. She moved to Los Angeles and went into a career producing television news specials. She and Bobby always kept in touch, but didn't see each other face-to-face until Bobby was asked to appear at a fund-raiser for California teachers. Bobby jumped at the chance, not only because he believed in the cause, but also because he knew that Courtney would be there to cover it. When they met, it was like no time had passed.

They were never apart again. Two years later they were married.

The two traveled the world. Whether it was for Bobby's research or Courtney's job, they saw places that most people only dreamed of. Together. When they wrote e-mails back to their friends, they always signed them: "The Travelers."

If there was one regret for either of them, it was that they never had kids. They wanted children, but it was not meant to be. Though they had no kids of their own, that didn't stop them from playing a big part in the lives of three very special youngsters. Their names were Allie, Claire, and Teddy. They were the children of Mark Dimond.

Mark was the one who followed the path that everyone expected. After high school he attended MIT. Where else? While there he was credited with designing technology that allowed 3-D images to be digitally broadcast and reproduced. The revolutionary technology was used not only for entertainment but for biological research, medical imaging, and communications. It made him a very rich guy. Not that anybody could tell. He still bought his clothes at discount stores and didn't get his hair cut often enough.

He married a girl from Boston named Marie, and settled there. Not a month would go by that they didn't see either Bobby or Courtney or both. They were like an extended family. Bobby and Courtney bought a house on an island off of Maine, where Mark and Marie's kids would often visit. Bobby would take them on adventures from the time they were barely old enough to walk. Bobby and Courtney took them backpacking in the Sierras and rafting down the Colorado River. Bobby taught them to scuba dive. And drive a boat. And rock climb. And fish. And drive. And and and . . . Bobby became the kind of uncle that everybody wished they had. He always said it was a no-brainer because he'd been taught by the best. He promised Mark that he would always be there for the kids, as Uncle Press had always been there for him. Bobby kept that promise. Bobby always kept his promises.

Bobby wasn't much for publicity, though he had one prized possession. It was a clipping from his hometown newspaper, the

Stony Brook Times. It was an article about two successful alumni of Stony Brook High, who had each gone on to do great things in widely divergent fields while still remaining best friends. Bobby had the article framed and he put it over his desk. Prominent in it was a picture of the two of them. Bobby and Mark. The framed article became even more precious when Bobby got a phone call that changed everything.

It was from Marie. She gave Bobby the sad and shocking news that Mark had suddenly taken ill, and died. It came with no warning. A heart attack before his fortieth birthday. Bobby didn't even get the chance to say good-bye. It was a harsh lesson that life is full of surprises and not all of them are good.

At Mark's funeral Courtney and Bobby both gave the eulogy. Courtney spoke of the importance of friendship and of inspiring people to follow their dreams. Bobby said that he was proud of Mark, not for the incredible accomplishments he made in his short lifespan, but for the fact that he lived his life doing something he loved. "That," he said, "is a lesson we can all take from Mark that is far more valuable than any of his inventions."

Bobby kept his promise. Both he and Courtney did all they could to help and support Marie and the kids. The Dimonds didn't need money. They needed friendship and stability. Bobby and Courtney were there for them. Always. The extended family stayed strong in spite of the tragedy. Or maybe because of it.

"Marie and the kids came by yesterday," Bobby said.

"All of them?" Courtney asked. She helped Bobby sit up in bed, moving the pillows and propping him up.

"Yeah. You know those kids aren't kids anymore. They've got their own little ones, for cryin' out loud, but they still call me Uncle Bibs."

"And they always will," Courtney replied.

The two were silent for a moment, then Bobby said, "I wonder if they felt like they needed to see me too."

Courtney sat on the edge of the bed. She didn't have to answer. Of course that's why they came.

They were holding hands. It was late. Past visiting hours. The room was silent. There were no monitors of any kind. Bobby wouldn't allow it. He didn't care what his vitals were. "If I'm breathing, that's vital enough for me," he'd say. The doctors didn't argue.

"It's okay, you know," Bobby said to Courtney. "I'm good with this."

Courtney nodded.

"You should be too," he added.

"I am," she said. "It's just that . . . I kind of got used to having you around."

"Did you ever wonder what would have happened if you hadn't come over to my house that night?" he asked.

"The night of the basketball game?"

Bobby nodded.

Courtney answered, "Nothing would have changed. Destiny is a funny thing. When something is right, it's hard to avoid it. We'd still be sitting here, two old farts, spending more time thinking about the past than living in the present."

"Speak for yourself," Bobby said quickly. "I'm enjoying this hand-holding business."

Courtney leaned over and gave Bobby a kiss. She liked kissing Bobby. Always did. They were interrupted by an unfamiliar voice.

"Uh, ooh, sorry. Excuse me."

They both looked up quickly, embarrassed that they'd been caught kissing. Standing in the doorway was a man who looked to be in his forties. He wore a long, light brown coat over jeans and a work shirt. His brown hair fell below his ears. It looked like he hadn't shaved in a few days.

"Didn't mean to interrupt," the man said. His eyes were on the ground, but Bobby could see that he was smiling.

"What's the matter?" Bobby called out in a thin voice. "Never seen a couple of lovebirds smooching before?"

"Please, don't stop on my account!" the guy said, and backed out the door. "I can come back."

"Stop!" Bobby called. "The mood's gone now, thank you very much. Who you looking for?"

The man walked into the room, still holding back his smile. He stood at the foot of the bed. "I'm looking for you, Bobby."

"Bobby?" Bobby exclaimed. He and Courtney exchanged surprised looks. "Nobody's called me that since I was a kid. Who are you?"

"I'm here to deliver something to you," the guy answered. "Is that okay?"

"Sure," Bobby answered. "So long as it's something decent to eat. Between the lousy food here and my diet restrictions, I haven't had anything edible in weeks. I could go for some French fries."

The guy chuckled and stepped back toward the door.

Courtney asked, "Why are you here so late at night?"

The guy answered, "Because it's time."

Bobby and Courtney looked at each other again. Who was this guy? The visitor leaned out the door, reached to the floor, and came back with a large, white cardboard box.

"That can't be for me," Bobby announced.

"But it is." The guy lifted the lid, reached inside, and pulled out a roll of yellowed paper tied with leather twine.

"Looks like a pirate map," Courtney observed.

Bobby added, "If you've come here thinking I might head off on some wild-goose treasure hunt, you're a little late."

"No, I'm right on time," the guy said. "But this *is* a treasure. Of sorts."

"What's this all about, young man?" Courtney asked, growing impatient. "Mr. Pendragon is not a well man. He doesn't need to be bothered by—"

"I'm sorry. I don't mean to bother you. But I would like you to do something for me."

"What's that?" Bobby asked.

"Read."

"'Read'?" Bobby repeated.

"That's right. In this box is a story. A good one. Told in thirty-seven chapters." He held up the roll and added, "This is the first chapter. The rest are in here. Some are in book form. Some are recorded with interesting technology that you can watch with a player. But they're all part of the same story."

"What kind of story?" Courtney asked.

"You'll have to read it for yourself, but I can say this much, you'll be glad you did."

The man held out the roll of paper. Courtney took it and examined it curiously. Bobby took it from her and did the same. He ran his fingers over the rough surface, as if trying to glean some information by touching it.

He cast a suspicious look back to the strange visitor.

"Do I know you?" Bobby asked. "You look awful familiar."

"I doubt you'd remember me" was the man's answer. "It was a long time ago."

"I remember everything, and you sure do remind me of somebody," Bobby said. "You ever been to Stony Brook?"

"Like I said," the guy answered, "it was a long time ago."

Bobby stared at the man. Something was tickling the edges of his memory. He had met this man before. He was sure of it. Then, like a light switch being turned on, he remembered.

"I know!" he exclaimed, sitting forward. Courtney held him back, as if the effort might do him some damage. Just as quickly, Bobby relaxed. His excitement was gone. "But that's . . . that's impossible," he said as Courtney helped him rest back against the pillows. "You sure do look like him, though."

"I get that a lot," the man said with a knowing wink.

Bobby kept his eyes on the visitor. Though he knew there was no way he could have been the man he remembered, there was something about this stranger. Something truly familiar. Something that told Bobby he should be trusted.

"All right, fella, I'll read your story," Bobby answered.

"It's not my story," the man corrected.

"Then whose is it?"

"Just read," the man replied.

"What do we do with this when I'm done?"

"I'll come back for it," the man replied.

"Gee, could you be a little bit more mysterious?" Courtney asked sarcastically.

Her comment made the man laugh. "That's perfect!" he exclaimed.

Courtney looked to Bobby and shrugged. The guy backed away, headed for the door.

"Where you going?" Bobby asked.

"Gotta run," he replied. "I've got nine more of these to deliver." He was about to walk out the door when he stopped and looked back. His expression turned serious. "You should read it now."

He said it like he meant it. Bobby and Courtney both understood.

He winked and added, "But first take a look inside the box. Good night, Bobby. Good night, Courtney. See you soon."

With that, he was gone. Bobby and Courtney sat there staring at the door for several seconds.

It was Bobby who spoke first. "You'd think I'd be a lot more confused about all that."

"I know what you mean," Courtney said. "Who did he remind you of?"

"Nah, it's silly," Bobby said dismissively. "Take a look in the box."

Courtney stood and went to the foot of the bed. She looked inside to see more scrolls of paper. Some were the same as the first, others were light green. She saw bound volumes as well as loose sheets, and even a small device that Courtney figured was the "player" the mysterious guy mentioned.

"Now this just keeps getting stranger by the second," she declared.

"Why?"

She reached inside and pulled out a small, white box with a thin metal handle. She held it up to show Bobby, saying, "Looks like he forgot his take-out Chinese."

"Close the door!" Bobby exclaimed quickly. "Hurry! I don't want those nosy nurses coming in and grabbing it away from us."

Courtney opened the lid, looked inside, and smiled.

"Smells good," Bobby said. "What is it?"

Courtney chuckled. "When was the last time you had some Garden Poultry fries?"

She tipped the box over, so that Bobby could see it was packed with the tasty, golden strips. Piping hot. Seasoned to perfection. Bobby's eyes went wide with delight.

"Reading can wait," he exclaimed.

The two polished off the fries in minutes. The experience brought back long-buried, delicious memories. Neither spoke while they ate. They didn't want to break the spell. When the last fry was gone and the last finger licked, Courtney looked to Bobby.

"Do you want to read it now?"

"I'm thinking we should. I need your help though. My eyes."

He didn't have to explain. Courtney understood. "I'd love to." She put on her own reading glasses, slipped off the twine that held the scroll together, and was about to unfurl the paper when she stopped and added, "We really had a great life, didn't we?"

Bobby held his wife's hand, squeezed it, and said, "The best."

She leaned over and kissed him on the cheek.

"Ready?" she asked.

"And so we go," Bobby answered.

Courtney gave him a puzzled look. "You always say that. What exactly does that mean?"

He shrugged. "It's something I say when I'm ready to move on. I'm always saying interesting things. Have I mentioned that before?"

Courtney chuckled and said, "Yes, I think you have."

In the grand scheme of all that was and ever will be, a few decades is no more than a blip of time. An eye blink. A fleeting moment. But for the souls who live in Halla, every short second counts. All time is precious. The challenge is to make the most of it. The ability to decide how to spend time is a great and powerful gift. Everyone controls their own destiny. Makes their own decisions. Chooses their own fate. Not everyone chooses wisely, but that is the way it was meant to be. The way it should be. The way it will always be.

Bobby Pendragon got what he wished for. A little more time. When it ended, he could look back and know in his heart that he'd spent it wisely.

It was time for him to return to Solara. Courtney would soon follow. However, before that final journey could be made, he had to be prepared.

For that, he had to read.

"Can't put my finger on it," Bobby said. "But I'm kind of excited about hearing this story."

"Then we shouldn't waste another second."

Courtney climbed into bed, leaned back into the pillow with Bobby, made sure they were both comfortable, and unfurled the scroll.

In a clear, confident voice, she began to read:

"Journal Number One. Denduron. I hope you're reading this, Mark. . . ."

THE END

August
2009